T0063241

Patricians:

Sinful Seven

Ryan Browning

AuthorHouse™ LLC
1663 Liberty Drive
Bloomington, IN 47403
www.authorhouse.com
Phone: 1-800-839-8640

This is a work of fiction. All of the characters, names, incidents, organizations, and dialogue in this novel are either the products of the author's imagination or are used fictitiously.

Published by AuthorHouse 08/12/2014

ISBN: 978-1-4969-3277-8 (sc)
ISBN: 978-1-4969-2956-3 (hc)
ISBN: 978-1-4969-3278-5 (e)

Library of Congress Control Number: 2014914554

Dedication

To those souls burden by the weight of their dreams, struggling against the world, and refusing to back down. I would like to thank my mom, Rob Micks, John Van Mil whose love and support made publishing this book possible.

CHAPTER 1

Truth and Tragedy

"Are you ready they are calling for you at the press conference Madame?" A soft voice echoed in the back of the woman's mind. The woman focused her attention on the earrings before her. Light reflected from white gold earrings dangling from the woman's thin fingers. Swaying in the air the delicate figure dangled. Eyes dilated focusing on the minute details sparkling in the light.

"I love you Victoria." Memories of the delicate features of Victoria's husband rushed into the center of her thoughts. Twenty years ago Victoria stood on that beach at a time when the future seemed uncertain. Memories of the smells of the beach the day the earrings were presented as a gift. During uncertainty Victoria let love and dreams guide her through the shadows. Looking towards the future it never looked so dark. Today uncertainty clouded the future like a thick heavy mist. Victoria came back to reality putting turning to her assistant.

"Tell them I need only a moment more Carissa." Looking into the mirror the image stared back from the cold glass showed an elegant, expensive, and stylish white couture dress. Sparkling white silver and gold radiated in the light of the stark dressing room. Victoria looked the role of queen prepared for public execution. Thoughts of how Anne Bolynne felt preparing for her own execution leapt to the woman's mind. The absurdity of the thought echoed the absurdity of the times.

Disappearance of Muse Industries CEO would have stockholders panicked and worried. Responsibilities of the CEO now rested on Victoria's shoulders. Faith existed to comfort the darkest hours when answers cannot be found. Faith told Victoria her husband would be ok. Keeping other peoples hopes up during such dark and troubled times remained the only pressing concern. The stockholders had to be reassured that the future of Muse Industries is not contingent on one man.

Of course it was a monumental lie. If anyone could sell that lie it was Victoria, but she knew all too well it was that genius that attracted her towards her husband. Henry Rollins Williams was one of a kind. Legend stated the man was a genius in both computers and medicine. Henry forged the modern age with the invention of cybernetic implants starting with the first neural data computer link. Muse marketed the implant calling it the Mind's eye.

Victoria and Henry were married the same year seen the meteoric rise of Muse industries on the back of the Mind's eye. Rags to riches wouldn't do them justice. The Williams family became one of the most powerful names on the planet Earth. Muse Industries wasted no time in gaining control of the entire cybernetic market they created. No one could compete with Henry's unique knowledge creating a monopoly.

Governments pay vast fortunes for their cybernetic research and development. Nations needed cybernetic implants allowing Muse to operate above the law. Power and prestige to rival the gods' one journalist exaggerated in the first few weeks. The journalist proved an oracle. Over the next several years unleashed the brilliant tactical planning of a modern day Caesar. Henry funded leading geneticists, engineers, and computer scientists.

Today Muse ranked the number one most profitable and wealthy of all multinational corporations. Henry now possessed power capable of shaping governments and nations. Muse drew the brightest minds and developed cutting edge technology. Henry didn't discourage competition, but the technology made it hard to reverse engineer. Cybertechnology allowed Henry to grasp a stranglehold on the future.

In an anarchistic state system all nations are forced to fight over limited resources and power. Multinational corporations operated in the same system with not enforceable international law. Self defense requires the maintenance of the most powerful military. In the past military power remained in weapon systems. Tools of war allowed ancient leaders to overlook the power of the individual. Only the exceptional soldiers stood out. The Achilles of war.

Muse changed all that. Cybernetic implants leaved the playing field between trained warriors and soldiers. Cybernetic and genetic modification revolutionized warfare far more than the invention of firearms ever had. One well trained soldier with the best equipment and weapons didn't equal one modified civilian. When the greatest warriors were implanted they become gods of war to make Mars and Ares proud. Soldiers now became the true weapons of mass destruction.

Henry's genius crafted the best cybernetic implants, and Muse controlled most of the genetics industry as well. Success comes with a price breeding envy and silent enemies. Nothing is more offensive than power to the powerless. Over the last twenty years several assassination attempts targeted Muse employees, families, and facilities. Victoria knew that her husband travelled with the best soldiers in the world, and recruited from the best government agencies.

The man in thermal optical camouflage standing invisible guard served the royal family until the assassination. Henry travelled with the best recruits handpicked by him and fiercely loyal to the ideologies of Muse. Victoria smile reflected back from the mirror remembered her husband called his body guards "the Williams 13th". Henry did have an eye for talent. Victoria blocked it all from her mind walking towards the door.

"I must confess Mr. Kincaide. I have grown quite use to your ghostly presence." The door slid open in response to Victoria's motion. Stepping out into the hallway individuals assailing the woman. One of the aids for the show ushered her forward.

"Mrs. Williams this way please Mr. Stewart is expecting you." Kincaide's steady hand and invisible presence kept a small opening behind Victoria for an escape route. Assistants led Victoria towards the stage haltering her at the entrance. Cameras turned getting ready to capture the entrance. Hearing the Cue Victoria took a deep breath before walking forward.

"I'm pleased to welcome to the stage the beautiful wife of Muse Industries CEO, and old friend of the Daily Show. Please give a warm welcome to Mrs. Victoria Williams." Jon Stewart's voice died off. The crowd greeted the woman stepping onto the stage with thunderous applause. Walking over at a brisk pace Victoria sat down face to face with the most intimating of the journalists wolf pack.

Jon Stewart remained a journalistic lion. The man redefined comedy and journalism over the last thirty years. Age wore the once young man's face down, but the characteristic charismatic smile and indomitable intelligence leapt from Jon's eyes. The lion had not lost hunger for the truth. All lies would be devoured between gnashing jaw of public opinion.

"Always a pleasure to have you Mrs. Williams" Jon greeted his guest.

"It's good to see you again Jon." Victoria returned a smile at the host. Sharing an empathetic moment both people they looked at each other across the desk.

"I must say the whole world is in tears tonight over the tragic events that took place only a few hours ago in Beijing. How is your family holding up?" Victoria smiled knowing the concern was legitimate, but sensing some real questions lurking beneath the surface.

"Jon as close family friends you know that my husband has the best body guards on the planet. I am certain that he will be fine and the situation will be resolved shortly." The show aired video showing the Muse Industries airplane coming under attack. News media claimed the attack came from a rogue paramilitary corporation. Explosions lite up the sky rocking the plane causing it to lose control. Video followed the aircraft crashing through several buildings landing in wreck in the lower wards of Beijing.

"Information is limited at this time as you know Ms. Williams, but we've heard that there is a ground fight. Social media is full of pictures of unidentified group of assailants moving into the area." Jon paused for a second to control the emotions inside. Silence fell over the crowd watching in the studio. Jon looked up at his guest with a question glimmering in his eyes.

"This leaves the whole world wondering at what point this behaviour becomes normalized. Every major corporation now owns their own private military. Adoption of PMC by corporations like Muse claimed for security purposes might cause events like today." The question was predictable and Victoria maintained composure.

"Jon I don't like guns. I run a charity that supports children victimized by war. I don't condone the use of privatized armies by corporations, and I have been outspoken against my husband's security policies in the past. The real culprit isn't the corporation that use these groups, but the leaders of the UN. World leaders that refuse to surrender power to allow enforcement of international laws. We are living in the corporate wild west on a global scale." The crowd roared in approval filling the studio with the thunder of clapping hands. Applause overwhelmed the stage for an entire minute.

"UN and world leaders need to take responsibility for governing this planet. With international laws Muse and many other corporations would not require security corporations. Many of my outspoken opponents have stated my views are Marxist and against free market economics."

"I have to agree with you Mrs. Williams. Tragedies like this one seem to set a real cost to the public." Jon turned on his charismatic charm.

"Jon the real cost isn't just to the public, but to every person on this planet. Not everyone celebrates Christmas but my family does. I have a teenage girl at home watching this on the news right now. Wondering if her father will get home alive and for Christmas. The price that is paid isn't just by the public it's paid by everyone and its cost is always the same. Freedom comes only with the sacrifice of blood." Victoria paused for a moment relying on well-honed instincts to draw her audience in. Sitting in silence the crowd hung on every word. Looking up Victoria turned towards a camera.

"I have only one message to anyone who uses violence and terror to try to change the world, and it's the same message I have for my daughter. We will we get through this and everything will be fine." Applause echoed in response to Victoria's words.

"You have always been a source of inspiration, and despite the events today is it not true that Muse Industries is preparing to release its New Year line up early?" Jon hit the solid questions. Now it was time for Victoria to talk about something positive.

"My husband decided this year in the spirit of Christmas and generosity it entails. Muse is offering 2034 lineup of cybernetic implants as free upgrades. This is Muse's way to thank our customers for their support." The crowd cheered again as cybernetic implants had become a staple of modern society. Almost every person in the world had at least one cybernetic implant.

"We want to share with everyone in the world the blessings the world has shared with us and our family."

"Victoria you have taken very stern stances against cybertechnology, genetic modification, and the political power structure. In Your book you claim governments place military power in the hands of seven families. How do your beliefs stand in line with your statements tonight?"

Victoria waited with the precision of a hunter for this question. Jon Stewart was the finest entertainer. The fact a comedian was the best journalist seemed the cruellest joke on journalism. The question showed The Daily show was the closest you could come to real news. Societies addiction to entertainment to drowned everything else.

"I love my husband and my family. First and foremost my job as a wife is to protect my family and take care of them. My political stances are not the same as my family politics. My book the sinful seven reveals what I know to be true. Remember I count my family as the first of the sinful seven. As a Senator of the United States of America I stand opposed to the tyranny created by the economic and political climate, but as a wife and mother I pray for the safe return of someone who I loved beyond all reason. Any wife just wants her husband to be safe and their family to be together. Tonight I am just a wife."

"We've got to cut to commercial but I am wondering can you stick around for a moment. We'll throw the rest up on the net." Jon eyes surged with empathy as his hand gently touched Victoria's.

"Sure Jon I'd love to." Victoria replied straight and poignant echoing with elegance and authority.

"The reports we are getting in right now are terrifying. Beijing police and military have been pinned down and cut off from the crash site." Terror trembled in Jon's voice now that only a few minutes ago sounded strong like a lions roar.

"I haven't heard anything from the ground team, but Muse Industries has sent in expert extraction teams. The last report I received that Henry is coordinating an escape with his team. Remember Henry has trained for this and this isn't the first time something like this has happened." Victoria smiled remaining calm as a leaf on water.

"Your family has been big supporters of New York City. People here on the streets are angry right now" Jon added.

"I thank the people of New York City for the support. This is why we call New York State our home." The interview concluded both people saying goodbye. Victoria met the awaiting bodyguard entourage. Led from the building the security team escorted the CEOs wife to a private VTL limo waiting on the roof.

"Madam I warned you about the dangers of flight at this time with the weather conditions." The gruff voice of the security detail bellowed. Victoria stepped into the car past the guard. Snowflakes whipped around outside. Engines hummed louder as the vehicle gained altitude at steady pace.

"Limited visibility will make this a very difficult target to hit and with the thermal shielding we are practical invisible in this weather." The tone of Victoria's voice carried the authority of command earned only through the rigors and terrors of actual combat.

"I'd ask you to relax Major Lee, but I know your upset you're not in the mud and blood with Henry." The lines of brooding etched lines across Major Edward Lee's face staring back at this woman in regal white.

"You and your husband are far too comfortable putting yourself in the way of danger for my liking." Victoria's delicate fingers grasped the thin stem of the crystal glass raising it to her mouth. A faint crimson colour stained the rim of the glass.

"You would think a real warrior would understand they died the minute they were born. You shouldn't worry about such a trifling thing as death. There are so many more important matters to contend with right now. Don't you agree Maj. Lee?" Lowering the glass Victoria smiled at the major.

Edward stared back at this woman in white. A major in the American Airborne 101st. Edward fought wars on every continent in his 20 years of service since he signed up at 18. War honed the man into a perfect soldier in mind and body. Edward saw the worst parts of war in his life and almost nothing scared him except Victoria.

"Madam my father once told me the most beautiful flower is the most deadly, but not until you did I understand what that meant." A smile crept across Victoria's delicate features.

"Thank you Edward for such a wonderful compliment, but now let us move onto the business of seeing that my dear husband makes it home for Christmas." Wind whistled past the car streaking across the sky. Snowflakes flung by the window in a streak of white. Looking out Victoria sipped on the champagne trying to silence her worry.

Chapter 2

Aftershock

Silence lingered in the hallways of the upper New York prep school. The Masters Preparation School ranked number one in the world for education. The cybertechnology boom had hit New York culture with the force of a tsunami. Sweeping changes washed away the old world leaving only the glistening new technology in its wake. The Williams family called New York City and state home. Wealth and influence that poured from the most powerful family in the free world led to the creation of renowned think tanks and academies.

Muse Industries intellectual power changed everything it touched like the mythological Midas. The Williams family were as close as you could come to American royalty. Powerful, rich, and successful people flocked to the locations the Williams spent time. The Masters prep school held the attendance of the world's brightest and best young minds. Shocking events of the day left the students horrified. Fear cast a cloak of silence throughout the school halls. Everyone feared how the only daughter of the most powerful man in the world would react to the news of the attack in Beijing.

Julia family status earned her a degree of respect from the other children. Striding down the hallway eyes darted away from the young woman as she passed her fellow students. Wearing the finest clothes in the school torn to shred, smeared makeup, and any other audacious behaviour that would draw attention from the crowd. Most students avoided eye contact and some even emulated their icon.

Each article of clothing had been carefully selected. The clothes echoed the angst filled teens mind opinions. Adorn in cheap jewellery was a statement against the distribution of wealth. Tearing the expensive clothing showed the poor students what they wore didn't define them. Henry instilled his daughter with a sense of confidence and pride. Julia wasted no opportunity to either speak or state an opinion. Growing up in the Williams family meant a lengthy education at a young age in the art of public relations.

Julia's hair styled into a mess of tangles perfectly shaped as a representation of the fierce mind that lurked beneath. The mess looked untamed and wild echoing of confidence. Unlike most teenagers Julia used the attention she got to promote universal ideals her family raised her to embrace. Passion lurked just underneath the skin burning bright and hot as the sun. Henry and Victoria taught their daughter everyone is responsible to help make the world a better place with what power they have.

Parents try to instil values in their children. Julia had a natural passion for what her parents taught her. Passion for a better world burned in young woman's heart and swirled in her eyes for all to see and feel. Julia stood out as an out spoken advocate against the ravages of bullying in the school and corporate society, raising funds for books for the poorer students on social assistance programs, and to her mother's great pleasure the best debater in the nation.

Rebellion and defiance were natural to Julia. The young woman's streak for social rebellion left a bad taste in most adults. Psychiatrists tried to diagnose Julia with oppositional defiance disorder. The diagnosis sparked an essay from the brilliant young mind that shocked the world. With great charisma and intelligence the essay central argument defined defiance as the very breath of liberty, and the only true source of freedom.

"Children do not rebel because it is fun, but because every child has the right to define themselves how they choose. It is the soul's instinct to create individuality. Self-determination is the very breath of liberty. Without art and creativity people become slaves. Do children not possess the right to choose their future and be judged on our actions not our personal tastes?"

The line was gobbled up by the media and projected worldwide within hours. Julia felt no fear of reprisal and some of her antics teetered on the edge of violence. Organizing student strikes against illegal rules and regulations pushed the administrators and staff to condemn some actions. School board held hearings to discuss the young woman's expulsion. When brought before the school board Julia presented her argument.

"Zero tolerance is a noose always tightened for the good of those strangled by such rules; and any law that does not have a rationale connection between objective and action is not law. Rebellion is justified when there is no access to peaceful revolution." Julia used lawful rebellion to defend her actions. Without any regulation to invoke the school board dropped the matter.

Teachers and administrators overlooked all but the worse behaviour. Julia didn't know if her arguments or the money her parents poured into the school caused the oversight. Family connections allowed early essays on poverty and social problems caused by technology to get published. Media attention earned the young woman a fair amount of prestige all on her own. Julia often wondered how much of her success came because of her parents.

Loneliness sunk deep into Julia's mind on days like today feeling like a birthright. Every student watched the news horrified by the images on the screen. News showed the explosion than the airplane crashing through the poor district of Beijing. Reports stated untold scores of people wounded or dead. Everyone existed in a state of shock faces frozen without expression. Watching the airplane crash devastated the young woman who needed to hide her shock and fear. Social status taught Julia to trust few people around her. Protecting the family remained an instinct that forced the young woman to isolate herself.

Growing up a Williams gave Julia a unique set of experiences. Responsibilities of CEO and Senate taught the young woman the value of duty at a young age. Experience taught Julia that everyone had an interest in getting something from her. Training and education taught self-reliance. Julia only trusted a young man named Robert Cross. The Cross family controlled the majority of the worldwide market of arms and security. Guns and security profits made Robert's family almost as rich as the Williams.

The greater the wealth and power the more problems. Neither Robert nor Julia could just walk through public unescorted without fear of something or someone making an attempt. Even average people would mob the children because of their celebrity status. The harsh realities of the world did come with a benefit. Robert and Julia confided in each other since they were kids. Each provided safety and shelter from the storms of life to the other. Julia's heart skipped spotting the distinguished athletic Robert walking towards her in the hallway.

"JULIA!"

Sound of the voice cracked the sanctum of Julia's thoughts. Robert rushed up wearing his normal dress clothes that would allow him to blend into to any formal event. The young man dressed in a very retro style of the roaring twenties wearing suits everywhere he went. Only sports got the boy out of his fancy clothes. Years of sports chiselled and refined the young man's physique. Robert towered over the other kids at the school.

"The football team just got back from the game. I heard about what happened to your father are you ok?" Julia's mask of stoic pride and self-reliance began to crack threatening to tear her apart from within. Robert noticed Julia's arms tremble and reached towards her grabbing her delicate shoulder to steady her.

"Julia lets go somewhere more private. We'll talk about everything." Calm washed over Julia renewing strength and steadied her. Robert was the only person she felt safe around. Safety threatened the composure usually maintained with ease.

"Could you walk me back to my door room?" The smile creased Roberts's lips as he took off his coat and put it over Julia. The jacket would prevent any of the children from seeing her shake.

"I would love to" Robert said with a smile. Walking down the hallway Robert supported Julia with his arm wrapped around her waist. Each footstep echoed the silence in the hallway ringing down sweeping corridors. Students and teachers stole glances trying not to be noticed. Whispers of gossip followed in wake of the couple. Lies and secrets drifted through the air like tendrils of smoke distorting everything. Children are cursed by the sins and successes of their parents.

Envy, greed, and fear reflected in stolen gazes. Age didn't seem to matter. Teachers and students of the school participated in the same behaviour. Adults often possess no more control of their own emotions than children. These two children born with a silver spoon in their mouths represented to some adults a great injustice. Wealth and power thrust upon them at birth wasn't a gift but a burden. Julia and Robert grew accustom to dealing with the swirl of emotions their heritage brought long ago.

Julia's single dorm room slide open as the two approached. Only the sound of footsteps of the two people entered the room as a greeting. Rushing shut with precision the door sealed the outside world away. Both people stood in the small dorm room with one bed and a small closet. Julia took off Robert's suit jacket and handed it back forcing a smile in appreciation.

"You don't know how much what you did means to me." Robert nodded in response smiling back.

"Have you heard anything at all about your dad yet?" Silence answered the question lingering in limbo. Julia's looked to the window trying to stop her nerves from shaking.

"I haven't heard anything. I can't even get through to my mom." Sitting on the bed Julia stared at the floor around her feet. Feeling powerless Robert watched helpless and unsure of what to say. After a few moments of awkward silence Robert moved over sitting next to Julia.

"Don't worry Julia. Your dad is one of the toughest guys on the planet. Even my dad fears him Jules which means I'm sure he'll make it through this." Robert stared into those bright green eyes beginning to well up with tears. A tear trickled down Julia's right cheek signalling the torrential storm about to be unleashed.

Mental walls holding the flood back gave away under pressure. Julia wrapped her arms around Robert clinging on. Sitting on the bed the young man became a massive rock jutting out of raging rapids that threatening to sweep everything away. Every muscle constricting in the woman's body squeezing like a great serpent.

Julia whispered "thank you I don't know what I would do without you Robert." Julia's whisper was just audible.

"For as long as you need me" Robert replied.

Julia relaxed feeling a sense of safety here in this moment, but struggled to hold onto the fleeting emotion. The world conspires against everyone to take the things they cherish. Julia hadn't felt safe since being sent away from home to boarding school several years ago. Trips to the Middle East and war torn parts of the world showed the young woman the world. Everywhere around the world people died over pointless conflicts. At seventeen Julia experience told her safety was just an illusion. The world was not a safe place for anyone.

"Incoming call from Victoria Anne Williams do you want to accept?" The soft feminine robotic voice broke the silence in the room.

"Answer" Julia commanded as instinct took over forcing her to push Robert away, stand up, and regained composure. Flickering into existence the image of Victoria Williams appeared in the center of the room. Victoria's stern features broke as she seen her daughter and regret filled her voice.

"Honey I am so sorry I couldn't contact you earlier, but you know the normal duties required when such events occur." Julia knew that her mother loved and cared about her, but didn't have much free time. Often these calls would come across as a business report.

"Your father is fine from the intelligence reports I have. We are not quite sure of the ground situation. Major Lee is co-ordinating the movements of the rescue teams. I promise you Julia we will bring your father home alive." Robert noticed the calming effect as Julia muscles lost tension at the sound of the news.

"Just tell dad I got him an awesome present. He has to make it home to get it!" Julia learned this technique of inspiration through watching her father. Pride would give strength. Unable to resist Victoria smiled at her daughter.

"When I speak to him I'll pass the message on. We're still on for tomorrow right?" Caught off-guard Julia's mind raced through memories trying to figure out what her mother was talking about.

"Oh the Christmas shopping trip! We planned to go to New York City on the way back home. Mom if you can't make it I'll understand. I know what needs to be done right now." Victoria admired her daughter's bravery.

"I wouldn't miss it for the world." Trying not to be noticed Robert stood in a corner feeling Victoria's gaze hovering on him.

"I see your spending time with the youngest Cross boy. There is no need for your family or any of their associates to hear of our troubles. I expect that you will respect the privacy of the conversation you just over heard." Robert froze. Victoria's holographic gaze pierced through the young man. Fear caused Robert to stumble over words trying to figure out what to say in response.

"Of c.. c.. course Mrs. Williams. I would never betray Julia's trust Mrs. Williams o.. o.. r yours." After a moment Victoria broke her stern gaze looking back to her daughter.

"Thank you Robert. I hope you both have a wonderful evening, but get to bed at a respectable hour. I will be arriving first thing in the morning." The hologram vanished leaving both Julia and Robert looking towards a wall.

"Is your mom always that scary?" Julia laughed turning around.

"My mom can bark but she doesn't have much bite most of the time. Don't let her phase you." Robert smile twitched with nervous energy. "Well I guess you do have to be tough to be a senator."

Trying to slough off the terror Victoria's gaze left Robert reeling. No experience prepared the young man for the feeling now overwhelming him. Texas provided plenty of adventure with its rugged landscape. Robert youthful energy and reckless behaviour provoked the ire of both his parents on more than one occasion. Not even the fearsome Colt Cross could cause such terror and dread with a gaze.

"Trust me my parents like you. Remember when our families were skeet shooting at that party last year My dad told me he admire the sharpness of your mind, and my mom said you were the very example of a fine young gentlemen. My parents don't even praise me like that" Julia opened the small fridge built into her nightstand pulling out a can of pop.

"Want a drink?" Julia offered the can to her friend.

"Thanks!" Robert took the can and popped it open with a hiss. Thirst gripped the young man glugging down the drink trying to moisten a dry mouth.

"That's the mix!" Robert turned to see Julia holding a bottle of whiskey in her hands.

"How did you get that past security and the scanners?" Julia opened the bottle and poured a fair amount into two cups with a coy smile.

"I have my tricks. A good magician never reveals their secrets." Pausing in both admiration and astonishment Robert looked at the young woman. Julia was bold, fearless, and free. Robert admired the confidence about Julia.

"Don't you ever worry about getting caught or the consequences?" Julia scoffed in response.

"You really think we are going to get in trouble for a couple of drinks?" Soft fizzing of carbonation as the pop mixed with the alcohol at the bottom of the cup. Silence filled the room for a moment. Both people sipped at the drink in hand. Shaking her head at the question Julia looked at Robert.

"I mean honestly I don't think most adults should be allowed to drink. Adults push their own insecurities onto us. You know what bugs me the most about the world. It's not the terrorists or the constant threat to my mom and dad. Not even all the bad things that happen just because of our last name. It's all the things we are told not to do because other people think it's in our best interests. My mom told me freedom is the most important thing in the world, and the only thing worth dying for. I don't know if she's right or wrong. I would rather do what I want and pay the consequences of my actions than to live in fear of what may happen. Besides who is this really hurting?"

Robert admitted that most of what Julia talked about felt true to him. That was the strange power the young woman possessed with her words. People listened to Julia when she spoke almost as if compelled by an invisible force. Some people listened to argue against what was being said. Some people listened because they sensed truth. Only ignoring the young woman seemed impossible. Julia poured her second drink and sat down next to Robert again.

"So are you going to the new year's Masquerade Ball in New York?" The annual New Year's plaza masquerade ball had been going on for ten years now. The event drew the richest and most powerful families to New York from all over the world.

"Of course I am going. My dad wouldn't let me skip it. The Cross kids are expected to show up. Just thinking about it bores me." Laughter echoed in the small room. Julia couldn't stop herself from laughing.

"Poor rich kids like us whining about going to one of the most prestigious events in the free world." Robert felt a sudden sense of shame at the statement.

"Hey it's tough being rich." Robert's half-hearted protestation fell flat. Staring with a look of disbelief Julia couldn't even blink.

"Come on Robert you can't be serious. You know I'm right. We should just be happy to be able to do the things we get to be, but all the kids our age treat what we have like it's such a burden." Robert's pride forced him to stand up to defend himself.

"Hey you know you're still upset about what is happening to your dad! You downed your first drink like water." Julia stared at Robert for a second trying to maintain composure.

"Yea your right I am upset, but I'm still not so tragically hung up on being rich." Robert felt uncomfortable sitting down with hesitation filled with a sense of shame.

"So I take it you're going as well?" Laughter burst forward again from Julia.

"Come on you know I have as little choice in going as you do. I am actually looking forward to it. These events are the most time I get to spend with my parents, and knowing I'll have a friend to talk to makes it a little more bearable." The compliment caught Robert off guard evident by the shocked look he wore.

"I never thought of it like that." Seeing Roberts' eyes widen with excitement brought a smile to Julia's face.

"That's because you never think. Well at least not with the right head any ways" Julia giggled poking fun.

"Hey that's not fair Julia!" Roberts's indignation at the joke filled his voice. "How could I know that Lisa was a trap to blackmail with a video?" Liquid spewed from Julia's mouth as she couldn't contain the laughter at the news. "Well if you stopped and thought things out for once you could have seen that a girl trying that hard wants something."

CHAPTER 3

Aggressive Negotiations

Smoke poured from the wreck of the aircraft. Crashing through the slums of Beijing caused little damage to the hardened reinforced plating of the vessel. The once sleek shiny exterior of the Boeing suborbital mercury class shuttle lay covered in debris and soot. Fire burned from the crafts main engines. Destruction of the main engine rendered the vehicle incapable of flight.

Lurching forward the escape hatch flew off the vessel landing a few feet away with a loud thud. Amidst the black fumes of smoke billowing into the night sky stood the shadow of a solemn man. The thin silhouette of the man carried the body of a much larger figure on his back from the wreckage. Placing the larger man down away from the crash the man checked for vital signs. The soldier in his body armor remained disoriented but had no visible damage on him.

Light revealed the figure to be Henry Williams when he stood up. Body armour showed through the rips and tears of the expensive designer suit. Henry was slender but well-toned. The two men were polar opposites in comparison. Armour clung to the well-developed muscles of a seasoned veteran soldier Looking down Henry checked over the man he had carried out..

"Charlie hold tight. I got to get the others out." Henry raced back into the black smoke. Coughing Charlie hacked up the smoke caught in his lungs. Moments later several more figures emerged from the smoke.

"Kendra is that you?" Charlie's voice sounded harsh and jagged.

"Yea it's me Charles. I got Max with me too." Kendra dragged an unconscious man wearing the same uniform. Muse security logo of a fist and book etched on the shoulder of both uniforms.

"Where's Henry?" Charlie pulled his canteen taking a drink.

"Henry got me on my feet and told me to get Max outside. You know the boss he won't leave anyone behind." Several more figures began to emerge from the ship. A small gathering of security forces and Muse employees assembled outside the aircraft wreckage. Standing up Charlie spit out some water onto the ground.

"That shit just doesn't get out of your mouth." Kendra chuckled holding the canteen to a near unconscious Max.

"Drink slowly Max. You got hit in the head by some luggage, but you'll be ok." Captain Max Anderson awareness increased with the daze of unconsciousness wearing off.

"Where is Henry?" Charlie pointed to the wreckage swishing more water around in his mouth.

"We have to get Mr. Williams to safety Kendra." Kendra looked back with concern on her face.

"Just relax Captain it's going to be alright. Mr. Williams is just getting the last employee out. The pilot's had an oxygen supply and the crash wasn't as bad as it could have been." Soldiers and employees gathered outside the crash watched for several minutes. Suspense and terror gripped those without any experience to draw on.

Henry emerged from the crash with the pilot clinging to him. The designer suit now caked in a layer of black soot staining the fine grey fabric, and the white dress shirt now stained black and crimson. The white of henry's eyes stared out from the black mask of his face. Everyone looked to the CEO for orders. Still holding on to the pilot Henry scanned for an escape route.

"Everyone we need to move now!" Henry commanded pointing towards a nearby sewer grate. Soldiers stood up and move towards the task. Several employees froze staring at each other with uncertain eyes. One of the employees stepped forward.

"Muse will have teams here in twenty minutes tops. Sir shouldn't we wait for a rescue unit?" Henry looked back to the co-pilot who had raised the objection.

"This crash isn't an accident. The people who shot us down are much closer than any rescue unit. If you value your life I would recommend you do exactly what I tell you when I tell you." The upper area of the slums echoed with the sound of Cantonese. Henry looked up attuning his cybernetic hearing implants to try to understand what was being said.

Several soldiers in Chinese army uniform appeared on the upper layer of the slums. Looking down from the vantage point the soldiers spotted the survivors. Shouting orders in Cantonese the soldiers pointed down at the group. Noticing the people wielding fully automatic gun caused civilian employees to start screaming in terror. Captain Anderson watched Charlie the heavy weapons expert attempting to open the grate with a cutting torch.

"No time we have to move now!" Barking the order Max drew his custom pistol taking aim at the lock. Several shots later the lock sparked and hissed. Metal creaked being pulled by Charlie ripping open the grate.

"Get into the tunnels now!" Henry's order provoked instant response. Civilian's flooded towards the open grate. Security force lead by Max took flank drawing their assault rifles aiming through the smoke at the enemy. Henry's presence and command let people filled into the tunnels with precision.

Charlie followed last after planting a fair amount of explosive on the outside of the tunnel. The force of the explosion rocked the tunnel causing dust, dirt, and debris to fall from the ceiling. Light flickering in through the entrance disappeared. Rubble covered the entrance leaving only one path to take.

"Good job sealing the entrance Lt. Compton. Sgt. Malarkey can you try to access the sewer systems maintenance records for a map or at least a location?" Henry looked over his people assessing the situation. At least everyone was safe for the moment. Taking a second Henry weighted the options available to him.

"Well we're safe for the moment. You got a plan or you playing this out by the seat of your pants as usual sir?" Looking at Henry waiting for an answer Max wore his worry on his face. Activating the neural implant to accessing nearby wireless systems Kendra began surveying the map of the tunnels.

"Max you would think after ten years with me you'd stop doubting me. You know my ability to assess any situation tactically." Henry smiled back at Capt. Anderson question.

"Someone has to keep you honest sir. We'll assume you have a plan to deal with the situation. Do you care to inform the rest of us of the details of your plan?" Max placed his hand on his friends shoulder leaning in. Downloading the sewer schematics Kendra turned to the group with a holoemitter in hand.

"We've got some problems. Where we crashed put us in a part of the sewer that only exits in one spot. This tunnel is a one way drainage pipe." Kendra uploaded the schematics of the sewer plans to a holoemitter she held. The holoemitter lit up displaying the location of the team on the sewer map grid. Kendra pointed to the exit on the map.

"That's an ambush for sure" Charlie stated with confidence.

"Thanks for pointing out the obvious Charlie" Max retorted.

"None of you sense a strategic purpose to everything that has happened?" Henry remained calm glancing at his team with confidence. The team froze turning to their commander staring at them. Everyone waited for Henry to explain the situation.

"The attack on the plane was a precision job that damaged only the engine. It would be far easier to just destroy us in the air with overwhelming firepower. Now we are forced into a sewer with only one exit. The soldiers who found us didn't fire upon us or make any aggressive maneuver against us. We are being maneuvered to this location for some unknown reason. Any of you care to guess that reason?" The entire group of people just stared with disbelief at Henry Williams.

"That seems to sum up the situation. I doubt that we are going to make it out of this one alive. It has been an honour sir." Charlie's voice resounded with determination not fear. Henry shook his head.

"Charlie you're a great soldier but if they wanted us dead we would already be dead. No whoever is pulling the strings to orchestrate this attack possesses powerful connections. If the Senate or the UN found out about Chinese military involvement it would spark a war. No whoever is orchestrating this is playing at a much bigger game. I would stake my life on the fact they want us alive."

Max nodded in agreement "you would make a very valuable hostage sir, but they aren't taking you without killing all of us." The other eleven members of the team grunted in unison showing their determination. Each person was ready to lay down their lives for their commander. Henry looked around at his team and in his mind a part of his family.

"We'll let's march to meet fate with sword in hand and death at our backs." Plodding through the sewage racing past the team marched behind their leader. The ephemeral smell of rot and decay overpowered the senses causing several civilian employees to vomit. The soldiers acclimated to death would have not been fazed, but enhanced scent implants blocked out the smell through filters. Sewer tunnels twisted and turned descending deeper into the slums.

Several hours passed while the team worked through the sewer with caution. Tunnels rendered communication with the outside difficult. Presence of communication blockers closed the small gaps any communication could pass through. After three hours of travelling through the long tunnel a sliver of light radiated from up ahead. Light beamed into the tunnel from the exit with blinding brightness. Instincts caused the soldiers to stop and take defensive positions. Sweat dripped down the faces of the survivors as ever single person could feel the cold chill of death in their nerves. Only Henry Williams remained unaffected.

"Capt. Anderson get a drone out there." Henry knew he needed to see what waited beyond the tunnel. Captain Anderson motioned towards Kendra who produced a small sphere from her tool pouch. With a click of a button the sphere hummed to life suspending itself in the air. The silver ball hovered still for a moment before streaked down the tunnel into the blinding light ahead.

"I've got visual coming in now sir." Kendra uploaded the video to the holoemitter she held. Holographic image from the device showed the surrounding terrain outside the tunnel. The sewer exited into what appeared as the base of the construction site for a new skyscraper. Sweeping around the drone transmitted video direct to the holoemitter.

"That's where I would go if I wanted to ambush someone." Henry pointed to the higher encircling elevation.

"Sir that is death ground as sure as I have ever seen in my life" Max stated.

"The only way we live Cpt. is if we make a break for it through here." Henry pointed to a wall only halfway complete. Video showed a half constructed wall near the sewer exit. Surrounding building support structure would provide cover.

"Charlie you still got the girlfriend with you?" Henry looked over at his soldier coming up with a plan.

"You know my baby never lets me leave without her." Charlie's hand fell to the smooth metal surface of the compact rocket launcher off his hip.

"I'll take Pvt. Jackson and set up position here. We can provide cover fire for your exit." Kendra pointed to the tunnel exit.

"Excellent idea but it would leave you too exposed. No we'll pop chaff and thermal smoke in the center right here." Henry pointed to the small elevation difference at the lip of the sewer exit. The holoemitter zoomed in on the footage. Henry looked over at Charlie.

"Then Charlie takes out the wall. Speed and misdirection is what we need." Henry's eyes shined with the glint of hardened resolve. The team moved forward with determination and the civilians in tow. Dead silence filled the air.

Tension crawled through everyone's nerves lingering palatable in the air. Hair stood on end. Each footstep drew the survivors towards the unknown. Charlie moved forward with Kendra getting into position. Max followed a few steps behind clenching grenades in hand. Charlie stopped just far enough back in the tunnel that he couldn't be seen. Everyone watched Henry waiting for the signal.

Henry studied the drone's feed through the holoemitter Kendra gave him. No sign of life was spotted, but that didn't mean there wasn't anyone waiting. Turning off the holoemitter Henry's eyes focused on Charlie, the tunnel, and the future possibilities being weighed out in the mind. Time marched on for the survivors waiting with patience. Henry felt the weight of uncertainty using his hand to signal.

The courtyard of the construction site lit up from flood lights within seconds. Grenades exploded releasing smoke into the air. Charlie charged forward firing a rocket at the wall. The rush of heat and force from the explosion shook the entire building reverberating into the tunnel. Red lines filled the air stopping on each person when the survivors broke out into the courtyard.

"Mr. William I request that you stop and give me a moment of your time please. I assure you there shall be no harm to you or your people." The thick Chinese accent bellowed from loudspeakers. Glancing around Henry couldn't see where the voice originated. Laser lines traced back to nothing.

Thermal optical camouflage hid the soldiers surrounding the construction site. Henry gritted his teeth. TOC was state of the art military technology few nations possessed. Surrender is never an option in the mind of a strategist. Henry stopped in his tracks standing stoic watching the laser sight rested firm on his heart. Urged on by the soldiers the survivors continued racing towards the exit. Kendra, Max, and Charlie surrounded their commander using their bodies for shields. Weapons drawn and aimed at the invisible assailants all around them the four stood defiant.

"This is State of the art ballistic combat armour. You better aim for the head!" Henry defiant statement filled the construction site. Using the distraction the survivors raced to cover. At least all the employees would survive Henry thought.

Red laser lines held steadfast in the air painting targets. Seconds turn into minutes without any movement. Watching from safety behind cover civilians and soldiers felt doubt and anxiety. Air shifted moving like smoke across water bending reality. Thermal optical camouflage disintegrated the illusion revealing the well-dressed Chinese man.

"I apologize for the inconvenience Mr. Williams I have had to impose upon you, but this is a matter of great concern." A middle aged Chinese man greeted the group. Well dressed in a business suit the man was not even six foot. Noticing the facial features Henry realized who the man was.

"You're Zhou Yun Sun the wanted terrorist!" Glancing over the man Henry weighed his worth and value. Zhou Yun was missing an index finger, tattoos could be glimpsed lurking under the clothes, and the man's seemed absent of human emotion.

"I see my reputation precedes me" Zhou Yun thick accent slowed the pronunciation of the words.

"Your connections both legitimate and illegitimate are well known to most of the world. You have been banned from legal entry into every country in the free world Mr. Sun. I've heard the UN wants to try you for crimes against humanity." Henry face scrunched up with judgment. Zhou

Yun Sun approached with confident stride. Watching soldiers stared down the barrel of their guns prepared for anything.

"Mr. Williams we do not live in simple times. I would ask you reserve judgment of me until you at least hear me out. You refused a direct meeting that I requested creating the necessity of my actions." Playing a game of words Zhou Yun measured the Muse CEO. Henry couldn't believe the audacity of lying the blaming for the attack at his feet.

"You shot down my plane endangering the lives of my people, injured numerous innocent people in the process, and almost killed me. I'm sure the UN would agree that the co-operation of the Chinese military constitute this is an act of war. You're playing a dangerous game. I hope your information is a revelation of equal magnitude to the actions you have taken." Henry face trembled with fury. Zhou extended his hand which grasped a tiny data chip housed in a protective casing.

"Mr. Williams your genius is legendary and the future of Muse industries is bright. This information shows your Asian shipping partner distributing your technology is playing you for a fool. Mr. Edward Tong is responsible for the attacks on your shipping, and has been stealing your goods to inflate the prices of your technology throughout the Asian Union. You're aware that this act creates crime and disorder threatening your business, and my hold of the criminal cartels in Asia. If crime cannot be maintained it threatens social order. If social order collapses many people lose their life in the ensuing chaos of violence." Zhou demeanour remained tranquil delivering the report with confidence. Henry stared into Zhou's eyes trying to glimpse motives of the mind lurking behind the dark black pools.

"Let's say I am inclined to believe you Mr. Sun. I would need to find another source capable of distributing my products throughout the Asian Union. From my understanding the only other person capable of such a feat is you Mr. Sun." Zhou Yun lips curled into a wide smile.

"You are correct Mr. Williams." Henry weighted the situation out.

"These aggressive negotiation tactics leave me little choice right now. What Mr. Sun keeps this deal working once the threat of violence lifts?" Realities of the situation told Henry the most prudent choice is the best choice. Keeping everyone alive is the most important job of a leader. Reading Henry's eyes told Zhou Yun that he needed to reassure his partner.

"Your former business partner is driven by greed and envy, but I do not care for profits. Dragon Enterprises and its subsidiaries will make far more profit from providing services to people with cybernetic implants. There has never been a prolonged war that has been beneficial. I am even inclined to offer your products at whatever price you wish to set Mr. Williams. I will give you complete control over your product, and of course ensure it gets to the people who will receive the most benefit from it." Zhou Yun stepped forward extended his hand with bold confidence. Looking down Henry allowed the hand to linger in the air.

"I expect full compensation for the damage done to my property, and any additional expense incurred because of your actions Mr. Sun." Henry took Zhou Yun's hand shaking reluctance. Laser lines dispersed from the air in response to the conclusion of the deal. Zhou Yun filled with ecstatic energy.

"Of course I shall reimburse you Mr. Williams. I never intended to do any damage to you or your assets. Please forgive my vulgar ways, but it is the way business is handled in the underworld. I will provide transportation for you and your personnel. I arranged for a limo to be waiting just beyond the construction site." Marching away Henry looked back with disbelief at his new business associate.

"This is indeed the beginning of a long and beautiful friendship Mr. Williams." Zhou yelled watching the survivors leave the construction site. Future associate with Muse would only increase the power of Dragon Enterprises. Fortune found its way to those close to the marvellous genius of Henry Williams. Thoughts of wealth caused Zhou Yun to smile in anticipation.

CHAPTER 4

Family connections

"Welcome home Mrs. Williams" a guard smiled greeting Victoria. Snow poured down from the sky with only two bright lights from the hover car cutting through. Large arched double doors swung open leading into the foyer of the massive stone mansion. Two guards held the doors open as the clacking sound of Victoria Williams high heels echoed in the midst of winters howling voice.

"Tony did your wife receive the food I sent for Christmas?" Victoria returned the smile stopping at the door way for a moment.

"My wife is very grateful for your generosity." Nodding in response Tony held the door.

"It is my husband and I who are grateful." Victoria touched Tony's shoulder walking past him. Aroma of food cooking in the kitchen wafted through the house. Walking through the house Victoria felt her stomach growl. Time pressures told the senator she didn't have time for food right now.

"Dinner can be served whenever you wish" a servant informed.

"Tony can you have the maids set up the dinner in the common room, and ensure the men take turns relieving each other. I want everyone to enjoy a good meal tonight." Victoria looked outside at the foul weather. The massive snow storm hitting the east coast buried the world in white in a few hours. Warm food and some time in from the cold would keep the guards morale up.

"You're not eating Madame?" Tony eyes filled with worry.

"The events of the day require my attention elsewhere at this moment, but if you will make you feel better Tony have some food sent to the study." Victoria held firm against the onslaught of emotions and exhaustion. Tony set about arranging the task leaving through the front door. Hurrying towards the study Victoria knew Henry sent a private message.

The white marble floor echoed the clacking sound of high heels. Victoria ascended the circular stairs towards the second floor of the mansion. A decorative carved oak handle rail trailed the paths of the stairs with emblem of a lion on the top. Large curtains made of fine silk trailed down from cathedral ceilings. Cloaked from sight the storm raged beyond the windows. Long corridors lined with doors to many rooms flowed from the stairway in both directions.

The mansion was the largest home in the world with the most up to date technology. Home of the richest family in the world built in opulent decadence. Technology blended in with ancient stone and wood. A palace that made the Whitehouse a squatters shack in comparison. Expensive and rare art hung from the walls as intellectual trophies. A large skylight opened to the atrium just beyond the foyer. Gardens filled with the rarest flora in the world could be seen from the top of the stairs. Home is where the heart is Victoria reminded herself drinking in the beauty before heading to the study.

Victoria pressed her hand onto the palm reader next to the large oak door of the study. Faint light from the sensor above the door scanned up and down the full length of body. Sensors read skin flake samples comparing them to the genetic markers of the handprint. The central computer security took only a fraction of a second to verify. Processing the information the computer hummed.

"Welcome Victoria Williams setting the study lighting level to your preference." The door opened without a sound. Flames burst into life in the fireplace next to the large desk across the room. Walking towards the desk Victoria passed many rows of bookshelves. Glow from the flames danced on the reflective surface of the polished dark cherry wood desk.

Wheels squeaked when the chair rolled out from behind the desk. Books cluttered the desktop with some open and half read scattered across the top. Machiavelli's The Prince lay wide open on top of the stack of books in the center. Victoria looked down at the book on top seeing only Chapter

XXI before turning her attention to the flashing intercom. Pressing the button to the intercom brought the system to life like an explosion.

"Sorry to disturb you Madame. You have unexpected visitors at the gate requesting to see you." Victoria peered out the large window trying to see the front gates. A veil of white proved to be impenetrable. Pressing the intercom Victoria wondered who would venture into this weather.

"Who is it?" Victoria curt tone shocked the guard who stumbled for a second to respond.

"Umm it looks to be Colt Cross and his eldest son Barrett." Grimacing from the report Victoria hated incompetence.

"Appearances can be deceiving. Did you preform the normal DNA scans and other safe guards before reporting to me?" Victoria's face scrunched up in anger. Cutting out the intercom went dead. Victoria waited for a response for several moments tapping her foot with impatience.

"I've just completed the scans Madame. Scans show that it is Colton Cross and his son Barrett. I was asked to inform you that their intention is to discuss the events of Beijing with you in private, and it was stated the matter is of exigent concern." The intercom fell to silence again for another few moments.

"Have my guests escorted to the study." The intercom shut off before the guard could even respond.

Victoria sat down feeling soft leather cushion of the chair returning the bliss of comfort to the senses. Swivelling the chair until its back faced the door Victoria looked out the window. Raging just beyond the pane of glass the storm continued to grow in intensity. Flames glowed dancing across the glass surface. Chaos of fire and ice forced Victoria into deep thought looking out at nature's wrath.

Why would the Cross's show up unannounced? The whole world is aware of the situation in Beijing. Only the Cross's attempted to make formal contact during this trying time. Victoria pondered the situation staring ahead lost in thought. Colt Cross the patriarch of the Cross family did have ties with law enforcement agencies around the world. Instinct kept Victoria's mind ever alert for the possibility of any threat to her family. Only by allowing this situation to play out could true motivation be glimpsed.

Deep thought warped Victoria sense of time. Echo of three sets of footprints resonated down the hallway outside the study. Footsteps drew closer stopping outside the study, and the door opened. Hearing the noise tore Victoria from her thoughts. A large well-built man in his late fifties sauntered into the room with all the grand bravado of a true Texan.

"Are you in here Victoria?" Colt bellowed in his thick Texan accent. Shadows hung across the study creating darkness in the recesses of the rows of books. Victoria turned and looked at Colt Cross standing before her with thumbs tucked into the sides of his belt. Barrett stood next to his father. Colt looked at Victoria beaming a wide grin.

"Well I'll be damned if you don't get more beautiful every time I lay eyes on you! Not a single mark of plastic surgery on you. That's how a real woman should look boy." Colt turned towards his son. Barrett in his early thirties looked like a mirror image of his father thirty years ago Victoria noticed.

"You should try to find yourself a woman of intelligence and respect like Victoria here boy. Women make or break a man boy." Colt patted his son on the back. Without expression or emotion Barrett nodded in agreement with his father.

Victoria hated the Cross family with the exception of the young son Robert. The Cross' represented the classical conservative views of the world. Victoria's democratic and liberal ideas took offense at everything the Cross family stood for. Colt and his family were tolerated because of Henry's close business and personal relationship. Both families were joint partners on several military funded projects by the appropriations department. Victoria knew Crossfire made high quality guns.

"I hope you don't feel too naked without your pistol Colt" Victoria smirked.

"Anywhere else and I would have told them where they could go taking my gun. After everything that's happened I can hardly blame you for being cautious. Even with an old family friend. You can never be too safe Victoria." Colton marched over towards the desk.

"Damn dad I think they own more books than the congressional library. Mrs. Williams what do you do with all these books besides let them collect dust?" Barrett stood in a distance looking at the many shelves of books in the library. Reading didn't make any sense to the young man. Books were a waste of time according to Barrett.

"My husband has read every single book in this library more than once. In a way these books represent the collective knowledge Henry spent his life building." Victoria unlocked the top desk draw with a key pulling out a sleek ebony box. Placing the box on the desk the woman unlocked it with a click. Opening the box revealed a line of the finest Cuban cigars.

"These Cigars were given to Henry by Fidel Castro before he died. Would either of you care for one?" Colt picked up one of the cigars taking a long inhale to smell the aroma of the tobacco. Memory told Victoria both her husband and the senior Cross loved cigars. Letting out a jovial laugh of delight Colt picked up a cigar placing it in his mouth.

"You know them communist don't do much right, but damn do they ever make a good cigar." Victoria pulled out the clippers and clipped off the end of the cigar dangling from Colts mouth. For a moment Victoria imagined the cutters were severing that annoying tongue wagging without purpose. Colt lit the cigar puffing smoke into the air. Tobacco smoke filled the room with thick aroma.

"So Colt what do I owe the pleasure of your company to?" Victoria's question sent an electric shock to the nerves. Both Cross men stiffened up in response to the authority of the voice commanding answers. Looking at each other with a hint of confusion both men stayed silent for a moment. Stepping forward Colt removed the cigar from his mouth.

"My boy and I are deeply worried for Henry's welfare. We heard of the attack by the insurgents on his personal shuttlecraft." Barrett placed his hand on his father shoulder as he stood to his right.

"Yea when dad seen it on the news we boarded our family shuttle and flew straight from England to New York." Victoria eyes grazed over both of the men. Standing by his father Barrett didn't care about anyone but himself. Empathy filled Colt's eyes looking at Victoria.

"My family and I are deeply worried about Henry. I warned him to not negotiate with those goddamn chinks, but your husband is a hard man to reason with once he gets an idea stuck in his head." Colt fumed with frustration.

Victoria smirked "I know this all too well, but it is an admirable quality is it not?"

"Admirable sure, but I think Henry forgets how many people rely on him, and it's not fair that he leaves you worrying so much about his wellbeing." Colt tried to contain a mix of anger and anxiety.

"Isn't your anniversary coming up?" Barrett eyes were fixed on the wedding picture on the desk.

"Yes my husband and I were married on New Year's Eve in 2013. We hold a party every year to celebrate it. We ask for charitable contributions to those less fortunate." Victoria wondered why Barrett changed subject. Stepping forward Colt puffed smoke into the air.

"My family will of course be there as always." Instinct told Victoria something was not right.

"My family appreciates it as always, but please forgive me if I ask you to cleave to the purpose of your visit. I have pressing affairs to attend to." Victoria stared Colt straight in the eyes. Barrett looked at his father with the cigar hanging from his mouth looking for a cue on how to react. Colt grasped the cigar with his fingers flicking ashes from it. Drifting down like gray snow the ashes fell into the receptacle on the table.

"Victoria it has been too long since we last spoke. My family and I would like to offer any support that may be necessary to help Henry and you during these troubled times." Offering a sincere smile Colt looked at Victoria.

Barrett chimed in "strength in numbers."

"What type of aid are you offering us exactly?" Victoria's blunt questioning pressed for the truth.

"Well if you need any assistance with troops for a rescue mission. I can help with the enormous workload of a CEO if you need me to. I would imagine senate business keep you busy Victoria." Smoke drifted from Colts lips with the last syllable rolling from his tongue. Barrett nodded in sycophantic agreement with his father.

"My family and I are here to lend aid in whatever capacity your family requires. Anything you need just ask." Victoria stared at both men's face weighing their intentions before speaking.

"Muse Security has been unable to establish communications channels with Henry and his security team since the incident." Colt paced with anger listening to the facts.

"You know those Chinese bastards and their control of information. It's 2033 facebook is still illegal. I have some connections that might be able to help out. I could reach out to for information in the Chinese embassy and local security forces of Beijing." Colt offer felt genuine to Victoria. Stern and gruff the old Texan's face etched with the lines of emotion mixed with time. Victoria pressed the intercom.

"Yes Madame" the guard questioned?

"Please have the guest wing set up for Colt and his son Barrett. The storm is getting worse every minute. I want to ensure the Cross's comfort until the morning or the storm breaks." Turning back Victoria smiled at Colt. At least everyone would be safe for the night until the storm passed.

"Of course Madame as you wish" the man acknowledged as the intercom cut out.

"Really the hospitality is appreciated, but I am sure my men and I can make it back to our hotel safe and sound." Colt stared at Victoria with a look of disbelief.

"None sense! You're a close friend of Henry and mine, and I will hear no more talk of travelling in this weather. Besides if you can get any information it will be easier to co-ordinate from here. Our guest wing is more comfortable than the best hotels in the world. My servants provide better service as well." Victoria shook her head stating her firm intentions.

"Thank you for your hospitality Victoria. My boy and I will head off and make some calls. We'll see what we can turn up. Come on Barrett let's leave Victoria to take care of her personal matters." Noticing Barrett expression of uncertainty Colt reassured his boy. The door to the study opened as a security guard entered.

"Please follow me Mr. Cross" the guard stated in a polite tone.

Victoria watched as Colt and his son Barrett were escorted out of the study. When the door to the study clicked shut the woman let out a loud sigh of exhaustion. Victoria pressed the button under the desk initiating the security system to ensure no one could record or eavesdrop. Once the system clicked on and turned green Victoria activated the computer built into the desk. The holographic emitters lit up. The screen displayed one saved message that arrived just before the Cross's showed up.

Encryption ensured only one or two of the best hackers in the world could crack it. Even then it would probably take years to hack in. Victoria waited for the encryption key to decrypt the information. Several minutes later the screen reported the completion of the decryption routine. Victoria opened the message feeling a mixture of anxiety and relief.

"Audio message only recorded at 12:43 am December 21st 2033 by CEO Henry Rollins Williams. Message is intended for recipient Victoria Anne Williams." The reporting automated voice dropped into silent beginning to play the recording.

"My dearest Victoria I miss you with all my heart. I am sorry for the stress the events of today must cause you. I sent this message as soon as I could. The situation in Beijing is almost resolved, and I am heading to the scheduled meeting now. One last loose end to tie up, and then I shall return to your loving embrace with great haste. I will call you in the morning, and know that you are never far from my mind and always in my heart."

Victoria seldom showed her emotions. Sudden relief of knowing Henry remained alive and safe broke the woman's mental armour. Water flooded from Victoria's eyes erupted like a ruptured dam. The hot water stained cheek and dropped to the floor. Victoria's face covered in tears she closed her eyes and clasped her hands.

"Dear lord thank you for the mercy you have shown to my family this day. Please continue to watch over and bless us. Let all people live forever under your countenance and wisdom. Amen." Victoria opened her eyes and whipped away the tears turning to look out the grand window.

The storm continued to rage on around her, but in this moment it didn't matter. The storm could keep raging on because love kept Victoria warm. Love and hope can endure any storm. All anyone needs in life is a clear purpose. Soon the sun would return and the storm would break as all things pass. Victoria relaxed as she stared off into to the swirling storm feeling nothing but peace.

CHAPTER 5

Breach of contract

Edward Tong paced within his office staring at the communicator on his desk. Anticipation caused time to drag on at a snail's pace. Perspiration beaded on Edward's forehead from stress while waiting for the computer to light up. The news of the attack on Henry Williams came hours ago. Silence filled both owners with a bittersweet feeling of excitement and dread. Chang watched his brother with worried stare.

"Edward you need to calm down. I am sure Mr. Sun would check in soon with good news." Edward glanced in frustration across the room at his second in command.

"News reported Mr. Williams's shuttle was shot down almost three hours ago. We have heard nothing Chang and that does not bode well." Chang stood silent for a moment. Prosperity or ruin on either side teetering with uncertainty. Both men felt tension wondering which way things would fall. Change understood why his brother worried but had to keep him calm.

"Mr. Williams is a resourceful man. Perhaps it is just taking longer to accomplish the task than Mr. Sun originally anticipated." Glass shattered crashing into the wall spraying the room with sharp shards and liquid. Chang predicted the response knowing full well the anger and frustration his brother felt. Edward wounded pride often exploded in violent outbursts.

"I do not care if it is taking longer than anticipated! Mr. Sun should keep me informed to the progress of the operation." Loud beeping emitted from the desk drawing the attention of both men. Edward pressed the button on his watch and activated the intercom screen on the wall.

"This had better be important! I am waiting for an important call."

"Sir I apologize for the intrusion. Mr. Williams is here for his scheduled appointment, and offers sincere apologies for the unanticipated delay." The guard at the front desk pointed to the man standing behind him. The image of Henry Williams standing in his designer suit without a scratch on him sent a chill down both men's spines.

"Please send Mr. Williams up right away!" Turning off the video screen Edward turned with a fury on his face. "How is it possible that Williams is here and we have not heard from Mr. Sun?"

"I do not know brother but what should we do?" Chang shrugged back in response. Perspiration raced down Edward's forehead rolling down his face. Drops of sweat fell towards the floor.

"Chang summon our personal guards into the office. We must prepare with all haste for Mr. Williams arrival." Both men knew the dangerous situation they were now in. The plan had failed and the details no longer mattered. Chang turned on his communicator. Edward nodded and his brother responded.

"Please report to Mr. Tong's office immediately." Within a minute four large guards steps into the office. Edward looked them up and down trying to measure the troops.

"These are our best?" Chang nodded in approval.

"Men you're orders are to stand against that wall. Don't move or say anything. If I raise my hand like this you are to draw your guns and execute Henry Williams." Edward placed his index finger next to his right eye resting his thumb on his cheek.

"That is the signal do you understand?" The guards nodded and lined up against the wall.

"Please Mr. William's wait here for just a moment. I am sure Mr. Tong will summon you soon." The employee standing at the front desk smiled motioning to the seating area just outside of the office. Henry didn't move or say anything in response. After a few minutes the front desk guard left to return to the front gates. Looking at the watch Henry waited for Mr. Tong with growing impatience. After several minutes the door to office opened up and Chang step out.

"My apologies Mr. Williams but the events of the afternoon caused my brother to grow very worried and upset. We need to straighten up the office to make it presentable." Henry followed Chang into the office without saying a word. Edward stood up behind his desk and walked over to Henry extending his hand and the two men quickly shook.

"Please sit Mr. Williams" Chang motioned to the chair as Edward returned behind the desk.

"I am so sorry to hear of the vicious attack on your shuttle this afternoon. I must admit it is a great relief to see that you are unharmed Mr. Williams." Edward plied his silver tongue trying to convince his associate of genuine concern.

"This is just the nature of business in today's world Mr. Tong. I can see from your increased security within this room you have safety concerns." Henry didn't even look back at the guards lined up on the back wall of the office.

"These are sad and horrible day's Mr. Williams. News reports had me and my brother worrying. We are both glad you could make the meeting today." Chang nodded in agreement with his brother. Picking up a drink Edward took a sip to moisten his throat.

"You and your corporation is the light of the world. The world will rejoice to hear you are ok Mr. Williams. You help so many people with your inventions, but I am curious as to why you called this meeting?" Both brothers appeared to be confused looking at one another. Pulling out a portfolio Henry laid the papers on the table.

"Well it is my pleasure to announce that our production capacity at Muse has been increased by 34%. With increased production and the shortage of our technology in China I see many lucrative possibilities. I figured we could discuss increased shipping. I do have some concerns with recent logistics problems. You have on lost or damaged15% of the units we have shipped to Asia over the last year, and this trend alarms me. I set this meeting up so we could discuss strategies on how to fix these problems since you are my primary distributor in Asia." Henry felt a devious smile creep across face. Looking at the information Edward turned his business associate.

"Mr. Williams I assure you I have taken every precaution to ensure safe transport of your goods. I am doing everything in my power to protect the good, but the news shows increased attacks by pirates over the last year." Edward turned on the video showing attacks by pirates on conveys of ships.

"You can see these men are well co-ordinated. I have spent a fortune trying to discover their location. The pirates have proven elusive in hunting down." Video showed the pirates offloading cargo from a ship. Watching the video Henry could see how the pirates proved problematic.

"I understand the pressures that such actions put on you. Your responsibility must be to foresee take adequate precautions against such actions. A theft from you is a theft from me Mr. Tong. You should know I do not tolerate weakness." Henry watched the videos feigning intent interests.

Edward bowed in respect stating "one thousand apologies Mr. Williams I vow I will not allow such actions to occur again."

"Can I offer you a drink Mr. Williams while my brother shows you our plan to eradicate the pirate problem?" Chang stood stoically next to his brother.

"No thank you" Henry responded staying focused on the task at hand.

"Mr. Williams can I ask what happened today? News reports present almost no information. Any problems that are yours are also mine." Edward tried to manoeuvre his business partner into dropping his guard.

"Well our plane was intercepted in the air, and before the pilot could react an attack knocked out the main engine. Forced to the ground we crashed in the slum district." Henry spoke slow expression shock and terror at the events.

"That is horrible! We must help Mr. Williams discover who has done this." Chang looked at his brother trying to conceal his worry.

Edward nodded in agreement stating "whatever you need. Anything that I can provide is at your disposal Mr. Williams."

"Please call me Henry, and thank you for your help. Have either of you heard of a Chinese nationalist by the name of Zhou Yun Sun?" Henry caught both men off guard with his question. Both brothers froze at the sound of the name staring at Henry from behind the desk.

"Rumours state he runs all the organized crime here in China. I've heard that he is the leader of the infamous Triad criminal syndicate. If Zhou Yun Sun is behind the attacks on you it is lucky you made it out alive. What happened to your security detail?" Edward tried to contain his fear in front of Henry.

"They all died ensuring that I made it out of the attack alive." Henry scrunched his face feigning remorse.

"The loyalty a man inspires in those who follow him is a sign of that mans strength. You are a blessed man to be so loved Henry." Chang lowered his head in respect.

"I wondered why you showed up with no security detail. If you need to borrow some of my security personnel I would be more than happy to help." Edward hoped his offer would get rid of any remaining suspicion.

"Thank you Mr. Tong. That would be most helpful, and while you're helping perhaps you can answer a question for me." Henry pulled out his holoemitter and activated it. Holographic images appeared in the air displaying information. Pointing at the information Henry looked at the brothers.

"You can see here this is the worldwide financial report of all property loss and damages from every company. As you can see here is Tong Distribution shows an annual loss on all goods of 16%, but your information shows 15% of your loses are from what I ship you. Now no other business in china suffers more than 4% loses to criminal activities including piracy. My question for you and your brother Edward is how did you think someone like me wouldn't notice this?"

Silence in the office shattered with the sound of glass window cracking. Four distinct holes appeared with lines weaving out. Four bodies hitting the floor followed within seconds of the glass cracking. Edward and Chang were frozen in place from the grip of terror. Staring into the brothers eyes Henry noticed the intercom nearby.

"I wouldn't bother calling for help. Your men have been dealt with and removed from the equation." Henry had not moved from his seat or even flinched when the bullets struck. The spectre of death swept through the room leaving only silence in its wake. Blood soaked into the carpet staining it crimson.

"I confess admiration at the audacity of stealing from the richest and most powerful man on the planet. You forgot that men should either be treated well or crushed completely." Henry watched his words gripped the brothers tight. Chang looked at his brother both men face perspiring from uncertainty of how to handle the situation. Trying to regain control of the situation Edward stepped forward.

"Henry I understand your fears and concerns. I assure you the only reason those numbers exist is not because of theft by Chang and myself, but because the pirates target technology first. Cybertechnology is a very rare commodity in Asia. There are no plants to manufacture the good here. I swear on the lives of my family I would not steal from you." Chang nodded his head in agreement with his brother trying to save their lives.

"Give my brother and I a chance Mr. Williams. We will hunt down these pirates and deliver you their heads if that will satisfy you." Chang threw himself before the great Henry Williams begging for mercy at his feet. Henry stared at both men with fury and murderous rage welling in the pupils of his eyes. Every muscle in the man's body tensed up preparing to lash out in violent explosion.

Henry spoke in a low guttural growl rasping off his tongue "I despise liars!" Bursting to life the video screen drew both Edward and Chang's attention. Information on the data chip Zhou Yun had given Henry rolled across the screen showing both men's bank account information, transfers to private individuals, and private communications between conspirators. Zhou Yun's thick Chinese accent filled the room.

"Gentlemen I am sorry to inform you that I cannot take your money for the assassination of Henry Williams. Instead I am required by honour to report all my findings directly to Mr. Williams. I am sorry we could not come to an arrangement in these matters, but I have calculated that it is not to my advantage to assist you in your endeavors. Gentlemen may you come to the attention of powerful people" the video screen shut off when Zhou Yun's voice stopped playing.

"I have video of you murdering four of my men. The Chinese government does not treat murderers well. Even powerful people are held accountable by the law in my country." Chang began to shake with fear glancing at his brother with absolute terror in his eyes. Edward stared into Henry's eyes trying to unnerve him. Everything seemed to be spinning out of control to some terrifying end. Each man in the room could feel the onslaught of inevitability.

"Your camera's stopped working the moment I entered your office. My new business partner seems to have much more influence with the Chinese government than you." Henry laughter revealed his superior position. Insult pushed Edward beyond the brink of sanity. Staring in disbelief Chang didn't know what would happen next.

Snapping under pressure Edward drew the gun from inside his suit jacket pocket bringing it to aim on Henry. Another loud crack filled the room. A fifth hole appeared in the glass sending lines splintered away from it in all directions. Chang dropped like a sack of brick slamming into the desk. Stepping forward Henry caught Chang's arm relieving him of the pistol before letting go.

Chang's body hit the floor with a thud. Both men stood with eyes fill of anger locked on each other. Fury could be seen in Edwards's eyes seeing the body of his dead brother. The door to the office flew inward. Captain Anderson pulled off the thermal optical camouflage hood over his face. A disembodied head floated in midair.

"The building has been emptied. We've secured all the information you requested." Reporting the information Max glanced through the room seeing the bodies on the floor.

"Your services have been exemplary and above your required duties." Henry didn't bother turning to acknowledge Max.

"We could leave him for Mr. Sun to handle, or hand him over to the authority's sir." Max could see how scared Edward Tong felt trigging a hint of remorse.

"No I am going to handle this myself. Gather the men and prepare our departure. I'll meet you downstairs in a moment." Henry ordered refusing to look away from Edward. Max could feel the murderous intent emanating from the gaze, but with reluctance followed orders. The office door closed leaving the room silent.

"Your reputation is not that of a cold blooded murder Henry." Edward hoped reason would save his life. Henry stared in silence weighing out the future in his mind. Morality complicated the situation. Reality demanded prudence in handling this situation. Henry knew he couldn't leave Edward alive or he would seek vengeance.

"Your right I am not a murder, but killing you wouldn't really be murder would it? Some of my cybertechnology I sent was intended for hospital. Your theft of my cybertechnology has killed how many? What about the lives of the crews that transported the shipments that were killed by your hired thugs? How about the surging crime rate caused by your inflation of the market price of my technology? How many lives have you snuffed out Edward because of your callous actions of self-aggrandizement? I don't think killing you would be murder at all. No it would be a step towards justice and better world to put down a ravenous wolf. It would be a step towards progress and a better humanity. Nothing is more savage than the progress of civilization."

Before Edward could retort the room echoed with the shot of the pistol. Smoke drifting from the barrel. Staring down the sight Henry's eyes filled with cold malice. Edwards's body fell back into his chair. Blood poured from the gaping holes in the front and back of his head. Blood and grey matter splattered on the window behind. Henry didn't even look down just bent over and placed the gun back in the hands of Chang. Moments later Henry exited the corporate building of Tong Distribution and into the awaiting limo.

"Mr. Sun agreed that everything would proceed as planned. Our team will dispose of the bodies and plant the necessary evidence." Max looked at his boss with a hint of worry in his eyes.

"Good idea to prevent my DNA and prints from ending up on the gun Max." Henry pulled off what appeared to be cellophane substance from his hand.

Max didn't respond at first sitting in silence. "Sir you've never killed anyone outside combat. How is what you did morally right?"

"You'll always look out for me Max. You know I would never do something I believe to be wrong, but that wasn't murder. That was an act of war. Once Edward stole from Muse and endangered lives my choice was removed. Edward would have sought vengeance even though he caused the first wrong." Henry placed his hand on his old friends shoulder.

Max had been the one of the first person recruited for Muse security, and the staunchest supporter. Loyalty remained the man's highest conviction. Henry valued Max's company and respecting his opinion above most others. Max relaxed feeling reassured realizing Edward would have sought vengeance for his brother. Henry knew no one would hurt his family with Cpt. Anderson standing by his side.

CHAPTER 6

Profiling

Gliding between the skyscrapers of New York City the black limo whisked along. Two guards sat in the back watching the Williams. Victoria looked at her daughter sitting across from her in the back of the limo. Julia clothes were not dirty, torn, ripped, and in fact would be the talk of any social ball. Dressing up remained a simple gesture to please a parent, but the clothes made the young woman feel uneasy as she was not herself. Public affairs required a certain taming down of the youth's natural rebellious streak.

"Thank you dear for dressing for the occasion."

"You know I only do this for you right mom?"

"Yes I know and I love you too dear." Victoria smirked at her daughter expressing a palatable enjoyment of the situation. Both guards tried not to smile and look the role of tough protector, but watching mother and daughter was hard to not laugh at.

"One of these days you should try dressing more like me mom. I bet it would help get you some youth vote's next election, and shock the senate." Julia teased her mother.

"Keep dreaming those big dreams of yours, and besides youth don't vote. Hell most adults don't vote" Victoria shook her head sighing under her breath.

Julia put on a stern look and said "mom if I have to wear this than you can't talk about politics at all today. That's the deal we made right?"

"So have you heard from dad yet?" Julia tried gauging her mother to see if she was hiding something about the situation in Beijing. Victoria caught off guard with the question almost spilled the drink she was pouring.

"Honey I am so sorry. I should have told you when you got into the car, but your dad called last night."

"What's the official story mom?" Julia sank into the seat with a brooding look half out of anger trying to get more information.

"The official story is that there was a malfunction in main repulsion drive core and a nearby plane came to assist. Before anything could be done to help the engine blew. The other plane was the one under attack by the rogue militia. Your father and his security got caught up in a situation they had nothing to do with. We're going to emphasis the fact there were no civilian casualties." Victoria knew her daughter was plying her for information because she needed know what happened.

"How much is it going to cost the company?" Julia paused for a few second to let silence linger

"Clever" Victoria hesitation revealed the truth bringing a smile to Julia's face.

"You can't lie to me mom. I'm smarter than you just accept it. Besides isn't that why you spent all this money on my education." Regretting the decision for a second Victoria glared at her daughter. Julia leaned forward and grabbed a soda from the bar.

"What really happened mom? It's just us and dads 13th. These guys would sooner die than betray dad." Watching Julia looked for any sign that might give her a hint. Victoria gave a stern look of disapproval, but surrendering the charade when she realized Julia wasn't fooled by it.

"A Chinese nationalist named Zhou Yun Sun came across data. The data proved your fathers suspicions about the Tong brothers and Tong distribution, but because of his criminal background." Julia and Victoria's voice meshed together. Both women said "refused to meet him."

"So dad got shot down because he refused to take a business meeting?" Julia burst out in hysterical laughter piecing the whole story together in her mind.

"Yes it is quite funny isn't it?" Victoria noticed the two guards were trying not to smirk.

"Your father got shot down because he refused to take a business meeting, but the event turned out to be quite profitable. Mr. Sun is taking over distribution. One possible threat to the company has been dealt with." One word stood out. Julia looked at her mother with concern.

"Dad thinks there's a threat?" Victoria regretted all that education for a split second. One word filled the young woman with worry. Parents try to protect their children from the harder parts of life. Victoria knew she couldn't avoid discussing the subject now.

"Yes your father noticed financial attacks on several of his Asian and European interests. He believes the attacks are designed to lure him out into the opening. I keep telling him to open up Muse to public trading on the stock market. Public trading would create trails we could follow to see threats and incoming attacks." Victoria explained the details she felt comfortable telling her daughter. Children had to be protected from the harshest realities, but also prepared for the future at the same time. Both Victoria and Henry struggled with how much to tell their daughter over the years.

"You think dad should put muse on the stock market?" Julia scoffed at her mother's statement. It was the most absurd idea the young woman had ever heard. Victoria stern gaze fell on her daughter before sensing that her daughter knew something she didn't. Looking across the car Julia decided to explain herself to her baffled mother.

"Mom you're a US senator. I get that you don't understand the way the market works. It's like legalized gambling on a massive scale. Think back to the independence wars. One of the causes of the war was British restriction on Lotteries. Now think about it from the perspective of a king. Lotteries allow the poor a brilliant tactic. Poor people could channel large pools of money under the guise of granting it to one person in one large sum. If any citizen could amass a large enough sum they could raise an army and threaten the monarchy. When America broke from England one of the first inventions was the New York stock exchange which opened in1792. The stock exchange allows the richest people in America to gamble with everything they own. The stock market is the biggest legalized gambling ring in the world. On several occasion the market has crashed or needed to be bailed out. Dad would never be stupid enough to put himself up for sale. You said in your book he's too prideful."

Victoria listened to her daughter agreeing with what she said. In fact looking back on the writing of her political dissertation she realized the oversight of the stock market. The financial power of the stock market created ever expanding wealth. In a world without the tyranny of kings and fear of great masses of wealth the stock was a money tree. Ideas fuelled the transfer of wealth from the poor to the rich.

"Still we can only guess. We can know where the threat could come from that your father is sensing." Julia shook her head in agreement knowing her mother spoke the truth.

"Well I mean it could be any one of the sinful seven as you dubbed them mom. I mean each of the seven most powerful families in the world have some interest in Muse Industries. I mean Muse is valued at what 113 trillion dollars or something. Reports show revenue of three times that annually. The family is the popular kid at school. Everyone wants to be us and everyone will take any opportunity to become us." Julia laid out her thoughts.

"I noticed you spending time with Robert Cross last night." Victoria smirked while the car fell silent. "You know his father and brother were at the house last night offering to help with the situation."

"I thought you said Robert was the only Cross you could stand?" Julia raised one eyebrow on a sharp angle revealed curiosity.

Victoria smiled "he's a good boy. I like that you hang out with him, but I can't stand that family."

"Robert always told me his dad is really selfish. That lines up with your profile on him in your book. It doesn't make sense that Colt would just show up and offer help." Julia's brow furrowed contemplated the presence of the Cross family. Victoria subtle laugh was caught by her daughter forcing her to reveal her thoughts.

"Colt has designs on the company that's to be sure. I am certain the purpose of the visit was to determine the odds of your father's survival." Julia hated being a Williams sometimes.

"You know people think wealth and power bring elegance and civility. Upper class society is a pool full of starving piranha's ready to devour each other to survive. The harder you work to succeed the more people claw into you to hold you back." Julia shook her head in disbelief. The holoemitter drew Victoria's attention away from the conversation.

"What are you looking at mom?" Victoria turned back to her daughter regaining senses.

"I'm going over the confirmation list for the twentieth anniversary charity ball on New Year's eve. With everything going on in with the business, the new product line rolling out, and the attack on your father I really think we should postpone it. Your father thinks that would be a sign of fear. It has been a world watched event for the last 10 years and raises a lot of money for charity." Victoria pressed buttons on the holoemitter contemplating the situation.

"So you're worrying like usual." Julia shot a disapproving look at her mother.

"One day you'll worry too. I got it from my mother and you'll get it from me. With all the current threats I don't think it's a good idea. Nothing good can come from putting the most powerful people in the world in one room." Victoria empathetic gaze pushed the realities of the situation on her daughter.

"At least you'll know where all your enemies are." Julia planted the idea in her mother's head. Truth of the statement remained impossible to deny within Victoria's mind. The annual charity event Henry put on for their anniversary would draw all his rivals into one building. Most guests on the invitation list were dangerous.

Victoria went over the guest list looking at the roster of enemies before her. The most dangerous was the Russian transportation magnate Ivan Vladimir Romanov. Romanov attempts to acquire Muse industries over the last decade filled the papers. Journalist made a vast sum of wealth reporting the disputes between both companies. Headlines dubbed the fighting between the two companies corporate warfare. News agencies echoed fear of damage caused if both companies used PMC's. Victoria knew that corporations used agents to infiltrate, sabotage production, and steal corporate secrets.

Corporate espionage became a raging problem within the modern era. The term "Shadow War" had been dubbed by political experts. The shadow war became the scapegoat anytime a criminal action couldn't be explained, or rampant large scale violence provided no suspects. Until the journalist started speaking about the shadow war it didn't exist. Reality changes to match narrative. Art imitates life, but life also imitates art.

Today Romanov remained a potential threat at all times. Ivan recruited his security from the most brutal of Russia's military training programs. In Victoria's mind the worst were the other players. King George upon ascending to the royal throne created ripples in the business world. George made a series of business maneuvers and corporate acquisitions. Either through intelligent cunning or skilful advisors the young king acquired massive corporate holdings.

"For the power and glory" had long been the mantra of the British monarchy. England's economy flourished in a golden age. Forbes claimed the young King one of the captains of industry in a modern revolution. London sat once again in the seat of cultural supremacy. George used financial power to draw business to England in flocks. Both Victoria and her husband admired the young king. Henry made careful choices in selecting business partners. Association with the young king had been lucrative, but Victoria knew her husband was well aware of the king's ambitions.

Victoria sighed realizing she'd have to see Catherine Assisi at the event. Just the thought of dealing with the fashion magnate brought on feelings of unease. Invidia Corporation owned all the major production in fashion from clothing to makeup. Victoria hated Catherine because the young woman was the very image of modern beauty. Of course Invidia Corporation had devoted fortunes to ensure society agreed with their idea of beauty.

Catherine used beauty and deception to acquire factories at the lowest rung of production. Once in control of production the woman manipulated that into control of the entire fashion industry. Victoria hated dealing with the woman's arrogance, but Catherine was a threat as well. Catherine used her money to buy and built a very successful PMC to protect both her assets. The fact the younger woman hit on Henry every chance she got only infuriated Victoria more.

The Argentinian business magnate of Sojourn Corporation would attend also. Victoria enjoyed the company of Diego Marquez and his wife Mariana. Diego acquired a significant amount of money from the death of his father. Rumours said the elder Marquez had been a legendary drug lord. Diego instead used the money to acquire every major resort and transport business in the world. Control of passenger transport and resorts allowed Diego to control the market of relaxation. To the unobservant Diego and his wife was the very image of modern nobility.

News documented the Marquez as elegant cultured philanthropists and social advocates. Henry showed Victoria the truth. South American military industrial complex had many backers. Diego used a series of container corporations and slush funds to keep indirect control of the military. Jaguar PMC remained the visible security force the Marquez's owned to protect their resorts and airlines. In the modern age no rich family could afford to leave their personal safety in the hands of corruptible government officials.

"Mom every year you worry something bad is going to happen, and every year nothing bad happens. You can't control the future." Julia's voice brought Victoria out of deep thought. Naivety lined the young woman's statement. Bad things didn't happen because they were prevented from happening.

Victoria knew the naïve thought revealed her success as a parent. Julia had never seen the real horrors of the world except on tv or the in passing conversation. Vacations and business trips brought the young woman close, but security always stood by ready to protect. Every parent knows the day will come when they would no longer be able to protect their children, but the day would be held at bay for as long as possible. Some might say that sheltering the child is not to the child's advantage. Victoria knew the truth that every parent knows. Each day longer with their child is worth any sacrifice.

"Your right Julia worrying won't do anything, and it supposed to be our day right?"

Julia nodded in agreement stating "besides that what you pay these guys for." The two guards in the card smile with pride.

"Are you inviting Robert as your date to the event?" Victoria's question caught Julia off-guard and unprepared to answer.

"Umm I hadn't given it much thought to be honest mom. I'll probably go by myself. Besides its not who you go with it's who you leave with right?" The sultry smile on her daughters face nearly drove Victoria into a rant until she realized the joke.

"Mom you know I am way too busy for dating. I have school work, studying, and extracurricular. I have my fun once in a while, but when I have ever not been responsible?" Victoria conceded the point. Responsibility had always been Julia's strong suit.

"It'll be fun mom! We don't to spend that much time together anymore. This event is one of the few times we get to have fun together." Victoria's heart sank hearing the truth in her daughter's words. The US senate and her political responsibilities kept her busy most of the time. Henry's responsibilities as CEO of Muse absorbed most of his time. Both parents hated that their jobs kept them away from their daughter so much.

"Well let's make the best out of this week than Julia." Victoria enthusiasm remained a rare sight.

"Don't we always mom?" Julia beamed back a radiant devilish smile.

"What is that you're writing?" Victoria noticed for the first time during the conversation her daughter writing on a data pad.

Julia groaned "another paper for school. The work never stops, but I'd rather be ahead when we get back."

"What is the paper about?" Victoria move next to her daughter in the back of the limo trying to steal a better view.

Julia sighed "it's a history paper. We have to pick someone who we admire and write a report on the events of that person's life." Victoria's interest was now piqued.

"Who did you pick?" Julia handed the pad to her mom. Victoria stared down at the title. The Modern Woman: Victoria Williams rise to power. Reading the carefully crafted first line brought tears to Victoria's eyes.

"Most girls grow up admiring one of numerous great women throughout history. All little girls have idols, but I am lucky to call the woman I admire most in history to be my mom." Victoria smiled wiping the tears from her cheeks.

"Stop mom! You're going to make me cry" Julia protested. Victoria hugged her daughter threatening to suffocate the girl from the fierce pride of only a mother could feel. Hugging back Julia didn't expect her mother to get so emotional. Victoria leaned close to her daughters' ear to whisper.

"That is the best Christmas present any one has ever given me." Mother and daughter turned to see the view of the largest mall in the world approaching."

You think I could just write a paper about dad for Christmas. You think that will work on him too?" Victoria laughed in reponse.

"No. Your dad is not as sentimental as I am." Julia smirked in agreement

"You were always the mushy one in the family." Both people laughed. Senators feared Victoria. Even Henry had learned to be careful about upsetting his wife. Only Julia had never seen her mother get angry. Leaning in Victoria wrapped an arm around her daughter.

CHAPTER 7

Paradise Lost

Swinging in the air with grace the limo descended through the sky. Hovering above the parking out front of the sky mall provided a magisterial view. Height allowed both women to look into the mall through the glass ceiling of the domed structured. Victoria and Julia could see people walking the promenade filled with lush vibrant colours of tropical plants. The tropical paradise soothing atmosphere permeated the building. Both women smiled at each other in anticipation of the adventures of the day.

Coming to a silent stop the limo rested just in front of the mall's main entrance. Both of the security guards opened the doors of the limo allowing the women to exit first. The guard stepped out of the limo first scanning around ensuring safety. After a moment of inspection the guards nodded at each other reaching into the limo. Stepping out from both sides the women exited the limo.

"The cost is clear ladies" one guard informed. Victoria Williams wore her fashionable black couture dress with a large brimmed fancy hat. There was a flash as a nearby patron taking the opportunity to take a picture. Hushed whispers could be heard from the crowd beginning to take notice. Before the women could even get to the mall a crowd began forming.

"Well at least we avoided the paparazzi." Victoria joked looking back at her daughter. Julia long flowing silver dress and hair flowed in the breeze of the warm winter day. Standing together the two women looked more like sisters than mother and daughter. Victoria looked at her daughter with a question in mind.

"So what exactly are you going to get for your father for Christmas Julia?" Julia walked alongside her mother heading towards the large arched entrance of the Skymall.

"Dad mentioned a book he was interested to read by John Milton called Paradise lost. I thought I would get him a copy of that." Julia smiled with delight at the idea. Books were always a good choice for Henry. Victoria felt sometimes books excited her husband more than she did. Envy lined the thought that Henry may be more interested in peeling open an old musty book than sliding off some lingerie. Victoria shook the negative thought from mind remembering doubt is the most destructive force.

Both guards walk beside the women only accelerating pace to open the door. People took pictures of the William's walking into the mall. Only the rich and powerful shopped at the Skymall due to prices for parking and shopping. No public mass transit arrived at the Skymall. Anyone wanting to shop had to possess their own transportation. The coercion of public opinion kept the Skymall for the elite wealthy few.

Crisp smell of fresh air generated by both abundant tropical plants and pumped in oxygen invigorated guests. The Skymall was a mixture of an exotic botanical garden, zoo, and place to shop. A group of rare tropical birds took flight across the sky landing above a store to look down at the people walking around. The animals were kept inside by implanted restraining chips and training. Sound of rushing water mixed with birds singing to create a relaxing ambiance.

"Where do you want to go looking first?" Victoria turned to Julia who shrugged in response.

"Mom you know I love this yearly shopping trip, but look around talk about wasted time. I mean come on how much jewellery can people need. I mean this place is packed year round with people buying things they don't need. Christmas is twice as packed with people buying stuff for other people."

Victoria shook her head "girls your age love the mall! I know I did at your age."

Julia glared at her mom "you should write a book about that! Hanging out in a mall all day sitting and watching people buy stuff sounds so interesting mom." Julia could not stand the mall. Only Victoria could get her daughter into the mall. Julia hated that most people expressed themselves through gifts instead of actions.

Mother and daughter bickered in jest with each other walking through the mall. Most people saw the security presence of the four guards and moved away. Security parted the sea of people like Moses. Packed shoulder to shoulder people watched Victoria and Julia walking through the mall with a bubble around them. Whispers filled the air around the mother and daughter walking past the crowd of people. Occasional camera flashes shocked the air with blinding light.

Stares of judgment alongside fury of whispers fazed neither woman. Being a Williams meant both women were well adapted to the situation. Walking through the arch of the corporate book store the elderly manager spotted both women entering. Staring from behind a stack of books the man appeared to be in his mid-fifties. Hints of grey hair speckled in a thick mane of black hair. Wearing a white and grey business suit represented the modern corporate uniform showed the status of manger. Corporations felt suits represented authority and eased customers into position of trust. Racing from behind the stack of books the elderly manager hurried his employees to empty the store.

"It is truly an honor to meet the both of you Mrs. And Ms. Williams." The manager bowed in show of respect. Victoria glanced at the glowing name tag on the suit vest.

"Nick perhaps you could help my daughter today with the printing of a book?"

"Mrs. Williams I have already spoken to your daughter. I've already got permission from corporate headquarters." Nick smiled looking at Victoria and her daughter. Victoria's eye filled with bewilderment as she turned to her daughter looking for answers. Stuck between anxiety and excitement Julia wait to find out about the book.

"So you were able to get it?" Julia entire body buzzed with excitement.

"Yes the book arrived today. I informed you in the message this morning. I have the oldest surviving printing of John Milton's Paradise lost. I have it in the safe under guard in the back of the store. I have already processed your payment and it is ready to be picked up." Looking through glasses Nick fit the role of a Liberian offering reassurance. Pointing towards the back the manager led the two women towards the back of the store. Victoria face hid the anger of being misled.

"How much did my daughter spend on a book Nick?" Julia shot a look at her mom that screamed don't embarrass me.

"Corporate head office was more than willing to help your daughter fulfill a Christmas wish for Mr. Williams. Your daughter paid only the cost to acquire the book at its fair market value of fifty million. Remember this is a historical piece that will only increase in value. I imagine being owned by the great Henry Williams couldn't hurt." Nick cordial voice did nothing to alter the anger that Victoria felt at receiving the news.

"Fifty million sounds like a reasonable price for a pile of old paper." Victoria's soft voice delivered the message cut with jagged words of anger. Nick stopped at the safe and opened it with remarkable speed. Nothing could bring Julia down right now. Pulling the book encased in transparent preserving glass Nick presented it.

"Don't worry it comes with a second readable copy since the original is quite old." Nick offered the book trying to avoid Victoria's stare.

Julia grasped it with glee exclaiming "Dad's going to love it!"

Victoria looked at the excitement in her daughter's eyes and the anger she felt vanish. Julia's choice in gift showed incredible thought and care in its selection. The expense was outrageous but could be forgiven, and the book sounded like it would be more valuable now. Victoria knew her daughter Julia wasn't prone to spending money without asking, and even admired how much work it must have took to keep it a secret.

"You know honey it's not nice to upstage your mother. There is no way I can compete with this gift." Julia turned with a shocked expression across her face.

"Mom you don't think there is anything you can give dad that can beat this? You really have been married for twenty years haven't you? You know what they say all the best things in life are free." Julia's jest didn't make her mother laugh. For the first time Victoria realized her daughter was on the edge of true adulthood.

"Maybe I just needed reminding honey, but we'll save private talk for later." Julia sensed that her words wounded her mother's pride.

"Mom dad called me thirty times to make sure what he got you was just perfect." Victoria smiled at the kind words remarking at the wisdom and intelligent flowering before her.

Nick smiled at both of them waiting for an opening before saying "I have guards to help escort you if you?"

Vibrations shook through the foundation of the mall. Explosions rippled through the air with violent force knocking people down. Shrieks of terror ripped through the mall mixed with sounds of gunfire. Panic shattered the idyllic tranquility. A great tidal wave of people surged in front of the book store. Nick and his corporate security guards looked around trying to figure what to do. Victoria turned to her security guards with loaded guns in hand ready to go.

"Take cover by the front door. Make sure no one gets in that way." Taking position at the door the guards scanned for threats. Julia tried to keep from shaking moving closer to her mother. Victoria turned her attention to the manager Nick.

"Is there any other way out of here other than the front door?" Nick nodded and pointed to a hallway off the back of the storeroom.

"The employee entrance runs underneath the building connecting the parking garage off that corridor." Victoria headed towards the back of the shop.

"Come on this way!" Victoria commanded grabbing her daughters arm before marching towards the corridor.

"Wait Mrs. Williams. You should take my security guards. They are not as well armed as your people but they might be able to help." Victoria turned to say thank you and seen Nick holding a pistol out towards her.

"2nd amendment rights, but I think you need it more than I do."

Looking into Nick's eyes and grasping the gun Victoria said "thank you." The security guards moved down the corridor providing cover for their charges. Both of the Williams women followed behind with the other guards.

Julia voice trembled with fear as she asked "what's going on mom?" Victoria didn't respond and in truth couldn't. There was no way to be certain if the gunshots and explosion were linked to the Williams family. Henry always told Victoria in dangerous situations to always do what seemed most prudent. Leaving seemed the most prudent thing to do in this situation. Descending the stairwell with the echo of rapid footsteps the group of people arrived at the door. Muse security guards opened the door and scanned the hallway for a brief moment. The long corridor appeared empty.

"All clear" the soft command resonated in the small square stairwell.

Covering the rear the corporate security stated "rear clear." Victoria motioned her security team forward. Entering the long corridor the group descended into the parking garage below the Skymall. Doors on either side exited into the long tunnel presented danger slowing the group down. Sounds of gunfire and screams resonated through the tunnel. Julia tried to contain the tears welling up. Following the group Victoria drug her daughter behind. Smoke lingered across the ceiling filling the tunnel with a dim haze.

Victoria and the Muse security guards stopped in front of the large doors to the garage. Corporate security guards followed from behind. Victoria pulled out a holodevice opening it up. The machine whirled to life projecting a holographic map. The map displayed the current location of the group relative to the limo parked underground. Images displayed the approximate distance between the group and escape to be a thousand meters. Gripping the pistol Victoria looked in the eyes of her men.

"Ok this is the plan. When we open the doors you're going to move in to take cover to provide fire support. I am going to divide the group up. Two groups of four mixing Muse guards with our bookstore guards. We'll displace and move from cover to cover until we reach the vehicle. Than the bookstore guards will provide cover while we escape. If the attack is aimed at us once we escape they will move to follow." Nodding in silent agreement the guards were well trained to follow orders of their superiors.

Doors flung open allowing two muse guards to run in and take position. Crouching behind the foundation support beam the guards motioned to the group. Two corporate guards moved across the lane to the far side taking up position behind a vehicle. Both women moved into the lane way. Gunfire lit up in burst through the dense thick black smoke limiting sight. Bullets twanged off cars striking concrete. Force of the impact from the bullets sent debris of rock flying. Victoria pulled Julia along moving towards cover.

Julia screamed in panic. Bullets tore in between both women. Fear took control of Julia causing her to pull away with all her might. Victoria lost her grip. Instinct drove Julia away from the gunfire. Helpless Victoria watched her daughter run back towards the corridor. Instincts of a mother screamed chase after but the security training told her to take cover. A dead mother cannot help her daughter. Victoria dove behind the cover and reached out with her neural implant to her guards.

"Get Julia out of her another way" Victoria commanded. Rapid gunfire tore through the smoke filled air. Julia raced towards the door until a piece of stone struck her above her right eye knocking her to the ground. Both muse guards rushed out grabbing Julia to pull her back into the cover. Sealing the door shut behind them the guards looked at each other.

"Lock that door and head toward the main exit. I'll route muse forces to your new location." Victoria's voice boomed over the neural link remaining steady in the midst of chaos. One of the muse men grabbed Julia hoisting her over one shoulder. Both guards raced back down the corridor followed by two of the bookstore guards. Victoria peered into the smoke unable to see the location of the exact position of the enemy.

"This is Victoria Williams calling for help. We are under fire at the Skymall. Repeat we are under heavy fire." The line remained dead. Moments passed with no response. Victoria realized the enemy must be blocking communication and began looking around. Spotting the cover to one of the internet hard lines that ran to the buildings. Victoria waited for a break in gun fire before moving with speed to the junction box. Bullets struck around the woman running through the haze.

Smashing the lock Victoria opened the panel to the internet access port. Drawing a thin cord from under her tangle of hair the woman plugged it into the port. Gunfire fell away. Information flowed into the mind through the neural cable. Victoria closed her eyes seeing the vision of the garage dim and light lines of the network. Neural implants allowed the occipital lobe to visualize the internet. Neural implants translated the electronic signal into a chemical signal the brain could process.

Hacking became a struggle between the willpower of a mind and the logic of mathematical networks. Math seemed to present truths of the universe. Math remained the language of computers and all security systems were based on equations. If an individual could understand the equation they could arrive at the answer. Hackers outthought computers in realtime through heuristics. Neural implants proved no computer could stand against heuristic thought process of the human brain.

Pulling the plug Victoria's senses returned to the real world. Soft hiss and the box slid open revealing the bundle of cabling. Victoria manipulated the communicator jury rigging it to direct interface with the network signal. The com blared to life receiving the signal. Victoria activated Muse only communications.

"This is Muse security please come in Mrs. Williams. We have troops outside." Victoria breathed a sigh of relief.

"This is Victoria Williams. I am trapped in the garage and under heavy fire." The com feel silent for a second causing Victoria to check signal strength, but the signal was still transmitting.

Breaking the silence a guff voice stated "Victoria this is Maj. Lee."

"Edward I've been separated from Julia and we both need help." Another long pause of silence on the com as gunfire continued in the garage. Trapped in the garage and separated from Julia left Victoria worried. Time feels like a weight in uncertain times. Victoria sat in the smoke with furious gunfire echoing around her feeling the weight of time crushing her.

CHAPTER 8

Homecoming

Dense traffic of shuttles filled the skies above New York City. Cutting through the sky a sleek outline of the new Muse Shuttle glided across the horizon. Passing the stoic statue of Liberty the shuttle approached New York City. Only a discerning eye could tell any difference between the new shuttle and the one shot down. Looking out the window of the shuttlecraft the captain saw the hustle and bustle of the city.

"This is the captain reporting. We are currently on approach to our Landing zone. We will be landing in about thirty minutes depending on traffic." Security force ignored the captain's voice on the intercom. Henry Williams sat in his spot reading the news on his data pad sipping some coffee.

"Please ensure my car is ready to take me to the office when we land Cpt. Anderson." Smoke drifted from the cigar Henry held in his hand. "Also make sure you get my wife on the line. I need to move the scheduled lunch back an hour." Cpt. Anderson reached out with his neural communicator.

"Mrs. Williams this is Cpt. Anderson. Could you please return this call at your earliest convenience?" Capt. Anderson recorded the message and sent it to Victoria. After a few minutes the automated system replied. The message informed that the recipient communicator was either shut off or out of range.

"Sir I can't raise your wife. The message says she is out of communication tower range. Perhaps your wife turned off her communication." Henry looked up from the news with a quizzical look. Uncertainty set the mind racing through every bit of knowledge. Henry remembered the date and where his wife and daughter would be. Anxiety and fear sent a shock through the nervous system.

"She's at the Skymall with Julia. Victoria would never turn off her coms for shopping." Henry's mind melded with the internet in an instant upon activating the wireless neural implant. Information poured into the man's mind slithering through the energy conduits of information. Henry accessed the Skymall's public system which reported it had been taken offline for maintenance. Next the consciousness flowed towards the public police department, and hacked through the digital defenses that protected the system from intruders. Henry's eyes filled with life as his mind rushed back to reality as he grabbed the communicator

"Get this shuttlecraft over to the Skymall now!" Muse security forces turned to look at their commander.

"What is the situation sir?" Cpt. Anderson senses buzzed with the instinctive knowledge that something was wrong. A picture can speak a thousand words and Henry's expression to the discerning eye show the only shred of fear left in the man.

"Victoria and Julia are under attack. Reports of gunfire and explosion are coming from the Skymall. Get your men organized this is going to be a hot drop in to a hostile zone." Taking command of the autopilot in the shuttle Henry rerouted the shuttle. Max could see worry in his friend eyes.

"Sir what is the situation on the ground?" Henry's mind consumed by the task ignored the question. Silence spoke louder than any words could have. Each man and woman in the cabin felt their worst fears confirmed. Each member of the team went to work. Tactical equipment and weapons began circulating the cabin.

"We're going in as soon as we arrive." Henry's orders his team into position. Not a single person spoke. Weapons clicked locking clips into place. Commotion filled the cabin. Each individual checked their equipment and the person next to them. Muse security was a family business. Each member of its team had a deep emotional connection to Henry, Victoria, and Julia. Feelings of dread purpose filled every man and woman. Inertia shifted when the shuttlecraft careened towards its destination.

Capt. Anderson broke silence to inform "the team is ready for your deployment sir." Henry just nodded in acknowledgement.

"Sir we are on final approach vector. Police request that we divert the shuttle away from the area" the pilot reported.

Henry stomped towards the cockpit almost ripping the door off its hinges. Police forces created a no fly zone around the Skymall. Officers on the ground surrounded the building running the standard police play book. Blue and red flashing lights of the police cars reflected off the glistening glass. From the cockpit Henry could see the inside of the mall looked like a war zone. Black smoke collecting in a dense cloud on the ceiling trapped inside by glass. Henry snatched the com from the pilot and brought it to ear.

"This is NYPD to Muse Shuttlecraft. Please reroute to a different zone now or we will be forced to open fire." Before anyone could do anything the com blared with Henry's voice.

"This is Henry Williams and I am landing at the Skymall! If you want to open fire I suggest you do it now. I wonder how your commanding officer will respond to you shooting this ship down. Perhaps you missed the news report on the damage in Beijing." Henry cut transmission and shut off the com channel.

"Interesting diplomacy sir" Cpt. Anderson joked.

Henry turned to the pilot "get us to the main entrance. Hover over top we'll rappel down. Once we are on the ground turn on the coms and follow the NYPD orders. If the NYPD detain you do not answer any questions till my lawyers arrive. Do you understand?"

The pilot eyes relayed the fear of defying the authorities but he responded "yes sir." Henry matched towards the back exit hatch of the shuttlecraft with Capt. Anderson. Both men walked stood at the exit hatch with the rest of the team right behind. Snapped their rappel lines and prepared to drop the team waited for the signal. Henry turned to face his troops with his hand on the door ready to open it.

"I am not going to lie to you. We are dropping into a warzone that my wife and daughter are trapped in. I do not know what to expect and we don't have time to plan." Each member of the team listened in silence. Every person could feel the worry emanating from the man. Henry could feel each person worrying about his wife and daughter.

"I trust each and every man and women on this team, because you are the best of the best. When we dropped from this shuttle we will be surrounded by enemies. Even the NYPD will stand in the way. Any man or woman who does not want to take part in this action can choose not to. I cannot ask you to do this."

Henry watched with a discerning eye. Not a single person faltered. Every one stood united in cause. Commanding people was not a gift, but a great burden. Henry knew he was endangering his people for his family. Worry etched the commander's face.

"I won't command you to do this, but I need your help. My wife and daughter need your help. Who is with me?" Roaring in unity the teams combined voices shook with thunderous resonation. Everyone standing united in support of Henry filled him with hope.

"All troops are prepared and ready to deploy. Just give the command sir." Cpt. Anderson looked into Henry's fierce eyes. Air rushed in as the hatch opened. Stepping into the doorway Henry looked back.

"Let's show these people how war is fought by real soldiers, and why we are the best warriors on the planet." Henry Williams and thirty of his troops repelled down to the main entrance to the Skymall. Police force assembled outside stared watching the heavily armed men and woman repel down. Approaching from the police barricade the commander officer stared at Henry.

"What the hell do you think you're doing? I ought to have you arrested! Who the hell do you think you are?" Muse guards ignored the officer standing behind their commander. Henry stared passed the officer berating him look taking in the situation.

"I am Henry Williams. Officer if you and your men don't step out of the way you leave me no other choice but to fight through you." Henry's calm and authoritative tone shocked the officer for a second.

"Sir I understand emotions are high right now, but you need to let the police do our job." Henry knew the commanding officer tried to calm the situation.

"What's your name?" Henry searched the man's uniform for a name and rank.

"I am Deputy Chief James Wayne." Henry drew his gun with lightning speed and aimed it at the deputy chief's head. Muse security forces raised their guns to back up their commander.

"Well James you seem to have a problem. You face a superior foe with superior firepower who has outflanked you." Cops watching from the barricade were confused. Some of the officers continued aiming forward while some turned to aim at the new threat. Guns pointed in all directions.

"James you got three seconds to come to a decision before I squeeze this trigger. Then I'll fight through your men. You can't stop us." James eyes flittered trying to assess the situation. Pressure of the situation bore down on the unprepared Deputy Chief. Both men stared at each other trying to peer into the future.

Henry voice resonated with force as he counted "one!" Guns clicked into action. Muse soldiers stared down the sights on their guns. Police officers looked at each other knowing they didn't stand a chance. Beads of sweat appeared on James head.

"Sir I understand your wife and daughter are."

Cutting the Deputy Chief off Henry stated with more force "two!" James felt the lives hanging in the balance trying to sense the right decision. In five minute the whole world seemed to flip upside down. Nothing made sense in James mind. Certainty of action wore on Henry face.

"Let them through." James ordered his officers still staring into Henry's eyes. Muse forces lowered gun in unison with their commanding officer. Sighs of relief could be heard from the officers. Henry began marching towards the entrance with his troops in formation around him. James raced up behind Henry moving alongside the man.

"Mr. Williams I should notify you that your wife is holed up in the parking garage. Another small team of Muse security is trapped inside the mall." Henry listened wondering why he was helping.

"Can you tell me about the situation?" Information could be the difference between life and death. Henry needed any intelligence on the inside situation. James showed a rare ability to look past a grievous wound. Most men would not respond well to a gun aimed at them, or a death threat. Even fewer men would than help the man who had pointed the gun.

"Insurgents breached the mall detonating a series of explosions. Teams assaulted every entrance with precision according to video footage. Within minutes the group secured the entire mall. Inside agents took out the communication except for the hard lines to the building. We have no clue what's going on inside the mall, and the perpetrators have yet to make any demands. Your wife was able to get out a distress call to bring reinforcements, and then all communications went silent." Wayne didn't hold any information back.

Weighing the situation Henry knew this was the work of a team of ghosts. Professional mercenaries contracting their service to corporations, governments, and anyone who could afford the price tag. James provided valuable information that gave insight into the situation. Muse forces around Henry listened to the report. Activating the neural networked Henry directed his troops.

"Cpt. Anderson split the team. We need one team to move on the garage. The second team will aid in rescuing the people trapped in the mall." Neural connection between Muse security personnel allowed the order to be said without words. In battle the speed of neural communication gave Muse soldiers an edge. Henry could use the connection to see through the eyes and access the memories of his people. Neural communication created a phalanx of the human mind.

"Word from your wife is gunfire separated her and your daughter. There is no way to know where your daughter is in the mall." Wayne's knew the situation looked grim but felt Henry needed to know the truth.

"Lt. Malarkey I need you to stay here. Work on establishing communications with the other team and coordinate information." Malarkey moved to purpose towards the nearby police communication. Henry scanned the horizon sizing up the building. Neurons fired connecting patterns. Hacking multiple network connections poured video feed through the neural implant. Strategy required as broad of a view as possible.

"Capt. Anderson take whoever you want to assist Victoria in the parking garage. Everyone else come with me we're marching through those front doors." Henry's words were followed with a commotion as the teams organized behind him.

"I'll have a transport take your second team to the garage" Deputy Chief Wayne's offered.

"For a guy who threatened to arrest me moments ago you seem to have changed your mind." Both men understood the nature of the situation. Wayne's couldn't fault a father trying to save his daughter. Hell in the reverse situation most men would do the same. War shows humanity the real value in the world. People are irreplaceable.

Wayne's shrugged "I might still arrest you afterwards, but if I can't stop you I might as well assist you." Muse transports and support helicopters swept in landing near Cpt. Anderson's team.

"Take care of my wife Max. That's an order" Henry's choice of words revealed his fears.

"I'll make sure she gets home safe and sound." Engines ignited expelling a roar of wind causing the transport to drift away from the platform. Rumbling of engines made speaking impossible. Henry watched for a moment before turning to the task at hand. Enhanced vision showed a handful of men hiding in cover just inside the main entrance. Five threats concealed themselves behind stone walls.

"Just beyond the entrance five people are waiting for our attack Lt. Compton." Every member of team could see through Henry's eyes the situation.

Lt. Compton looked to his commander asking "What your plan sir?" Henry's mind churned through the strategic options available. Construction scenarios inside the mind entire realities swirled in a chaotic vortex of possibilities. Each reality created and destroyed in fractions of a second. Weight options Henry searched for the right solution.

"We have to move on them hard and fast to overcome them. We should assume they have advanced imagery. We won't catch them by surprise. No grenades people tight quarters with civilian hostages." The troops standing around Henry nodded agreeing in silence. Every single soldier waited in anticipation. Searching for a strategy caused a memory to come to the surface. Henry looked at the doors the walls thinking about misdirection and deception.

"Lt. Malarkey do you have access to the malls security system?" Kendra's mind buried deep in the matrix of the mall's network nodded in agreement. Henry smiled forming a picture of the future he could create. Superior strategy could overpower the force with easy. Henry knew this battle had already been won.

"I want you to activate the sprinkler system." Kendra responded by activating the fire suppression system. Sprinklers deployed sparking to life spraying in all direction. Water poured from the shop ceilings and pipes over the tropical plants. Henry ordered the fire team into action. Muse forces moved with alacrity flanking the sides of the front door. Henry watched straight ahead waiting with calm patience at the center of the hurricane of action.

"Why activate the sprinklers?" Wayne's turned to Henry with a quizzical expression revealing his confusion. Without blinking Henry stared forward waiting for something. Water filled plants and flooded the floor. Oozing out from under the door water pooled on the platform.

"Kendra I want you to activate every single threat suppression system in the main entrance." Overriding safety protocols Kendra hacked the system to activate it. Threat suppression systems used motion sensors and cameras to track a threat. Once the system acquired a target it fired a single accurate Taser dart. Activating the entire system sent hundreds of darts flying through the air. Electricity arced as the men behind covered fell to the ground convulsing.

Wayne's quizzical look shifted to one of shock and amazement. Within a minute every single threat behind the door had been eliminated. Waiting for the Taser system to shut off Henry gave the command for muse forces to move. Troops swarmed into the main entrance of the mall in a flurry of action. Within moments the main entrance had been secured. Marching forward Henry entered the mall with several officers in tow.

"Sir the enemies had some sort of neural poison that killed them. I am guessing that the system was remote triggered." Henry bent down and pulled back the black mask. Toxins putrefied while acid eat the flesh on the face of the dead man. Most ghosts used some sort of stored viral and acid system to protect their identities. Clients used ghosts to maintain anonymity, and demanded such systems to protect their identity..

"Ghosts as I thought" Henry muttered.

"So this is a corporate job" the deputy chief stated.

"These ghosts are after something in this building. My instinct points say these people want my wife and daughter. Deputy Chief Wayne my fire team will create a path and funnel any survivors to you can your team handle that?" James looked around at the scene. Bullet holes splattered across the walls as smoke rose from craters.

"Yea I'll handle the civilians and you get your daughter. You know I am definitely getting fired for this." Henry watched his fire team move forward into the mall looking at James.

"I'll do what I can to make sure that doesn't happen, but if it does come see me." Deputy Chief Wayne watched Henry follow behind his men. One of the officers walked up beside him.

"Can you believe we just met Henry Williams?" James recalled hearing stories about Henry Williams from other cops but couldn't help admire the man.

"Wish we met under better circumstance. Now get in there and get those civilians to safety." The officers scurried off to do their jobs before the Deputy Chief got any more upset. James watched the Muse team moved down allowing Civilians to funnel out of the mall. Scared people raced out of the mall in a panicked stampede. No experience prepares someone to meet a man like Henry Williams. James felt the strange mix of fear and awe after standing next to a living force of nature.

CHAPTER 9

Dazed and Confused

Disorientation weighed Julia's mind feeling a sharp pain radiating from her forehead. Crimson drops fell from soaked tendrils of hair splashing into the ground below. Vision blurred for the young woman watching the floor sweep by in swift motion. Julia brought her hand to her head feeling intense pain whipping her mind. Sound of gunfire seemed to come from some immutable distance echoing through the corridor.

Julia's eyes fixed on her hand trying to see straight. Blurred vision made it hard to see anything at all, and pain made it impossible for the young woman to focus. Thick dark liquid coated Julia's hand dripping off her fingers. Racing down the tunnel Muse soldiers carried Julia towards the bookstore. Arriving at the door to the bookstore the group gasped for air. One of the guards looked back watching for movement. Trying to open the door the other guard accessed the computer. Julia didn't even realize she still clenched the book in her other hand.

"Damn the door is locked from the other side!" Frustrated the guard pulled a data pad hooking a cord to the door. Accessing the computer triggered a password breaking program to launch on the data pad. Muse security combat training instilled a sense of calm, but the corporate guards training fell short. Both of the corporate guards were wound tighter than a spring. Time ticked away on the password breaking program assaulting the lock.

"Just a minute or so before the hacking tool locks onto the passcode." Julia hung over the shoulder of the guard. Dangling like a sack of potatoes the young woman tried to muster control of her tongue. No words came out. Locking in on the code the program finished its routine. Creaking to life the door slid open. Guards moved into the small square room at the bottom of the staircase.

Pulling the hacking tool free the last guard stepped in pulling a cutting torch. Corporate guards helped pushed the doors back shut. Sparks leapt from the cutting torch igniting with a whoosh. Applying the torch the guard knew welding the door would take a minute. Both corporate security officers' eyes showed the terror gripping their minds.

"We are not trained to deal with this kind of shit. Those are professional soldiers coming to get us. How are we going to escape?" Setting Julia down against the wall the Muse soldier examined the wound on her forehead. Both Corporate guards paced with worry in the small room. Julia hissed from pain when the guard wiped away soot and blood from the wound.

"My name's Tim O'Neil. Hold still I am going to seal that wound on your forehead." Spraying grey anti-septic foam caused searing pain to shoot through Julia returning her senses. Tim applied pressure to the wound causing nerves to spasm. Julia's eyes darted around trying to figure out where she was at first.

"Where is my mom?" Julia struggled to stand up. Looking around the young woman tried to discern where she was and what had happened. Standing in small square stairwell exit sparked memory. Julia remembered coming under fire and the soldiers dragging her to safety. Blurred pictures rolled through memory coming in bits and pieces.

"Slow down Julia. You took a nasty hit to the head. You need to relax so I can treat you and we can get moving." Julia's eyes seen her blood soaked hands causing her to start screaming in panic. Both corporate security guards leapt from shock at the sudden noise. Tim placed his hand over the girl's mouth to seal the screaming cries echoing through the stairwell. All eyes fell on Julia except the guard welding the door shut.

"I am going to take my hand off your mouth now, but you can't scream or someone is going to hear you. Do you understand?" Julia nodded in agreement. Tim removed his hand with hesitation. Julia looked at the guard sealing the door, the two scared bookstore guards, and back to Tim.

"Where is my mother?" Julia question was answered with silence and averted gazes. No one knew how to say the truth. Victoria remained trapped in the garage fighting for her life. Everyone feared how Julia would react to the news. Tim looked back towards the door before answering.

"Your mothers trapped with the other half of the team in the parking garage. We came under attack when we tried to exit the mall. I am under orders to get you to safety Julia, but I need to seal that wound on your head ok?" Julia looked at Tim's hand seeing the surgical spray foam for sealing wounds. Calming down the young woman let the man inspect the woman on her head.

Julia mustered the courage to ask "is it going to hurt?"

Tim eyes widened with empathy responding with a curt "yes."

Julia bit into her lip to prevent from screaming feeling the spray set her nerves on fire. After a few seconds Tim looked at his patient. Artificial flesh began to harden pulling the skin together. Julia grimaced feeling the goo sink deep into the cut and harden. After a few moments the wound vanished to all but well trained eyes.

"Good as new" Tim smiled offering his hand to help the woman up. Julia took the offer of help still feeling a little woozy. Tim braced the young woman feeling her teetered back and forth against the wall. Julia looked at Tim's big brown eyes offering hope to her.

"Take it easy now Julia. You're probably still suffering from shock of the blow to your head." Tim ran a couple checks on his patient. Machines reported strong vitals. After a few minutes Tim was satisfied with the results. With Julia back on her feet the group could get ready to move out.

Tim looked at his friend by the door asking "Kurt that door sealed?" Shutting off the cutting torch Kurt removed the goggles from his eyes. Thick metal slag covered the door seam holding it shut. Studying the weld Kurt believed it would hold against most attempts.

"Yea it'll take a bit to get through this thing without explosives. You got a plan?" Once spoken the question revealed that everyone was wondering the same thing. Tim weighed out the possibilities. Burden of command fell on the highest ranking officer.

Tim looked at the two guards "I want you two on point. We're going to have to make a break for the main entrance. It's the only choice left."

Both corporate guards shook with nervous energy. Tim could sense neither of the guards was prepared for the situation they now faced.

"Keep calm and we'll get out of here" Kurt tried to sooth and calm with words.

Tim looked back and asked "Can you walk Julia?"

"Yea I think so." Julia still clenched the present close to her chest with one hand. Tim braced the young woman steading her to help her walk forward. Legs wobbled when Julia tried to walk forward. Each footstep seemed an Olympic feat to the young woman, but each step came easier than the last.

"You two take point" Tim ordered. Ascended the stairwell with weary minds the team felt anxiety racing in their veins. Each person knew that an uncertain future waited at each corner. Tim's hand held steadfast to Julia shoulder offering continued support and encouragement. Each step towards the top came slower than the last. Tension gripped each person's mind in a stranglehold. Terror gripped all but the most prepared mind in Tim's experience. Halting at the door back to the bookstore the team prepared themselves. Tim looked at the team waiting in position for orders.

"We have no clue what is on the other side of the door. Julia I want you to stay back until we make sure the area is clear of danger. Kurt hand her your cutting torch. If we encounter resistance I want you to seal this door behind us. That should buy you some time for help to arrive." Kurt passed the tool to her and placed the googles on her head. Julia grasped the cutting torch with her blood soaked hand.

The door to the book store whisked open without noise. Both book store guards moved into the hallway leading to the store room. Tim and his partner Kurt followed behind taking up the rear position. Gunfire echoed in the hallway from the promenade. Slow careful footsteps allow the team to move forward without sound. No signs of movement or any life met the advancing team.

Both teams of armed guards moved into the storeroom taking cover behind printing machines. Julia glimpsed into the storeroom seeing Tim motion for her to move forward with his hand. Soft clacking footsteps of the small woman echoed in the empty hall. Tim pointed to an enclosing behind a dense metal printing press that offered exceptional cover.

"Wait here Julia. I am going to investigate the main shop." Tim and Kurt moved into the bookstore now devoid of any of any human presence. Both men scanned the windows of the book store seeing the chaos of the mall promenade. Blood stained the mall floor. Bodies lay strewn everywhere. Innocent shoppers riddled with bullets created a gruesome tapestry. Smell of burning flesh filled the air with putrid aroma.

Glaring out onto the promenade Tim couldn't spot any movement. Taking up position the two bookstore guards flanked both sides of the arched entrance. Julia moved forward taking cover behind the shop counter with her guards. No solution to the precarious situation presented itself. Tim knew perception can be deceiving. The promenade seemed devoid, but instinct told each person to ignore the illusion.

"Julia this is what we are going to do. Kurt and I are going to head onto the promenade with the other guards. We'll try to create a diversion for you. Once the enemy engages I want you to bolt towards the main entrance without looking back. These will slow you down." Tim bent down removing the high heel shoes from Julia's feet.

"What about all the broken glass?" Julia's eyes dilated in fear. Tim pulled bandages from his supply kit on his side wrapping them around the diminutive feet. Several laps of the bandage created a thick glove of protection. Tim and Julia looked at each other seeing the fear reflected back from the other person eyes.

"The bandages will protect you from the glass, but regardless you need to block out any pain. We will do our best to protect you and draw any gunfire. Once you start running do not stop under any circumstance. No matter what you hear or what happens just keep running until your free." Julia nodded in silent agreement.

Tim and Kurt raced from behind the counter with steadfast determination. Both men darted towards the arched entrance taking cover behind the pillars. Hand signals ordered the corporate guards to move forward. Breaking from cover both bookstore guards darted across the promenade taking cover behind planters. Thick trunk of a large palm tree raced towards the sky from the cement planter. Scared and isolated both guards crouched down glancing back and forth. Sounds of gunfire echoed from all around, but there was no sign of movement.

Tim watched and waited. Smoke drifted through the promenade. After a moment Tim and Kurt darted around the corner of the entrance. The promenade seemed clear after a moment of inspection. Tim and Kurt pressed their backs firm to the shop wall for cover. Gunshots rang out in the distance at random intervals. Tim leaned through the broken window giving the signal with his hand.

Julia raced from behind the counter pushing her legs with all the force she could muster. Tim watched ahead searching the horizon for any sign of movement amongst the sea of corpses. Julia's heart hammered in her chest powering her to surge forward from the shop onto the promenade. Roaring to life a powerful sniper rifle echoed through the mall. Julia caught the book store guards head exploded in a bloody torrent of gore.

Screaming in absolute horror Julia drowned out the gun fire echoing throughout the mall. Tim turned in time to see the guard toppling over. Twitching nerves caused gunfire to rack across the ground when the man fell over. Scattered fire in front of Julia knocked her off balance preventing her escape. Tim watched his charge toppled and slam into the floor with a loud reverberating thud. Within seconds the next shot rippled through the air echoing through the mall. The high calibre round slammed into the planter tearing through the cement. Blasting through the cement the bullet took out the second guard. Julia recoiled in fear clawing at the ground trying to get behind cover.

Tim scanned the horizon with methodical precision trying to spot the shooters. Flashes of gunfire from above the shops revealed the enemies position. Tim motioned Kurt to the direction of the shooter. Both men took aim and opened fire. Bullets tracers shot through the air leaving a distinct momentary trail of red. Julia pushed herself from the floor feeling glass shards cut deep into the palm of her hands. Adrenaline surged in the young woman blocking any sensation of pain.

"RUN JULIA!" Tim's shout rang soft sounding like it came from a great distance to the young woman. Panic set in and the instinct to flee over powered the senses. Julia pulled herself back to her feet dashing across the promenade without a thought. Gunfire hailed down shattering the pots of plants and ripping apart the tiled floor. Glancing back to watch Julia's escape Tim continued to fire in steady bursts at the target.

Chaos consumed Julia's mind. Explosions of debris shot in every direction filling the air. Erratic breathing caused air to be consumed in violent gasps. Pushing the muscles with fear addled determination Julia felt a fiery backlash of pain. Muscles burned demanding more energy. Tim's words repeated in Julia's mind acting like a mantra pushing away the encroaching terror.

Footsteps hit the ground with powerful purpose propelling the young woman. Julia couldn't resist the terror pushing back the last vestiges of reason from her mind, and glimpsed back to look at Tim. Explosions erupted sending the limp lifeless body of Kurt sailing through the air. Julia couldn't scream, couldn't run, and froze up. Kurt slammed with force into the ground. Cracking bones created a distinct sound that would never be forgotten. Flesh squished beneath the force of impact. Tim watched Julia freeze and stare at the body of Kurt mere inches away from her.

"KEEP RUNNING!" Rapid gunfire absorbed Tim's screams. Bullets ripped into the ground near the man. Julia's eyes widened with horror watching gunfire tear through Tim's shoulder. The second and then a third shot tore through Tim's chest armour dropping him to the floor. Julia remained frozen in time compelled to watch the horror transpiring around her. Tim crawled across the floor his mouth uttering words that couldn't be heard. Blood stained the floor beneath the wounded guard struggling forward. Tim waved his hand trying to signal Julia to run.

Air seemed to shift. The optical illusion vanished revealing a large man wearing black armor and a face mask. Julia watched the man marching towards her with slow confident strides. Tim heard the sounds of footsteps behind. Rolling over gripping the assault rifle Tim tried to aim at the target. The unidentified assailant shot Tim in the head without breaking eye contact with Julia. Honed instincts of a predator told the assailant he had won. Stalking the prey the assailant walked around the woman drinking in the victory.

"I have secured the target." The assailant spoke into a communicator with a voice distorted by some electronic device. Staring up Julia stared into the black goggles concealing the eyes of her assailant. Mirrored glass of the goggles reflected Julia's terror stricken eyes back at her. Reaching down the assailant grasped a chunk of hair in his hands pulling the woman to her feet. Holding Julia's hair allowed the man to control her every move. With a sharp violent pull of hair the assailant drug Julia behind.

"Ghost one this is command. We are sending in the extraction team." Another distorted voice responded over the communicator. Dragging Julia behind in tears didn't concern the man. Extraction teams would be here in a few moments. Successful missions are what separate life and death to a ghost. Some people call ghosts terrorists and others called them heroes. All the assailant cared about was getting paid.

Julia whimpered "please don't hurt me."

"Stop struggling little girl or I'll make this much more painful for you." A malicious laugh bellowed forth from the assailant dragging his target towards the open atrium. Pain shot through Julia's mind again causing her to stumbled and fall. Before Julia could regain senses she felt a gun barrel pressed against her forehead. Pushing the barrel hard the man tore open the medical gel sealing the wound. Julia howled in pain feeling the wound ripped open.

"Are you going to be a good little girl?" Julia winced in pain nodding her head in agreement. Rumbling in the distance a vector thrust craft roared closer each second. Standing up the assailant released his victim's hair. Pulling Julia to her feet by the back of the neck the ghost pushed his gun against the back of her head.

"Don't worry girl. This will all be over soon. You'll be home with your family in time for your fairy tale Christmas. You can sit around eat chocolates and watch stupid cartoons and movies soon enough." Julia looked up seeing the approaching military attack ship racing towards the mall in the distance.

"You know my father will hunt you down. There is no where you can run that he won't find you." Julia squeezed the book she held close to her chest. The book represented hope. Somehow Julia held onto the book keeping it safe and undamaged in its case.

"Henry William's reputation for audacity and fearlessness is legendary. Will your father risk the life of his beloved daughter to satisfy his vain pride?" Sounds of gunfire echoing from below and throughout the mall stopped. Only the sound of rapid footsteps approaching from behind filled the air. The assailant turned to facing the group of muse soldiers approaching.

"Looks like the Calvary arrived quicker than I anticipated. I guess we get to see exactly how much your father cares for his darling precious princess. Let's see how the man measures up to the legend." The distorted voice taunted from behind the black mask. Julia stared forward eyes full of terror. Pulling Julia into a chock hold turned her body into a shield. Facing the sound of footsteps the ghost pressed the gun to the side of his victim's head. Hope and terror mixed in Julia's mind at the thought of her father rescue.

CHAPTER 10

A Father's Resolve

Henry followed his men in the rear. Muse soldiers pressed forward through the mall. Tactical training allowed precision movement. Soldiers displaced moving to new cover, hunkering down, and moments later displacing again. Clarity of purpose pushed each person forward and silenced doubt. Julia's life hung in the balance. Each team member connected to Henry's mind felt his pain and fear. Glass vibrated from the loud roar of air signalling the approach of an aircraft.

Kendra reported "Sir we got attack gunships inbound." Henry didn't respond pushing the thought from his mind. Only the thought of saving Julia remained. Henry resigned himself to save his daughter or die trying. Every member of the team felt the cold resignation in the neural link. Henry's love for his daughter knew no bounds, and no sacrifice would be too great.

"Have you been able to reach Victoria yet?"

Kendra's soft voice responded "You wife is moving towards the promenade from the opposite side. I'll patch her through to you." The com line went dead for a few seconds. Adrenaline pumped through Henry's veins. Sparking back to life the communication filled with static noise. Kendra worked her magic amplifying signal strength to cut through interference.

"Henry if you can hear me we're on our way. I sent soldiers back with Julia towards the main entrance. Keep your eyes open." Victoria's voice broke through the static.

"I haven't found her yet. Nothing is going to happen to our baby." Henry gritted his teeth grinding down with the force of frustration. Emotions needed to be kept from decision making. Years of struggle and running a corporation taught Henry that lesson in spades. Sounds of a struggle against something echoed over the neural link. Henry knew he needed to keep his wife calm.

"The door back to the book store is sealed from the inside. We are blasting through with an improvised explosive. We'll link up with you in a few minutes." Henry turned the communicator off rounding the corner with his men. The man held Julia in a choke hold with his arm. Henry eye's flared with rage staring into the black glass of the goggles.

"Well if it isn't the great Henry Williams in the flesh" the distorted voice of the assailant bellowed out. Surging next to Julia's head deafening shots rang out next to her ear. Henry dodged behind a large column along the garden path. Bullets slammed into the column just missing the intended target. Henry's men took position trying to aim at the assailant. Ducking behind Julia the assailant used her to cover most of his body. Soldiers looked down scopes trying to find a shot.

"Sir we can't get a shot. The chance to hit Julia is too great with her in the way." Words echoed inside Henry's mind from the wireless network. Digital information flowed between the people. Each person could see, hear, and feel what every other team member could feel. Henry's willpower dominated the networked minds unifying purpose and dispelling fear.

"Jackson can you get a clear shot?"

"Not a good one sir." Jackson peered through the scope at the assailants head waiting for a shot. The assailant held Julia in front leaving only a few inches to hit the target. Henry heard the distinct roar of the aircraft coming to rest overhead. Variables turned in the mind like giant cogs. Henry could feel the pressure of the situation bearing down trying to crush him.

"Stay in cover people. Make sure that aircraft can't get a clear shot at any of us."

"Looks like our rides here. Guess daddy won't be saving you today princess." The assailant squeezed harder on Julia's neck making her squirm in pain. Henry watched as the man tortured his daughter fuelling his anger. Aiming the pistol upwards the assailant fired a single shot. Explosive rounds hit the glass and detonated. Shards of glass rained down behind Julia. Dangling down from the aircraft a line lowered through the hole.

"Let my daughter go now, or I swear I will devout fortunes to your long painful death." Henry hoped the threat would provoke compliance, but if not compliance than a moment of hesitation. Malicious laughter echoed through the promenade from the assailant. Henry knew everything he needed to from the unusual response. Both men were willing to die to complete their objective.

"Those who hunt monsters with self-righteous certainty often become that which they hunt." The assailant taunted Henry with a malicious laugh.

"Team prepare to take a shot." Henry felt time and hope slipping through his fingers watching the assailant step towards the rope. Desperation flared across the neural connection. Everyone could feel Henry's desperation and fears. The soldiers worried the emotions compromised Henry's ability to strategize. The neural connection fragmented into dissenting voices. Different voices raged in Henry's mind.

"Sir it's too dangerous. Your daughter is too close" a cadre of minds urged in unison. Splintered voices echoed a mix of loyalty, doubt, and anxiety. Many members of the team remained silent in the neural connection. resigned to their commanders' fate. Not a single team member feared their own death, but every person feared for Julia's safety.

"There is no choice! Just be prepared to take the shot when the opportunity presents itself." Henry surged with motion breaking from cover without warning. Each stride powered by the grim determination of a father's love for his child. Henry strode forward across the promenade towards his daughter. Hovering above the mall the gunship tracked motion locking in on the moving target. Twin cannon barrels spun whining louder picking up speed.

Thundering forth cannons blared to life pouring a stream of gunfire down on the target. Glass ceiling panels exploded into thousands of shards raining down razor sharp fragments. Bullets tore through cement and plants. Debris flew the air creating a maelstrom around the solemn man. Nothing could stop Henry from rescuing his daughter. Shards cut the skin. Echoes of glass tinkled hitting the tiled floor. Henry marched through the storm unfazed.

Bullets grazed past the man missing the target by a breath. Henry's clenched his pistol using his cybernetic eyes to zoom in on the assailant. Giant tropical leaves prevented the gunship from getting clear visual of the man. Kendra had been using a wave generator to interfere with the optics preventing accurate lock. Henry waited for the moment the assailant moved to take the shot. Staying calm the father marched through chaos and destruction swirling around him. Julia watched the gun drift in front of her vision. Horror filled the woman's mind watching the assailant take aim at her father.

"DADDY!" Everyone heard the woman's scream booming over the fury of gunfire. Julia pushed back off her feet slamming the back of her skull into the man's face. Instinct took over. Skulls collided with resounding force causing the assailant to stagger releasing the chokehold. Taking advantage of the maneuvering room Julia spun around driving her elbow backwards into the man's chin. Disorientation caused the man to fall backwards losing balance.

Henry raced forward trying to help his daughter. Julia grabbed the gun ripping it from her assailants grasp while he fell. Crashing into the ground the assailant looked up at the former victim. Julia eyes filled with rage before opening fire. Shot after shot rang out. Soldiers watched on powerless. Julia emptied the clip into the body of the assailant still pulling the trigger long after the gun ran out of ammunition. Tears fell towards the ground in a steady downpour from Julia's eyes.

Henry sprinted forward towards his daughter. Muse soldiers opening fire on the aircraft lingering above. The steady barrage of bullets from the ground forced the gunship to retreat away with haste. Henry grabbed his daughter and spun her around wrapping his arms around her. Julia felt her fathers' tight embrace threatening to suffocate her. Henry and Julia feel to their knees holding onto one another. Tears poured from both father and daughter.

Henry whispered in his daughters' ear "your safe now baby." Every muse soldier could feel Henry's thoughts fill with a relief. Most of the members of Muse Industries watched Julia grow from childhood. Everyone felt the ecstasy of joy seeing the young woman safe. Few people ever seen Henry eyes more than moistened by sadness, and the onslaught of tears brought everyone watching to tears.

Marching behind the Muse soldiers Victoria gripped the pistol tight in her hand. Maj. Lee's team raced out from the store room of the book store. Looking around the promenade Victoria saw Henry on the ground holding Julia. Emotions took control overwhelming the mothers' senses. Charging across the promenade Victoria raced towards her child and husband. Tears burst forward and the woman dropped the gun which clattered to the floor. Victoria dropped to the floor embracing her daughter and husband as relief washed over her.

"I would have never forgiven myself if anything happened to you." Victoria stared in to her daughter's eyes brimming with tears. Surrounded by carnage and death the Williams family held each other close. Police aircraft covered the sky trying to keep air traffic from the scene. Several reporters zoomed in broadcasting live feed of the Williams family embrace surrounded by bodies. News broadcasts around the world played the live feed.

"Let's get you out of here" Henry stated. Victoria helped her daughter to her feet. Shock set in pulling Julia to a distant place while the world hummed on around her. Henry saw the blood soaked bandages wrapped around his daughters' feet, and the shards of glass sticking out. Crimson soaked the bandages. Henry scooped his daughter into his arms and hoisted her up.

"Let's go home baby." Deputy Chief Wayne's walked towards the Williams examining the carnage with police officers following behind. Bodies littered the ground all around. Blood stained the ground pooling in the bullet holes in the floor. Once a place of joy and fun the mall transformed into a visual of the dread spectre of death.

"Have your men seen any survivors?" Henry shook his head no in response carrying his daughter in his arms.

"I would like to get my daughter home after the events of the day. Please excuse us Deputy Chief."

Wayne's looked at Henry "The media is outside and the feeding frenzy has already started. You know I am going to need statements from your wife and daughter at some point later." Maj. Lee and Cpt. Anderson formed troops up around Henry, Victoria, and Julia. Deputy Chief Wayne's surveyed the damage noticing the shimmering case from the book.

"What's this?" Wayne's muttered to himself as he bent over and picked up the container.

"Dad that's your Christmas present I bought for you" Julia pointed towards the Deputy Chief. Henry turned and looked at the container in Wayne's hands. Marching over Victoria approached the deputy chief. Wayne's inspected the book feeling a tap on his shoulder.

"Excuse me Deputy Chief. That book you are holding is the reason Julia and I came to the Skymall today. If it's not too much trouble we'd like it back." Victoria glanced at the container in the Deputy Chief hands. Wayne's wondered how much something like the old book cost, but pushed the thoughts aside.

"You have a very thoughtful daughter Mr. Williams" Wayne's smiled handing the container to Victoria.

"I'll be in touch in a day or two. Is that that ok Deputy Chief" Henry asked?

"No rush Mr. Williams. It's going to take me a month to write up all the paper work on this." Wayne watched the Williams family walking away wondering how he would explain everything. Henry and his family walked at a slow pace toward the main entrance of the mall. The Williams family held onto each other in silent relief. Muse Security forces formed a tight perimeter around the family. Maj. Lee looked back at his old friend Henry holding his daughter than to his second in command.

"Hell of a family picture" Lee noted.

"Hell most families today won't even help their kids go to school let alone die for them." Cpt. Anderson nodded in agreement.

Edward smiled "reminds me of my grandpa. You know back when people had values." Max looked ahead seeing the ambiance of flashing lights. Sirens and commotion grew louder. Media swarmed the landing platform outside. Hundreds of people gathered out front holding cameras pointed at the mall. Paparazzi were parasites feasting on the corpse of human tragedy to earn money. Muse security most often acted to shield the Williams family from the media.

"The worst part is after enduring one tragedy we get to walk through another. I almost prefer the gunship over what's waiting outside." Cpt. Anderson glanced around drinking in the scene. Sirens flashing strobe glared through the glass of the Skymall entrance. NYPD forces enforced a cordon. Officers tried to keep the onslaught of TV reporters and journalists from getting inside. A sea of journalists discussed the events while recording segments with their camera crews. Clamour of motion and voices filled the air outside.

From a distance the mass of journalists appear a school of piranha stuck in shrinking waters. The term applied to the media attention to newsworthy events was aptly named the feeding frenzy. Each piranha snapping for scraps of information and devouring each other if necessary just to survive. Reporters struggled to record the most compelling version of the story. Tragedies and successes emotional appeal would be heightened by succulent news framing.

When the twin towers fell in 2001 the real causality was the destruction of journalistic integrity. Modern journalism became pseudo indoctrination best captured by the word truthiness. Scientists called the behaviour framing, or the selective telling of the facts to manipulate public opinion. Propaganda wasn't a new invention. Even the best news networks made sure every view felt true even when it was the opposite of truth. Every tragedy reported by the news was sold to the public through fear. Fear and wonder kept the masses distracted.

Modern day journalism treated the news the way the Roman Republic treated gladiators in the arena. Every triumph and tragedy needed to be coated in honeyed rhetoric matched to compelling spectacles. Every event told to the people through stories that stroked the public's emotions. Journalist spun the web of the story into one that could happen to anyone. Of course the story focused on the Williams, but betrayed the family as the villain of the story. Every story had to be enthralling. Reporters needed to pull the viewer in and connected them to the experience. News pandered to the lowest common denominator of simple human emotions of anger, joy, and fear.

Corporations are driven by profits, and the News industry is no exception. The cost of increased profits for news organization came at the expense of public awareness. The value of truth eroded in the era of digital media. Lies pushed across the airwaves saturated the truth to the point where truths and lies appeared the same. Twisting public opinion to the advantage of powerful individuals and to entertain the masses ensured profits. News sold lies like PMC sold soldiers to causes. Public opinion was a never ending war.

Maj. Lee and Cpt. Anderson stepped from the Mall first. Lights from the hovering news cars turned to capture the people exiting the mall. Blinding bright white light beamed down on the Williams family exiting the mall. Henry led his family towards an awaiting shuttle. Police cleared an area for the vessel to land at the far end of the main entrance. Distance forced the police to make a barrier to contain the sea of journalists.

Henry carried Julia with Victoria hanging onto his right arm. Lights tracked the family walking down the steps. Journalists' flew into motion causing uproar. Every single camera turned on the Williams. Muse security team escorted the family towards the shuttle. Police kept back the surge of journalists pushing on the police line. Journalists yelled and scream questions gnashing their teeth at the story inches away. One Journalist recorded a segment with the Williams in the background.

"When people think of Christmas they think of families gathering together. Today the Williams are appreciating being together after surviving a tragedy. Today December 23 2033 will be remembered forever as a tragic day for New York to rival that of 9/11. U.S. Senator Victoria Williams and her seventeen year old daughter Julia were shopping today. A group of insurgents attacked the Skymall trying to kidnap Julia Williams. Victoria Williams is the wife of Henry Williams's founder and CEO of Muse Industries. Today cybertechnology is a multitrillion dollar industry. Henry Williams was attacked in Beijing yesterday. The tragedy today makes it clear that the Williams family have become the targets of some group. What will the government do about this, or will anything be done at all? Police refused to comment on survivors at this time, but from all accounts the casualties are high. This is Victor Wolfe reported for Owl news where the wise get their news."

Henry stared at the charismatic German reporter. Victor stood just over six feet tall with a well-built frame. The young reporter still in his early thirties dressed impeccably with the style of the times. Every single news agency sought after the man. Victors' short and wild hair resembled more of mane than a haircut which complimented his goatee well. Henry admired the way Victor was able to influence the audience to persuade them to his conclusions. Owl news desired the man because of his popularity and republican views.

"Take care of Julia and ensure she is comfortable." Maj. Lee nodded in agreement to Victoria's request. Henry handed over Julia staring at Edward with a concerned look. Muse security helped Victoria on the shuttle staying close to her. Lee turned to board the shuttle when Henry marched towards Victor Wolfe. The sudden action caught all the guards by shock. Journalists watched the man approaching feeling excitement surge at the possibilities. Leaping over the cordon in one stride Henry noticed his security team trailing behind.

"Hey Victor you want the real story?" Victor turned in a state of shock from Henry's sudden presence. The journalist couldn't find words. Camera's flashed enhancing Henry's personal presence. Floating nearby a camera drone linked to Victor's mind turned towards the titan of business. Straightening the suit jacket Victor tried to regain composure, but still couldn't find anything to say.

"The real story is innocent people are dead because we don't live in a perfect world." The automated robotic camera zoomed in recording Henry. Live feed flooded the news room of Owl news being directed by satellites. Video streamed all over the world in a matter of minutes. Executives watched viewer numbers soring across all media platforms from television, online streaming, and holoemitters playing the footage.

"There are people out there that pay people to hurt other people, and some people out there like to make money hurting other people. Governments can't stop them or don't want to. Mr. Wolfe what you're doing here is a disservice to the dead and that's the real story." Henry turned storming away with his men right behind him. Journalist surged around Henry shouting questions hoping they would be answered. Microphones hung in the air hoping to catch a stray noise that could be used.

Cap. Anderson moved in close and asked "What the hell was that?"

Henry smirked for a second before answering "political spin." Both men walked back towards the ship. Owl news would try to spin what had been said to discredit and promote a different agenda. Henry knew the world would respond to the real emotion he had put behind the words. The only way to battle slander was by standing up to it.

CHAPTER 11

Post Traumatic Stress

Sun reflected off the sleek shuttle ascending into the Sky. Henry watched the clamouring crowd fade into the distance. Feeling the loving embrace Julia rested her head on her father's shoulder. Maj. Lee and Capt. Anderson sat with their troops watching over the Williams family. Events of the day filled the cabin of the shuttle with a sombre ambiance that everyone felt sink in. Sudden weightless feeling of gravitational inertia from the shuttle foreshadowed the future.

Holding the most important things close Henry felt relief wash over him. Holding one arm Victoria rested to in her seat with eyes closed. Looking down Henry smiled daughter cuddled up to him. Everyone who knew the William's described the family as affection, loving, and private. Henry was a proud family man from a family that had ever reason for their pride. When bad times struck the family pulled together and endured.

Soft leather cushions drained tension from Henry sinking deeper into his seat. Memories of the events of the day replayed over and over. Examining the memories Henry tried to gleam any new piece of information. Today's events would define Julia in unpredictable ways for the rest of her life. Henry tried to focus his thoughts away from the worry pulling at his mind. The future is always uncertain like a raging river of rapids. How the event would shape Julia would only be seen in time.

Henry knew that the real problem with people is you can never know what is lurking behind their eyes. The best scientific theories measured observable behaviours to form patterns of thought and action, but freewill meant at any moment that pattern could change. Experience taught Henry that life is a struggle between organized reason and chaotic violence. People lived in ignorant bliss at the dangers all around them expecting police, firefighters, and doctors to solve every problem.

Henry watched most people struggling to survive putting forward minimal effort. Success demands effort. Life defines the individual by pushing people past their breaking point to see how much they can endure. Looking down Henry thought about how much his daughter surprised him today. Julia never surrendered choosing to fight back unarmed and without training. Nerves surged with a terrible mix of pride, terror, and helplessness when Henry watched his daughter fighting back.

The ordeal at the mall would be talked about for weeks in the news. Realization swept through Henry knowing how much this event would infect Julia's school life. Every student and teacher would be talking about the event. Henry knew the real struggle would be answering the questions still to come. Political and corporate enemies would seek to use the story of the tragedy to their advantage.

Half-truths, rumours, and lies would descend with hurricane force swirling around Julia at the center. Henry knew there was nothing he could do to shelter his daughter from public opinion. Every parent wants to protect children from the horrors of the world. No feeling is worse than powerlessness. Utter futility to prevent a tragedy weighs on everyone with equal strength. Wealth and power didn't protect children, but create even more danger.

Silence lingered in the cabin of the shuttle during the trip back to the William's estate. Snowflakes danced just beyond the window of the shuttle. New York City drifted away and skyscrapers vanished into the sky. The William's estate rested on the Long Island sound between New York State and Connecticut. The family home boasting fifty acres of beach front property, two offshore islands, and an almost fourteen thousands square foot old French renaissance Mansion.

Sweeping over the copper beech trees the shuttle approached the landing zone. Thrust from the engines of the shuttle tossed the titanic trees back and forth like tooth picks. Descending into the clearing the shuttle hovered to a stop over the landing pad. Lights flashed from the landing pad reflecting off the shuttle in steady strobes. Hues of amber and orange broke through the dark grey clouds gathering in the early dusk skies.

Disembarking first Maj. Lee led the security team off the shuttle in single file. Following the security team Henry helped his wife and daughter off the shuttle. Muse Security forces escorted the William's family down the winding path towards their home. No sanctuary existed for the rich and powerful. The idyllic home rested in the gated community that resembled a military base rather than a luxurious home. Creating a perimeter around the family Muse security remained Vigilant.

Home sweet home was an idea lost on a man of such power and influence as Henry Williams. Restoring the ancient French renaissance mansion turned the home into a palace fit for a king. Underneath the house rested an underground complex with facilities to house a legion of troops. Hidden from plain sight were all kinds of measures to ensure the protection of the Williams family. Henry took no chances with the safety of his family.

Marching forward at a brisk pace Cpt. Anderson opened the door for the approaching family. Max noticed the look of worry concealed in the families faces. Both parents wore a sombre look on their faces. Julia's face haunted max the most. Exhaustion lined the features of the young woman's face. People described Julia as a radiant ball of energy and passion, but Max seen a broken shell of the girl he remembered.

"Welcome home." Max smiled at the family walking into their home. Julia broke away from her parents upon entered the home. Henry and Victoria watched their daughter in a moment of silent empathy. No one knew how to help Julia deal with what had happened. Henry and Victoria knew the best way to help their daughter was to offer unconditional love and support.

"I am going to go lie down" Julia turned and offered a forced smile.

"Ok honey, but remember the Cross family is coming tomorrow for Christmas Eve dinner." Victoria intended to keep her daughter focused on what needed to be done. Distraction would prevent any slip into deep apathy or guilt. Julia dreaded the thought knowing it had to be done. Reputation is everything in life. The words almost echoed in Julia's mind.

"I'll be fine I just need to get some sleep and wrap dad's present." Julia walked up the stairs attending to how her parents would be studying her behavior. Walking speed, body language, and facial expression could all reveal the truth hidden beneath the surface of flesh. Focusing on walking steady and poised Julia headed towards her room trying to push thoughts away. Raging emotions tore under the skin threatened to break through the mental dam of willpower.

Julia never lied to her parents, but in this situation there was nothing anyone could do. Walking down the hallway to the bedroom each step caused another crack in the emotional dam. Nerves trembling from memories flooding Julia's mind filling her with anxiety. Gunfire and explosions rang out seeming real in the mind. Flashes of people lying on the floor snapped in Julia's vision.

Each step required more concentration sapping mental strength. Reaching out Julia pressed the button to open her bedroom door with hesitation. Sliding open the door revealed a pit of darkness. Staring into the pit of darkness Julia felt her emotions surging with uncertainty. Automated sensors detected movement causing lights flash to life. Memories of disorientation flooded Julia's mind in response to the sudden flash of lights.

Familiar surroundings distorted in a mist of confusion seizing the woman for a moment. Struggling to contain the confusion Julia lingered at the entrance to her room. Memories of blood dripping to the floor echoed through the senses with the force of reality. Julia bolted into the room closing the door behind her. Rapid deep breathes echoed in the empty room. Leaning back against the door Julia slid to the floor gasping for breath.

Blood retreated away from the skin leaving it pale. Julia's incredible facade came crashing down with the force of a tumbling skyscraper. Vision blurred blending memory into reality. Malicious laughter rang in Julia's ears. Tears dripped to the floor accompanied by soft sobs. Gunshots rang out tearing through the black mask in Julia's looping memories.

Retreating to the safety of the bedroom offered Julia solace away from prying eyes. Nerves flared from the emotions pulsing through the woman's body. Julia looked at her own hand noticing it shook to no particular cadence. Each finger possessed by its own erratic unknown purpose. Taking control Julia slowed her breathing pushing herself to her feet.

"Alfred do I have any Christmas wrapping paper left over from last year?" Focusing on wrapping the present would keep Julia's mind preoccupied.

Alfred's digital voice responded "yes Madame it is in the closet located to your left." Julia looked at the book in her hand, took a deep breath, and walked over to the closet opening the door with a push of a button. Light flooded the small dark space revealing a roll of wrapping paper in the corner. Pushing clothes aside Julia grabbed the roll and headed towards her bed. Unrolling the wrapping paper caused a crinkling noise sounding like boots on broken glass. Julia trembled from memories flashing in her mind.

Shaking caused the crinkling noise to increase only heightening the intensity of the flashback. Julia tried to maintain focus on the task of wrapping the present. Trembling nerves made wrapping difficult. Julia tore the wrapping paper several times from muscle spasms. Forty five minute later the present looked perfect with a big bow on top. Feeling accomplishment caused Julia to relax a little.

Muscle tension washed away from the woman replaced by overwhelming feelings of exhaustion. Picking up the present off the bed Julia placed it on the nightstand. Accomplishment faded into the silence of the room. Exhaustion drained Julia's remaining energy. Sleep called out with its siren song beckoning on a subconscious level.

Laying back on the bed Julia closed her eyes stilling her breathing. Darkness only offered repeating images of the two guards being shot. Screams and gunfire tormented Julia preventing her from falling asleep. Fear bore down like a great weight onto the woman in the darkness of her own thoughts. Sitting up straight Julia looked around for anything to preoccupy her mind. Wrapping the present had been difficult, but it had brought a moment of reprieve from tormented thoughts.

Only a dressing table with large mirror, walk-in closet, and large canopy bed sat in the large room. Nothing in the room seemed to offer anything to divert the mind. Looking at the vanity Julia remembered she kept a stash of whiskey there. Julia didn't drink often and had never passed out from being drunk. Unconsciousness seemed blissful in comparison to the haunting memories. Exhaustion pulled at every muscle in Julia's body demanding sleep.

Escape fuelled the decision. Marching over to the vanity Julia withdrew the bottle from the hidden compartment. Light glinted off the amber liquid in the glass container. Picking up the bottle from the compartment Julia placed it on the vanity. Liquid splashed across the bottom of the glass filling it a quarter full. Corking the bottle Julia placed it on the vanity before grabbing the glass.

One loud gulp echoed in the room for a brief moment followed by a deep inhalation of air. Whiskey burned Julia's mouth causing her to shake her head trying to stop the sensation. For a beautiful moment the pain pushed back the memories. Muscles relaxed in Julia's body feeling the numbing sensation replace the pain. Alcohol warmed the stomach radiating its heat outward.

Looking into the mirror Julia didn't recognize the unfamiliar image reflected on the surface. Exhaustion filled the young woman's face with lines. Tears caused the eyes to turn red and cheeks to puff up. Julia once radiant features now mired in despair and torment. Only thoughts of the alcohol brought peace to the young woman. Tension pulled every single muscle in Julia's body. Moments passed into minutes.

Popping the corked caused a distinct echoing in the room. Refilling the glass Julia set the bottle back down not bothering to replace the cork. Swift motion delivered the drink to be swallowed. No burning sensation followed the second drink. Proceeding to refilling the glass Julia focused on numbing the pain. No hesitation between drinks to wait for the effects to kick in. The third drink followed by a fourth drink.

Looking at the bottle of whiskey Julia noticed a third of the bottle gone. Alcohols' subtle effects presented themselves in the woman's mirrored reflection. Balance and coordination were causing Julia to struggle to put the cork back in the bottle. A loud thud rang out when the bottle hit the wood floor. Grabbing the glass Julia walked towards her bed with a stumble. Hitting the vanity caused the whiskey bottle to stop rolling.

Julia crashed into the soft pillowed bed spread without sound. Whiskey splashed back and forth in the cup spraying drops onto the bed sheet. Swallowing the last drink Julia slammed the glass down on the nightstand. Comfort beckoned Julia to lay down feeling weights pulling her eyes shut. Darkness brought no comfort.

Traumatic memories surged when Julia closed her eyes. Cushions of soft fabric pushed on the skin while sharp jagged memories cut from within. Trying to block the memories Julia pleaded inside her mind for the alcohol to kick in. Smell of gun smoke filled the air, screams echoed, and flashes of pain shot through every nerve. Julia tried to push the thoughts out feeling herself twitch from the impulses shooting through her body.

Warmth spread from the alcohol pumping through the veins. Pressure seemed to release from Julia's mind. Alcohol pushed back the haunting memories. Simple desire for a cessation of pain drove Julia's struggle with the flood of traumatic memories. Time seemed to stop from anticipation. Seconds seemed meaningless. Julia kept being drawn back to the repeated gun shots, the man in the black mask, and the feeling of killing the man.

Guilt ravaged inside screaming "murderer!" Voices mocked and tormented within the shadows of Julia's mind refusing to grant respite. Only the salvation of drug induced sleep offered any sanctuary or hope. Julia pulled the pillow over her head attempting to silence the voices raging inside her mind. Alcohol didn't reduce the pressure of the voices, but reduced the ability to resist the message.

Alcohol wore down Julia's ability to resist the surge of the superego's self-righteous anger at taking a life. Societal rules crashed against animal instinct to survive. Conflict raged inside Julia's mind fighting over the inherent evil of the action. Society teaches all killing is wrong, but the situation left no choice. People call soldiers murders. Doubt tore away at Julia's thoughts.

Sleep eluded Julia forcing her to think about what her mother said about difficult times. Victoria told her daughter to pray to god for help when you're desperate or need guidance. One day when Julia was ten she asked her father about god. Henry told his daughter that life is governed by chance not destiny or providence. Neither idea brought Julia any peace in this moment. Howling wind rattled at the windows. Julia sobbed into her pillow until she passed out.

CHAPTER 12

Strategic Concept

Henry and Victoria watched their daughter walking up the steps. Cling to each other both parents were filled with a foreboding sense concerning their daughter. Holding a report in hand Maj. Lee waited with patience. Julia disappeared around the corner. Catching the look on Maj. Lee's face told Henry something important needed his attention. Stepping away Victoria let her husband attend to the business at hand.

"The President of the United States of America is at your front gate." Edward offered the report to his boss.

Henry begged "will this day ever end?"

"Escort the President to the study Maj. Lee." Victoria placed her hand on her husband shoulders. Tension tightened Henry's muscles in his shoulders. Kneading the muscles Victoria tried to relax her husband. Trying to determine what the president could want set Henry's mind racing with possibilities.

Edward nodded "of course Madame." Henry responded to the soft tug on the inside of his arm turning to walk upstairs with his wife. Marching down the hall the couple headed towards the study security terminal. After scanning both people the door whisked opened. Henry stormed into the room with Victoria right behind him. Lights sparked to life illuminating the study. Henry caught his wife between the door and his body.

"What were you thinking taking Julia to the mall with only four guards?" Fury etched Henry's features. Victoria had seen her husband mad on a few occasions, but never furious beyond reason. Nostrils flared with each deep breath Henry took. The day's event left questions demanding immediate answers.

"Why would you send Julia off all by herself?"

"I would never jeopardize our daughter's life! I only did what I thought was best. I should have brought more guards, but once we were under attack I did what I had to do to keep Julia safe." Victoria pleaded with her husband. Husband and Wife stared into the others' eyes searching for truth. Henry broke his hold and stormed towards his desk.

"I'm sorry Victoria. I shouldn't have acted like that, but it's been a stressful day."

Victoria raced behind her husband warning "it's about to get more stressful. What do you think President Woods wants?"

"I would bet it has something to do with the attack on the mall today." Henry pulled open the top desk drawer pulling out the cigar box. Cigar cutters sliced the tip of the cigar off with a quick snip. Henry placed the cigar in his mouth. Soft hiss of the match filled the room with the smell of sulphur. Flames burst into life casting a soft glow. Henry puffed on the cigar bringing it to life and exhaled the cigar smoke.

"I am sure President Woods is going to look for a way to leverage this tragedy to his advantage." Henry knew the U.S government wanted his research. Muse had been doing into cybernetic prosthetics for the last five years. Governments demanded cybernetic implants for their soldiers. Every world government tried to leverage Henry to concede to their desires.

Victoria thought carefully before replying "he'll demand you pay for the damages and support the initiative for firearms regulation."

"Do you think President Woods is stupid enough to gamble his political currency on firearm reforms? America is the only civilized nation in the world that allows military weapons to be owned by civilians." Henry tried to sense the game being played. 2nd amendment rights turned America into the wild west of corporate warfare. Rampant gun problems only allowed corporate agents to leave less evidence.

Victoria stated "if he offers I think you should accept and help endorse his campaign."

"You want me to support gun reform to minimalize Crossfire Securities influence in North America? I am not sure what kind of blowback would occur from such an action. Colt would be pissed." Henry responded with a quizzical look trying to gauge his wife's stratagem. Pouring two drinks Victoria turned to her husband.

"You stand to lose nothing. First you get public relations boost after the attack by appearing to attempt to prevent more attacks. Colt will understand you're just protecting Julia." Victoria knew that if the initiative passed it would redefine America. Fewer guns would limit corporate warfare in America. The Williams produced most of their cybernetic implants in North America. Improved public relations would create a boost in sales for Muse industries as well.

Henry smiled at the thought saying "well thought out my darling wife. I knew I married you for a reason."

Victoria offered her husband his drink. "I thought you married me for love?"

"I married you because I couldn't imagine living without you next to me." Henry placed the drink on his desk before pulling his wife into a tight embrace. Victoria felt her knees weaken staring into his husband's eyes. Love burned bright between the Williams even after twenty years of marriage. Henry leaned in delaying the meeting of lips for a moment before kissing his wife. The couple got few moments of respite, and savoured each one.

Knocking resonated from the door breaking the couple from the moment. Henry broke from the embrace to press the button under his desk. A loud click echoed for the retreating lock bolt. Maj. Lee opened the door leading a tall well-dressed Asian American towards the desk. President Adam Woods was the first Asian American president. Confidence poured from the youngest president in American history.

Adam Woods had worked under four of the previous presidents. At thirty two years old the native of Washington controlled politics in America. Woods formed his own political research corporation. The US administration used Wood's company to form the foundation of a technological bureaucracy. Governments automated most of their bureaucratic processes attempting to reduce government expenditures. Adam Woods used the success of technological innovation to change the political battlefield securing a presidential election.

"Henry it's good to see you my old friend. I know how much you love those Cuban cigars." President Woods presented a box with a smile on his face. Henry took the gift and opened the box. Tobacco fumes filled the study with a sweet aroma.

"I wish I had known you were coming." Henry sealed the box placing it in the desk still puffing on his own cigar. President Woods remained a staunch supporter or cybertechnology in the America. Many of the religious institutions railed against the evils of cybertechnology. Christianity called cybernetic implants a corruption of the body and atrocity against god. Many institutions tried to get governments to ban the technology for a variety of reasons. Cybernetic implants changed how society functioned, and not everyone liked the change.

President Woods smiled back stating "No need Henry. I just wanted to come by and say merry Christmas and congratulate you on becoming the world's first quadrillionaire." Rhetoric and pandering were lost on a man like Henry who could see the game being played. Everything in the modern day was a form of propaganda. Henry stared into President Woods's eyes exhaling smoke in a puff.

"Thank you Mr. President. I hadn't realized I had hit that mark yet. Please sit down lets discuss the real reason you're here." Standing on tradition never suited Henry. Pulling out the chair Maj. Lee motioned for the president to sit down.

"You can't tell me a man in your position doesn't watch the news. News reports are filled with the tragedy at the Skymall. Victoria is it true you and your daughter were there during the attack?" Empathetic soft words belied the real purpose the President aimed at. Henry's lips curled into a smirk admiring the game. President Wood's showed himself a master at playing the political game. Artful conversation revealed a great deal of information on the presidents' political rivals.

"Julia and I were at the mall during the attack today, but we are both fine Mr. President. Thank you for your concern." Victoria responded maintaining elegant tact in her response. Success in politics depended on a person's ability to fuse truth and lie in seamless speech. Nature's fury battered against the walls shaking the Williams house.

"To be a victim of such a tragedy so close to Christmas is heart breaking. Do you have any idea who caused the attack?" Henry could see the purpose in the dilation of President Wood's eyes. Poker and politics relied on gleaming information from behaviour. Woods searched for information in physical or emotional reactions.

"I am afraid the world we live is far less safe for our children than either of us would like." Pulling a cigar from the gift Henry snipped the end off. The piece of cigar fell into the trash can below the desk. Victoria watched the two men banter back and forth reminding her of the senate. Word exchanges without purpose or meaning just burning away time. Both men tried to say as little as possible waiting for the other to slip up. President Woods accepted the cigar offered by Henry.

"Your generosity is much appreciated on such a cold night." President Woods held a lite match to the cigar and puffed at it. Smoke hung across the ceiling of the study filling the room with the aroma of tobacco. Noticing the lack of a secret service escort Henry looked out the window towards his driveway. Four black vehicles sat outside the palatial home. Henry wondered why the president came alone.

"Is your secret service all equipped with thermal optical camouflage now?"

"I came alone. We have important business to discuss in private." Exhaling the cigar smoke Adam tried to cover a bit of a cough. Victoria motioned for Edward to leave with a nod. Without a sound or notice Maj. Lee turned exiting the room at a brisk pace. Only the three people were left to conspire in private.

"Tell me how your trip to China went. How does business with Mr. Sun look from your vantage point?" President Wood's puffed on his cigar waiting for an answer. Muse Industries expansion into the Asian markets became a growing interest to western nations. Taxes on cybernetic implant trade gave America a huge boost on the value of the dollar. The cybernetic market expanded all of the western democracies economies.

"Mr. Sun appears to care more about public order than profits. Dragon Enterprises will handle all the shipping of my cybernetic implants and genetic modifications. The new arrangement will allow Muse industries to bid on Chinese military contracts." Thinking about the possibilities caused Adam's face to scrunch from deep thought. Zhou Yun Sun still remained a wanted criminal in most nations of the world. Politics often create the necessity for deals with devils.

"Your one hundred percent sure you can trust Zhou Yun Sun? You have read the intelligence reports on his actions?" President Woods hoped that Henry would see reason on the subject. Politicians in America couldn't really argue against their patrons. Cunning won Woods the election, but Henry's financial contributions made him indispensable. Woods knew he was walking up a slippery slope on this deal.

Henry scoffed "the C.I.A. sees threats everywhere. I find the dossier provided on Mr. Sun to be no reflection of the actual man." Henry aided the government when it worked to both parties interests. The U.S government had been trying to get a foothold into china's economy for a decade. The balance of trade swung in the favour of China. Henry told the Chinese leaders that he wouldn't sell his technology to any country that supressed any human rights.

In the last 10 years China reinvented their society. New laws brought the country into accordance with UN international laws of the Geneva Convention. Chinese government craved the social and military benefits of cyber technology. Every nation struggled for military supremacy in a world with no leviathan. China needed an edge over the Russian's and Middle East troops. Cooperation alleviated western fears that cyber technology would end up in the hands of terrorists.

"The U.S. could use the boost to revenues trade will bring" President Woods congratulated. Henry allowed Woods to believe he was interested only in the money. Millions of people in china needed medical implants. Industrialization filled China's air with pollution making breathing difficult. Cybernetic implants could filter out the pollution in the air and save thousands of lives.

Neural implants allowed medicine to diagnose problems using the bodies' nervous system. Cyber technology helped treat injuries and damage that would otherwise kill, and sped up the recovery of patients both physically and mentally. Limbs could be replaced, muscles strengthened, bones reinforced, and brain damage repaired. Technology changes people lives, and Henry Williams irrevocably changed the course of humanity forever.

"I don't mean to pry, but do you know who is behind the Skymall attack yet?" President Woods looked at William's with empathetic eyes.

"No Mr. President we have no idea who is behind the attack at the Skymall today. I assure you I will discover who ordered the attack. Considerable assets have already been moved to that purpose." Henry stared across from his desk at the President. Information is the key to success in any conflict. Pride filled Henry with a sense of anger. Not knowing the source of the attack felt like a splinter you can't pull out. You can pretend the splinter isn't there, but the wound will still get infected.

"You should cancel your New Year's Anniversary charity Ball" Woods urged.

"With all due respect that charity helps hundreds of thousands of people. People stuck below poverty all around the world. I will not cancel such an important event out of base fear of what could happen." Experience told Henry that appearing weak would only create more attacks. Victoria smiled supporting her husband but she agreed with the president.

"I doubt the attack at the mall had anything to do with my wife and daughter. The New Year's charity masquerade ball is attended by the most powerful families. These families own the most powerful security forces in the world. No one would be stupid enough to attack with that much security present." Henry exuded his utter confidence in his ability to protect his daughter.

"The safety of your family is nothing to gamble on" President Woods responded. "However we should discuss how to deal with the public's backlash. I know you haven't watched the news, but Owl is already on the offensive. Victor Wolfe is claiming you're making enemies all around the world. You need to start making some friends."

Henry rocked the glass back and forth. Motion caused the liquid at the bottom of the glass to swirl around. Victoria knew the president well enough to sense where the conversation headed. Gun control laws could prevent some of the worst violent crimes raging throughout the U.S. Woods now searched for the words to convince his political ally to join his cause of gun regulation.

"I think we need to bring forth some kind of legislation controlling weapons sales. Cybernetic implants are only one threat. We need to limit the damage in these situations" President Woods urged. Studying the president Henry wondered how well the idea had been considered.

Victoria supported gun control reform but her husband agreed with the constitution.

"I am not sure Mr. President. The American people are ardent supporters of their 2nd Amendment rights. I am not sure you're capable of reforming gun laws. I have to consider if such reforms will be advantageous to Muse Industries and the Williams Family. Would you like a drink Mr. President?" Henry walked over to the bar and refilled his drink turning to ask"

"With you and your wife in support I believe that we can succeed." Confidence beamed from the young president's smile. Strategy requires moving your opponent along the path you set out for them. Henry knew the key to success lay in seducing the opponent into wanting to go in the chosen direction. Both men needed something from the other. Henry would ensure he got the upper hand out of the trade.

Victoria interjected "perhaps the law will succeed, but is it in our best interests?" Adam paused for a second working out a stratagem to convince his opposition. Handing the drink to the president Henry sat back down behind his desk. Only difference between conversation and war were the weapons employed. The key to Henry's success lay in never letting his opponent know what he wanted. The president needed the William's support and would pay to get it.

"I can offer concession in taxes and import breaks. I heard your looking to develop new facilities in North America. The U.S. government would be happy to help you with business grants." President Woods offered anything he thought might convince his ally. Most people wanted money and would sell their souls for it. Cut from a different cloth Henry never cared for money. Only the future mattered.

"I am still not convinced" Henry shook his head no. Wiggling like a worm on the hook the president squirmed looking for something he could offer. President Woods looked at Victoria realizing that she was the way to get what he needed. Henry still had to keep his wife happy like every other man. Victoria's ambition would provide the clearest route to success.

"What if I ensure your wife is made the chairperson of the appropriations committee?" Henry stroked his chin thinking about the possibilities. The U.S. government didn't deny Muse industries many contracts, but Victoria as chairperson could push any agenda through the appropriation committee. Funds and land could be acquired to fund Muse's newest research projects. More power would only entrench Victoria further into the institutions of government.

"I think we have a deal Mr. President." President Woods face lite up with delight. Excitement boiled in Victoria forcing her to contain her elation at the turn of events. Republican backing a democrat would only increase the senator's substantial influence. Thoughts raced through Victoria's mind realizing she might be able to run for the presidency.

"Mr. and Mrs. Williams I believe we cannot be stopped. Our political triumvirate will shape the future. Working together we will bring stability to this great nation together." Taking a deep inhale of the cigar President Woods extended his hand and exhaled. "We have a deal Mr. Williams."

Henry leaned across the desk and shook the president hand. Standing up president Woods bowed showing respect. Victoria knew the possibilities the future now held were limitless. After exchanging pleasantries the President left the study claiming important business matters. Victoria looked her husband with eyes brimming with lust.

"You never need to buy me a present ever again." Henry reached out and pulled his wife close. Both bodies slammed against the desk shaking it. Passionate kissing now the only sound emanating in the study. Pressing hard against the desk Victoria pulled her husband close wrapping her legs around him. Soft kisses on the inside of Henry's neck stroked his urges. Victoria pressed against the desk pulling her husband on top of her.

"Finding the perfect gift for a woman with everything is an Olympian endeavour." Victoria stared deep into her husband's sparkling cybernetic eyes. Troubles and woes washed away in the rising tide of passion. For a moment the world and its problems faded from thought. Only the flickering light of the fireplace illuminated the dark room. Intense love burned in the couple's hearts mirroring the fires intensity.

"You have given me more than I could ever have hoped for." Slow and delicate Victoria undid the buttons on her husbands' shirt sliding the fabric off. Muscles rippled beneath Henry's skin with anticipation. Victoria stroked her husband chest tracing her finger up the center. Caught in the moment of lust Henry tore clothes off in a flurry of motion. Soft noise from kisses filled the study. Drinking in the soft naked flesh Henry admired the curves of his wife delicate body.

Victoria pushed forward knocking her husband to the ground landing on top of him. Remnants of clothes dangled from both bodies stretched across the floor. Henry could feel his wife's legs squeezing around him. Shedding the last pieces of clothes left the two lay naked in the glow of the fireplace. Wind continued to howl in the distance covered by the grunts and moans of the two lovers. Henry and Victoria lost themselves in the moment.

CHAPTER 13

Family Friends

Scintillating light filtered through the bay window in the bedroom. Something stirred beneath the shifting mass of pillows and blankets on the bed. Breaking free from the tomb of comfort Julia stretched her arms yawning. Sunlight beaming into the room revealed the time to be sometime after noon. Glaring into the vanity mirror Julia saw her wild messy hair and the present reflected back.

Opening the bedroom door allowed sounds emanated from the kitchen downstairs to be heard. People talking and laughing echoed throughout the mansion. Julia walked down the hall and descended the circular staircase putting her robe on. Wrapping paper crunched underneath the robe. Aroma from delicious food wafted in the air of the vacant mansion halls.

Julia looked into the den from the bottom of the stairs. Multi-coloured light radiated from the Christmas tree beckoning from the living room. Presents stacked high under the tree revealed the Cross family had arrived. Julia walked to the living room bending over to place her present beneath the tree. Lights on the Christmas tree created a glowing aura around the ten foot pine tree. Following the sounds of laughing and talking Julia walked towards the kitchen. Servants raced by the girl in a hurry trying to prepare the massive Christmas dinner.

"Thank you again for the invitation for Christmas dinner." Pricilla's voice resonated from the kitchen. Julia approached the kitchen leaning around the corner to see her mother and Colt's wife drinking wine. Growing up with the Cross children Julia knew that her mother and

Pricilla loved wine and gossip. Servants raced through the kitchen cooking the food around the two women.

"I'm so glad both of you are safe Victoria. How is Julia doing?" Pricilla talked in a thick southern accent and dressed like a southern belle from history books. Julia lingered at the doorway eavesdropping for a moment. Both women chatted away.

"My daughter's fine and probably still sleeping. I am sure she'll be up soon and you can ask her yourself." Victoria took a sip of her white wine trying to avoid the question. Gunshots echoed from outside the mansion. Startled by the noise Julia spun around, lost balance, and tumble into the kitchen. Victoria and Pricilla watched the young woman crash into the floor with a loud thud.

"Good morning dear. How was your sleep?" Containing laughter Victoria watched her daughter stand up and regain composure. Julia could feel both women staring at her with a curious looks on their face. Looking at one another the three women sat in awkward silence for a moment.

"I slept fine mom." Another series of gunshots rang out. Memories rushed back triggered by the sound of gunshots. Julia struggled to keep composure in front of everyone in the kitchen. Each gunshot triggered another set of flashbacks causing nerves to tremble.

"You know how much Colt and your father love their Christmas Eve skeet shooting. Those two only fight about where to do the shooting at." Blunt honesty was Pricilla's gift and curse. Every year Henry and Colt argued about where to have Christmas dinner. Neither man ever seemed to agree on anything. Priscilla refilled her glass holding up the bottle of wine as an offering.

"Do you want some dear?" One of the servants offered a wine glass. Taking the glass Julia watched white wine pour from the bottle. Priscilla filled the glass almost to the brim. Social functions always called for copious amounts of alcohol, and high society remained true to convention.

"There you go dear" Pricilla radiant smile beaming at the young woman. Wine and food went hand in hand whenever Victoria and Pricilla socialized. Sitting down at the table Julia sipped the wine to prevent it from spilling. Covering the top of the table was a buffet of chocolate delicacies, miniature pies, and biscotti. Victoria offered a plate of treats to her daughter.

"Dinner should be done soon dear, but Pricilla brought some treats to tide us over." Julia's stomach rebelled with a groan from the thought of food. Hearing the groan Victoria took notice of her daughters act. High society groomed the children of the rich and powerful to keep constant awareness on their behaviour. Tabloids represented a cautionary tale to children of high society.

Sex scandals, Affairs, Drinking binges, and rampant drug use by the rich and powerful could start month long public opinion campaigns. Money and power couldn't shield against the force of public outrage. Julia never cared much for what other people thought despite her parents' pressure. Paying close attention Victoria could see something was wrong with her daughter.

"Are you ok Julia you look a little pale" Pricilla inquired? Victoria noticed the difference in skin colour last night, but hoped a good night sleep would fix the problem. Struggling against the anxiety Julia tried to resist the anxiety. Using food to distract the guest Victoria provided cover for her daughter. Another loud bang echoed throughout the house.

"Robert your shooting has improved since our skeet shooting in Texas last Christmas." Henry praised the boy wrapped in a head lock under his arm. Praise seemed a foreign concept to Robert. Even success in football made the young man feel insecure. None of Robert's accomplishment got much praise from his father. Each success rewarded with a lecture on how things could be improved.

"You should take that as a compliment. Not many soldiers have ever outshot the good doc here. Back in the army we used to joke that Henry's second choice in weapons was the scalpel." Colt prodded his friend with an elbow in time with his joke. Barrett sulked behind with a gruff expression reflecting his wounded ego. Both Robert and Barrett fought over everything trying to earn their fathers praise.

The group of men burst through the thick oak doors of the dining room marching into the kitchen. Grinning from ear to ear Robert managed to widen his smile at the sight of Julia. Henry handed the guns to several servants to be locked up in the gun cabinet. Almost spilling the wine Pricilla hugged her boys welcoming them back. Panic shot through Julia causing her heart to race at the sight of the guns.

"I don't know I think it was just luck" Robert said in a humble tone.

"Colt are you sure this boys yours and not adopted, because I've never met a humble Cross before." Colt filled the kitchen with his jovial laugh. Servants began carrying food to the dining room in a steady stream. Victoria directed people flowing from the kitchen in single file. Ants carried the food in column for their queen.

"Boy gets his humility from his mother, but the shooting that is from his dad." Colt sauntered behind everyone else bragging about his boy. Both families organized themselves sitting down behind the long dinner table. Everyone gathered around a massive turkey sitting centered surrounded by stuffing, ham, cranberry sauce, soups, several salads, hors d'oeuvres such as oysters with crème fraiche, and dauphinoise potatoes. Food spread across the table top presented a feast for the senses.

Colt looked to Henry "may I have the honor of saying grace?" Henry contained his grimace at the thought of prayer. Each man stood on opposing side of the question. Religious upbringing taught Colt to never question things you can't find answers for. Science looked at observable and testable facts. Treating patients in the worse shape showed Henry how cruel the world could be.

"Of course Colt the honour is yours." Henry believed in reason and logic. Reason stated the food on the table had been purchased, and not gifted by any beneficial deity. Henry found it difficult to tolerate the Christmas season and its hypocrisy of commercialism. Everyone around the table followed Colt in putting their hands together and bowing their heads.

"Thank you god for the plentiful bounty you have given us today. We thank you for your infinite mercy and compassion. We ask today that you bless this food and the families gathered here today. Amen. Now let's eat." Colt raised his head grabbing his plate before anyone else. Henry grabbed the knife carving into the turkey. Everyone passed the various sides around the table until every plate was filled with delicious food. Victoria looked at her daughter sipping wine with a near empty plate.

"Are you not hungry dear?" Julia felt the sudden shift of attention caused by the question. Everyone could see the sparse amount of food on the young woman's plate. Anxiety swelled up causing Julia to take another drink of the wine. Worried faces stared down the table. Robert could see the stares made Julia even more uncomfortable, and resigned to not make the situation worse.

"I am just not very hungry right now mom" Julia deflected the question.

"Dad how did you and Mr. Williams become friends." Robert changed subjects with the question. Everyone at the table turned looking at Colt. Sinking into the chair Julia felt relieved the attention was off her and her heart beat slowed. Colt wrapped his arm around his youngest boy with a smile of delight.

"My boy knows that I love to tell a story."

Henry chuckled "something every man who served under you learned to dread." Colt glared across the table for a moment. Both men liked to taunt each other trying to provoke some kind of reaction. For a second Henry thought he could see his friend getting angry from the verbal jab. Shirking off the jest Colt turned back to the table prepared to tell his story.

"You see Henry and I fought in the same unit during the Middle-east wars. You remember the war started when Iran funded a terrorist group to detonate a nuclear bomb, and that blast destroyed Ottawa back in 2015. Canada joined the Union of the states. Henry here signed up for the war right out of school. Henry is one of those prodigies that managed to graduate with a medical degree at a very young age. How old were you again?"

Memories carried Henry back through time. The destruction of Ottawa still brought tears when heard by anyone who remembered Canada. Canadian Government collapsed in absent of the House of Commons and prime minister. Many of the government officials died in the initial attack. Remaining officials demanded an immediate sovereignty referendum. Without leadership the provinces voted to secede from Canada and join the U.S.

"I was eighteen when I earned my PhD from the University of Western Ontario." Henry took a drink of the whiskey in front of him. Memories brought back a flood of emotions. Love, Sorrow, and hatred flooded into Henry's mind. Julia could see her father going through the same situation. Empathy passed between father and daughter staring at one another.

"So this 18 year old kid is assigned to my unit to be our combat medic, and I was furious. I admit to disliking Henry when I first met him. This eighteen year old arrogant punk was supposed to save the lives of my men.

I thought whoever sent this kid to me had to be an idiot." Around the table everyone had stopped eating enthralled by the story. Colt chewed a piece of turkey and swallowed while everyone stared at him.

"One day I am forced to go check on an important assignment of troops. When I arrive the situation turns out to be an ambush. I got hit pretty badly." Colt pulled his shirt away from his neck to reveal a scar on the side of his neck from a bullet. Scar tissue shined under the chandler lighting.

"I wake up in the hospital a week or two later in the hospital. How long was it exactly" Colt asked?

"Nine days, fourteen hours, and sixteen minutes." Henry eyes rolled back recounted the event from memory.

"When I wake up my second in command Edward Lee comes over. The man looks like he's seen a ghost. Turns out the bullet blew out the back of my neck damaging my spine and spinal cord. Lt. Lee informs me that the only reason I am alive is because of the young medic. Henry overheard the distress call from my unit, stole a jeep, and raced to the site. My men pursued the thief and both arrived in time. Lt. Lee tells me the man who saved my life is locked up awaiting court martial. I ordered my men to bring Henry to see me. Henry gets led to me in cuffs with a defiance simmering in his eyes. This arrogant young man explains how if it wasn't for his revolutionary technology how I would be dead. Citing regulations verbatim Henry explained that it was his duty to defy any order that jeopardizes the lives and safety of the regiment, and how he was obligated to steal the jeep and save my life."

Colt paused to take another bite of food. Henry hated to admit that Colt did have a way with telling a story. Only Colt's plate had any food missing. Everyone waited for the story to continue. Listening to the story allowed Victoria to hide her worry about Julia that prevented eating.

"So what happened next?" Robert hung on every word in awe. Washing the turkey down with a glass of wine Colt turned back to his audience.

"I've seen enough death to last two lifetimes son. No force on this earth or otherwise could make me order the death of a man who saved my life." Barrett looked at his father with curiosity trying to piece the information together in his mind.

"So is that why Grandpa helped Mr. William's start Muse industries?"

"Your Grandpa was a smart business man. Dad always told me good business is supporting other smart people in succeeding." Silence washed over the table. Priscilla glared at Barrett trying to silence him. Cutting into the turkey Henry noted the behaviour. Barrett intended to hide the insult in the form of a question.

Henry raised his glass declaring "let us toast the great Thomas Cross." Colt raised his glass clanging it on Henry's. Soft chimes of glass rang throughout the dining room. The table still brimmed with food long after people finished eating. Everyone sat around the table filled to content. Henry pulled cigars from his chest pocket offering Colt and his sons' one. Pungent tobacco fumes assaulted the aroma of the food.

"Don't throw the food away. Instead have it delivered to the guard barracks please Helen." Victoria smiled at Helen her head of the house hold servants. Servants emptied the table in several trips. Both families sat around drinking wine for several hours discussing politics and business.

Smoke drifted thick in the dining room. Victoria and Priscilla laughed about the gossip that flew around New York like a high school. All the men sat around smoking cigars and drinking whiskey. Henry and Colt discussed business. Time seemed to stop in a moment of happiness and tranquility. Snow furrowed from wind sweeping white mist across the landscape just beyond the windows. Everyone felt the world's problems and stresses fade away in the company of friends and family. Even Julia had been lulled into sleep by the serene setting.

"The poor dear must not be feeling well from yesterday." Pricilla noticed Julia passed out in her chair. Exhaustion wore the young woman out. Sleep brought only nightmare for Julia but exhaustion kept her slumbering. Henry turned to see his daughter sleeping in the chair.

"She's been through a lot in the last couple days." Walking over Henry scooped his daughter up into his arms. Julia looked at peace despite her eyes fluttering from torment of nightmares. Holding the door open Robert watched his friend carried off to bed. Traversing the circular steps Henry activated the door to Julia's room.

Lights flashed on revealing the events of the night before. Lying in the middle of the floor was an almost empty bottle of whiskey. Henry's mind bubbled with worry for his daughter's mental condition. On the night stand a glass lay on its side. Henry carried his daughter over to her bed and tucked her in with loving care.

"Sweet dreams baby. I love you." Henry leaned over and kissed his daughter on the forehead. Faint residue of alcohol lingered in the air. Henry picked up the glass and placed the bottle back in his daughter hiding spot. Nightmares caused Julia's nerves to twitch. Standing at the door Henry prayed for the first time ever for his daughter.

CHAPTER 14

Gifts from the Heart

"Come on Legionnaires attack the gap" Henry shouted at the holographic screen. Colt cheered on the Texas Rangers watching the two teams collide. Warzone became a worldwide craze in the past decade. Two teams played on a football sized field trying to place a ball in a basket from a distance. Teams could also score points by moving a majority of their team into the end zone for a conquest.

Players wore shields and padding trying to outflank, out manoeuvre, and pinned down the other team. No weapons were permitted in Warzone but beyond that tackling, hitting, and checking were permissible. Football sized teams squared off against each other. The field of play consisted of defensible walls and one hill on each side. Warzone focused on aggression with few rules calling for play stoppages. When either team forced the ball out of bounds it signaled a switch of offense.

Warzone combined the physical contact of football with the sudden burst of speed of basketball. The Williams owned the controlling interests of the New York Legionnaires representing one of the six original teams. Colt founded the Texas Rangers trying to compete with his friend. The contest between the Legionnaires and Rangers represented the contest between the two CEO's. Economists even joked that you could predict corporate profits based on which team won last. Time dwindled down in the first half with the Rangers ahead by only a few points.

"The Legionnaires look out of shape Henry. Your team must have eaten a big Christmas dinner." Taunting caused Henry to grit his teeth in frustration. The whistle blew signalling halftime. Both men turned hearing soft footsteps approaching in the hallway. Henry caught a glimpse of Julia staggering towards the kitchen.

"Are you going to come open your presents?" Julia ignored her father's question continuing towards the kitchen searching for coffee. Cackling laughter filled the kitchen from Victoria and Priscilla. Bright glint blinded Julia from the new necklace adorning her mother's neck. White gold sparkled in the morning sunlight filtering through the kitchen window. Henry asked his daughter to help pick out the gift weeks ago.

"Merry Christmas honey" speaking soft showed Victoria knew her daughters pain. Julia rummaged through the cupboard grabbing a bottle of ibuprofen. The cap popped off with an echo. Each sound caused Julia's head to throb in rebellion. Rattling pills on exacerbated the pain from the headache pounding in the woman's skull. Taking two pills Julia popped them into her mouth.

Pricilla poured a cup of coffee "here you go dear to help with those pills." The kitchen almost looked barren in the absence of its normal servants. Only the William's and Cross's remained with a few body guards. Sipping the coffee Julia thanked Pricilla with a smile. Victoria wrapped her arms around her daughter trying to comfort her.

"There is nothing merry about this morning." Julia looked at her mother with a disdain in her eyes.

"Dear this is what happens when you drink on an empty stomach." Priscilla tried not to laugh watching the young woman sip the coffee with her mother hugging her. Mother and daughter created an interesting juxtaposition of emotions. Heredity showed in the faces of both Victoria and her daughter. Breaking free of the hold Julia turned back to face her mother.

"Did Dad open my present for him yet?" Victoria looked out of the kitchen towards the Christmas tree.

"Your father refused to open his present until you were up" Victoria answered. Looking into the living room Julia could see her present untouched surrounded by presents. Barrett sat in one corner of the living room playing with a brand new hunting rifle. On the other side of the room Robert played with a holographic football game. Julia smiled seeing her friend enjoy her gift. Christmas wrapping paper littered the ground.

The mess covered the room as if a tornado ripped through the living room a short time ago. Walking into the living room Julia retrieved the present for her father.

"Dad I got this for you." Henry took the gift from his daughter unwrapping it with care. Paradise lost glared through the paper with its leather bound cover and centuries old pages. Henry felt a rush of emotion and a tear rolling down his cheek. From a young age Julia had always been daddy's girl. Each year Henry was shocked at the unique gifts his daughter would find for him.

"This is an original printing how did you find this?" Henry looked at his daughter with amazement. Opening the container released the musty smell of old paper and leather. Henry picked the book up tracing his fingers across the old leather binding. A lost treasure for the mind lay beyond the cover. Turning the pages with delicate care Henry studied the text with delight.

"This is the best gift anyone has ever given me." Henry placed the book back into the container before hugging his daughter. Sneaking towards the tree Robert fetched the present he brought for Julia. Henry kissed his daughter on the forehead than pulled the book back out. Rare moments allowed Julia to see her father happy, and each moment was a gift to be cherished. Robert crept closer with the present clenched tight to his chest.

"Julia I got this for you. I know it's not much, but I hope you like it." Julia turned around hearing Robert's meek offering. The small rectangular gift contrasted against the large hands presenting it. Robert could feel his heart beat faster from the mix of anticipation and fear.

"Robert you didn't need to get me anything" Julia replied taking the gift without hesitation. Ripping the paper off revealed a small bound book. The book title read "On life, Liberty, and the pursuit of happiness a collection of essays." Staring at the book Julia wondered who the author was. Opening the book Julia was shocked by the words written on the page.

"I took all the essays you have written and bound them together for you. I really love your writings, and I think the rest of the world would enjoy them as well." Trying to fight back the rush of emotions Julia couldn't stop the river of tears from spilling. Robert couldn't figure out if the tears were joy or sadness. Henry, Colt, and Barrett looked at each other confused about what caused the commotion. Feeling anxiety rising Julia raced out of the room without warning. Silence remained in the aftermath. Everyone stared at Robert with confused expressions except his brother. Barrett laughed at his brother.

"I thought she would like it. I didn't mean to upset her" Robert defended himself.

"What are you waiting for boy? Go after her" Colt urged his young son. Robert looked to Henry sitting in his chair with open book in his lap.

"I've been married for twenty years and my wife still doesn't make sense to me sometimes. Don't take it personally Robert. Go see if Julia's could use a good friend right now." Encouragement filled Robert with hope sending him dashing after Julia. The only clue to follow was the sound of footsteps in the hallway.

Robert raced up the circle stairs pursing Julia towards her room. Soft hiss of a door sliding shut beckoned the young man from down the hallway. Arriving at the bedroom door Robert lingered for a second before knocking. Loud knocking provoked no response from inside the room. Julia held her head in her hands with her back against the bed. Hot tears raced down the woman's cheek. Unable to hold back the flood Julia could feel tears drip off her face.

Teardrops collected on the hard surface of the book cover. Robert stood at the door waiting for several minutes before knocking a second time. After a moment the soft clicking sound echoed from inside the room. The door slid only part way open. Julia stood on the other side with her face stained red from tears. Staring at each other neither person knew what to say in this moment.

"I'm sorry Julia I didn't mean to upset you" Robert apologized. Wiping away the tears Julia allowed Robert to enter the room. The door slid shut locking again with a resonated click. Robert looked at his friend clenching the book close to chest and felt worried. Both people remained quiet feeling the awkward tension in the air.

"I really wanted you to like the present. I swear I didn't think it would upset you at all. Honestly I kind of hoped you would think it was sweet." Robert beamed his charismatic smile trying to cheer his friend up. Wiping away the tears Julia managed to regain composure.

"Robert I wasn't upset by the gift. This book is one of the most thoughtful gifts I have ever seen, and I will cherish it forever." Julia noticed the confused look in her friend's eyes and body language. Nothing seemed to make sense to the young man. Trying to make sense of the situation filled Roberts mind with even more questions.

"If you like the present then why are you crying?" Robert tried to understand the emotional outburst. Julia always remained in control of her appearance. During four years of friendship Robert had never seen Julia cry in public. Julia could see that Robert just wanted to help. Emotions raged tearing the young woman apart inside. Emotions pulled Julia between revealing the truth and staying strong.

"It's not you Robert or your gift. I just couldn't take everyone staring at me. I can't stop remember the attack at the mall. Memories keep repeating of gunshots, smelling the burning flesh, and the man aimed his gun at my father. I can't close my eyes without reliving it all over again Robert. It is almost impossible to sleep, and when I do sleep I have nightmares. I feel like I'm fading away." Julia felt relief the moment the words passed her lips.

Listening to the story Robert swallowed hard. No words existed capable of quelling the woman's pain. Robert felt powerless witnessing his friend breaking under the pressure of emotions. Every action seemed futile against such pain and suffering, and the young man could only empathize with his friend. Robert pulled Julia towards him hugging her tight in his strong arms.

The warmth of the embrace allowed Julia to let go. Mental barriers collapsed allowing emotions to pour out. Buried into the soft folds of the shirt Julia allowed tears to explode forth. Robert felt the warm tears soaking through the fabric of the shirt. Holding on tight Julia felt relief wash over her for the first time since the attack. Whispers filtered through the cloth up to Robert's ear.

"Thank you Robert." Julia pulled away from the embrace wiping the tears from her red swollen cheeks. Staring into each other's eyes both people got caught in the gravity of the moment. Embarrassment stung Julia's pride when she caught a glimpse of herself in the mirror. Tears left trails running down both cheeks. Glass reflected swollen, puffy, and bloodshot eyes.

"I look like an absolute mess" Julia stated seeing the evidence in the mirror.

"You don't ever look a mess Julia." Robert plucked some tissues from the nearby vanity and handed them to his friend. Wiping away the tears Julia gazed back at her reflection. Mirrors don't lie. Tissues hadn't taken away any of the redness from Julia's face.

"I look pretty awful right now, but I feel so much worse. I'm sorry I didn't mean to make you think I was upset about your sweet gift." Julia sat down in front of her vanity to apply makeup. Concealing powder covered the puffiness and concealed the redness. Standing there watching Robert wondered what he could do to help.

"If you ever need someone to talk to I'll always be there for you." Offering to listen seemed like the only thing Robert could do. After a few minutes of applying makeup Julia looked almost normal. Only distance remained in the woman's eyes revealing the truth. Makeup acted like a mask concealing away the pain. Julia turned backwards looking at Robert.

"Two days ago I was excited about the next semester. I couldn't wait to move ahead in life, but now it feels like that life never exists. My whole life seems like a vague dream twisted into a nightmare. First the attack on my father then the events at the mall leaves me feeling like the worst is yet to come. It feels like my future has been stolen. I don't know if that makes any sense to you."

Listening to Julia explain how she felt caused Roberts heart to sink from sorrow. Both kids were caught in the riptide of depression. Robert couldn't imagine what Julia had been through at the mall. News reports mentioned the attack but failed to reveal any specific details. Only the small mark on Julia's forehead gave a clue to the violence she suffered. Slippers covered up the cuts from the glass. Hidden behind makeup, a sweet smile, and green eyes were scars that might never heal. Robert knew that the real damage had been done to Julia's mind.

"Maybe you could talk to your dad and see someone who can help you with all this." Julie spun around with anger and worry in her eyes. Henry respected strength and perseverance in other people. Only thing that mattered to Julia was her fathers' love. All most children want is the love of their parents.

"You can't tell anyone what I just told you especially my dad!"

"Your dad just wants to help you" Robert pleaded.

"If anyone ever found out what happened to me it would make my dad look weak. Any sign of weakness would provoke attack. Do you understand that I will never allow myself to be used to harm my dad?" Words seemed hollow and futile in changing Julia's mind. Robert stared into the eyes filled with zealous fury and clear purpose.

"Of course Julia you know I would never do anything to hurt you." Robert reassurance caused Julia to hug him again.

"I knew I could trust you. You're the only person I can trust. Thank you so much." Tears threatened to pour forth again. Julia felt a mix of admiration and desperation in this moment. Robert looked into Julia's radiant green eyes pulled in by an invisible force.

Both people stood fixed with eyes locked onto each other. Robert felt overwhelmed by the intense love he felt. Pools of radiant green sparkled in the sunlight. Certainty filled Roberts mind. Poetry told the young man that love is the most powerful force in the universe. In that moment Robert knew he loved Julia beyond needing reason.

Julia lingered in the embrace savoring the closeness and intimacy she longed for. Loneliness caused by being Henry Williams' daughter weighed heavy on her for years. Henry's love caused him to build an impregnable cage of people to protect his daughter. Safety had taken Julia's freedom long ago. Guards and schedules made dating impossible. No previous experience prepared the young woman for how she felt now. Fear heightened the sense of everything while excitement pushed Julia forward. Julia felt a strange and powerful emotion drawing her towards Robert.

Fate conspired to make things difficult for both children. Fear caused Julia to hesitate and pull back. Corporate life didn't leave a lot of room for love. Julia nuzzled her head into Roberts shoulder turning to look out the window. Sitting in front of the window Robert ran his fingers through Julia's hair. Neither person needed words in this moment. Robert and Julia cuddled together looking out the window enjoying this moment.

CHAPTER 15

Schemes

Henry and Victoria worked night and day setting up their 20th anniversary charity event. Chef's, caterers, entertainment, and security arrangement needed to be arranged. Preparations for the charity event filled the house with chaos. Julia remained in her room for the last couple of days. Constant traffic of people coming and going created too many opportunities for a panic attack. Victoria spent most of the time at home working on the seating arrangements and the VIP list. Sitting behind the desk in the study Henry smoked a cigar bickering on the holophone with a business associate.

"Samesh this is an important dinner. I don't care about the cost just get me everything on that list, and stop wasting my time checking in. I need you to focusing on getting this event organized. I trust your judgment Samesh." Henry pounded the off button almost breaking the machine from force. Endless hours of fighting over costs and time tables could drive any man insane.

Implementation always caused problems whether logistics or team work. Henry found that it didn't matter how much preparation went into planning anything. Every event found new problems at the last moment. Nothing ever went according to plan. The intercom rang out forcing Henry to he hit the button again.

"You know that I am trying to work up here right? What is so damn important now?" Henry's frustration couldn't be contained any longer. Silence lingered over the intercom for a second. Henry knew time is a resource that could never be recouped. Running a corporation shackled the CEO with certain time constraints. Wasting Henry's time always provoked frustration and anger.

"Sir there is a Deputy Chief Wayne here to see you. I can't seem to find an appointment. I tried to send the Officer away, but he keeps insisting it is urgent that he speak with you." The guard reported with trepidation resonating within his voice. With the all the hectic commotion of organizing the New Year's event Henry forgot about the police report. Julia needed to go to the station to give her report on the attack.

"Ask Deputy Chief Wayne's what the urgent matter involves." Sitting behind the desk Henry waited for the response. Stacks of papers lay scattered across the desk waiting to get attention. Henry continued to work away trying to pass the time and stay productive. The intercom sprung back to life after a long pause.

"Deputy Chief Wayne's stated the matter is concerning Julia sir." Henry wondered why the deputy chief would come all the way to the William's estate for a statement. The NYPD could have sent a lower ranked officer to get the statement. Questions about the Deputy Chief's motives raised some alarms in Henry's mind. Wayne's dossier laid on the table buried under some papers.

"Escort the deputy chief to the study please." Picking up the dossier from the table Henry opened it flipping through the records. Muse Security did full surveillance and intelligence profiles on every officer on the scene. Henry knew that attacks could come from anywhere. Information remained the only guard against subversive tactics.

Wayne's file showed that he was an average officer. Henry studied the profile but nothing remarkable popped off the page. Only a few black marks stood out from Wayne's early career. Page after page revealed nothing of consequence on the Deputy Chief or any of the other officers. Henry lost track of time reading the profile until the knock at the door startled him. Opening the door Maj. Lee stepped in to announce himself.

"Deputy Chief Wayne is here to see you sir." Maj. Lee led the Deputy Chief into the study. Opening the drawer Henry slid the portfolio into his private collection. Wayne's eyes filled with amazement at the size of the study and the sheer volume of books. Henry motioned for the Deputy

Chief to sit down in the chair. Bewildered James stumbled into his chair before regaining focus and sitting down.

"I am sorry to interrupt you Mr. Williams. I am sure you're very busy with your upcoming event, but I have critical information in regards to Julia. I just need a few moments of your private time to discuss the matter in detail." Maj. Lee hated leaving his boss all alone with an armed man. Henry waved his head of security out of the room without a second thought. Waiting until the study door closed Wayne produced a pile of papers from his jacket.

"I could get fired for what I am about to show you Mr. Williams. I came across some alarming evidence during the course of my investigation. First let's begin with the gunship involved in the attack. There is no official report by the USAF, but cameras and photos show the vehicle is military property. I tried to dig but hit a wall of federal red tape. I use outside connections discovering a report of a fire at Fort Drum. I tried to contact any of the personnel responding to the fire. Every last one of them died within a day or two of the fire."

Henry took the files from the Deputy Chief perusing them with diligence. Multiple satellite images show the gunship taking off from the USAF airbase. Dates on the images revealed the pictures were taken the same day of the attack. The gunship took off only an hour before attacking the mall. Leafing through the various reports Henry could see multiple inconsistencies. Official reports and direct evidence contradicted each other.

"Sir I understand this sounds like a conspiracy theory, but I have more evidence. The pistol used by the man who held your daughter. I cross referenced every gun patent, and this gun design does not exist. It would be impossible to track down the guns point of origin, but advanced composition of the pistol requires powerful industrial equipment. The weapon uses some advance nanotechnology construction process. Only about a dozen businesses possess facilities capable of producing this gun. Three have factories in America."

Pictures and photos showed the process of deconstructing the pistol. Henry saw his fair share of firearms, and noticed the advancements in the gun. The firing chamber used a magnetic rail system instead of gun powder to propel the bullet. Each clip contained a battery capable of firing the bullets in the clip. High powered magnetics shot the projectile at near light speed. Henry realized bullets from this gun would have been able to penetrate his armour.

"I was able to collect samples from the man holding your daughter hostage. Ghost agents use a special genetic virus to render their DNA unrecognizable. Poison released from nodes under the skin cause rapid breakdown upon death preventing identification. My private lab found a correlation between groups of inherited genetic traits that remained intact. Fifteen years ago the Russians tried to create genetic super soldier. UN inspection teams discovering the program shut it down filing the genetic code used. There was a 99% correlation between the code used by the Russian and your assailants."

All the information in the report had citation and collaborating evidence. Henry admired the Deputy Chiefs vigilance in piecing together disparate strands of information. The report read like a high level intelligence briefing. Medical charts showed the genetic testing done on the sample. Henry could feel the gravity of the situation sinking in.

"You know there are CIA agents incapable of creating such a profound report. I fear your talents are going to waste at the NYPD." Information in the report showed Henry the truth. Only one of the seven powerful families could orchestrate the attack. Bribing that many officials would require a vast sum of money. Ordering the attack required a vast network of connections inside the American government. Henry scoured the report trying to gleam the motivation of the attack from the evidence. Nothing in the report pointed to a culprit.

Deputy Chief Wayne looked at the last piece of paper in his hand, and handed the page over with reluctance. Henry couldn't believe what he was reading. A judge approved court order charging Julia with third degree murder. The court order showed the arrest date set for January 2nd 2044. Henry looked up at the Deputy Chief unable to contain his shock.

"That order comes down from the District Attorney's office. I tried to inquire in how to enforce it, but I was stonewalled. No one in the DA's office will answer my calls or questions. I have been ordered to arrest Julia on the appointed date with twenty officers. Footage from inside the mall shows Julia acted in self defense. I don't understand why the DA is pushing to have Julia charged." James eyes betrayed the empathy of a father replacing the stern glare of a deputy chief.

Henry slammed the report down on the desk. Only one motive made sense. Whoever ordered the attacks intended to send twenty officers to die. Henry wouldn't allow his only daughter to be arrested without proper legal justification. Any fighting between Muse security and the police would spark international outrage. The incident could even start a war. Muse Industries security forces and assets outnumbered the U.S military. The scheme intended to use public opinion to destroy Henry. The attack targeted the one thing that could destroy Muse industries.

"Thank you for your concern and this information Deputy Chief." Sliding the desk open Henry pulled out his cheque book. Deputy Chief Wayne watched with curiosity. Henry filled out the cheque to the sum of two hundred and fifty thousand dollars. Wayne's feelings of guilt wore plain in his facial expression.

"Mr. Williams I can't accept any money for the information I gave you. Even giving you the information is against the law."

"I believe your wife works in research and development at Mount Sinai hospital?" Henry filled the cheque out to Deborah Wayne with a smile.

"How is where my wife works relevant Mr. Williams?" Wayne watched Henry produced a legal contract from the desk.

"Have your wife sign these forms before she cashes the cheque. This will make your wife a contracted medical research consultant for Muse Industries. The contract will take care of the legalities. I am not asking you to break the law Deputy Chief. I wish to thank you for the information you brought today by your own volition. If you have any further moral crisis please feel free to contact me at any time. I have the greatest respect for the law and those that enforce it. After all the purpose of the law is to protect life and prevent harm. We are all obligated to do whatever it takes to protect innocent people."

Deputy Chief Wayne took the papers and cheque off the desk. The cheque represented several years of police salary. Wayne knew the money could pay off most of his family's debt. Enough money would be left over to help fund Deborah's research. Holding the cheque in hand Wayne felt a great weight of guilt bearing down on him. Weighing the pros and cons only complicated the issue to the man.

"Mr. Williams I am not sure I am comfortable with this. I know you're not asking me for anything, but this doesn't feel right." Watching the officer struggle with the moral dilemma brought a smirk to Henry's face. The verbal protest had not been followed by any attempt to return the cheque. Henry knew greed corrupts everything it touches, but power doesn't corrupt it just acts. Bringing the information had been James choice, and the reward another choice. People would claim the reward was a bribe, and could get the Deputy Chief fired.

"Think of it as an open ended agreement. If pangs of conscious ever lead you to feel the need to bring more information it will be rewarded. I would love to hire someone like you for my private security detail, but I doubt you would leave the police force. Too often in life good deeds go unrewarded. I seek to balance the scales of justice. Karma demands repayment for the good will you showed my family today, and the lives your actions have preserved. Please you would do me a great honor in accepting my generosity."

Rhetoric twisted inside the Deputy Chiefs mind. Every instinct screamed to return the cheque and walk away. Life's harsh reality demanded James to take the money because of the good it could do. College funds for the Wayne's children and freedom from financial debt. James struggled to help his wife pay off her student loans, but the debts continued to pile up. Morality gave way to prudence. James rationalized it was best to not offend the most powerful man in the world.

"Thank you Mr. Williams my family appreciates this. I will think about what you said, but I am not sure I can bring you information in the future." Business needed people to do what was necessary. Only a cunning person could motivate workers to push past pressures to reach goals. Mastered the art of influence Henry used the skill to build Muse Industries. Persuasion and manipulation were tools of influence in the political world of business.

Departing the study James held the cheque in hand. Hearing the door shut Henry turned attention towards the District Attorney. Thoughts churned into the man's mind trying to discern how best to handle the situation. Looking down Henry glimpsed a book hidden under some papers and pulled it out. Pages flipped in rapid succession until Henry stopped on the page he knew by memory.

War can never be avoided to one's advantage, but only the advantage of others. Machiavelli's words glared up from the page at Henry. All that mattered was discovering who was behind the attacks against Julia. Henry thought a visit to the District Attorney may shed light on who the puppet master was. Protecting Julia made the reward outweigh any risk.

CHAPTER 16

Intimidation Tactics

Stars twinkled in the sky over New York City. Soft starlight reflected from the hull of the limo sweeping across the night sky. Slowing down the limo hovered in front of a massive grey skyscraper. Limo doors whisked open with a whoosh. Stepping out Cpt. Anderson led Muse Security and established a perimeter.

White moon light highlighted the ebony combat armour worn by Muse security. Only the white logo of a hand over a fist stood out on the uniform. Henry William's stepped out of the limo marching straight towards the office. Guards flanked the CEO marching towards the door to the office building. Automated sensors scanned the approaching people triggering the main doors to open.

Henry strolled through the double doors with four guards following behind. Six security guards stood watch at the base of the District Attorney's office. Cameras tracked Henry and his team marched towards the group of security. Noticing the armed escort building security looked at one another with worry. One of the guards stopped Henry by stepping in his way.

"Excuse me sir, but I don't see any visitors on the log. I am going to have to ask you to identify yourself." Henry motioned with his hand for the team to stop. The other guards stared at the large assault rifles Muse security troops held. Tension filled the air from the darting glances of the people gathered in the lobby. Armed only with pistols the security guards knew the inferior position they were in. Oblivious Henry dusted dirt from his shoulders before answering.

"Henry Williams. I am here to see District Attorney Richter."

Behind a mahogany desk District Attorney Kyle Richter perused through the case files. Massive stacks of papers towered on the one side of the desk threatening to topple. Kyle groaned running his hands through his hair pulling strands from frustration. The work load had piled up in the pattern resembling a losing game of Jenga. Callous digital time on the watch blared at Kyle showing it was quarter after eleven pm, and the workload would take hours to finish. The intercom buzzed to life interrupting the quiet ambiance of the office.

"I hate to disturb you sir. I have Henry Williams stand here asking to see you." The report only added more stress to the district attorney. Within seconds Kyle realized the reason for the visit at this hour. Henry must have found out about the charges pending on his daughter. The holographic display showed security guards standing opposed to Henry with his armed security team.

Weighing the chain of consequences Kyle tried to decide the best way to handle the situation. Henry Williams possessed power and influence making it unwise to refuse the meeting, but the prosecution of Julia made it unwise to allow entry of her father. The report on the Skymall attack and Henry's behaviour sat on the desk. Having read the report made Kyle feel weary about allowing entrance, but refusal could be much worse. Video showed Henry staring with impatient at the guard standing by the silent intercom. Staring at the intercom Kyle couldn't break through his the indecision gripping his mind.

Henry waited with patience watching the security guard talking over the intercom. After a few minutes the guard exited the booth leaning in to whispering something to his partner. Taking an aggressive stance the entire security group approached Henry and his team. Security guards rested their hands on the pistols at the hip revealing their hostile intentions. Each of the security guards eyes darting watching for slightest sign of hostile intent. Nervous energy added to the tension in the air.

"Tell Mr. Williams he can come enter if he comes alone and surrenders any weapons. Otherwise you are to prevent anyone from entering this building." Turning the intercom off Kyle stared at the door resigned to the choice. Time tightened the hangman's' noose with each second that ticked away. Video zoomed in on Henry so Kyle could watch the response when the guard delivered the news.

"Mr. Williams the District Attorney is pleased to hear of your visit, but requests that your security team remains here. Also I am going to need to ask you to surrender your sidearm in your jacket. You must comply in order to be allowed to enter." Reaching into the jacket pocket Henry withdrew a legal document presenting the paper. Snatching the paperwork the guard examined the document. License and documentation from the government gave rights to carry concealed weapons, and permitted Henry to carry his pistol into any government building.

"I am legally licensed to carry this weapon at all times. I can carry my pistol everywhere in society by the federal government. I am more than willing to leave my men behind. A man in my position must think of his safety at all times. It's a preposterous notion that I have come here with any intention of harm towards the Mr. Richter."

Looking over the legal documentation the Guard scanned for evidence of forgery. After several minutes of scrutiny the guards looked up with disdain. The security guard motioned Henry to move into the scanner. Loud humming emanated from the machine. Blue light swept up and down scanning the devices target. Watching the readout the machine identified the various cybernetic components, genetic modifications, and the pistol in the jacket pocket.

"I am going to assume you have the required forms for your other equipment?" Henry shot a charismatic smile producing the papers handing for the guard. Anger marked the man's face studying he paper work with diligence hoping to find something wrong. Defeated the guard waved Henry through them machine. Motioning to be followed the guard walked towards the elevator at a slow pace.

Both men stopped in front of the elevator. Watching the elevator descend Henry could feel the tension in the air. A soft ding announced the elevator's arrival and doors slid open. Both men stepped forward onto the elevator without looking at one another. Pressing the button for the top floor the guard waited for the doors to close.

Inertia shifted when the Elevator lurched into motion. Magnets pulled the metal car up to the top of the building. Travel to the District Attorney's office only took only a few seconds. Neither Henry nor the Guard uttered a word during the trip. Dinging marked the arrival at the destined floor breaking the silence. Exiting the elevator the securities guard led Henry down the hallway. Approached the double set of wooden doors to the District attorney's office the guard stepped forward.

"After you Mr. Williams" the guard said opening one of the doors. District Attorney Kyle Richter stared from behind a document seeing the figure in the doorway. Walking into the office Henry observed the stack of law books on one side, the artwork on the walls, and the mound of paperwork covering the desk. Closing the door behind the guard stood outside in case he was needed. Henry pulled out one of the chairs in front of the desk sitting down. The sound of a loud snip caused Kyle to look up in time to see the end of a cigar hit the office floor.

"You can't smoke in a federal building it's a ten thousand dollar fine Mr. Williams."

"I must have forgotten District Attorney Richter. Let me offer my sincere apologies." Henry produced a piece of paper and pen. Looking down at the piece of paper Kyle discerned that it was a cheque. Filling out the cheque Henry slid it across the desk. Kyle read ten thousand dollars on the cheque made out to the corporation of New York City. Striking the lighter caused sparks to flash causing flames to roar to life. Holding up the flame Henry lit his cigar in defiance.

"I believe that should satisfy the good people of New York. This will also help you with your conviction rates at the same time. I like it when everyone wins." Tobacco smoke drifted through the room from the cigar. Savouring the flavour for a second Henry blew the smoke at the District Attorney. Powerless to act Kyle could only glare in anger. Henry William's statement was not lost on the lawyer. Double jeopardy laws ensured that each offense could only be charged once, and it was only civil offense punishable by fine. Crossing his arms Kyle watched Henry puff on his cigar for a few moments.

"Mr. William I assure you it is quite the honor to meet you in person. Do you have any particular reason for your visit?" Kyle legal training taught him to never admit to anything first.. Taking stock both men stared at each gauging the opponent. Even years of training didn't prepare Kyle to read the poker face of his opponent. Henry took his time before pulling the cigar from his mouth preparing to answer.

"I felt that I've been remiss. I should have visited when you took office District Attorney Richter. I have heard of your successes in the war on crime and drugs in New York. You're making quite the name for yourself amongst the rich and powerful elite. I don't imagine you get much rest working for the city that never sleeps. I wanted to give you my personal thanks for your tireless and diligent work." Relaxing in the seat Henry exuded an aura of calm to throw his opponent off.

Acute instinct told Kyle that the honey words coated a venomous intent. Henry played the game of words trying to lure his opponent into dropping his guard. Years of experience handling trials taught Kyle how to control his outward appearance. Neither man flinched in resolve. Two titans stood opposed to another divided by a wooden desk.

"You're much smaller in person than I expected Mr. Williams. Your legend paints you as a titan of business, but I find the real man to be much more human. I do appreciate your visit. I suspect you have heard of the indictment of Julia for manslaughter. I think that is the real reason you have come here at such a late hour. Do you intend to use some sort of intimidation tactic on me? Perhaps you intend to threaten me with violence? You can see I have a lot of work to do so could get to the point Mr. Williams."

Henry's feigned shock on his face. Each word represented the movement of another piece on the board. Kyle designed each word and sentence with the purpose to distract, infuriate, or attack. Henry knew words can be the most devastating weapons. Both men struggled to sense the next attack from their opponent. Business taught Henry the war of words.

"I had no idea you intended to prosecute my daughter. I wonder how you could even attempt such a thing against the evidence. I have dozens of witnesses willing to testify to Julia's situation. My daughter endured the ordeal of attempted kidnapping and the traumatic site of the mall. I cannot fathom why you would want to hurt an innocent girl who defended herself. Julia is preparing to embark on the start of her adult life. I mean unless you were using the prosecution as a weapon. I understand how a man of limited foresight would think that hurting my daughter would hurt me. Now what advantage could the District Attorney gain from using my daughter as leverage?"

Scanning the desk Henry spotted a picture frame. Silver framed the picture of Kyle Richter with his wife and two young children. Henry reached onto the desk grabbing the picture. Desperation filled Kyle's face when he tried to grasp the picture before Henry could see it. Each inhale on the cigar caused the heater to glow red illuminating the man's face. Henry looked at the picture with the cigar dangling from his lips.

"I see you are a family man. I wonder how you would act if someone were to threaten your daughter. What lengths would you go to protect your child?" Air bended and shifted distorting Kyle's view from smoke wafting in front of him. The loud thud echoed from the hallway before the room door opened. Wide open the door showed the guard lying unconscious on the ground. Kyle's eyes widened with fear staring at Henry.

"Well it looks like we have some time alone Mr. Richter. Mr. Kincaide is here, but I promise you that he won't tell anyone. Please enlighten me to reason why you're attacking my daughter. A man of your education would know that such action would be a direct attack against me." Henry drank in the reaction from his opposition. Shock left Kyle speechless.

"Your silence reveals you understand the situation all too well. You're going to tell me who put you on this course of action." Exhaling a puff of smoke Henry savoured the emotions in his opponent. Unable to control the emotions Kyle felt panic grip his mind. Polished metal from the pistol gleamed from the half open desk drawer up at the man. Glancing towards the pistol Kyle realized there was no way to get to it.

"Mr. Williams you seem to think someone put me up to this. My indictment of Julia is my own personal crusade. I have taken down every major criminal in New York in the last eighteen months, but I am force to confess the worst criminal runs lose. Mr. Williams since you opened up Muse Industries your actions have left a wake of blood and suffering. Your actions cause chaos on a global scale because you believe you're above the law. I can't hold you accountable to the law. Even if you left evidence I couldn't convince the people to convict you."

Choosing words with care Kyle voice was a mix of terror and conviction. Henry gauged the character of the man before him. District Attorney Kyle Richter's war on organized crime had become a legend throughout New York City. Newspapers called the District Attorney the modern day Elliot Ness. Everyone in New York City adored the forty year old district attorney. Henry could sense the conviction and truth behind the words spoken. Instinct told him the District Attorney was working alone driven by self-righteous conviction.

"I am sorry you think that Mr. Richter. I will not try to change your mind. The next time you decide to attack please have the dignity of coming after me. The only thing keeping you alive is your conviction in the law. You can believe whatever you want and attack me. If you're going to declare war you should be prepared for the consequences. If you ever come after me again through my family the consequences will be dire. I will devote immense fortunes to ensure you're no longer a threat.

Henry slammed his cigar down extinguishing it on the desk top. Staring at each other neither man wanted to break the gaze first. Only after a few moments did Kyle looked towards the picture of his family. The picture was a symbol of what the man held most important. Turning away Henry walked towards the door certain one threat had been dealt with. Kincaide still held the door open waiting for his boss to leave. Turning back to face the district attorney Henry could see the emotions tearing inside the man.

"Tell your technicians I am sorry about the inconvenience. Mr. Kincaides presence causes electronic devices to short out. Think of it as my way to promote job creation." Henry used words to twist the knife. Few people could stand to be insulted in their own office. Fuelled by rage Kyle stood up in defiance.

"You know Mr. Williams I was wrong. Your legend doesn't do you justice. I've heard of the William's pride is something awesome to behold. You really could kill a District Attorney without feeling a hint of remorse. The government would be forced to prosecute. Muse Security would defend you like you were Julius fucking Caesar. Governments would be forced to draw lines between revenue and alliances. If governments side with your action the shadow war would increase in violence. The world would drown in the tidal wave of chaos. I believed monsters were fairy tales for children until I met you. You're so deluded by your pride you have yourself convinced your making the world a better place."

Henry stopped dead in his tracks reaching into his coat pocket. Looking down at the pistol Kyle wondering if he should reach for it. The invisible guardian Kincaide prepared himself to prevent any action by the

District attorney. Spinning around Henry drew an object from inside his jacket pocket. Kyle launched backwards diving for cover behind his office chair and desk. Henry walked forward and placed a formal invite on the table. Heavy breathing echoed from behind the desk.

"Now I remember why I came here. My wife sends you her regards with that invitation to the charity event tomorrow. See you at the party Richter!" Henry waved good bye over his shoulder exiting the office. Cowering behind the desk Kyle looked up seeing the empty office. Sitting in the center of the desk was the invitation glaring up at Kyle.

CHAPTER 17

The Witching Hour

Cold winter air raced between skyscrapers stretching into the darkness of the night sky. Wind shrieked through New York City creating a terrifying ambiance. Pale moonlight broke through holes in the clouds swirling in the sky. The old city street of New York City fell into disuse with the invention of the gravity engine. Cracks etched through the pavement next to pristine sidewalks. Towering glass monuments rose from the decaying sprawl of the metropolis. From above corporate towers resembled weeds leeching the life from soil of the city.

Outside the building the Muse limo hovered over the pavement. Henry stepped out of the District Attorney's building followed by his honour guard. Muse security guards opened the limo door for their boss. Entering the limo Henry found reprieve from the cold winter night. Cpt. Anderson sat next to the now visible Achilles Kincaide. Achilles eyes were shut in a meditative trance.

Kincaide wore skin-tight thermal optical camouflage over reinforced combat armour. Thermal optical camouflage semitransparent outer layer resembled cellophane when not active. When activated the suit mirrored the surrounding environment. Powerful microcomputers allowed the outer layer to adjust quicker than the human eye. Thermal optic camouflage created the illusion of invisibility while blocking out any other emissions. Achilles suit made it impossible to see any defining personal characteristic even when visible. Only the eyes remained visible in thermal optical camouflage suits. Achilles appeared a silhouette made flesh.

Energy pulsed from the limo engine vibrating the frame. Gravity engines generated energy through spinning liquid magnetic metal at high speeds. The engine generated an electromagnetic field the same polarity as the Earth's core. Magnetic repulsion caused the limo to ascend into the night sky. Electric engines whirled to life thrusting the ship forward using turbines. Sitting in the back of the limo Henry stared at city skyline blurring past him.

"Do you think it was wise to threaten the District attorney Sir?" Cpt. Anderson asked out of concern. Looking across the car Henry saw the worry on his friends face. Maintaining a calm demeanour Max anger still filled his eyes. Staying quiet Henry allowed his friend to vent his frustration.

"Not to mention that you broke the law bringing thermal optical camouflage into a government building. I can even figure out what you're thinking." Careful wording allowed Max to speak his mind. No one else dared to speak up in support, but everyone agreed in silence. Henry knew that his friend only worried because he cared.

"You worry too much Max. Kincaide disabled the security cameras with his jammer before anything incriminating happened. The district attorney won't act against me without solid proof. The only disappointing part of this excursion was that Mr. Richter appears to be operating of his own volition. Information regarding the source of the attack on the mall continues to prove elusive."

Ringing out through the back of the limo a chime indicated the incoming call. Turning to answer the call Henry stopped seeing the hand signal from Max. Pulling out a personal holoemitter Cpt. Anderson moved through menus and information. The device connected to the limo's communication systems. Using the holoemitter Max accessed the incoming call trying to trace the source.

"Sir the message is encrypted with a very powerful encryption algorithm. I can't see who is calling or where they are calling from. The only information I can gleam is that the call is coming from within New York City itself." Sighing from frustration Henry reached from the phone. The voice was distorted beyond recognition, but sill clear enough to understand.

"Mr. Williams I have important information that I must give to you. Time is the enemy to both of us. I would ask you to come to the construction site of your new corporate tower. You must come with haste. I will wait for you at the location until midnight. You have ten minutes to show up before I must depart."

The abrupt ending of the transmission filled the limo atmosphere with tension. Cpt. Anderson looked to his men seeing worry on their faces. Still mediating Kincaide seemed unfazed by the nature of the message. Henry calculated the intent behind the message trying to visualize every possible future. Multiple possible futures flashed by in an instant in the man's mind. Only one lingering question remained. Did the risk outweigh possibility of reward?

Pressing the intercom button Henry ordered "driver get us to Jupiter tower in five minutes." Careening through the sky the limo accelerated blurring the passing cityscape. Stoic pride caused Max to sit still and quiet. Cpt. Anderson instinct told him to never go into any situation blind, but experience showed that Henry Williams had an appetite for risk. Humming louder Kincaide tried to calm the tension in the air of the limo with his meditation.

Orbiting around Jupiter tower the limo provided a view of the construction site. Henry looked out the window seeing nothing but equipment and materials. Wind howled through the top of the construction site. Tarps flapped caught in the gale force. Scanning in every visual spectrum available to the cybernetic eyes revealed nothing to Henry.

Moving closer to Jupiter tower the limo fought against the high wind. Coming to a rest at the edge of the unfinished top floor the limo door opened. Wind whipped through the back of the limo intensified by the small enclosing. Stepping out first Cpt. Anderson scanned the roof before leading troops out. Stepping out Henry did up his suit jacket feeling the cold chill in his bones.

Looking down Cpt. Anderson felt overcome by the feeling of vertigo. When completed Jupiter Tower would be the highest tower in the world. The new headquarters of Muse Industries towered over the sprawling city below. Powerful wind threatened to throw the people over the edge with each gust. Looking down Henry read his watch seeing only one minute from midnight.

No one appeared to be on the top of the tower. Henry focused on hearing a faint whistling distinct from the wind. Approaching closer the noise grew louder. Instinct forced the security team into position using steel girders and machines to provide cover. A soft tune could be heard through the howl of the wind. Air distorted revealing the image of a man whistling the tune bad moon rising.

"Ah Mr. Williams it is good to see you again. If only we didn't seem to always meet under such dire circumstance." Henry recognized the thick Chinese accent. Muse security team aimed their guns at Zhou Yun Sun. Henry wondered what could be so important to bring Zhou Yun Sun from his sanctuary.

"You know if you get caught on American soil they would execute you as a terrorist. It's a brave move leaving the safety of China's borders. I am assuming the information you have forced you into such a desperate gamble. You continue to surprise me at every turn." Zhou Yun bowed showing his deep respect to Henry.

"You honour me with such praise that I am unworthy of. My coming to America was motivated by selfish reasons. You may not be aware of how much control I possess over worldwide organized crime. The information my agents brought to me threatens my business and the stability of China. I am a loyal Chinese citizen and agent of the Chinese government. I swore an oath to defend my nation. If my life ends in service to the people of China than I will die a very happy man."

Studying the man Henry tried to suss out the true motives in Zhou Yun's mind. Asking a favor could have been handled over a secure communication unless it was criminal. Digital footprints were too hard to cover in the digitalized world of 2033. Zhou Yun could be behind the attack using this situation to draw attention in another direction. Henry raced through the possible motives in his thoughts.

"I have had enough intrigue for one day Mr. Sun. If you have important information give it to me. If you came to ask for a favor than ask it, but whatever reason you're here you need to make it known." Henry chose the direct path desiring to go home. Cold wind howling made the night inhospitable to man and beast.

"I am not here to ask for a favor Mr. Williams. I am here to do you a favor. There are rumblings in the criminal world of some sort of machination against your interests. Your interests are tied to my own. The attack on Julia is on the lips of everyone throughout the world. Whoever is behind the attack is looking to gain leverage over you, but I am sure you know that. I believe the attack on Julia is the prelude to a thrust against Muse Industries itself. China needs your medical technology Mr. Williams. Too many people could be saved by your technology. It is necessary to try to save as many lives as possible for my goals to succeed."

Henry listened with great care trying to discern any lies. No evidence existed that Zhou Yun would have any reason to betray the business arrangement. Evidence from China revealed truth behind the medical urgency of the nation. Money ensured Zhou Yuns would be motivated to expand business opportunity through implants. Henry couldn't see the moves that it would take to conquer muse, but understood why Julia was the target. Whoever held Julia could force Henry to take the company public making it vulnerable to attack. Pacing back and forward in thought Henry looked towards Zhou Yun.

"I assume you didn't come all the way to New York City to tell me things I already knew. You do not seem to be the kind of man who makes himself vulnerable for no reason. If you had information regarding who is behind the plot you would have presented it. I would like to know what benefit you can be to me in this matter before we freeze to death. Why did you come all this way Mr. Sun?" Producing a small data chip Zhou Yun offered it to his associate. Henry grasped the small data chip wondering what information could be on it.

"There is a recording of a torture I directed. The man revealed that a ghost team known as the Wolf pack took a job contract for an attack set on New Year's Eve. Sadly the man knew little else of value. The Wolf pack is the most expensive ghost team in the world. Not even my own network has been capable of discovering who they are. Instinct tells me that your charity event tomorrow is the target, but there is no evidence to prove it. I have lost several agents and a small fortune trying to acquire any evidence."

Inserting the data chip in to the holoemitter displayed the scene of torture. Several unidentifiable men were peeling the man's finger nails off using a machete. Zhou Yun voice asked questions from off camera. Each unsatisfactory response provoked another fingernail cut off. After several minutes the man broke down screaming for mercy.

The man rambled off names of people smuggling weapons and technology into China. Zhou Yun pressed again to reveal who was behind the attack on the Skymall. Swearing ignorance the man continued to beg for mercy. Running out of fingernails the men hacked a finger off. Sobbing the man swore the only thing he knew was that the Wolf pack were offered the job first. The wolf pack refused because the price was too low, but the failure of the attack on the Skymall brought a new offer. An offer so high it would allow the entire team to retire and live comfortable the rest of their lives. Video recording cut off ending in a black screen.

Zhou Yun grimaced "it pains me to bring this information to you Mr. Williams. What I am about to advise you to do is perhaps even more painful. Your enemies are using deception and distraction to stay hidden. All the power your enemies possess relies upon their staying hidden and unidentified. Without a target to strike even the great Henry Williams and his army is rendered powerless."

Words conveyed clear truth to Henry's mind. Agents and information sources revealed no evidence on the enemy planning the attack. Blinded from the lack of information forced defensive reaction to whatever happened. The acute feeling of being at a disadvantage filled Henry with frustration. Zhou Yun could see the resistance of pride on his associates face.

"I can't cancel the event less than twenty four hours away from it. I won't show such weakness on the world stage." Henry spoke over the howling wind his voice conveying intention. Anger pushed hot blood through the veins. Steam rose from Henry's skin into the cold night air.

"Nor would I advise you to do such. Mr. Williams the reality is one day your enemies will succeed in abducting Julia. Even the venerated Muse Security force cannot protect your daughter forever. Learn the lesson that great emperors failed to. Enemies will always use family because it is the greatest weakness any person can have. You can't protect Julia. Even if you could what kind of life would your daughter have with such confinement?"

Tapping his foot with impatience Henry listened to Zhou Yun. No father wants to be unable to protect his daughter. Powerlessness offends everyone with equal power. Henry felt the stinging frustration of powerlessness. Logic behind Zhou Yun's analysis of the situation showed the strategic reasoning he possessed.

"What are you advising Mr. Sun. You seem to allude to purpose with your words. I will not abandon my daughter, yet as you say I cannot protect Julia either. You speak in riddles and I would have you point cleave to your purpose. What do you purpose I do in my situation?" Henry's agitated expression revealed the strength of emotions stirring in the man's mind.

Diplomacy required delicate application of truth. Delivering the message required tact so Henry would not be offended. Zhou Yun paused thinking how to best bring the message forward to avoid provoking a backlash. Waiting for a response compounded the tension Henry felt pulling at his muscles. Realizing there is only one way to say delicate truths Zhou Yun resigned himself to his fate.

"Mr. Williams if you cannot protect your daughter than there is only one strategic option left. You must allow your daughter to be taken." Henry marched towards Zhou Yun trying to contain his murderous rage. Muse security forces took aim under Cpt. Anderson's order. Wind howled unable to break the tensions building between the two men. Staring into Zhou Yun's eyes Henry searched for the truth.

"You dare suggest I let my daughter get kidnapped. Perhaps you're behind all this Mr. Sun. Perhaps your death is the price of my daughter's freedom. A price I would pay in a second if I knew it to be true. Strange coincidence that the attack on my daughter came just a day after you attacked me. If I kill you now Mr. Sun do all my problems cease to exist?"

Zhou Yun never flinched when Henry came face to face aiming his pistol. Watching from behind cover Cpt. Anderson waited for the signal to open fire. Holding the gun Henry finger hovered over the trigger. Tarps flapped with explosive power in random burst from the wind. Neither man seemed fazed by the cold, noise, or wind. Standing in opposition Zhou Yun and Henry kept their gaze locked on each other.

"I have come here unguarded and unarmed to show the truth of my intentions. You know my death would not save your daughter. I believe you to be one of the greatest strategic minds in the world. Whoever wants Julia has no interest in killing her. Your daughter is more valuable alive and unharmed to use as leverage. No one would suspect the great Henry Williams would allow his daughter to be kidnapped. Allowing your daughter to be taken will smoke your enemies out into the open."

Emotion clouded Henry's thoughts. Constant protection would rob Julia of any chance at a happy life. Zhou Yun's argument rolled over in Henry's mind. Truth of the argument battled against the father's natural instinct. Henry felt the weight of life and death pulling his mind into the mire of uncertainty. Zhou Yun watched Henry for any sign of what he was thinking.

"Mr. Williams are you aware that the Chinese written symbol for crisis can mean danger or opportunity. You know the truth is danger and opportunity is the same thing." No matter how much the plan made sense Henry felt compelled to rebel against it. Pride clouded the vision. Raising one hand Henry gave the signal for his team to back off. Cpt. Anderson covered his men falling back into the limo.

Turning away Henry put his pistol back into his jacket pocket. Zhou Yun couldn't tell if his plan had been accepted or not. Marching back towards the Limo Henry still debated what he should do with the information. Cpt. Anderson fell back last using his body to shield his boss. Stepping into the limo Henry looked back at Zhou Yun one last time.

"Thank you for the information Mr. Sun." Henry still didn't know what to make of the situation, but the information would be useful. Closing the limo door Cpt. Anderson banged on the driver compartment barrier. Henry wondered if he should trust Zhou Yun watching him disappear. Engines whined causing the ship to drift away from the tower. Information allowed Henry to prepare for the attack regardless who directed it, and the first step to avoiding any deception was preparation.

CHAPTER 18

Preparations

Stepping from the limo Henry, Victoria, and Julia walked towards the plaza hotel. The iconic look of the Plaza hotel towered twenty stories into the sky. Several employees of the hotel came rushing out to assist the Williams with their bags. Muse security stood at attention scanning for any trouble. The flags of various nations hung stoic above the door tossing back and forth in the mid-afternoon breeze.

Walking into the hotel the Williams were greeted by the massive chandlers hanging over head. Sun gleamed off the polished marble floor. Hotel staff rushed around in a flurry of activity surrounding the Williams. Every employee attended the family like they were royalty. Spotting Henry Williams and his family the head manager approached with haste.

"Welcome to the Plaza hotel Mr. Williams. Everything has been prepared for your arrival. Your wife submitted the guest list and we've seen everyone to their rooms. Your head of security Maj. Lee is already overseeing hotel security per your request. Mr. Williams it is always the Plaza's greatest pleasure to serve your family." Bowing before Henry the manager hoped to leave a good impression.

Maximizing safety required the entire hotel to be closed for business. Complete control of internal and external security would be under Muse Security forces. Hotel staff was placed at the whim of Henry Williams and his guests. Bellhops carried the family baggage behind the Williams following the manager to the elevator. In order to put on the first annual Charity event Henry purchased the entire Plaza Hotel.

Various celebrity figures owned some of the penthouses in the Plaza. Henry offered twice the market rate spending a ridiculous fortune on the building. No one said no to the CEO of Muse Industries. Refusing to remodel the rooms Henry kept the unique flare of the previous owner of each penthouse unit. The purchase of the Plaza hotel along with other real estate in the early days of Muse Industries caused controversy, but the publicity fueled the legend of the CEO. Henry restored the old building to their original condition blending modern technology into the design. Everything touched by the Williams prospered.

Sectioning off the largest penthouse units for honoured guests kept the units free most of the year. Henry kept the largest unit for a personal private get away and special occasions. Victoria often stayed in the hotel when working in New York spending a fortune on decorating. Overlooking central park the William's penthouse unit was a triplex with an open balcony. Each guest received lodging in their own luxurious penthouse unit for their stay.

Exiting the elevator the manager escorted the family towards their suite. Simple elegance of classical style greeted the William's family when they entered their suite. Julia showed the way to her room to the bellhops carrying the bags. Henry sat down on the couch looking out into central park through the massive living room windows. Maj. Lee approached handing the report detailing security placement to his boss.

Muse Security were positioned on the roof and posted at every entrance to the Plaza. Roving guards patrolled the hallways. Every room had been searched and nothing abnormal found. Hundreds of Muse security personnel had been stationed around and throughout the hotel. Reading the report brought Henry some sense of security.

Victoria rushed around followed by a cadre of people directing the organization of the event. Only six hours remained until the dinner party started. Only the richest and most influential people in the world were invited to attend. Everyone would gather into the Plaza ballroom for dinner and the New Year's party. Select guests were invited to the private party in the Williams suite after diner. Exploding inward the front doors flew open. Colt Cross sauntered into the room wearing a jovial smile. Swaggering across the floor Colt looked around the condo whistling at the sight.

"I see your wife redecorated again Henry. You always pull out all the stops for your annual shindig. I still think you should let me call in my Crossfire boys to lend a hand. You should have gunships overhead and double the men you got right now." News played on the holoemitter displayed above the fireplace mantle. Reporters set up broadcast just outside the plaza allowing Henry to watch the activity outside.

Police forces blocked off the street and set up a perimeter just beyond the Plaza entrance. Henry invited world leaders, business CEO's, and celebrities to the annual event requiring the city to protect the rich and powerful. In the frame you could see the SWAT van to the left creating the line between police and protestors. Thousands of people gathered outside to protest the One percent. Signs waved in the cool air calling the CEO calling him Dr. Death, A modern Caligula, and an international criminal. Some of the signs construction revealed the dubious nature of the certain protestors.

"We are gathered outside the Plaza hotel today. Preparations for the Annual Charity Dinner and Masquerade ball are under way. Guests have been showing up since the early morning for the biggest event of the year. Protesters gathering out front have created a large crowd. Cries denouncing Muse Industries monopoly on Cybertechnology can be heard in the background. Rumours speak of secret government research into simulated experience. Public outcry has never been louder over this issue. Muse Industries refuses to put Simex on the market. Simulated experience is the ability to upload and download memories using a neural implant. Government officials refused to address the rampant social problem caused by Simex shops springing up in every city."

Clicking the off button on the remote Henry stood up in frustration over the news. Colt could see the frustration etched on his old friends face. Henry felt a hand touch his back trying to calm him. Snow danced across the window whipped around by the wind Looking out the window Colt leaned closer to Henry.

"You know that old adage that no good deed goes unpunished. The public wants this technology because it has an unending thirst for entertainment. The people don't' care if something is bad for them." Colt reminded his friend of the truth of the human condition. Thinking about history Henry seen parallels in ancient civilizations.

During the Roman Empire people in the coliseum howled for entertainment in the form of blood. Monarchs used public executions both for public entertainment and terror to keep people in line. Television, Movies, and the internet pushed entertainment to new heights. Neural implants allowed people to experience things they couldn't otherwise. Henry understood why the people were angry, but the people didn't see the dark side of simulated experience.

Simulated experience and real experience could not be separated in a persons mind. Henry knew widespread distribution of Simex would cause even further social unrest. Neural technology allowed digitization of the human conscious. The human mind became a vast organic computer. In the world of digitized consciousness the question of the nature of the human soul became poignant.

Once people realized memories could be manipulated real experience would lose value. With the ability to manipulate memory came the ability to hack the human mind. Henry worried what would happen in a world where memories were only digital information. Wireless neural implants turned each human mind into one node in a worldwide neural network. Each person mind and memories open to the world. Each person would be one neuron in the Earth's consciousness.

"Why are you not marketing the technology" Colt questioned? Simulated experience would make a fortune in a world with no regulating laws. Driven by greed Colt couldn't see the cliff he raced towards. Most people were driven to succeed. Society defined success in material wealth and possessions. Henry had more money than he ever needed. Neural technology created to help humanity now threatened to push humanity over the edge.

"Don't you ever wonder how far the consequences of our actions go Colt?" Colt stepped forward pulling Henry close with a jovial laugh. Just beyond the window protestors cries echoed through the city streets below. Henry wondered how his friend maintained his invincible happy attitude. Nothing seemed to faze Colt at all.

"You're always so serious. Look at all the good you've done with the technology you've created. I'm alive because of your neural implant. There are people walking with artificial cybernetic legs who couldn't walk before. Cybernetic eyes have given the blind people the ability to see the beauty of the world. If people choose to use your tools as weapons you can't be blamed. I don't make guns to hurt people, but sometimes that how people use guns."

Staring at the old Texan Henry marvelled at the power of rationalization to justify everything a person does. The way the human brain pushed negative information out of the way so the person can continue their pursuits. Crossfire industries remained one the few firearms business to conduct only legal business, but the security dilemma meant that nations supplied other nations with weapons. Colt seemed unbothered by the source of his wealth. The entire Cross family fortune had been built on blood and death.

Henry watched his daughter enter the room wearing an elegant sheer silk formal dress. Light reflected off silver frills of the black dress. Julia's standing next to her mother revealed the striking similarities. Victoria and her daughter looked like mirror reflections of each other. Only age told the two women apart. Henry's mind turned to thoughts of what the Williams family legacy.

"Now are you going to let me get my gunships and troops in here to lock this place down?" Colts stared at his friend waiting for a response.

"Gunships and heavily armed troops will only frighten people. I have confidence in Maj. Lee's ability to ensure the safety of the guests. Many of the guests will be bringing their own security forces. I think Muse security has the building secured. Full militarized force presence could excite the protestors outside into violent action. Public outcry to a militarized force would also be significant. I don't want this party to cause any more public disorder than necessary."

Colt looked at the stoic expression on Maj. Lee's face. Years of military service engrained the idea of taking all precautions. Colt flared with frustration struggling to understand the situation. After two recent attacks Henry still refused to bring in more security. Colt couldn't contain the frustration.

"All due respect Henry but I would think you would do anything to protect your family. Two attacks in the span of twenty four hours centered on your family. I know the last week has been calm, but you should be prepare for the storms still coming." Watching the two CEO's debate Maj.

Lee felt inclined to agree with Colt. Henry hadn't given any definitive answer to Zhou Yun Sun proposal.

Lack of vigilance towards security left Maj. Lee wondering. Edward studied Henry's face trying to gleam the thoughts inside the man's mind. Pride could be blinding the CEO to the real possibility of an attack during the night's events. Maj. Lee didn't think Henry was capable of sacrificing his own daughter. Muse Security forces were spread throughout the building at every major point, but there is no such thing as too much security. Henry pulled his friend close with a smile.

"With you looking out for me Colt what could go wrong? We both have to learn to relax a little. You're going to have another heart attack if you continue. I appreciate everything you and your family have done. I am blessed to have a friend like you Colt. Let us have a drink before we head down to the dinner." Henry motioned for his friend to follow him.

Creeping across the old Texans face his lips curled into a wily smile. Walking over to the bar Henry cracked open an aged bottle of whiskey. Pouring the liquid into the two cups Henry offered a glass to his friend. Taking the glass Colt brought the glass to his lips and sipped the drink. Whiskey burned the tongue and throat leaving a sweet aftertaste.

"Your one crazy man Henry, but you do have a damn fine taste in drinks. You know my father loved you like a son. I got to say I don't agree with you on the security issues, but I do respect your opinion. Here's to your bright future my old comrade." Henry tapped the glass together causing a chime. Both men tipped the glass back downing their glass drinks in a gulp. Victoria walked over tapping Henry on the shoulder to gain his attention.

"Julia and I are going to head down to help oversee the guests to their table. Colt and you can follow when you're done. Just don't be too long. Maj. Lee you make sure my husband doesn't drink too much before the party." Several security guards formed up on the two women walking towards the door. Victoria wrapped an arm around her daughter. Both women turned waving goodbye.

Henry watched his beautiful wife and daughter leave with dresses flowing behind them. Glugging the whiskey poured into both glasses. Seeing Henry pour the liquid Maj. Lee hoped that he would pace himself. The New Year's party was one of the few occasion in which Henry would get drunk. Despite Victoria's orders Edward knew he couldn't prevent his boss from drinking. Colt watched the amber liquid pour into the glass feeling saliva fill his mouth in anticipation.

"I've never been known to turn down a good drink." Henry raised his glass into the air motioning for Colt to do the same.

"Let's toast to the future. May our days ahead contain more glory than the ones that have past us by. Let love and dreams be our North Star guiding us to our soul's purpose. To our families and continued success in 2034. We'll change the world and make it a better place for everyone."

Glasses chimed striking together from the men's toast. Colt admired his friend's way with words. Looking down on the protestors below Henry wondered what the future would hold. Central park swept out before the two men staring out the window. Snow collected on the trees. Cries rang out from the street below. Sipping the drink Henry pushed the feelings of unease from his mind.

CHAPTER 19

Red Carpet

Journalists and photographers clogged the hallway leading to the Plaza ballroom. Snapping cameras took pictures of celebrities heading into the ballroom. All the guests wore the finest designer clothing and sparkling jewellery. All the wealth glistened on the world stage for one night. Words flung through the air in furious verbal assault on the celebrities passing by.

Guests flowed through the journalist's gauntlet berated with innocuous questions. The whole world teetered to hear the word from up high spoken through prophets of wealth and power. Everything in society bent to the whim of the rich and powerful. Entire magazines devoted to the lifestyles of the rich and famous. Henry stood back behind his guards watching from a safe distance.

World leaders filed towards the ballroom with their security entourages. Politicians passed reporters trying to avoid the constant barrage of questions. Berating the people the journalists thirsted for answer. The scene in the Plaza resembled a nature documentary. Snapping jaws unleashing hisses in the form of word exchanges. Soft pleasant purrs mixed with angry roars. The human zoo thrived on the paradigm of survival of the fittest.

Ivan Vladmir Romanov walked through the door with his entourage. Everything stopped as all attention shifted to the third richest man in the world. Security escorts wore magnificent full body hardened combat armour painted crimson red. Young beautiful women hung off the fifty year old man's arms. Designer clothes hanging on the cadre of women covered very little leaving bare flesh to allure the senses.

Henry knew that Romanov's men were part of his dreaded Cossack security forces. Ivan named his security force after the Cossacks to create the image of imperial power of Russia. The thick combat armor covered a hardened ex-Spetsnaz soldier underneath. Painted on to the helmet's face mask was the visage of a skull. Everything about the armour was designed to strike terror into the Romanov family enemies. Ivan's entire security force wore military grade equipment from head to toe.

Journalists often repeated the same question they had asked other guests. Ivan Romanov seemed the center of the media frenzy. Questions railed out about the completion of a worldwide Magnetic rail system. Romanov could transport goods all over the world both fast and cheap. None of the journalist asked how the reduction in transport costs could benefit humanity. Profits and competition were the only thing people were interested in.

News agencies fed on the conflict of any story trying to keep the public interested. The public didn't care to know that the new magnetic rail trains increased trade and reduced prices on goods. Good news faded too quick proving to be unprofitable to news organizations. People cried for drama and the news delivered. Nothing is more tyrannical than the needs of the people.

Journalists spotted the arrival of the young twenty year old King George. British SAS formed the core of the King's personal entourage escorting their king with pride. George had an impeccable flair for fashion and style. Adorned in a royal red and white designer suit produced by his own designers George strode like a peacock with feathers plumed to impress. Questions flew at the young king who devoured them whole. George responded with great charisma and intelligence.

"You see the royal family has a duty to guide Britain in its affairs. While it is true the crown holds only symbolic power. The British monarchy remains a symbol that brings peace and order to the Commonwealth. My ventures into Business will only increase the power of Britian and our allies." Answering with a boyish grin George pushed the media frenzy to untold heights.

Henry's cybernetic eyes showed the thermal increase in woman swooning over the King. The entire group of journalist's hung on every word George spoke listening in silent awe. Everyone loved the Monarch.

George returned that love answering ever question pushing the interview pass twenty minutes. George gave a sly smile bidding farewell with a regal wave.

"I must be going now, but know that Britain wishes the world a prosperous and joyous New Years!" Just as the King entered the ballroom another powerful person walked through the doors. Catherine Assisi entered the grand lobby of the Plaza hotel. The fashion magnate drew camera attention. Digital camera snapped perfect pictures of the woman posing for the journalists.

Catherine wore a silk dress fashioned in a modern expression of the ancient roman toga. The couture cut just below the thigh line breaking into folds of silk fabric between the legs. Sheer silk draped down Catherine's long legs. A perfect cut revealed Catherine's ample cleavage with silk ruffled between. Magazines and articles dubbed the fashion magnate Assisi the Queen of beauty.

Catherine walked down the rep carpet passing the onslaught of questions. Journalist asked who the fashion CEO was dating, new products, and popular vacation spots. Vicious hard hitting journalists transformed into sycophants filled with benign questions. Journalist's behaviour revealed the public's opinion at any given moment. News organizations were inclined to avoid incurring the public's wrath. Journalists learned to fear the tyranny of the majority reflected in profit losses.

Journalist stood waiting for the meal of the hour to come from behind Muse security. Henry stood poised behind his guards trying to push off the inevitable storm on the horizon. Catherine Assisi noticed the iconic CEO blowing a kiss towards him. Camera's snapped in rapid secession catching the sensational flirting. Henry knew this would become a major tabloid frenzy lasting months. Victoria's adamant hatred of Catherine Assisi caused recurring tabloid stories over the years.

Whispering intrigue into the public's ear siphoned money into the tabloids hands. Henry didn't even flinch at the voluptuous Catherine walking towards the ballroom. A soft ding echoed in the lobby drawing Journalists attention. Elevator doors opened revealing the well-dressed Latin American couple. Diego walked off the elevator with his beautiful wife Mariana wrapped around him.

Diego Marquez inherited his wealth leading to rumours that his father was a Columbian drug lord. No evidence existed to confirm the truth in the rumours. Diego turned drug money in to luxury and relaxation creating a vacation empire with no rivals. Journalists called the Marquez family royalty of luxurious relaxation. Diego and Marianna smiled waving to the crowd of reporters.

Wearing simple and elegant clothing the sensational couple walked through the lobby with no great hurry. Marianna would stop to point out the significant of a piece of decoration, or a beautiful arrangement of flowers. Diego spotted Henry standing on the stairway behind guards waving to him. Smiling back Henry wave watching the Marquez's continue towards the ballroom. Journalist asked questions about where the next luxury resort would be built, plans for the future, and about the state of affairs between South America and U.S. with growing trade disputes. Diego laughed in response to the questions before answering.

"The U.S and South America have been friends a long time, and sometimes friends fight." The Marquez's managed to slip away when the media storm turned to see Zhuge Sun striding through the door. Zhou Yun placed his brother Zhuge in charge of the legitimate business operation of Dragon Enterprises. Unable to contain the excitement Journalists broke ranks and charged with camera and microphone towards the door. Acting in the capacity of CEO of Dragon Enterprises Zhuge formed the company at sixteen. Zhou Yun ensured no evidence existed of his involvement with the company.

Only thirty three years old Zhuge seemed young for a CEO. Dragon enterprises ranked the fourth richest company in the world. Despite all the interesting facts about the young Zhuge Sun the media focused on his brother. Question flung with fury and force from the surrounding journalists. Questions circled about the current relationship between the known terrorist and Dragon Enterprises.

Microphones darted out like spears towards the CEO's face. Questions crashed down with the force of an avalanche. Zhuge remained calm walking forward denying any involvement with his brother. The CEO denied that the Chinese government refused to prosecute Zhou Yun from fear of reprisal. Zhuge ignored claims that the Chinese government funded Zhou Yun's illegal activity.

"There is no situation in which China would use criminal activity to gain power. Dragon Enterprises focuses on distributing legal goods to increase the standard of living. Our goal is to reduce prices while improving the lives of our clients by meeting their shipping needs. Ever increasing demands for cybertechnology worldwide needs to be met. Distribution rights to cybertechnology in China were concluded with Muse Industries just before the holidays. I want to assure the public that Dragon Enterprises does not support Zhou Yun Sun ideologies."

Zhuge answered each question with authority. Henry admired the young CEO's ability to stay calm under fire. Dragon security personnel smiled holding back the onslaught of reporters, but pushed no one away. Henry walked through his guards deciding he needed to give Zhuge a chance to escape. Muse security followed a step behind their boss marching through the pack of journalists.

Pushing through the crowd Henry used minimal force to move through the reporters. Zhuge continued to answer the journalists pouring outrage into their questions. Henry broke through the last line of reporters extending his hand towards the young CEO. Both men shook hands greeting each other with warm smiles. Camera's snapped up the photo opportunity gobbling up money shots.

"Mr. Sun it so good to see you again. I hope your journey was not fraught with too many perils." Posing for the press corps the two business men remained locked in grip for several moments. Henry could only imagine the headlines this action would spark. Breaking the handshake Zhuge bowed before Henry.

"Mr. Williams I would like to thank you for the confidence you have shown in Dragon Enterprises. I look forward to future business opportunities that come from such an alliance. A bright future lies for both Muse Industries and Dragon Enterprises in 2034." Journalists circled like a pack of wolves stalking entrapped prey. Henry and Zhuge security forces joined together to push through the crowd.

Questions snapped out from multiple journalists filling the air with a clamour of voices. Journalists searched for a moment of weakness from either CEO. Questions about whether Dragon Enterprises would distribute Simulated Experience technology, how much cybertechnology would be shipped to China, and what the exact role Muse intended for Dragon

Enterprises. People starved for cybertechnology feared the dilution of the limited pool of available implants. Limited supply mixed with increasing demand kept viewers glued to the news reports. Henry and Zhuge broke through the ranks of Journalists after several minutes of struggle. Muse security forces turned forming a human barrier holding back the tide of reporters. Henry turned towards Zhuge with a smile.

"Head into the ballroom and leave this ravenous pack of reporters to me." Turning back to face the throng of reporters Henry paused. Reporters surged forward seeing the opportunity to have questions answered. Waiting for the clamour to die down Henry watched the crowd. After a moment reporters quieted down sensing an opportunity.

"I must be brief ladies and gentlemen of the press, because I have a lot of guest waiting inside for me. I can only give you a few minutes for questions. All I ask is that we conduct this interview with civility. Only one question at a time please." Henry laid out the rules of the press conference. Several hands went up in the crowd of reporters following the instructions like obedient dogs. Henry perused the group of people with questions avoiding the most extreme reporters. The CEO pointed to a young woman near the back of the crowd.

"Mr. Williams there are a lot of rumors flying around about the attacks on your family. Are the attacks in both China and the Skymall linked?" Holding the microphone out towards the CEO the young woman waited for a response. Tension rose in the crowd watching and waiting for an answer. Coughing Henry cleared his throat.

"Concerning the tragic events in both Beijing and here in New York I would first give my condolences. Many people lost loved ones in both attacks. Muse Industries intends to set out money and resources for anyone affected by the tragedy. There is no conclusive evidence at this point that shows the attacks are linked. I will continue to use all the resources at my disposal to discover the culprits. My daughter was caught in the attack on the Skymall. I intend to bring the people responsible for such reprehensible acts to justice."

Hands shot up the moment the first question had been answered. The crowd of reporters hungered for more information. Victor Wolfe stood near the front with his hand raised. Henry despised the man for his bias presentation of the truth. Victor stared at the CEO challenging the man to let him ask a question. Henry pointed to Victor to hear his spin.

"Mr. Williams you claim you want to bring those responsible to justice. Muse Industries is responsible for breaking multiple anti-trust laws. How can you claim to care about justice while breaking the law yourself Mr. Williams?" Victor's question riled the crowd around him. Henry shook his head in disbelief.

"It is true that Muse Industries has lost multiple anti-trust lawsuits. Every fine imposed by recognized courts has been paid in full. I am the founder and creator of the first cybernetic implants. I have trained countless surgeons, engineers, and doctors in the functioning of cybertechology. There will be a day when other companies compete against Muse in the cybertechnology market; however cybertechnology is still in its infancy. I cannot be faulted that the best and brightest scientists wish to work for Muse. I wonder if your news agency would still attack me if I were a republican."

One after another questions shot out forcing Henry to endure the interrogation. Journalist's questioned whether or not the Williams marriage constituted a conflict of interest within the senate, views on the effects of privatized military companies on world politics, and the effect Muse had on the military industrial complex. Questions assailed Henry in a vicious assault on everything related to him. The unending river of questions flowed forth from the spring of reporters. Looking at the time Henry raised his hands silencing the crowd.

"I am sorry to cut this short but I must now ask you to please leave the building. I have kept my guests waiting too long. I wish you all and everyone in the world a happy new year." Waving for the cameras Henry turned towards the ballroom. Muse security pushed back against the throng of reporters.

Marching towards the door Henry realized the real test was beyond the ballroom doors. Security opened the doors allowing the ambiance of the ballroom to flood into the hall. Looking in Henry could see his guests already discussing a multitude of issues. Cold crept through the nerves sending a shiver racing throughout the man's body. Maj. Lee placed his hand his bosses shoulder to help steady him. Henry hoped the night would fly by, but dreaded the events to come.

CHAPTER 20

Courtiers

All the guests gathered together in the grand ballroom of the Plaza hotel. Waking into the room Henry surveyed the large gathering of people. Maj. Lee followed behind his boss with several guards in tow. The grand ball rooms golden hue and style had been well maintained in its 1929 opulence. Guests turned to acknowledge Henry's arrival. Loud clapping welcomed the CEO to the event.

Scanning the crowd Henry looked for his wife and daughter. Small cliques of mutual interests spattered across the large ballroom. Business people associated with other business people, politicians discussed world affair with other politicians, and celebrities and movie stars discussed the latest gossip. Walking through the room Henry was greeted by everyone. Guest sipped the finest champagne waving to the passing CEO.

The ballroom held the most powerful and influential people in the world. Victoria set the seating plan placing like-minded people together. President Woods approached Henry with his secret service standing a few steps behind him. The president and Muse CEO shook hands out of formality. Pulling Henry close the president whispered in his ear.

"Thank you again for the invitation Mr. Williams. I noticed Muse security forces are spread out everywhere. Are you expecting trouble tonight?" Ignoring the question Henry turned to face the beautiful First Lady. Selene Woods ran several non-profit charities and contributed to various humanitarian programs. Charming and elegant the first lady commanded respect. Henry shook Selene's hand looking at both the president and his wife.

"It is always good to see you First lady. I hope that both of you are enjoying the evening so far. Mr. President in regards to what we discussed last time we spoke has there been any progress?" Several people standing around the group tried to eavesdrop without being noticed. Glancing around Henry noticed people averting their gaze to avoid detection.

Decreasing volume in the surrounding conversations revealed the extent of the attention the group drew. Everyone paid close attention to the conversation between President Woods and Henry Williams. Courtiers clung to the rich and powerful trying to gain their favor no different than the ancient courts of history. Power acted like a magnet drawing everyone towards it like moths to the flame. President Woods nodded in response to Henry's question.

"Yes I have moved matters forward in regards to your request Mr. Williams. I think we should both see the fruit of our endeavors in the New Year." Spotting Victoria standing across the room Henry smiled. Forming a political triumvirate seemed necessary to future plans for Muse industries. Henry returned his attention to the President and First lady.

"That is excellent news Mr. President. I am thrilled to be working with you on this project. We should arrange a vacation together so that our family gets more time to spend together. Julia misses hanging out with your son. I hate to cut this short, but I think my wife is waiting for me. Let's continue this discussion at the party later." Shaking hands again Henry nodded goodbye to the President and First Lady.

Walking away Henry could hear the whispered gossip surrounding him. Questions circulated to the nature of the deal between the Muse CEO and President. Smiles and polite greetings veiled the contempt driven by envy and jealousy hidden behind a mask. Smiling and waving back Henry masked his contempt for upper society. Journalists may be a pack of wolves, but the rich and powerful were lions with endless appetites. No amount of money or power could ever sate the appetites of the modern day patricians.

Single men adorned their arms with beautiful women wearing fine jewellery. Beautiful women cavorted around the room wearing alluring clothes leaving little to the imagination. Successful single women surrounded themselves with the finest male company drawing in groups of admirers. Henry looked around at the guest gorging themselves on money, sex, and power. Most people seemed slaves to their senses Henry noted.

Most of the wealth and power of the world was controlled by the guest gathered in this room. Henry walked by several people discussing the growing problems of poverty, rising civil disorder, and the social fragmentation caused by social media and neural implants. Social problems remained a key topic to the elite. Conflicts often threatened business interests. War and civil strife caused serious effects on every business including the massive entertainment complex. Henry spotted the French entertainment mogul Jean Jocques Decartes approaching.

"Mr. Williams I wanted to extend my thanks for your invitation to this event. I wondered if you care to share you insights into the growing neural entertainment market with my friends. They seem to undervalue the power of the neural matrix your implants have created." Jean Jocques Descartes used his company Imagine Incorporated to revolutionize the gaming industry. Imagine neural cafés sprung up in every city in the world. Descartes started a lawsuit with Muse attempting to force simulated experience to be made available to the public.

Entertainment industries sprung up around neural implant technologies. The gaming industry converted production of games around the access to the human mind. All the video games were now played inside the mind. Games used the brains natural creative powers to forge immersing realism in game environments. Scientists studied the phenomena of gamers becoming so involved in the fantasy world they stopped responding to reality. The group hurried to form a circle around Henry waiting to hear his predictions for the future of cybertechnology.

"I agree with you Mr. Descartes. The purpose of neural technology has always been to allow minds to connect to each other. Forming a matrix of mind remains the underlying principle of neural implant technology. Neural technology will indeed push the boundaries of gaming to unimaginable limits. I am not a gamer myself, but I have heard of the financial success of your neural cafes. I have to wonder what will happen if you get your way and force public distribution of simulated experience." Henry hid his contempt under a layer of tact.

"Mr. Williams you mistake my intentions. I admit I would love to have access to your research on Simex for my games. Gamers demand the best technology, the best equipment, and constantly push the limits of what technology is capable of. I cannot see how making Simex available to the public would be a bad thing. Both business ventures would be made rich by it." Descartes tried to fake an expression of shock and dismay at the allegations, but failed to convince anyone in the group. Falling silent the crowd watched the exchange between the two CEO's with great interest.

"Of course you don't see the damage caused by placing false memories in a person mind. People struggle to separate games from reality today. Allowing the gaming industry to use false memories to create a more vivid gaming world seems repugnant to me. Of course Mr. Descartes you haven't even considered the social impact of false memories on society. Muse industries research shows that false memories can be addictive. Addiction to false memories seems to be influenced by the positive nature of the false memory." Henry shook his head in amazement at the short sighted vision of Jean.

"Mr. Williams there are plenty of industries whose products are addictive yet still function. Gambling creates addiction but there is no shortage of casinos. Tobacco and alcohol are also addictive yet both are thriving businesses. Of course any business should try to reduce the negative impact of their products, but negative impact should not deter business. Muse Industries sells neural implants despite recorded attempts of neural hacking. The world craves Simex and the people will get it whether you or someone else sells it to them." Jean lashed back in retort.

Henry sensed truth to Jean's words. Decartes Imagine incorporated had been funding Simex development for the last several years. Industrial espionage reports revealed Imagine lagged far behind Muse in development. Still the reality remained that it was inevitable for some corporation to discover the science behind Simex. Henry extended his hand and shook Jeans with force.

"We should setup a meeting in the New Year. Perhaps Muse Industries and Imagine incorporated can come to a mutual beneficial agreement outside of the courts. I don't mean to cut this short but my wife is waiting for me to start the dinner." Pushing through the crowd Henry marched through the room towards his wife. Victoria stood near her seat at the head of the long table in the center of the room.

Several senators and celebrities discussed affairs with Victoria. Henry walked across the ballroom trying to dodge any further attempts by guest to start conversation. Guests hoped to share their ideas with the Muse CEO hoping to attract his patronage. Henry's support could mean the difference between success and failure for a new business venture. Zhuge Sun approached the Muse CEO extending his hands revealing a small box. The small box had been wrapped with care and adorned with a silver ribbon.

"Mr. Williams I would like to extend this gift as a token of my appreciation for your business. I would also like to thank you for helping me out with the journalists. This gift is just a small representation of the prosperity our mutual association will bring to the world." Bowing in respect Henry accepted the offered gift. The package was diminutive in size.

The brilliant intricate design on the paper revealed the time and energy put into wrapping the box. Even the bow had been tied in a complex design showing time and care. Unwrapping and opening the box Henry peered inside. A small statue of a lion carved in jade rested at the bottom. Picking up the figurine Henry marvelled at the delicate carved details of the jade.

"Mr. Sun this is a beautiful gift that must have cost you a fortune. I cannot accept such an expensive gift when it's your company that is doing me the favor. Dragon Enterprise will ensure the people of China get the needed cybernetic prosthetics and neural implants." Placing the figuring back in the box Henry tried to offer the box back. Zhuge Sun refused the gift bowing in respect.

"Mr. Williams please take this gift in the spirit in which it is given. It will give me great delight to know you look upon this figurine and think of our friendship. Together I believe we will make the world a better place. The lion is a symbol of strength and nobility. The strength offered to humanity through cybertechnology is a gift to the world. Mr. Williams you are like a great lion tending to the needs of his pack. I would be greatly honored if you would accept my gift."

"Thank you Mr. Sun for this thoughtful gift. I will place it in a special place where I can look at it often and be reminded of our friendship. I look forward to shipping the first bundle of cybertechnology through Dragon Enterprises in the coming week." Holding the delicate jade lion figure Henry marvelled at the value of such small things. Cybertechnology often came in small packages with value far beyond its size. The nature of the gift delivered a careful message Henry couldn't miss.

Zhuge bowed in appreciation at the acceptance of the gift before stepping out of the way. Henry returned the bow before heading towards his wife. Victoria distracted by the conversation with the Senators and celebrities failed to notice her husband's approach. Henry wrapped his arms around his wife sneaking up behind her. Leaning in Henry kissed his wife's cheek.

"Sorry to keep you dear. I hope our guests have been able to keep you entertained while you waited. Is the dinner ready to start yet?" Guests fell quiet allowing Victoria to turn to address her husband. Henry gazed into his wife's beautiful blue eyes mesmerized by their hypnotic appeal. The couple kissed embracing each other while the guests watched.

"Henry you have never been on time in the twenty years we've been married. I kept myself busy with Senator Klein and Jones discussing world issues. Everything is ready for the dinner, and we can begin whenever you like." Henry grabbed an empty glass from the table and picked it up along with a fork. Tapping the fork on the side of the empty glass filled the room with a distinct chime. Guest quieted down. Everyone in the room turned their attention to Henry.

"First I would like to welcome everyone. Victoria and I would like to thank you all for gathering here today to celebrate our twentieth anniversary. I would also like to thank you all for your generous donations to the War Orphans and veterans fund. With your generosity we have raised almost one hundred million dollars to help those affected by war." Thunderous clapping filled the ballroom from the crowds' ovation. Henry looked at his beautiful wife standing next to him.

"My wife and I would like to tell you dinner will be served soon. If you could return to your seats the feast will be brought in momentarily. Thank you all for kindness and generosity once again." People began heading towards their assigned seats. Henry sat next to his wife at the center of the crowd.

Everything seemed perfect to Victoria looking at her husband and daughter beside her. Business and politics separated the Williams family too often. Henry wasn't a perfect man but he did have his moments. Victoria hated to admit it that her husband still surprised her from time to time. Sitting at the head of the table of the sinful seven Victoria knew the dinner would not be uneventful.

CHAPTER 21

Rapacious Lions

Guests hurried toward their seats causing the entire ballroom to burst into motion. Henry and Victoria sat with Julia at the head of the main table. The long oak table sat in the middle of the golden aura of the grand ballroom. Ivan Romanov sat with his beautiful entourage seated around him. Romanov security stood only two steps behind their CEO leering over the table.

Catherine Assisi broke away from her retinue of admirers taking her seat. Victoria stared at the fashion magnate concealing her hatred for the woman. Watching the two women glaring across the table filled Henry with anxiety. Even the tabloids didn't know where the rivalry between the two women started. Staring at the gather Henry could feel tensions in the air between the guests.

The sinful seven seated around the table in order glancing at each other with weary eyes. Trying to remain inconspicuous guests glanced at the main table at random. Diego Marquez sat conversing with his wife. Colt sat near Henry with his wife on the other side and children close by. Sitting on opposite sides of the table Robert smiled across the table at Julia.

"Julia you look exceptional tonight in that dress." Blushing ensured Julia couldn't hide her embarrassment. King George brushed away his SAS body guards taking his seat next to Julia. Zhuge ordered his guards away sitting opposed to Henry at the far end of the table. Gathered together the sinful seven filled the table with a tense silence.

Waiters dressed in elegant white uniforms rushed out into the ballroom carrying giant platters of food. Platters covered in oyster with caviar and a Japanese ponzu sauce. In unison the platters were placed in the center of each table. Hor d'oeuvres on a second platter consisted of smoked Berkshire ham with aged cheese and a crostini. Food piled the table top waiting to be devoured. Christina reached over a plucking an oyster and slurping it down.

"Henry do you have any plans to make your sublime cybertechnology public in the coming year?" Attention shifted to the CEO sitting at the table head. Eyes from nearby tables also glanced to see the man's reaction. Cybernetic prosthetics had become the pursuit of every major nation in arming their troops. High maintenance on a regular basis presented the only drawback to cybernetic prosthetics, but the combat value of such technology stripped away any concerns. Soldiers with prosthetic replacements functioned eighty percent better in field tests. Cybernetic implants obsoleted human frailty.

"I have serious concerns over the social implications of selling military grade cybernetic implants and prosthetics." Ivan scoffed at the idea. Everyone around the table turned to attention to the Russian CEO. Relationships between Ivan and Henry had been strained when Muse switched distributors. Catherine looked at her own fair skin and complexion.

"Imagine the beauty applications of cybernetic prosthetics. Plastic surgery is outdated in a time when technology can keep anyone young and beautiful forever. Henry you and I should work together on a beauty line of prosthetics. Something less military oriented. Alliance between Invidia and Muse would bring wealth beyond imagining. We could make immortality a reality for humanity." Catherine smiled at the thought of eternal beauty.

Waiters stood nearby watching the platter of appetizers. Taking the form of statues waiters ensured the tables brimmed with food. Devouring the delicious food with alacrity the families discussed business. Conversation spiralled towards furious argument. Everyone at the table had an interest in cybertechnology. King George looked around with shock written across his face.

"Cybernetic prosthetics already have a well-established black market. Advisors tell me every major nation is struggling to contain the illegal sale of cybernetic prosthetics." Gulping down the wine in front of him Diego hung on every word. South America had been ravaged by several guerilla style revolutions in the last decade. Modern revolutionaries augmented themselves with as much cybernetic prosthetics as they could. Loyalist forces blamed other nations for arming the militant insurgents.

"Less developed nations have struggled with the invention of cybernetic modification. Henry your kind contributions to the South American nations towards developing a modern police and military is appreciated. I fear that using fire to combat fire will only escalate further conflicts. Pirates armed with Cybernetic implants and prosthetics have begun targeting my cruise liners." Crime and civil war hit the Marquez profit margin. No one wanted to vacation in a warzone or ganglands.

Listening to the conversation circling the table Henry thought about the problems. Thoughts turned in the CEO's head that small minded people never have great foresight. Muse Industries developed cybernetics far beyond what the Governments and people knew. Research funded by Henry's own profits worked on creating the first cybernetic brain. Simulated experience had only been the offshoot of research into transferring consciousness. Henry felt the human brain was the last great mystery of the universe.

A vast network of the world greatest minds came to work for Muse. Muse and its employees shared a dream. Henry founded the company on the simple dream of a world where technology could better the lives of all humanity. The ability to digitize and transfer a human mind into a machine would change the world. Social media and neural networking from implants pushed social disintegration to break point. Laws attempted to reach beyond the realm of humanity and into the lawless environment of cyberspace.

"What happens when we can digitize the human consciousness and transmit it?" Resonating across the table the question caught everyone by surprise. The idea of transferring a mind swept the room like a great fire roaring inside the ballroom. A social virus spreading through the air infecting everyone it touched. Ivan scoffed again turning to face henry.

"I suppose like all the other technology produced by Muse you'll get the lion's share of power. Hoarding all the power of your inventions Henry, yet claiming to be a symbol of social justice and democracy. You may control cybertechnology now but someday soon you will be dethroned Henry." Preparing a verbal counterattack Henry lost the initiative to his wife. Victoria glared across the table at Ivan clearing her throat with a soft cough.

"It is well known that Romanov industries have been attempting to reverse engineer cybertechnology. I read some reports about your recent test subject Ivan. I remember the vivid pictures of the man whose brain haemorrhaged. Perhaps if Russia took a stronger stance for funding public education you would have more success. I find it interesting that a communist society doesn't care about the proletarian base of the nation. There is a reason most of the scientific community supports Henry." Delicate words chosen by Victoria hit home with explosive force.

Silence fell across the table. Ivan glared back at Victoria trying to find an appropriate response. Henry admired his wife's ability to stay calm while waging verbal warfare on her opponents. Mastering the art of tact gave Victoria an advantage in the realm of politics. Henry wished he possessed the art of tact at times. Ivan seethed trying to contain the fury written across his face.

Waiters brought in soup on large silver platters placing the bowls at each table in front of the guests. A faint aroma of jasmine and spices filled the room from the steam rising from hot bowls. Remaining quiet Zhuge brought the spoon to his mouth listening to the discussion rage on. Henry noticed that his daughter remained silent during the conversation which struck him as unusual.

Sipping at the soup Julia tried to keep her mind off the commotion playing on her nerves. Instinct allowed Victoria to sense her daughter's growing unease. Anxiety raced through Julia's veins causing her heart to pound away in her chest. Under the table Victoria placed her hand on her daughter's knee offering reassurance. King George admired the young gorgeous woman sitting next to him.

"I've heard of Julia's legendary social activism and rebellious streak. What do you think about the impact of cybertechnology?" Provoking a sudden rush of attention the question caused Julia's anxiety to soar out of control. Everyone at the table stared waiting for an answer. Julia focused on her breathing forcing herself to take a deep breath.

"There is not stopping the cybertechnology craze sweeping the world. Even if my father quit producing and selling cybertechnology someone would step in to fill the void. I think humanity is rushing towards a dangerous cliff. Overpopulation is already a problem. Another problem is technology is only available to the wealthy and powerful. What happens when cybernetic prosthetics create a limited form of immortality as Ms. Assisi suggests?"

Silence filled the table. Everyone entered deep thoughts considering the question posed by Julia. Glancing eyes from surrounding tables fell on Julia heightening her sense of anxiety. Victoria glanced at her husband feeling the tension rise in her daughter. Henry looked at his little girl with admiration. Julia's mind had always been very precocious even at a young age.

"King George is your SAS body guards equipped with cybernetic prosthetics?" Trying to deflect attention the question drew everyone back to Henry. Placing the spoon back into the soup the young King looked around. George wondered at the purpose of the question. British spies worked hard to keep statistics on cybernetic modification from public hands. Struggling to find the right answer George cleared his throat biding time.

"Well as you know the Royal Air Force acquired several different models of cybernetic prosthetics. Most military forces in the world have specialized cyborg forces. My guards have the standard cybernetic prosthetics to fill their role." Answering with delicate precision revealed the truth of the situation to Henry. Muse sales and research showed most elite military personnel were over eighty percent modified.

With a sly smile Henry retorted "very expensive body guards indeed. I see Britain spares no expense on its soldiers. Cybernetic limbs, Eyes, and reinforced muscles and bones I believe. I am glad to see my British division is doing such fine work your majesty. It does leave me with one question. How long do soldiers have to swear to serve in order to receive such modifications?"

Provoking a chilling silence the entire ballroom hung on the question. Henry words crafted with care side stepped all non-disclosure agreements.

With Precision the CEO never once divulged classified information. Instead the statement put the young King in the position to expose the truth. Smiling in admiration at the cunning behind the question George took a bite before responding.

"With the extension of life that cybernetic implants and prosthetic limbs offer we ask fifty years. Recruitment has never been easier. Volunteers often sign on for even longer than that." Henry looked towards Ivan causing both men to lock gazes. Romanov troops standing behind their CEO had scarce amount of their natural bodies left. Russian elite forces were true cyborgs with only their original brain remaining.

"Now we all know the Russian elite troops are true warriors. Russian military keeps only the brain, and even modifies that to ensure obedience. Ladies and gentlemen I think the real question lies right before us. Are you going to let these people return to society with their new prosthetics once their service is up?"

A loud gasp echoed in the air from Mariana before she grasped her husband. Diego held his wife close reassuring himself his own reserve of security forces would be enough. Jaguar security remained funded by the Republic of South America. Diego kept his own cybernetic modified soldiers hidden from sight using thermal optic camouflage. Fear raced through the room when people realized the truth. Cybernetic implants changed the very nature of the world.

"You must sell these implants and prosthetics to the public. People must be able to defend themselves." Wealth made the elite ever rapacious lions always hungry for more power. Cybertechnology offered health, beauty. and power to all who could afford it. Henry believed technology could lift the poor from the enslavement of poverty, but business demanded profits. Muse funnelled money from the governments into solutions to the world problems. Creating a market for private cybernetic implants and prosthetics would siphon the wealth from the elite. Henry redistributed the wealth he collected in sales to poor parts of the world.

Colt looked at his old friend "We need to talk about some collaborative research in the New Year. My daddy always did say you're a brilliant man." Sitting back and listening Ivan stared at Henry with the mix of anger and respect. Romanov industries had never been able to get a spy inside

Muse. Intelligence reports showed the Henry reserved the top of the line cybernetic implants and prosthetics for himself.

America stayed quiet out of necessity. Henry gave the United States of America the lion's share of production. Ivan admired the cunning and ruthlessness of his rival. Henry's ideals kept him from wielding the power. Ivan worried that one day his rival would be willing to use all the power he possessed.

"Mr. Williams do you think you can rewrite human nature with technology. Humanity will always be a pack of sheep, wolves, and lions. Sheep are always passive and fearful running with panic at the first sign of any danger. Running from danger causes the sheep to trample each other from mindless fear. Wolves hunt the sheep careful not to gorge themselves too much. Aggression drives the wolf to prey on the sheep's meek nature, but never devouring the entire herd. Wolves need sheep to survive. Above all these lesser animals you have the magnificent lion standing proud and defiant. Violence is the realm of the lion devouring all before him both sheep and wolf alike. Lions rule to the benefit of the wolves and sheep of the world."

Anger rose up in Henry from the speech. People were not animals to be devoured to the benefit of those higher in society. Ideals like equality and freedom filled Henry with anger and frustration. Life didn't need to be a predatory act. Human consciousness gave people the ability to create tools and techniques to make life easier.

"Dividing us Ivan is one simple idea you cannot fathom. You believe people exist to make you powerful. Wealth and privilege used like weights to hold people beneath your boot. People don't exist to slave for each other, but to serve and help each other. You think people are animals waiting to be slaughtered. You forget that the lion lives and dies for the collective good of the pride."

Waiters brought the next course of pan roasted fish. Delicate smells of citrus and spices infused the air wafting through the room. Coated in a truffle puree with pomme frites adorned the fish on the plates. Henry and Ivan exchanged venomous glances. Eating the food the group of people ignored the tension between the two CEO's. Animosity seethed between the two men causing the table and the Ballroom to fall to silence.

Victoria signalled the waiter to bring the main dish without delay. Platters of roasted frenched spring lamb were placed on the table. Roasted vegetable with a red skin potato ragu dressed in a gorganzola cream accompanied the lamb. Everyone seemed to be enjoying the meal except a few people. Henry and Ivan continued to glare at each other. No longer at the center of attention Julia managed to calm her nerves. Henry waited for everyone to finish eating before he stood up chiming his glass.

"Just one announcement ladies and gentlemen. I am going to be heading upstairs with my family to prepare for the masquerade. Enjoy your desserts and join us in about half an hour." Victoria and Julia stood up at the end of the announcement. Henry turned and walked away from the table with his wife and daughter behind him.

King George turned his attention towards the incoming dessert. Almost everyone in the Ballroom returned to their previous activity. Ivan stalked Henry with his eyes watching him walk away from the table. Rage filled the Russian's eyes. No one slighted the great Ivan Vladimir Romanov. A waiter placed the dessert down in front of the Russian CEO. Savouring the dessert Ivan's thoughts of revenge on Henry Williams filled each bite.

Chapter 22

The Masquerade

Exiting the bedroom Julia wore the mask of Venus. Behind the mask the young woman noticed the masquerade party already underway. Guests wore a variety of costumes and masks. Guests in the main room mingled with Victoria wearing the mask of Diana goddess of the moon. Standing out on the balcony Henry puffed on a cigar looking down at the protestors below. The mask of Apollo sat on the balcony rail ledge.

Clacking footsteps approached Henry from behind. Protest chants echoed up from the streets below the Plaza. Commotion cloaked the approaching footsteps. Lost in a train of thought Henry remained oblivious to his surroundings. Catherine snuck up from behind whispering with a soft voice.

"It is a very beautiful view you have from up here. Do you mind if I join you out here Henry?" Catherine walked around Henry dragging a finger across the back of his neck. Shocked at the audacity Henry was stunned into silence. Pulling out a cigarette Catherine placed it in her lips. Lips stick marked the cylinder dangling from the vice of pink flesh. Henry could see desire lurking in Catherine's eyes.

Guest covered the apartment filling every room. Anxiety shot up inside of Julia surrounded by the crowd of masked faces. Victoria spotted her daughter moving through the crowd. Feeling a soft touch on the shoulder Julia spun around startled to see her mother's mask. Heavy breathes tried to draw air through the thin slits of the mask. Julia's heart thundered so hard in her chest she felt it would explode.

"Mom you scared me! What are you doing sneaking up on me like that?" Victoria gazed through the mask with great concern at her daughter's behaviour. Knowledge of how trauma could affect the mind filled the concerned mother's thoughts. Memories showed Victoria how she reacted after the first time she had been attacked. Fear paralyzed the mind entrapping the victim in a vicious cycle.

"Julia perhaps you would like to mingle with me. We never get enough time together. School keeps you busy, and work absorbs most of my time." Mother and daughter looked at each other for a moment. Julia took her mother's hand walking together through the crowd. Zhuge Sun noticed the approaching ladies and broke from conversation.

"What a beautiful sight to behold. We are in the presence of goddesses." King George lustful eyes studied the curves of both the women. Victoria curtseyed with an elegant flare greeting the two men. Embarrassment caused Julia's face to blush from the compliment. Admiring both women George drank in the beauty before him.

Fine details hand carved into the Chinese warlord mask sparked both fear and awe. Wood twisted into a demonic visage masking the face of Zhuge Sun. George concealed his face behind a feathered mask of black and red. Feeling the king's eyes Julia held onto her mother trying to keep calm. Admiring Zhuge's mask Victoria turned to face him.

"I hope both are having a wonderful time. Can my daughter and I join you in whatever it is you were discussing?" Wearing the feathered mask covering only half of the face showed King George's sly smile. Julia chose to keep away from most of the kids in school to avoid awkward situations. Glancing up and down the young woman's body the king didn't notice his effect. Since the attack any attention caused Julia to panic, but emotions of anxiety mixed with excitement. George took the young woman's hand inviting both women to join him and Zhuge.

"Mr. Sun and I were discussing a simple business arrangement. I heard Henry switched distribution from the cheaper Romanov magrail delivery system to Dragon Enterprises. I am just inquiring into Mr. Sun's services that enticed the great Muse CEO." Talking to the group George didn't break eye contact with Julia. Looking around Victoria couldn't see her husband anywhere in the apartment.

Flames shot from the lighter sparking to life. Catherine brought the flame to bear on the cigarette dangling from her lips. Soft suction from the woman was followed by a louder exhale blowing smoke into the night sky. Catherine stood at the edge of the balcony observing the horde of protestors below. The mass of people pushed against the wall of police like waves crashing into cliffs. Examining Catherine's body language Henry sensed the game being played.

"Wow it looks like your party has drawn quite a crowd of crashers Henry." Catherine swayed to show her sultry figure to Henry. Ivory skin reflected the light dancing across the soft flesh. Dangling the pleasures of the flesh like bait the Fashion CEO perfected the art of seduction. Catherine allowed Henry to gaze over every curve on her body before she pulled out a data pad.

"Invidia Incorporated has come up with an idea for a beauty cybernetic prosthetic. I was wondering if Muse Industries might be interested in a partnership." Reaching out to grab the data pad forced Henry next to the gorgeous woman. Catherine used the opportunity to create body contact. Forcing Henry to look down from above the shorter woman held the data pad outstretched.

"As you can see the design uses nanoconstructed glass layers for the fingernails. Muse would supply the neural connection between the display chip on the glass and neural implant. The co-development deal would revolve around muse programing the basic system for display on the glass fingernails. Invidia would create and sell the software and fingernails. Muse sells the implants and gets a percentage of the profits from Invidia sales on software. How does twenty percent sound?" Henry looked over the data on the pad considering the proposal.

"What do you say Henry. Can we get into bed on this deal?" Catherine turned to face the Muse CEO pressing her body up against his. Henry had to admit the merits of the business plan. Research statistics proved the venture would be profitable. The only loathing condition was working with Catherine. Looking into the woman's eyes Henry could see the lust and desire. Catherine desired this one man above all others.

Weighing the possibilities Victoria realized that George was looking for a pipeline to sell older cybernetics. Demand for cybernetics meant there was great fortune involved in the sale of cybertechnology. King

George was using Dragon Enterprises to create a pipeline for the older British cybernetic implants. Governments sold older cybernetics to stay on the cutting edge of innovation. Victoria sensed the opportunity for artful spying.

"When considering traditional transporting Henry saw a value in less automated processes of shipping. Dragon Enterprises employs approximately two million people worldwide. The other notable factor was the lowest rates in damage during shipping and better security. Mr. Sun is my information correct?" Admiration marked Zhuges face behind his mask.

"You are correct Mrs. Williams. The information you present is accurate. Dragon Enterprises has the highest efficiency in the world for customer satisfaction." Zhou Yun ensured criminals did not prey on the merchant navy of Dragon Enterprise. Zhuge worked hard to ensure his company had the best reliability in transportation services. Dragon Enterprises ranked number one in service and reliability. Victoria noticed George's eyebrows rise revealing his interest in the subject.

"Really I was not aware of those facts. I am glad that Henry recommended your services to me. Escalating conflicts in the Islamic Republic of the Middle-east required looking at other shipping options. Rising pirate activity in the oceans and seas around the world threaten British interests. Theft of valuable goods cannot be overlooked. Mr. Sun does Dragon Enterprises offer Muse such a guarantee on cybertechnology shipping?"

The question confirmed Victoria's instincts that King George was selling cybernetic goods. Henry told his wife of his suspicions that Ivan Romanov was stealing from him. Romanov industries reported a rising percentage of damaged goods and stolen cybertechnology during shipping. Victoria noticed the cutting edge cybernetic implants on Cossack Security. Mr. Sun paused considering how to address the question.

"It is one of the reasons I believe Mr. Williams chose my company. Dragon enterprises maintain an effective navy under Dragon PMC. Pirates and criminals have never been successful in attacking Dragon conveys. Dragon Enterprises seeks to keep its customers happy. We have no problem guaranteeing shipping form everything but acts of god." Zhuge failed to mention that pirates often acted as mercenaries for his PMC.

Snowflakes drifted past the balcony falling from the sky. Cold air blew across the balcony sending shivers through both people's bodies. Catherine gazed into Henry's eyes her pupils dilating to focus on her desire. The dress the fashion CEO wore didn't block much of the cold breeze whipping past. Henry looked over the proposal feeling Catherine stepping closer for warmth.

"I must admit I do see merit to your proposal Catherine. There is no doubt in my mind how you were able to go from model to magnate in the fashion world. Submit this through Muse Industries regular R&D process and I will fast track it along. We can meet sometime in the new year to discuss initial development." Henry handed the datapad back with a smile.

Catherine took the datapad stepping back when it was pushed towards her. Slipping out from between the woman and the guard rail Henry moved towards the balcony door. Catherine wore a coy smile radiating through hot breaths forming vapour in the air. Snow melted on the woman's hot skin and clung to her hair. Standing at the Door Henry looked back to Catherine.

"Neither of us will regret your decisions Henry. I look forward to the long hard hours of work ahead of us. Together we will see these plans to climax. It will build a closer physical relationship between Invidia and Muse, and that will be pleasurable for both parties I'm sure." Catherine delivered each word with clear enunciation to add to effect.

Words did not attempt to conceal the envious lust raging in the woman. Catherine shaped the words to convey her true meaning. Shrewd business instincts told Henry to use the lust to his advantage. Catherine raised her white feathered mask and held in her up to her face. The mask concealed the delicate and beautiful features of the gorgeous woman. Only Catherine's big brown eyes stared through the mask.

"I look forward to consummating our new relationship in the New Year Catherine. Please enjoy the party and imagine the future possibilities of our new partnership." Double doors swung open allowing Henry to walk into the main room from the balcony. Masked faces turned to greet the CEO. Multi-coloured feathers and extravagant styled masks filled the Horizon.

Henry spotted the marble white masks of Diana, and moved through the crowd pushing people aside with gentle nudges. Maj. Lee followed from the balcony behind his boss. People clung onto Henry greeting and hugging him. Both men waded through the thick crowd. Zhuge Sun turned to address the arrival of Henry with the group.

"Mr. Williams this is quite the grand party you have put on for us all." Raising the mask of Apollo Henry put his arm around his wife. Julia waved to her father and hugged him. Standing together the Williams family took on their masquerade as gods and goddesses of the room. Several groups of people turned to listen and watch the family.

"Sorry honey I got busy mingling. What is everyone discussing over here?" Wrapping an arm around Henry's waist Victoria looked to the group waiting for a reply. Julia noticed King George averted his gaze in the presence of her father. Zhuge looked to George to explain the topic of discussion to Henry.

"Mr. Sun and the King were discussing shipping matters I believe. King George expressed interest in securing more efficient transportation of cybernetic cargo. The rapid breakdown in relations between the Islamic Republic of the Middle East and Israel raises shipping concerns. Does that about sum it up?"

Stating the fact and leaving a question Julia left both men speechless. The accurate break down of the hidden nature of the conversation shocked George. Henry smiled with pride from his daughter's ability to read the situation. Julia now showed a much brighter visage in the security of her father. Even George couldn't help but admire Julia who possessed both beauty and intelligence.

"Yes Henry your daughter is right. You know the situation in the Middle East is threatening to alter the balance of power. Britain is looking to find ways to continue shipping in case of a war." A loud gasp echoed from the crowd overhearing the conversation. Whispers spread like wildfire when the elite heard the first confirmation of the possibility of war.

Fear crept across the crowd of guests. Conversation from the crowd divided into differing opinions. Several loud conversations broke out about whether to fight in the war or oppose it. Arguments heated up between multiple groups fueled by the ideological divide. Groups fractured from the ideological chasm tearing across the room. With earthquake force people divided in to pro-war, anti-war, and several different neutral positions.

"I am sorry but if you don't mind Mr. Sun I need to borrow King George. We have important business to discuss." Henry turned to hug Victoria and his daughter motioning for King George to follow. British SAS and Maj. Lee with a detachment of Muse guards followed behind. The sudden departure revealed the urgency behind the event to the crowd. Henry and King George left the room with their entourages. Looking to both women Zhuge Sun changed the conversation topic.

"Victoria I have heard your daughter is a talented political writer. You must be very proud to have raised such a brilliant daughter. You bring your family great honour Julia." Victoria appreciated Zhuge's attempts to lighten the spirit surrounding her husbands' departure. Muse guards at the door allowed Ivan Romanov and his Entourage of women to enter. Fate had other events planned.

Ivan wore a red and black mask with a hat to the party. The fully armoured troops of the Cossack PMC marched behind their CEO. Scanning the crowd Ivan searched for Henry. Victoria hoped the man would not see her and Julia. Ivan couldn't see his nemesis through the thick crowd, but spotted the group. Zhuge noticed the Russian moving towards the group eyes fixed on Victoria.

"Yes Mr. Sun I am very proud of my daughter Julia." Zhuge turned to face the approaching Russian CEO. Ivan marched towards Victoria with his half naked entourage dangling from his arms. Nerves buzzed with energy allowing Victoria to sense the man approaching. Ivan stepped into the group glaring at the mother and daughter wearing the masks of goddesses.

"Ah Mrs. and Ms. Williams what a beautiful party you have thrown for us tonight. On your wedding anniversary isn't the husband supposed to be with his wife. What is so urgent to call Henry from his beautiful wife's side?" Ivan's words dripped from venom thoughts lurking inside his mind. Reputation told Victoria what to expect from the Russian. Whether pride or insecurity fuelled Ivan's rage remained unknown, but reputation stated the man would avenge any slight.

Tension filled the air around the group causing the crowd to step away. Everyone could see the rage burning in Ivan's eyes. Victoria hoped business would keep her husband busy for a while to avoid any conflict. Any fight between Ivan and Henry would be on the front page of the news. Victoria hoped to avoid starting the new years with a scandal. Public relations were already low after the attacks in Beijing and the Skymall.

CHAPTER 23

Royal Audience

Sounds of boot steps boomed down the hollow halls of the Plaza. Henry and King George crossed the hotel to another condominium. The room chosen had already been swept for listening devices and cameras. Henry picked this condo turning it into a safe house with bullet and sound proof glass. Muse security installed a white noise generator and isolated the computer system. Limiting outside access to computer networks prevented hacking.

Entering through the door Henry greeted President Woods who stood at the table waiting. Lines of worry etched the face of President Woods. Walking with a hurried pace Henry and the King approached the table. Gathering around the large table the men looked at each other. Maj. Lee clicked a button activating security measures.

"We have no time to spare gentlemen. I have already dispatched diplomatic envoys to allies around the world. I was notified moments ago that intelligence reports coming in from Israel are alarming. CIA operatives on the ground show enemy fortifications being raised on the I.R.M.E side of the border." President Woods laid out the briefing to start the meeting.

Placing a holoemitter on the desk President Woods looked around to ensure privacy. Windows shifted in colour distorting vision into the room. A strategic map of Israeli forces lit up on a detailed map of the Middle East. Henry looked at the array of forces of Israel and I.R.M.E troops surveying the situation. Israel appeared to be surrounded and cut off from any aid.

"Israel will ask the U.N. general assembly for assistance. Russia will veto in order to sell arms to the Islamic Republic. What is your planned proposal President Woods?" Pressing a second button on the holoemitter President Woods brought up trade maps. Lines raced across the globe showing the various shipping networks. Each line coloured in a different hue to designated different businesses.

"Mr. Sun has agreed to the plan to provide secure shipping in the case of war. The Chinese government wishes to remain neutral in the conflict. Henry your timing for building a friendship with Zhou Yun and his brother Zhuge is prescient." King George pulled a disk from his suit handing it over. President Woods inserted the Disk and the filter adjusted to show modified Dragon Enterprise shipping information.

The real information had been passed to Henry by his wife Victoria. Spectres of war had haunted the Middle East since the end of the Second World War. When the Islamic Republic of the Middle East formed in 2021 Henry began making preparations. Political scientists rumoured the war in the Middle East would become the grounds of the third world war. Scientist agreed that this would be the first cybernetic war.

"Did you prepare everything I asked you to in our last meeting?" Henry looked to his ally for an answer. Nodding in response King George pulled another data disk passing it to the president. Holoemitter shifted to show the details of a trade proposal. The computer program projected income and expenditures for the scenario of war.

"I have arranged for your interests to be protected in the E.U in case of war. The British army has set detachments to defend your factories in Britain. I also managed to set up a trade deal with Mr. Sun to sell the outdated stock of the U.S and E.U to China throughout the war. Mr. Sun was very agreeable to terms you set out Henry. I also ensured the British government detached our best special service units. The units are prepared to disrupt the I.R.M.E forces should they attack."

"We must now lay the preparations for war with diligence gentlemen. Until Israel is attacked by I.R.M.E. forces we cannot take action. I suggest we produce as many cybernetic implants and prosthetics as possible. Mr. Williams please explain your plans to contribute to the war effort." Breathing a sigh of relief President Woods could feel tension drain from his body.

President Woods pointed to the holoemitter on the table. Henry pulled his data disk from his jacket pocket putting it into the machine. Data filtered on the screens showing production information from around the world. The bulk of cybernetic modifications were built in civilized countries of the European Union and U.S. Henry planned production of into specific parts of the world to prevent disruption to production.

"As you gentlemen can see the bulk of military cybernetic prosthesis is produced here in the U.S and in Britain. Medical prosthetics are divided into former Canada and safe parts of the E.U. far away from the war. I have been down playing my production to stockpile a vast sum of cutting edge implants. Once war is declared I will cut off military equipment sales to the I.R.M.E. and its allies. Redistribution of the I.R.M.E's supplies will be divided amongst the U.S, Britain, and China."

King George and President Woods were impressed by the new numbers displayed by the holoemitter. Millions of cybernetic prosthetics and implants would cause a rapid increase in military power. Henry tried his best to avert the war through international funding promoting peaceful progress. War seemed certain now. Henry wanted to see the effects of cybertechnology on actual warfare. President Woods turned to Henry with a question.

"What about the Detroit plan?" The Detroit revitalization project was the latest in a series of developments by Muse Industries. Revitalization projects gained partial funding from the government. Detroit had been a major center of industrial capacity created during the need for tanks in the Second World War. Falling into decay over the last century had left Detroit in tatters. Henry planned to rebuild the city making it the center for cybernetic technology. Government grants would cover profit losses. Corporate boards needed a carrot to follow.

"Yes I have acquired the required land necessary. Several major industrial factories are already being converted for cybernetic construction. The construction of a massive corporate building is funding the regrowth of the economy. War sales guaranteed in the contract should have Detroit back to glory inside a few years."

Henry planned the Detroit factory to produce cybernetic brain and full body prosthetics. Current facilities located in Germany and Sweden housed the starting research producing prototypes. Henry developed the technology of cybernetic brains and full body prosthetics in secret. Muse security protected the secret research for the last ten years. Funding from the government allowed Henry to finally put the plan into action.

Muse industries profits paid for the construction of the various facilities. Corporate lawyers awaited completion of the project to file patent and copy rights. Henry tried to hold war back to prevent the necessity of releasing the technology. Now technology would save a multitude of lives crushed by the horrors of war. Digitization of the human consciousness meant soldiers could be saved before their bodies gave out. Placing the holoemitter down on the table Henry gauged the reactions of the president and King. Both men were impressed by the information presented. President Wood's expression showed he still had concerns.

"I am concerned how you intend to deal with the alarming increase of neural hacking reports. Governments around the world are trying to keep the news from the media, but it is not long before neural hacking becomes a media sensation. CIA reports show there were three neural hacking attempts on U.S. government employees. The neural hacking attempts originating in the Middle East over last week. The U.S. military is concerned with reports of indoctrination capabilities of neural hacking."

Muse Industry research confirmed the capabilities of hacking the human mind through neural implants. Henry held back on simulated experience trying to minimize neural hacking attempts. Manipulation of memories could create sleeper agents. Only through intense neurological mapping could false memories be identified. Muse kept their advanced barrier systems hidden from the public. Barriers were built into each neural implant. Multiple mazes created a barrier between each unique mind and outside influences. Each conscious mind formed the last line of defense, and hacking became a struggle of willpower.

President Woods looked to Henry for answers. Standing back King George weighed the situation in silence. British intelligence had some experience with neural hacking. Reports of terrorist attacks on British interests and citizen property pinned neural hacking as the source. Britain still had the one of the best intelligent agencies on the planet. Henry looked at the worry apparent on the young Kings' face.

"Neural hacking is one of the drawbacks of neural implants. Muse industries barrier programs have kept the vast majority of the public safe.

I'll have new barrier software updates scheduled on a regular basis for all government employees." Both men felt reassured by the explanation. Government agencies worked with Henry to ensure world leaders possessed the best barrier programs.

Henry kept the best barrier program for himself. All the men in the room ran the latest neural implants with wireless capability. Wireless capability allowed the mind to be hacked from anywhere heightening the fear of hacking. All the reports indicated breaches of neural hacking were on obsolete barrier programs. Documented neural hacking reports remained isolated to a few dozen worldwide.

"If Russia decides to side with the Islamic Republic there will be a corporate war. Henry what are your plans for containing a war between Romanov and Muse Industries?" Henry had wondered if the world leaders would realize how far the war would reach. Romanov's removal as primary distributor and shipping for Muse industries created an antagonistic state. With loss of revenues and supply of cybernetic implants curtailed by war Romanov would act.

Corporate war seemed almost certain to follow any war in the Middle East. Henry remained certain Ivan had already attempted industrial espionage and sabotage, but lacked evidence to prove any crime. A shadow war between corporations in the Middle East had already been recorded by the media. Intelligence reports on the CEO of Romanov industries made him a known quantity. Ivan had served in the Russian military and was an ardent patriot.

Intelligence revealed Ivan had been falsifying damaged and stolen good reports on Cybertechnology. Shipments of cybernetic equipment were redirected to Russia. Cossack forces recruited from the government revealed a layer of mutual support. Empowering Russia allowed Ivan to build his own private military. Using the argument at dinner Henry intended to provoke Ivan into foolish action. Public relations could convince the public with the argument of self-defense. Henry still needed to reassure his political triumvirate.

"Gentlemen please calm yourselves. Corporate war between Muse and Romanov was suspected long before either of you conceived of the idea. I suspect Mr. Romanov is at the party fuming over my absence. Muse industries has never been infiltrated or sabotaged. My people have loyalty to the long range goals and ideals of Muse. I asked for military support in defending my property to allow Muse Security to strike back against any threats. I have laid careful preparations to defend against any aggressive strategy Ivan may have prepared."

"Well it looks like everything is prepared to move forward. I must take my leave now to push the agenda forward on my own end. Thank you for your hospitality Mr. Williams. We'll discuss the developments in the situation when they occur. Your majesty I pray your flight home is safe." President Woods grabbed his coat preparing to leave. Secret service agents followed the President out of the room.

George looked at the Muse CEO. Henry studied the information on the holoemitter for a few moments. Whirling noise emanating from the machine died down after the King clicked it off. George handed the data disks to a SAS officer. The officer pulled out a little tray and filled it with lighter fluid.

Whooshing to life the fire covered the tray. Henry watched the officer throw the disks into the fire. Within moments the data disks liquefied into a paste consumed by flames. Picking up the holoemitter Henry wiped all data from the machine. King George watched the thorough process of data deletion before looking at Henry.

"Well I suppose that takes care of everything. You should head back to the party before your absence causes alarm or suspicion. I was told you have a secure connection in this room. Do you mind if I use the connection in this room to transmit a report back to London?" Nodding in agreement Henry reached down and picked up his mask. Muse security escorted their CEO to the door stopping with him at the threshold. Henry looked at the mask of Apollo in his hands causing him to turn to King George.

"About the other matter we discussed in private. The plan requires timing and finesse leaving no links back to either of us. Have you set everything in motion in that regards?" King George hesitated for a minute trying to recall the important message from earlier that day. For a moment the information slipped through the cracks of the young Kings mind. Excitement and the events of the day clouded recollection.

"Ah Yes I remember now. No worries Henry I have already taking care of all the arrangements. I assure you this will be a night your daughter never forgets." Henry felt reassured pressing the button to open the door.

World war seemed inevitable at this point. Survival required adapting to new conditions.

Heading away from the room Henry tried to turn thoughts away from his daughter. Setting the plan in motion required everyone to follow through to the very end. Henry knew the rewards were worth the risks. Reports show Ivan's erratic and violent behaviour when angry. Marching with determination Henry focused on the confrontation with Ivan Romanov.

Fist fights in the middle of an upper society party needed to be avoided. Henry knew the situation required delicate application of pressure. Ivan had to be manipulated into striking Muse first out of revenge. Governments waited for Israel to be attacked first to claim self defense. Defense remained a valid argument for the application of force. Walking alongside Henry the security detailed remained close.

Leading four men Maj. Lee walked next to his boss. Each soldier could feel tension from an unknown source assaulting their senses. Maj. Lee wondered why his boss asked the young King to spend time with his daughter alone. Most fathers tried to keep their children away from young men. Activating the neural connection Maj. Lee connected to Henry's mind.

"I don't know what you're thinking sir, but that's the last man I'd leave my daughter alone with. I understand you are trying to give your daughter some company and entertainment for an evening. Julia does live a secluded life even at school from the reports. Do you believe the young King can be trusted?" The neural link stayed quiet for a moment. Maj Lee wondered why his boss failed to respond to his question.

"I don't trust him with my daughter Maj. Lee. I trust my daughter. I also trust that you will ensure nothing happens to Julia when she is with the young King. Every child deserves to be a kid. If only for one night I want Julia to have a semblance of a normal childhood, or perhaps even the hope of a fairy tale." The group of individuals continued to march down the hall in silence. Henry hoped Maj. Lee would understand and everything would go as planned.

CHAPTER 24

Star Crossed

Listening to the conversation Julia stood near her mother. Victoria discussed affairs with Zhuge focusing on the matter of business. Scanning through the crowd Julia looked for Robert hoping for some company. Colt and his two boys stood discussing targeting programs with Jean Jocques Decartes. Spotting Robert caused Julia's heart to race with excitement. Soft digitized classical music resonated through the air providing a calming atmosphere. Surrounded by a sea of people Julia tried to distract herself wondering what Robert was thinking.

Ivan Romanov left the group when Victoria refused to tell him where Henry went. The Russian CEO now occupied a couch surrounded by his entourage of sycophantic models. Both of the Cross Boys watched their father read a data pad. Colt viewed the information on the screen mumbling as he read. The information consisted of the breakdown of the advanced targeting systems games used.

"I think we got ourselves a deal partner. This information gets me excited about a co-development deal. You make sure to get a hold of my people in the next week and set up a meeting." Jean's information highlighted how easy the software could be converted to military application. Colt handed the data pad back to its owner. Bored of the conversation Robert glanced across the room noticing Julia looking at him.

Colt tipped his cowboy hat in farewell before sauntering towards Victoria with his wife on his arm. Walking a few feet behind Barrett and Robert followed their parents. Walking up to the group Colt beamed his

Texan smile behind his half face mask of a court jester. Priscilla waved to Victoria from behind her elegant feathered mask. Hoping Robert would come over Julia fretted with nervous energy.

"We want to wish you a Happy New Year's Victoria and Mr. Sun. I've been looking for Henry for some time now. Any of you know where he went?" Colt glanced around trying to spot his friend. Boring conversation took a toll on Julia's nerves. Noticing the stare Robert wondered what his friend could be thinking about. Anxiety sparked by the volume of the crowd compelled Julia to act. Robert felt a tap on his shoulder turning to see the Mask of Venus looking back. With Arms crossed Julia stood in front of the young man.

"Would you care to escort me to get a drink?" Caught off guard Robert hesitated for a moment fumbling for an answer. The mask concealed Julia's embarrassment and rising anxiety caused by the absent answer. Colt glared at his son trying to provoke him to answer the question. Before Robert could respond his father spoke up.

"What are you waiting for boy? Be the gentlemen and escort Julia to get a drink. Priscilla you should be teaching the boys how to treat a lady. Stop standing around with your hands in your pockets Robert. Get going boy and take Julia to get a drink already." Colt patted his son on the back trying to push him forward.

Frozen from the visage of beauty before him Robert seemed to be a statue. Thundering with each beat Robert worried someone would hear his racing heartbeat. Anxiety washed over Robert when he extended his hand. Time froze in that moment. Taking the young man's hand Julia felt her anxiety wash away. Turning to the group Robert seized control over his voice.

"Please excuse us, but we shall return in a few minutes." Both parents watched the young couple walk through the crowd towards the bar. Victoria noticed Priscilla wiping a tear from her eye. Wearing a proud father's smile Colt puffed on his cigar. Barrett watched the two walk away concealing dark thoughts behind his blank expression.

The crowd parted for Robert and Julia walking through the sea of people. Both parents began discussing their children's futures. Both parents watched their children feeling a sense of pride. Barrett slipped away from the group unnoticed. Walking through the crowd Julia felt safe for the first time all night since her father left. Robert walked a few steps away unsure of what to say forcing him to be silent. Julia wrapped her arm around Robert's linking the two together.

"Thank you for getting me away from the conversation. Another minute and I would have ran and jumped off the balcony. These parties are so boring." Robert laughed drawing some attention from the crowd. Sensing awkward energy Julia marvelled at how different her companion seemed. Approaching the bar Robert raised a hand to get the bartenders attention. Julia pulled her companion away from the bar with a tug on his arm.

"I got better stuff to drink just follow me. I'd rather get away for just a few minutes." Leading the way Julia headed towards her bedroom down the hallway away from the party. Muse security stationed to prevent guest from accessing the private rooms blocked the path. Julia and Robert walked past the guards without a single word spoken.

Standing back in the crowd Barrett watched his brother and the girl walk down the hallway. Envy sparked in the young man's eyes. Barrett couldn't stand the sight of his brother with the woman he desired. The door shut behind the couple after they entered the bedroom. Standing back Barrett waited watching the door with patience.

"I needed this short break from that hell." Soundproofing ensured the room remained in absolute silence. Tranquility reigned in the bedroom. Robert looked over the pictures of the Williams family together spread throughout the room. Stacks of books piled about in a disorganized mess. Julia sat down on the bed placing the mask of Venus next to her. Hearing a deep sigh of relief Robert turned to see his friend lying down. Stretched out on the bed covered in smooth silk Julia stretched out on her bed. Keen observation showed Robert that Julia had been anxious and stressed all night.

"I noticed you were really anxious out there. I can imagine the attack on the mall still has you shaken up. Julia if you need anyone to talk to about it. I know you can't tell your parents so I can offer my shoulder. Anything you need Julia just ask. You know I'll do whatever I can to help you in any way possible."

Blood rushed to Julia's cheeks unable to stop herself from blushing. Robert's kind sentiment caused the young woman's heart to flutter.

Julia noticed that her anxiety had disappeared when Robert came over. Emotions waged war inside the young woman's mind. Strange new feelings both puzzled and excited Julia.

"You know the worst part of the attack is what it showed me about my life. All my life I've lived in a dream world. Other children are excited about driving and living life. We've had chauffer's and personal security since we were kids Robert. The attack showed me how everything we see as luxury is really the cages of our cell." Sitting up Julia looked at Robert with a serious expression on her face.

Words rattled around inside Roberts mind bring harsh reality to light. Crossfire security kept a close guard on the Cross boys since childhood. Looking back Robert realized the truth in his friends' statement. Truth of the words painted the grim reality of the life of luxury. Colt instilled his children with the ideas of duty, responsibility, and family.

"Our entire lives have been forced upon both of us by necessity. The one thing I'll never ever have is freedom. Without freedom what is the point of life Robert?" Confusion wore across Robert's face revealing he didn't have an answer. Freedom was an ideal that never seemed important in the Cross family.

"I think freedom is doing what you want. If you could anything in the world right now what would you do?" No one had ever asked that question to Julia before. Victoria spoke of the ideals of freedoms with her daughter on a regular basis. The William's family lived the ideals of freedom, yet Henry with all his power could not secure freedom for his daughter. Robert looked at the sad expression on Julia's face.

"I've never really thought of it." Julia struggled to search for the answer to the question. Freedom seemed to be the most important thing in the world to the young woman. Writing papers on freedom was easy enough to Julia, but how to use freedom remained elusive. Schedules didn't leave Julia much room to make decisions about anything. Security required every event be planned out ahead of time. Nothing spontaneous occurred around Julia.

"I think I would travel and see as much of the world as possible. If I was lucky I might even fall in love and get swept away in romance." Robert had never seen this side of Julia before. Remaining reserved the young woman detached herself from the other students at school. Sitting on the bed next to the girl of his dreams Robert stared into her green eyes. Every instinct told the man to act while anxiety held him still. Julia wild eyes brimmed with desire for adventure and excitement of love.

"There is so much that I want to see and experience in this world. I realize now the loneliness I felt at school is caused by my lack of freedom. It's only around you I feel free to be myself." Confiding in Robert filled Julia with the first true sense of freedom. Truth can set you free the old proverb resonated inside the young woman's mind.

Growing up Robert's parent always had high expectation of him. Children of society's elite were given every advantage. In return for the advantages of wealth and power came the expectations of inevitable success. Parents raised children like gamblers betting on the odds. Most parents expect their children to grow up and become such adults. Both children had been groomed to be successful and had high expectations piled on top.

Robert and Julia had been sent to boarding school for high school. Boarding school teachers pushed both children harder to reach preplanned goals. Robert's choices in classes and extracurricular activities had been chosen by his father. Julia's parents influenced her into politics and business. Sharing school experience created a deep connection between the two children.

Close connection between the Williams' family and Cross's allowed both children to grow up together. Here in this moment Julia and Robert were becoming adults with long held feelings bubbling to the surface. Tension lingered in the air of the bedroom. Both Julia and Robert could feel the rising heat in their bodies. Fear, excitement, and lust mixed together in symphony of emotions.

"You're the only person I feel comfortable around too." Letting down emotional guards Robert looked at the beautiful woman sitting across from him. Words slammed against the dam holding Julia's emotions back. Rising anxiety compelled Robert to act. Words alone couldn't express the true depths of feelings. Staring into each other eyes Robert and Julia couldn't resist their emotions.

Fires of love pumped through Robert and Julia's veins drawing their lips together. Surrendering to each other the couple kissed with passionate force. Lips locked together with a smack. Roberts grazed his fingers down the smooth skin of the back of the neck. For the first time since the attack

Julia didn't feel any anxiety or fear. Caught in this moment of desire overpowered the woman's rational thought. Only after several minutes of passionate kissing did both people break free to look at each other. Desire burned in the both minds of the young adults sitting on the bed.

"We should probably return to the party. I mean we've already been gone for quite a while." Reason returned to Julia mind coming down from the emotional high. Fear filled the young woman's eyes when she realized the boundary the two had crossed. Julia didn't fear the change in relationship only she was unsure of Roberts's feelings.

"Yea of course I hadn't thought of that." Robert could see the fear in Julia's eyes and worried that he overstepped. The sudden desire to return to the party weighted on the young man's mind. Julia stood up and looked at herself in the mirror to straighten her clothes and hair. Still sitting on the bed in silence Robert couldn't stop worrying.

Pulling out makeup Julia touched up her face and applied new lipstick. The mirror reflected the smeared lipstick marks caused by kissing. Fixing the lipstick Julia relived the memory with a pleasant smile. Daydreaming pulled the young woman from reality for a moment. Standing up Robert walked up behind Julia.

"Are you ready to return?" Robert's gentle touch startled the young woman looking into the mirror. Julia spun around breaking from the fantasy to see Robert towering in front of her. Looking down Robert looked into Julia's green eyes. Julia emotions flared again pushing her to leap forward. Lips locked again filling the room with the soft noises of passion. Robert lost balance and crashed back onto the bed. Both people sunk into the embrace of the blankets that surrounded them.

Caught between the silk fabrics of the dress and surrounding blankets obscured Roberts sight, but Julia's angelic face floated in front. Surging passions compelled Julia to give into her secret desires for an instant. Pressures of school, parents, and life became distant memories for an instance to the woman. After several minutes Julia broke away again to take a deep breath of air. Robert lay on the bed lost in a mixture of shock and happiness.

"We really need to get back to the party before our parents come looking for us." Regaining senses the young man knew being discovered would complicate the situation. Standing up Robert looked at Julia with a reassuring confidence. The message of mutual attraction had been received loud and clear. Reapply makeup and lipstick for the second time Julia looked back at Robert standing by the door.

"Your right we should get going before either my dad or brother come to find us. Last thing we need to explain where we have been." Looking down at the watch Robert realized a half hour had passed already. Julia could see the shock on Roberts' face and decided to look at her own watch. Seeing the time Julia applied the make up in a hurry. Robert opened the door and looked down the hall. No one appeared to be approaching.

"Coast looks clear." Julia took Roberts arm exiting the bedroom. Neither person looked at the other walking down the hall. Approaching the party loud music and conversation washed over the couple. Muse Security parted the way to allow the young couple to pass. Walking through the bar Julia scanned to see people's reaction. None of the party guests seemed aware of anything out of the ordinary. Julia hoped that both her and Roberts parents would not notice anything either. Looking around with impatience Victoria spotted her daughter's return.

"Well I hope you two had fun leaving us to worry about you." Both Julia and Robert looked at their parents trying to gauge their reaction. Victoria seemed annoyed at something other than her daughter's absence. Robert could pride beaming from his father's eyes. Both parents seemed oblivious to the situation.

Chapter 25

Iron Hand

Sitting on the couch Ivan mauled the beautiful woman surrounding him. Guests watched in a mix of horror and intrigue. The Russian CEO waited with growing impatience for Henry Williams to return. The situation galvanized in Ivan's mind with one phone call. Muse Industries submitted their decisions to not renew the transportation contract with Romanov Industries.

The loss of profits had put Ivan into a terrible mood. Anger etched lines across the aging Russians face. Ivan stared at the door preparing his arguments. Walking towards the party Henry could sense the impending situation with Ivan. Maj. Lee reported Ivan's mood to his boss before they entered the apartment. Muse security at the party attached pictures and audio of the Russians anger.

Digital music and loud clamour of the guest assaulted Henry's senses when he entered the party. Victoria waved her Husband over to the group. Looking over towards the door Ivan spotted Henry's arrival. Pushing guest out of the way Cossack security cleared a path for Ivan. Approaching the group Henry leaned in and kissed his wife before addressing the group.

"I hope I haven't missed too much." Eyes shifted in the crowd watching the Russian storming through the party. Marching footstep echoed in the tune with the drumbeats sounding Ivan's approach. Tapping Henry on the shoulder Colt pointed to the approaching problem. Cossack Guards stopped before the group and separated allowing Ivan to step forward.

"Mr. Williams this is absurd!" The gruff voice of Ivan drew the attention of everyone at the party. Henry stared at the Russian CEO noting the rage across the man's face. Pride fuelled the anger overpowering the normal control Ivan chose to wear. Plans moved towards fruition in Henry's mind churning like a great clockwork machine.

"You're switching from the most technological advanced transportations service to archaic boats. You claim to be an honorable man yet break your contract with Romanov without warning. Mr. Williams this will provoke serious repercussions." Ivan intended to use aggression to back his opponent down in order to not disrupt the party. Disbelief washed over Henry caused by the lack of strategy from such an educated businessman. The Russian CEO expected to be pulled aside and addressed in private. Henry clenched his teeth preparing his response.

"Muse Industries had the option to renew our annual transportation and distribution contract with Romanov. Due to the nature of some new information the contract came under scrutiny." Watching the exchange Victoria could see the rising anger in her husband. Ivan stood only a few inches away from Henry. Face to face the two men stared back at each other.

Neither person intended to back down. Henry reached into his pocket pulling out his holoemitter. Setting the device onto broadcast it synced up with the nearby device for the living room. Soon Ivan would regret his grave miscalculation in dealing with Henry. The holoemitter transmitted all the data it held. Information about theft and damaged goods flooded the screen. Every guest at the party stood by and watched in absolute shock.

Video showed various goods being stolen from Romanov by Ivan's Cossack PMC. Figures and chart displayed the corresponding declaration of theft and damaged goods in Romanov accounts. Insurance payouts showed illegal profits. Detailed reports flew across the screen creating an orgy of evidence. Looking at the information Ivan felt his fury rising.

"All this information could be falsified. You have created bogus reports and information to attack my reputation. I am going to drag you into court for this!" Tapping a few buttons on the device Henry brought up a second set of videos. Pictures danced on the screen showing Ivan discussing Business in his office late at night.

"Williams will never know the difference. Magrail Trains may be the fastest and most efficient transportation, but that doesn't mean packages don't get damaged or stolen. I'll make sure to keep the lost and damaged goods well under any figures that would cause alarm. Everything will go as planned so stop worrying. We will divert the cybernetic implants to the Russian government minus costs." Video paused on Ivan's smug look standing before his corporate board.

Gasps filled the room from the crowd resonating with shock from the information. The information displayed on the screen was hard evidence to refute. Henry looked at Ivan seeing him seething with rage. Long range strategy relied upon layers of plans circling in chaotic patterns. Remaining calm Henry formed a polite smile looking into his adversaries eyes.

"The decision was nothing personal Mr. Romanov. I made the decision I felt to be the best interests of Muse International. I have already filed the necessary legal papers to bring charges against you in both the U.S and Russia. I doubt anything will happen to you in your homeland, but the US and International laws will view this as theft." Delivering a one two punch of words Henry watched to see the effect.

Standing there shocked Ivan struggled to find a reply. Watching the interaction with intense focus the crowd whispered of the possibilities. Ivan ears heard the words thief and criminal whispered stroking his rising anger. Both men waged war on the other in their minds without breaking their stare. Desire for vengeance clouded Ivan's mind provoking him to action.

"Mr. Williams I would prove that information to be fabricated in a court of law. You do realize that the lies you're fabricating right now could cause the first corporate war. When violence and blood fills the street because of these deceptions the people will know it is your fault." Patience would prove the victor in this power struggle between CEO's. Tapping into the device again Henry pulled up new video feeds.

Several images of Romanov troops being held hostage by Muse Industries flooded the screen. Corresponding news reports showed the attacks by Romanov on Muse holdings earlier that night. Each report showed that a small group of individual tried to infiltrate a cybernetic lab. Journalists extolled the virtues of joint team work by private security and public forces to prevent terrorism. The video feed zoomed into reveal the

Romanov markings on each captive's armour. Long range strategy allowed Henry to outthink his opponent at every move.

"Recognize any of these men on the screen? Each of them volunteered to testify that it was your orders that set them to task Ivan. I think the public will know who talked about corporate war while starting it. If these attacks had been successful then the world would be starved for cybertechnology. I believe you are trying to disrupt production just in case a war breaks out in the Middle East. Cybertechnology stolen from Muse Industries would be worth a fortune during such a shortage. You're not the first man to create demand by creating scarcity."

The information revealed the deepest secrets of Romanov Industries. Failure of the agents to succeed in their task filled Ivan with a terrible trembling fury. Insult of being captured on top of failure threatened to drive the CEO into madness. Romanov troops standing behind Ivan scanned the environment preparing for trouble. Anxiety of the crowd filled the air with a tangible tension. Everyone watched the two CEO's standoff. Ivan glared realizing the mistake he made underestimated the cunning of his opponent.

"I shall prove how baseless your accusations are in a court of law Mr. Williams." Ivan stood defiant before his rival and the evidence. Heavy breathing forced hot breath into each man's face standing almost toe to toe. Henry studied his opponent trying to discern the next action. Ivan had no intention of starting any fight here at the party.

Searching for the right tool Henry wanted to goad his opponent into acting first. Walking past the group a waitress carried a platter of glass filled with champagne. Picking up two glasses from the tray Henry presented one as an offering. The olive branch dangled between the two men. Ivan glared at the cup for a moment.

"What is the meaning of this?" Offering the glass Henry looked into Ivan's eyes that revealed his confusion. Distraction would serve a better purpose than aggression in this situation. Guest hung in delicate rapture feeling the uncertainty hanging in the air. Henry held the glass in front of his adversary.

"This is just business. No reason we can't drink and leave business for its own time and place. It is New Year's Eve after all. Let us celebrate together and forget the days gone by." Henry used the simple magnanimous act to push his rival over the edge. Unable to contain the spite and anger any longer Ivan leaned forward.

"Typical you act with cruelness and conceal it behind a curtain of lies. You offer me a drink as if we are friends while preparing the dagger in your hand. You are the serpent waiting for the opportunity to strike. You act like you are a kind and generous man concealing the truth of yourself behind more deception. Mr. Williams you are I are not that different except that I can accept my nature. Men like us must rule with an iron hand, and my only mistake is thinking the velvet glove your wearing is your real hand. Now I see the velvet glove on your hand conceals the iron claws behind it. You called me a wolf at dinner, yet forget the wolf backed into a corner bites deepest."

Henry watched the Russian CEO and his guard storm away in a hurry. Following behind the entourage clacking of high heels sounded retreat. Ivan reached the door stopping to look at Henry for a second. Both men stared at each other in a moment of silence. Unable to resist the current of emotions Ivan need to say one more thing.

"You will regret your actions today in the future Mr. Williams. One day the mighty Muse Industries will fall, and I will be standing there watching the destruction. There is an old saying I have learned to trust. Pride comes before the fall." Striding through the door Ivan stormed from the party. Cossack Security and models followed their master's exit.

Walking down the hallway towards the elevator Ivan wondered how much of what he had seen was truth. Taking a moment the CEO accessed the Romanov Industrial network servers using his neural implant. Information showed several teams sent on disruption missions failed to check in. Probabilities suggested that Henry's videos of captured Romanov troops were accurate. Ivan moved through the system and activated the Chimaera protocol.

Tapping several button Henry turned to the crowd. Holographic displays turned off. Everyone looked up to Henry awaiting his guidance. Stepping up onto a table Henry addressed the people. Everyone quieted down to hear Henry speak.

"I am sorry for the interruptions my friends. There is plenty of drinks and food to go around. Let's continue the celebration. Enjoy your evening because these are the last few minutes of 2033. My wife and I wish you all the best in 2034." Henry stepped down looking to his wife.

Victoria could only stare with disbelief wondering what her husband was thinking. With the attack on Julia in the mall the other day inciting Ivan to anger seemed dangerous. Most of the circumstantial evidence pointed to Romanov industries. Ivan and Romanov Industries stood to benefit the most from abducting the William's daughter. Henry turned to the rest of the group looking at Zhuge, Colt, and his family.

"Mr. Williams no one should endure dishonesty in a relationship." Nodding behind the Chinese warlord Mask Zhuge understood the reasons with perfect clarity. Weakness is always exploited in the world of business. Business expressed the truth of the world rooted in the philosophy of Survival of the fittest. Better to be cruel and safe than weak and afraid Zhuge thought.

"You both are crazy. That Russian is ex-military and backed by the Russian government. Henry you know those attack tonight on Muse will be the first of many. Damn boy I told you to let me bring in more security." Reaching into his pocket Colt brought out an older model communicator. Henry reached out and stopped his friend before he could radio for more troops.

"We can't show any signs of fear. Life is risk my old friend." Henry patted Colt on the back. Many philosophers discussed fate and the idea of risk. Audacity served Henry well in the past. Few people had the courage to change the world, and fewer had the perseverance to follow those dreams.

"Henry with all due respect you have to protect your family. Think about what happened at the mall. You need more security just in case Romanov has something planned." Henry wondered what his friend could be thinking. Colt didn't realize his voice had been overheard by the crowd.

The crowd began to take notice of the whispered conversation occurring around Henry Williams. Guest began to stop talking again turning their attention to eavesdrop. Oblivious to what was going around Colt fumed about the situation. Whispers filled the room from the crowd. Noticing this happen Henry leaned closer to his friend.

"Colt you need to act like nothing is happening. I assure you I have everything taken care of. The guests are growing alarmed at what you're talking about." Taking a deep breath Colt calmed himself down. The truth of the situation could be seen by anyone looking into the eyes of the crowd. Guests tried to hide the fear of the night's events; however the atmosphere of the party had changed. Tension from the disagreement between Henry and Ivan lingered in the air. Colt pulled out cigars passing one to his friend.

"You know your right. Just the military in me buddy. You remember how I use to get back in the field." Taking the cigar Henry placed it in his mouth and lit it. Glancing through the dim of smoke Colt looked into the eyes of his friend. Henry possessed bright green eyes that seemed to hold infinite wonders, but also terrible cunning lurked behind the green orbs.

"Colt we've been friend a long time and survived many dangers. We'll meet the future tomorrow when it comes. We should enjoy this moment together with our family." Henry thought about how moments of true happiness with his family were fleeting. Sometimes Victoria looked at her husband and only seen a stranger, and this was one of those moments. Sensing the divide Henry turned to his wife placing his arms around her and his daughter.

Victoria accessed her husband's wireless neural implant to create a communication connection. High level detection software secured the communication line preventing eavesdropping. Victoria activated encryption just in case someone managed to breach the communication. Once every security measure reported in working the message was sent. Inside Henry's mind he could hear his wife's voice

"We need to talk about what just occurred with Ivan Romanov." In a second the moment was gone. Henry snapped back to reality and its pressures. Victoria needed to be told about the events with the president Woods and King George. Henry knew his behaviour must look strange from his wife's point of view. Staring with intensity Victoria pulled at her husband's arm. Pausing for a second Henry searched for an excuse to tell Colt.

"Hey could you and Maj. Lee go check to make sure Ivan left without a problem?"

"We can do that Henry. Come on Maj. Lee let's get this over with." Leading the group Colt marched towards the door. Watching the group walk away Henry felt his wife tugging on his arm again. Impatience forced Victoria to turn to Zhuge.

CHAPTER 26

Ripples

Upon entering the quiet master bedroom the couple stop and looked at each other. Neural connection between husband and wife allowed voiceless communication, but important issues required both people talk. Henry walked over to the window and drew the curtains shut to prevent anyone from watching from outside. The lock on the door clicked breaking the silence in the room for a second. Turning away from the door Victoria looked at her husband with a mixed look of fear and anger.

Anti-espionage devices prevented outside sources from tapping into the neural communication occurring. White noise generators prevented anyone outside the room from hearing anything. Husband and wife stood next to the bed in the center of the room staring at each other. Neither person knew what to say first. Necessity caused Victoria to break the silence first.

"Do you think it is wise to agitate Ivan Romanov?"

"Perhaps it is unwise but the situation is necessary my love. Ivan has already attacked several Muse facilities tonight." Henry tried to convey the necessity to his wife. Wondering if the information had been fabricated upset Victoria even more. Henry noticed tears welling up in his wife's eyes.

"With everything that has happened how can you put your family at such risk?" The question was not an easy one to answer. All the memories and knowledge that Henry had accumulated over his life could not be vocalized in words. Victoria watched her husband reach for a neural patch cable offing one of the ends to her.

"My love you know my intentions. I would never jeopardize my family. Plug in and we can sync memories." Reaching out Victoria took the neural cable without hesitation. The process of neural syncing of memories took only a short period of time.

Victoria clicked the connector into the neural implant on her neck activating the memory sync. Memories flooded across the cable transferring from one mind to the other. Victoria felt her husbands' consciousness within her own mind. The process of neural syncing caused disorientation often accompanied by headaches. Victoria's eyes twitched in response to the synchronization to her husbands' memories.

Memories of the meeting earlier that night played in the minds of both husband and wife. Studying the memories Victoria absorbed the information presented at the meeting. Tactical information recorded by Henry's implants provided the revelation needed. In this moment both people were of one mind. Lies couldn't exist in such naked conditions. Henry and Victoria souls spoke to another through the cable.

"So the Islamic Republic of the Middle East is preparing to launch an offensive against Israel. You think that Ivan Romanov is preparing to take advantage of the declaration of war through manipulation of stocks. Do you believe Ivan is preparing a corporate war in prelude to Russia's declaration of war?" Neural linking allowed Henry to know what his wife wanted and needed. New memories flooded into Victoria's consciousness in response to her questions.

Information recorded by Henrys cybernetic eyes poured forward. Scans of the Romanov's Cossack security showed state of the art cybertechnology. The information revealed all the technology implanted in Ivan's personal forces was stolen from Muse. Henry's neural hacking of several of the guards presented itself in the stolen memories. Ivan prepared to move against Muse regardless of the cancelled contract.

"War can never be avoided to your own advantage, but only to the advantages of others." Henry pushed the thought into his wife's mind. Perusing the stream of data Victoria looked at the situation with clearer perception. Ivan already set up sales and distribution in preparation for the cybertechnology demand he would create. Economic laws spoke of supply and demand. Ivan had been preparing to attack Muse Industries for several years.

"Then Ivan must be the one behind the attack on Julia at the mall." Without responding Henry redirected the flow of memories. Accessing cybernetic recordings from the day of the attack revealed the soldiers had little to no cybernetic implants. There was no way to link the insurgents to Ivan. Collaborating reports flooded showed Ivan's character through business decisions.

"I cannot rule Ivan out as a suspect in the attack on the mall, nor can I confirm the attack on Julia was ordered by anyone else." Favouring hostile takeovers and brute force the Russian CEO conquered his empire by force. Looking through the information Victoria did not know what to think. Henry sensed his wife's confusion at the staggering amounts of data. Fusing in purpose both husband and wife together formed a neural network creating a human supercomputer.

"You cannot protect your daughter forever." Victoria focused in on the memory. Looping the memory of Zhou Yun put pressure on Henry. Information stolen from Colt and Maj. Lee showed the concern for increased safety and more troops. Victoria switched the flow of data pushing her own thoughts to her husband.

"I am trying to understand why you wouldn't increase security to protect your daughter. Are you considering allowing your enemies to kidnap Julia as this terrorist suggests?" Victoria gazed into eyes of her husband. Information exchanged minds, but one area of Henry's memory remained clouded. Unable to access the memory Victoria wondered why her husband would keep secrets from her.

"I will die protecting the two people I love more than life itself." Henry eyes filled with anger at the question. Sharing memories and emotions Victoria could feel the sting of her question. Responding in anger Henry's memories took on emotional overtures. Memories showed the position of Muse troops in the building with no entrance to the hotel left unsecured. Mental image of the city of New York revealed Muse security and gunships stood on the ready less than five minutes away. Symbols flashed through the memories revealing layer upon layer of coordinated plans.

"I would never jeopardize my family ever. It is a shame that in twenty years of marriage you haven't figured that out Victoria." Memories darkened with Henry's emotional state. Victoria felt the stinging pain of betrayal in her husband's mind. Surging emotions showed the only thing Henry valued in one simple image. Julia.

"I am sorry my love. You know I don't doubt you at all, but I am struggling to understand the purpose behind your actions." Victoria pushed her own memories towards her husband. Memories blurred together revealing to each person how the other felt. Feeling the love behind each memory Henry calmed.

"I am trying to smoke my enemies out by appearing to look weak. By offending Ivan and provoking him I am trying to discern if he is the one behind the attacks." Memories containing security arrangements traveled from husband to wife. Victoria felt calm wash over her upon learning the information. Muse security forces placed on high alert could provide a rapid response to any attack.

Security files from the Plaza showed several pictures of the Ivan's furious departure. Moving data showed the Russian CEO immediate departure from the Plaza. Moving the data stream from the Plaza cameras to Ivan's arrival revealed no baggage. Henry pushed his memories towards his wife. Scanning the information Victoria caught up to husbands thought process.

"There was no stop to pick up any belongings." Victoria echoed her worries in the neural link.

"This shows that there was no intention to attend the party to conclusion. Ivan had some intention with this party, but I cannot figure out the exact plan." Henry's thoughts raced through images trying to discern patterns. People called the ability intuition before the age of neural networks and digitalized memories. The human brain is a pattern recognition engine built on personal experience mixed with instinct.

"Don't you have to understand the strategy in order to beat it?" Looking at the information filled Victoria with worry. Reeling through the data flow Henry directed his wife to the cybernetic vision feeds from security. Uncertainty travelled the digital lines linking the two people's brains together. Purpose drove Henry to continue weighing out possibilities.

"I have tried to prepare for any attacks that could come. The reality of my situation is every action I take creates ripples. Even lying still trying not to act is an action that will push other people to act." Data feeds brought up the image of the Earth and showed every active neural implant on the planet. Circles symbolized wireless neural implants of people in society.

Referencing the circles a memory of Henry throwing stones into a pond filled Victoria's mind.

"Every single human being on this planet is a stone. Life is a pool of water. Every word and action ripples across the surface affecting every other action. Multiple actions coalesce into larger ripples travelling further causing more ripples. No one person can see the future, and so no one can predict the outcome of the ripples each individual's actions cause." Certainty in belief filled Victoria's mind from the transmitted memories.

Various new reports from around the world filtered through the data stream between husband and wife. News reports showed how actions caused by Henry affected the entire world. Cybertechnology changed the very functioning of human thought and civilizations on Earth. Victoria realized how much weight rested on the shoulder of one man. Every action Henry took needed to be scrutinized.

"Henry you can't bear the burden of the weight of the world. You alone cannot fix all the world problems. We are only responsible for the safety and wellbeing of our daughter." Empathy poured through Victoria's thoughts. Henry couldn't understand his wife at times. Husband and wife stood on opposing sides of an ideological divide.

Anger filled Henry's eyes staring in disbelief at his wife. Information from satellites and world news show the rising level of poverty across the world. Conflicts raged around the planet. Pictures of burnt children killed by military airstrikes filled Victoria's mind. Disasters ravaged cities and nations. People starving for food and water begged for help in videos. One idea rang through Victoria's mind. Purpose of everything Henry built was not to fix all the world's problems, but to fix just one.

"We are not responsible just for ourselves and our child. Every human being is responsible for the choices they make. Everyone just accepts how things are. How can you ask me to turn my back on the world when there is so much horror that needs to be changed?" Victoria looked up wiping away the tears from her husbands' eyes.

"You have to trust there is a reason for this and leave it the hands of god." Memories on human history Henry studied poured into his wife's mind. Sensing all the pain and suffering Victoria knew this was the source of the great love she had for her husband. Most people accepted the world the way it is with all the pain and tragedy. Henry raged against the world, refused to accept things the way they were, and defiance drove the man to change everything.

"If there is a god my love he abandoned us a long time ago. I know you believe in god and divine providence. Perhaps you are right and I am wrong, but this I do know beyond all doubt. I cannot endure the world the way it is. The gifts I have can make the world a better place. I won't refuse to act holding myself in place out of fear of being wrong. Instead I will continue to act. If I am wrong I can fix the problems my actions create. I am prepared to pay any price. I will sacrifice whatever is necessary to see humanity escape this conflict cycle repeating itself since time immemorial."

Victoria knees gave way under the force of the pain and suffering attached to the data being transmitted. Looking down Henry held his wife keeping her from falling to the floor. For the first time Victoria understood why Henry created neural technology. Sifting through the memories of all Henry's patients the truth blared out. Neural technology allowed painful memories to be erased, but Henry had collected the pain and suffering of all his patients. Every memory existed for a reason.

"You believe by understanding human nature, pain, and suffering you can fix the world's problems. Trying to unite humanity through technology into a global consciousness could work. Did you ever considered what will happen to you if your mind doesn't prove strong enough to contain these memories. Thousands of these memories from other people could change who you are. What happens when all the pain and suffering you've absorbed begins to affect your decisions?" Victoria touched on the crux of the problem of neural implants and cybertechnology.

"Now you see the problem." Pausing for a moment Victoria reached out to her husband mind.

"You already realized this a long time ago didn't you Henry. Now I understand why you haven't pushed neural implants further. It makes sense why you haven't shared Muse research into cybernetic brains with the world. I sense your fear that neural technology is doing the opposite of what you intended. You're afraid of how the world would use your technology."

Feeding data streams from new organizations reports on neural implants into the data synchronization. Neural implants allowed humans to connect to one another on a deeper level, but people used the technology for entertainment and power. Reports showed alarming increase in people using neural games to retreat away from society. Social disintegration caused by social media only increased with the invention of neural implants.

"My love my actions have created ripples that stretch across the planet. No one man can be the all-seeing prophet of god any more. Humanity is no longer enthralled by mysticism but by technocracy." Able to understand Victoria looked at her husband with a look of fear and admiration. Henry's mind still caused his wife to have chills when she touched it. Nerves twitched throughout Victoria's body from the mix of excitement and terror.

"I have never sought to hide anything from you honey. I must deal with something's all on my own. My actions have altered the path of humanity forever, but what will that legacy be?" Pictures of Julia from small childhood through her life flooded through the data stream. Both parents loved their daughter more than anything in the world. Memories synchronized filling both parent's minds with a gray fog. The ambiguous blob of grey mist represented the uncertain future that lay ahead of Julia.

"I do not know Julia's future any better than you do." Victoria felt the stream of data shift with her husbands' thoughts. Fabricated memories represented Henry's ideas. News footage showed another attack on the Williams family. Memories of attack after attack flowed through the data stream. Weight of the memories threatened to crush both parents.

"Our daughter is cursed by the name Williams. Julia will have to fight one day to define herself as an individual, but I cannot predict the costs those actions will have." Pulling the neural connection line free Victoria looked at her husband with worry. Free from the memory synchronization both parents looked at each other in silence. Words were not necessary after sharing such an intimate connection between two people.

Henry and Victoria shared empathetic looks. Both of the parents realized neither of them could protect Julia forever. Leaning in Henry kissed his wife. Time waits for no person. If this was the last kiss Henry intended to enjoy it. Victoria looked at her husband's green eyes.

"I understand now why you keep so many secrets from me."

"I would never jeopardize Julia, but I'm frustrated at the fact I can't figure how best to protect her. War is in the air and corporations will fight over the limited power available. Enemies will always try to use Julia

CHAPTER 27

Security Gaps

Standing around watching the party caused Julia to grow more bored with each passing minute. Conversation with Zhuge became the stale discussion of business and politics. Glancing around through the crowd Julia couldn't spot anyone near her age to have a conversation with. Feelings of loneliness washed over the young woman despite standing in a sea of people. Walking through the door King George returned to the party. Guest turned to greet the young king scanning the environment looking for Julia.

Commotion at the door to the apartment drew the attention of the guests. Julia spun to see the charming young prince making his way through the crowd towards her. The two young people's eyes locked across the room. Lost in the beautiful green eyes of the young woman King George pushed his way through the crowd. Stepping into the group King George bowed before Julia and Zhuge.

"I am sorry that I was away for so long. Where did your parents go Julia?"

"My parents wanted some alone time on their anniversary, and I would imagine they will be back soon." King George looked at his watch showing less than fifteen minutes till midnight. People danced only a few feet away to the digitalized music filling the room. Offering a hand George looked at the beautiful young woman before him.

"If it is not a problem with Mr. Sun would you like to dance Julia?"

"I fear I am too boring for you young kids. Go have some fun." Zhuge hid his smile behind the mask covering his face. Glimpsing towards the dance floor Julia admitted it looked more fun than standing around. Leading the young woman onto the dance floor George heard the music switch to a slower song. Everyone around the two young adults embraced dancing to the slow tempo. Julia took Georges hand as the two embraced on the dance floor.

The mask the Kings wore did little to hide the glances of his eyes. George admired the beautiful girl's body while dancing. People moved with delicate and subtle movements following the rhythm of the song. Sensing the lustful gaze Julia looked into the eyes of her partner longing for Robert's return. A soft touch of the Kings hand ran down the bare skinned back of his partner. Cadence of the music provided a subtle soundtrack to the allure of George's actions. Nerves tingled with excitement causing Julia's mind to break away from thoughts of Robert and the bedroom. George heard the distinct whisper.

"Thank you for getting me away from that boring conversation." Tension in back muscles revealed to George the stress the young woman was under. Julia's face revealed no hints of the strain she was under despite being hidden by her mask. The young king could not see any hit of stress in his dance partner's body language. George leaned close to his partner in the next flourish of moves.

"It is you who are doing me the favor Julia. I've endured many hours of dancing and speeches, but never have I enjoyed the company so much." Venus's visage hid Julia's blushing underneath. Reputation did say the young king had a way with words. Taking a step back Julia pulled away creating space between dancing partners.

"I am sure you have danced with many women in your life King George." Julia's tone revealed her hesitation. Dancing together both people never broke eye contact. There was no point in denying the truth to the young woman. Royal life required George to attend many formal events.

"Yes it is true I have danced with many women Julia. It is my duty as King of England to show diplomacy and tact when attending to affairs. It is a very rare thing when my duties are enjoyable to perform, and I must admit I quite enjoy dancing with you." Confidence filled every syllable of the words George spoke. Julia didn't know whether to believe the young king or not but she sensed truth. King George spun his dance partner around in a flourish of moves to a sudden change in tempo of the music.

"You don't enjoy your personal entourage and security?"

"We are both prisoners of our heritage Julia. Most of my hours are spent learning and acquiring knowledge. What free time I get is consumed by public appearances. I fear we will both be forever trapped by the luxury of our lives." Looking into the kings eyes Julia felt a connection between them. Looking around the young woman saw SAS operatives attended to every move of their king. Circumstances revealed the truth behind George's words to Julia.

"It would seem you and I have something in common your majesty." A charismatic smile beamed on George face. Pulled along by the music Julia felt swept off her feet. Excitement filled the air. Holding Julia close George's face hovered inches from hers.

"I long for the moments of escape in quiet tranquility from intruding eyes. Perhaps you might be interested in leaving the party with me?" Pausing at the question Julia felt unsure. Both stood still in the center of the dance floor. George could see the glimmer of curiosity in the green eyes behind the mask.

"Do you want to get out of here for a bit with me?" Reasserting the question George hoped to provoke a response. Julia remained hesitant to answer the question. Muse and Royal SAS troops positioned throughout the party would make slipping away unnoticed difficult. Every single exit from the apartment had guards posted at it.

"There is no way any of the security will let me leave unattended. I would love to be anywhere but here right now George, but how can we slip past the security?" Waiting for an answer Julia continued to enjoy dancing with the young King. The sly smile on Georges face hinted at a plan. Julia felt the strong safe grip of her partner lowering her in a freefall before sweeping her back up. Face to face George stared into the eyes behind the mask leaning in close for a whisper.

"A few years ago I learned that the best way to sneak out was in plain sight. Neural implants allow me to access the guard's vision and simply remove myself from their sight." Julia tried to not gasp at the thought of neural hacking. The grim stare of determination told the young woman that the King could do what he stated. Dilating eyes revealed Julia's mixture of hesitation and interest in the plan.

"You intend to hack the minds of the guards?" Music came to a slow stop signalling the end of the song. The crowd applauded the two young adult dancing skills. Everyone smiled at Julia and the king. Walking off the dance floor George held his dance partner close. Hot breath fell on Julia's ear.

"I have already managed to hack the neural implants of every guard in the building. We could leave now if you wish Julia and not a single person would notice." Nodding in agreement Julia followed the young king off the dance floor. A large crowd of people on the dance floor made it hard for anyone to move. Pushing through the flow of people the King led his companion towards the door.

"Just don't draw any attention from the guests. The only people who can't see you are the guards." Julia noticed the Muse security guards scanning the crowd but not noticing her at all. Pushing through the thick crowd King George led the way. Guards watched the king approach with one hand tucked behind his back.

Approaching the security checkpoint at the door Julia felt her anxiety rising. Muse Security would not be fooled by a neural implant hack and would stop both of them. Certain of the outcome Julia remained quiet. One of the security guards stopped King George. Glancing over the young King the security guards' face showed concern. George looked at the door guards with a tired look.

"Your majesty we hate to ask, but could you please tell us where you are going so close to midnight?" Holding onto Julia's hand the King felt her tight squeeze. George smiled at the two guards standing before him. Thunder heartbeats caused Julia to worry the guards could hear the noise. Tension gripped every muscle in the young woman's body. Remaining calm George looked at both the guards displaying an expression of annoyance.

"I am going to go to my room to get something I forgot to bring to the party. I intended to bring Ms. Williams a gift. You can imagine with my schedule it is hard to remember every single detail. If Mr. Williams asks tell him I should return before midnight." Exuding confidence George made every lie indecipherable from the truth.

Lingering for a second the guards checked the records. Every instinct told Julia the guards would catch on any second. When the guards asked where Georges SAS escort was the whole story would collapse. Julia couldn't stand much more anxiety waiting to see the outcome. Both guards scanned the room again.

"Security can't seem to locate Ms. Williams anywhere in the party. Your majesty you were just dancing with Julia a few moments ago. Could you tell us where she went?" One guard continued to scan the crowd searching for Julia. Pointing towards the master suite George prepared his story.

"Julia went to her parents' bedroom to check up on them." Both security guards looked at each other before stepping out of the way allowing the King to pass. Elation overtook Julia walking past the guard into the corridors of the plaza hotel. The apartment door whisked shut behind the exiting people. Shocked the ploy had worked Julia looked at George marvelling at how it was possible.

"How did you do that?" Stopping George turned to face the young woman wearing a wily smile.

"A simple computer virus that infects the vision processes regulated by neural implants." Looking around Julia felt no constraints holding her back for the first time. George led the way down the hallway. Taking deep breaths Julia felt the excitement overwhelm her anxiety. A deep feeling of understanding washed over the young woman's mind. Julia realized one emotion could overpower another.

"Where are we going?" Julia followed holding onto the king's hand. Walking down the long corridors King George pointed towards a door. Approaching the door Julia noticed it was the stairwell access to the roof and ground floor. Pushing open the door George looked back at his companion.

"I have always enjoyed looking out from the top of a tall building. It's the one place in the world I feel free. I've never seen New York City on New Year's eve." Ascending the staircase Julia admired the kings' audacity. Footsteps echoed in the small passageway of the stairwell. Julia admired the intelligence behind the creation of the virus that allowed escaped.

"That virus of yours is quite an ingenious idea. I've never been able to go anywhere without scheduling it with my father first." Glancing back George felt sympathy looking into those radiant green eyes. Life of royalty was constant attention to duty. George adapted to the life at any early age.

Looking into Julia eyes the king felt she was the only person that could understand the loneliness he felt.

"I can show you a few secrets uses for your neural implant." Remaining weary Julia pulled out a neural patch cable from inside her purse. The lure of the new information blocked out the fear of uncertainty in synchronizing thoughts. Julia never allowed anyone except Robert to access her neural implant. Picking up the cable King George attached it to his neural output.

Slipping the connector into the neural implant Julia finished the link. Information poured through the data link. Every memory King George possessed on neural hacking synchronized with Julia's mind expanded it. New neural connections formed in the synapsis between neurons. Julia's powerful mind threatened to overwhelm the king.

Neural synchronization allowed transfer of knowledge and memories, but often the memories transferred first were current memories. The attack in the mall consumed Julia's thoughts, and so the information about the attack poured out first. Watching the attack and feeling the emotions of the event overwhelmed George. During neural synchronization the stronger mind dominated the exchange of information. George had not expected Julia's mind to be able to overpower his own.

No safeguards could resist the powerful willpower hammering against it. Nothing stopped Julia moving without effort through Georges mind. Childhood memories of isolation filled the young woman's mind. Hours of studying and learning filled the vast majority of George's memory. Julia found little traces of memories of parents which related to her own situation.

"I am sorry if that was too forceful, but I don't neural link very often." Learning everything about neural hacking from George's mind Julia broke the connection. Reality rushed back at the young king. George stared with mixed feelings of awe and fear. Memories of the attack at the mall carried the emotions lurking in Julia's mind at the time.

"You weren't worried about yourself at all during that attack. All of your fear and anxiety are about your father. You're afraid you can't protect your father." Feeling the emotions of the memory George understood where the fear and anxiety came from. Julia didn't worry about bad things happening to her. George couldn't contain his disbelief having never encountered a woman like Julia.

"I know my father's enemies will use me against him." For the first time in his life George felt speechless. There existed no clever grouping of words that would offer comfort to the young woman. Julia felt naked in front of the king. Taking another human life wasn't the source of the pain. Instinct blurred the memories, but standing there holding the gun Julia felt righteous protecting her family.

CHAPTER 28

Missing

Muse security guards walked down the hallway to Julia's bedroom door. Loud knocking on the door provoked no response from inside the room. Both guards looked at each other with hesitation. Opening the door one of the guards scanned the room. Ruffled bed sheets were the only sign of activity in the room. Walking back towards the party the guards activated their neural implants.

"Julia is not in her room." Ten minutes remained before the ball dropped to signalling the beginning of the New Year. Guest danced away to the music unaware of the events transpiring around them. Security walked through the party scanning the faces of the guests. Several guests had gone outside in the steady snow fall to cool off. Scanning both outside and inside guards found no trace of Julia. Completing the pass through the party the security guard opened up a neural communication channel.

"Maj. Lee there is no sign of Julia anywhere at the party. How should we precede Sir?" Looking outside at the massive crowd of protestors outside Maj Lee heard the report. Scanning the protestors with cybernetic vision revealed over two thousand people gathered outside. Maj. Lee worried about the crowd outside. The limited number of police couldn't stop the protestors if they decided to become violent.

"I am in the main lobby with Mr. Cross and his sons. Henry and Victoria's GPS transponder shows him and his wife are in their room. Please inform Mr. Williams that we can't find Julia." The guard muttered in frustration walking towards the master bedroom preparing to deliver the bad news. Guests at the party continued to dance, drink, and eat while the party raged on.

Approaching the master bedroom door the guard stop for a second taking a deep breath. Knocking resonated throughout the room alerting the occupants. Wondering what was going on Victoria watched her husband walked over towards the door. Opening the door the Muse security guard stood waiting on the other side. Instinct told Henry something was wrong.

"I don't mean to disturb you sir, but there is a problem." Henry waved the security guard into the room. The door shut with a soft thud behind the guard. Stepping in the Guard saluted his bosses. Slapping the hand down with impatience Henry glared with intensity expecting a report.

Walking over Victoria stood next to her husband waiting to hear what the problem was. Standing there in silence the security guard searched for the words to communicate the situation. Henry tapped his foot from growing impatience. Unable to muster the courage to inform the parents of their missing daughter the guard froze. Tension filled the air telling Henry something unthinkable had happened.

"Tell me what you have to report now soldier!" Henry demanded immediate answers.

"I am sorry to inform you but about ten minutes ago Muse security lost track of Julia. We've scoured the entire apartment and can't find a single trace of her anywhere." Without a thought Henry accessed the GPS system of his daughter. The system reported that the selected neural implant had been disengaged. Scouring through Camera feeds and internal hotel security revealed didn't reveal Julia's location. Henry could see the concerned look creeping across his wife's face. Scouring memories Victoria had a sudden epiphany.

"We left Julia with Mr. Sun before we came in here perhaps he will know where she went?" Set to purpose Henry marched out of the bedroom with his wife and security following. Standing in the same spot Zhuge watched the guests at the party enjoy themselves. Glancing through the congested party Henry could see that Mr. Sun hadn't moved from the original spot. Victoria followed behind her husband with the security guards. The group pushed their way through the crowd without thought of the guests. Noticing the return of Henry and his wife Zhuge waved at both of them.

"It is good to see you both return before midnight. What happened to your masks?" Zhuge failed to notice the worried expression on the William's face when they approached. Neither Henry nor Victoria answered the question. Guards stood on edge surrounding the couple.

"I understand now why the William's parties are legendary in the business world." Zhuge watched the young men and women dancing throughout the room. Lost in the moment guests gyrated on each other. Bodies rubbed against each other in rhythm to the music playing. Henry reached over and pulled Mr. Sun closer to hear his whisper.

"I have a delicate situation. It appears my daughter has slipped away and turned off her GPS. Do you have any idea where Julia could have gone to?" Concern filled Henry's eyes revealing his desperation. Guards moved through the crowd renewing their search.

Zhuge could see the desperation in Henry's eyes and scanned around the room. Growing presence of Muse Security forces around the Williams revealed the severity of the situation. Noticing the British SAS searching through the party told Zhuge that King George was also missing. SAS soldiers spotted Henry and began walking towards the group of people.

"Last time I seen of Julia she was dancing with the King. It would appear the SAS are also looking for the King's location at this moment." Zhuge pointed to the approaching SAS officers. Scanning the party Victoria noticed the absence of the King. The lead SAS officer forced his way through the guests. Sensing the growing tension in the air Henry addressed the approaching SAS officer.

"Is there a problem?" The SAS officer came to a halt before the group of people.

"It would appear that his royal Majesty King George managed to slip away unnoticed. After a careful sweep of the premises there is no trace of the King or your daughter Julia. Do either of you know where they went?" Looking into both eyes the officer could see the confusion on both parents face. Trying to discern how both King George and Julia slipped through the security left Henry puzzled.

"How could two people just disappear without any of the security noticing them?" Pondering the question the SAS officers fell silent. Accessing building security through the neural implants Henry scanned through reports. Security logs showed King George departure time only a few minutes ago. Following behind Henry the entourage of SAS, Muse security, and Victoria marched towards the door. Stopping at the door Henry looked at both guards.

"There is a security log showing King George left the party a few minutes ago. We can't find Julia anywhere and her neural implant has been shut off. Was the king accompanied by my daughter?" Henry glared with intensity demanding answers from the guards. Looking to each other both guards were shocked by the question.

"No sir King George was by himself when he left the party." The group of people at the door had begun to draw attention from the party guests. Henry accessed the neural implant of the two guards scouring through data discovering the virus. Evidence told Henry that George and Julia had chosen to leave the party unattended.

"We should continue to discuss this matter outside away from prying eyes and ears." Henry led the group out into the hallway. Only a few guests noticed the group leaving the apartment. Doors whisked shut sealing away the noise from the party. Glaring at Henry the commanding SAS officer demanded answers.

"What is going on here?"

"I believe King George and Julia used a virus to blind themselves to both SAS and Muse Security. My security forces were unable to see my daughter while SAS couldn't see the king. We need to figure out where Julia and the King would be going." A soft ding echoed in the corridor announcing the arriving elevator. Maj. Lee and Colt walked off the elevator noticing Henry and the group of security.

Looking around Robert wondered what was going on. Colt sauntered down the hallway towards Henry intent on learning what the commotion was about. Edward picked up pace followed by Colt and his boys. The Muse security neural network buzzed with activity. Every guard in the Plaza searched the building looking for Julia and George.

"Have you brought yourself up to speed on the situation Major?" Henry looked at his head of security. Glancing around Colt could only wonder what was going on waiting to be informed. Completing the anti-virus program Henry uploaded it to the Muse security net. Everyone stood in a circle around the CEO waiting for instruction.

"A few moments ago we believe King George and Julia used a virus to blind security to their movements. GPS in both individuals' neural implants have been shut off. We need to determine the best way to find the king and my daughter." Henry took command of the situation. Everyone looked to the Muse CEO for answers.

"Do you believe that King George is behind the virus?" The question from the commanding officer revealed the truth to Henry. Julia had no experience in neural network hacking. British SAS prepared the King for neural hacking by teaching him how to hack. Henry accessed the SAS security network and uploaded the anti-virus.

"I believe it was either Julia or George, but that is irrelevant information Colonel Traynor. The real problem is that the building camera feeds were also hacked. There is no footage of either Julia or George leaving the party, but video shows the door opening long enough to allow two people to exit." Henry uploaded the video footage from the Plaza Hotel Security system to the SAS. Examining the footage in detail Colonel Traynor watched for any clues.

Worry began to bubble up inside Robert turning his thoughts to the attack on the mall. Trauma from the attack left deep wounds in Julia. Some people never recover from trauma. Robert didn't want to imagine how he would feel if something happened to Julia. Sensing the worry Colt patted his boy on the back.

"Don't worry we'll find Julia boy. I know they didn't head down stairs because I don't use your fancy technology Henry. My eye sight is as sharp as a cougar at midnight." Pointing to the obsolete neural implant Colt proved he couldn't be hacked. The plaza hotel was a large area to search. Henry felt a growing sense of anxiety.

"That still leaves most of the Plaza hotel to search for Julia and George." Accessing the Plaza security system Maj. Lee searched for clues. Hundreds of hours of video feed from multiple cameras would take too long to search. Inside Maj. Lee's mind he created hundreds of panels of video feeds. Pictures rolled by in a blur of motion. Catching a stair well door slamming shut Maj. Lee grabbed everyone's attention.

"Sir I got a recording from only a few minutes ago. Video shows a stair well door opening and closing. Cameras don't show anyone either in the corridor or stairwell. Unless you believe in ghosts it has to be Julia and George." Maj. Lee uploaded the video to his allies. Studying the video footage Colonel Traynor patted Edward on his back.

"Well done old boy. I guess you yanks aren't as poor at soldering as your reputation suggests." Ignoring the insult Maj Lee continued to sift through information. Stairwell camera had been turned off lending more support to the theory. Colt's stepped forward commanding the entire groups' attention.

"I say we divide up into two forces. One group goes up while the other group goes down. How long can two kids outsmart these military trained boys and girls?" Henry wasn't shocked his former commanding officer favoured action over deliberation. Information revealed no definitive destination that George could be leading Julia towards. Henry couldn't discern any pattern of strategy behind the action. King George was supposed to entertain Julia and show her a good time not put her in danger. The situation seemed senseless to Henry.

"The information doesn't reveal a final destination. There has to be some piece of information somewhere that reveals where the King is taking my daughter. Colonel Traynor has the king ever done anything like this before? Colonel Traynor remained reluctant to speak. Hesitation told Henry his instinct had been right, and this had happened before.

"His royal Majesty has never hacked neural implants before, but the King is fond of his alone time." Glaring at the colonel Henry needed more information. Col. Traynor was still struggling to piece the puzzle together while overlooking a major piece. The best way to attack is to attack strategy. Perhaps the King's particular tastes would reveal a discernable pattern Henry thought.

"When the King takes these little sojourns is there any place he likes to go?" Colonel Traynor smiled finding a pattern.

"The king prefers to go somewhere high up such as the rooftop of the palace in London." Hearing the information Maj. Lee accessed the neural network to access the roof top security.

"Well hot damn about time we figured this out. Henry get security on the roof to hold the King and Julia there until we arrive." Slapping his leg Colt celebrated the impending success he believed was coming. Searching through the Muse Security net Maj. Lee discovered an official order from

Henry. Peeling open the data file Edward scanned the authenticity of the order to remove Muse troops from the roof.

"Sir did you order the rooftop security out of position?" Henry stood in shock at the question. Scans showed the authenticity had been forged to fool the Muse security network. No evidence remained showing the identity of the hacker. Henry arrived at the same conclusion.

"The source of hacking on the order to remove the roof security looks the same as the code of the virus. We need to get to that rooftop as soon as possible." Activating the neural communicator Victoria sent a thought to her husband.

"You go get Julia and I'll return to the party to contain the situation." Leaning in Henry kissed his wife. Victoria watched her husband, Colt, and the Cross boys walk away before returning to the party. Guests continued to dance oblivious to the commotion in the hallway. There was nothing Victoria could do but pray for her daughter's safety.

Henry looked at Colt "You take the SAS with you to the lobby. Maj. Lee and my men will take the elevator to the roof. I will take a few men up the stairs to the rooftop." Watching the discussion Robert looked with concern. Emotion tugged at the young man demanding he go find Julia himself. Stepping over Robert stood next to Henry.

"Do you mind if I join you Mr. Williams?" Looking for approval Robert worried that his father would stop him. Startled by the request Colt glanced at his youngest son with curiosity. How much could Julia mean to the boy Colt wondered. Henry could see the worry on the boy's face.

"I don't have a problem with that if your father doesn't mind of course." Henry looked to his friend for his approval. Colt could see the strength of conviction burning in his sons' eyes. Standing confident behind the decision Robert refused to budge. Nodding in agreement Colt looked at Henry.

"I tell you girls make young men act crazy. You take care of my youngest boy Henry. We'll be right behind you." Colt and the SAS waited for their elevator to arrive. Simultaneous dings preceded both elevator doors opening. Holding Maj. Lee back Henry communicated over the neural com channel.

"Keep your eyes and ears open Edward. I have a feeling there is something more going on here. Proceed with caution and keep communication channels linked to me at all times." Troops stepped onto the elevator with Maj. Lee who looked back at his boss. Henry put his hand on Robert shoulder trying to reassure everyone including himself.

The elevator door closed sealed the occupants inside Anxiety filled the small chamber of the elevator. Everyone felt the gravity of the precarious situation pulling on their muscles. Henry accessed the hotel security giving control to himself and Maj. Lee. Marching towards the stairwell Henry led Robert and a few guards. Henry couldn't still the worried thoughts berating his mind.

CHAPTER 29

Stolen Moments

Julia followed behind George climbing the staircase towards the roof. Footsteps were the only noise in the empty stairwell. Walking ahead George thought on the memories he downloaded. Soldiers were trained to sacrifice themselves for an ideal. Julia's memories carried with them the pure sense of family devotion. Memories triggered George's own memories on sacrifice, duty, and love.

Looking through the memories a pattern appeared to the king. Memories from Julia coalesced around George's memories of the death of his parents. The tragic death of William and Kate shocked the world. People loved the elegant and generous King and Queen of England. George would do anything if he could bring back his parents. In that moment George realized Julia was perhaps the only person in the world who could understand his pain.

"Come on were almost at the roof" George urged his companion.

"Hey wait up for me!" Picking up the pace Julia raced up the steps. Looking at the watch George saw there was only fifteen minutes until midnight. Rapid footsteps from Julia echoed down the stairwell. Glancing backwards George noticed his companion falling behind.

"We don't have that much time. It's quarter to midnight already. We got to be back to the party before anyone notices. You can run faster than that can't you?" Spurred on by George's challenge Julia raced after him.

Loud footsteps from both people echoed off the close walls of the stairwell. Anyone coming up the stairs would be able to hear the two people from ten floors down. Lost in the moment both people raced towards the roof. Soccer and track gave Julia speed and endurance allowing her to pass the king. George watched the young woman sprinted past him on the stairs.

"Hey you told me to slow down. That's cheating!" Glancing back Julia shot a sly smile back at the king. Rounding the steps George chased behind unable to catch up. Surrendering complete control Julia gave into the flow of the moment.

Enthusiasm drove each footstep propelling the young woman towards the rooftop door. A loud bang echoed from the door bursting open. Cold night air mixed with falling snow hit Julia in the face. Warm breath created vapour lingering in the air. Bright lights of New York City assailed the senses. Breathing in deep Julia felt absolute freedom in this one moment. Julia's pupils dilated drinking in the vast cityscape across the horizon. Slamming into the shutting door George announced his arrival with a loud bang.

"It is a beautiful sight to behold isn't it?" Julia didn't hear the question lost in the world in front of her. Free from the constraint of pictures, car windows, or security guards the world took on a magical splendour to the young woman. Hover cars swept by at high sweeps with a loud whoosh. Walking up behind George looked over Julia shoulder.

"Now you see why I love looking out at cities from a good vantage point. From up here anyone can see there are no boundaries except for the ones we create for ourselves." Hearing George's soft voice brought Julia out of her trance. The entire world seemed to race around both people standing on the roof. Glancing back at the king Julia smiled with a thought.

"The whole wide world is full of endless possibilities." Stepping in George wrapped his arms around the young woman's waist. Julia felt the king's tight embrace from behind. Both people lost all sense of time for a moment. Everything felt perfect to Julia in this moment. George leaned over the woman's shoulder speaking direct into her ear.

"I wanted to show you my favourite place because I think you feel the same loneliness I do. The sad reality is for us our destiny is already chosen by what family we were born into. There are no possibilities for us only duty and responsibility." Neither person spoke. Howling wind blew snow casting a white haze across the horizon.

"So did you bring me all the way up here to show me the tragic reality of our lives?" Julia realized the feelings she felt were a tragic illusion. The world existed just beyond the horizon out of grasp for either person. Turning around Julia pushed George away slipping out of his grasp. George stumbled to find the right words.

"I just wanted to share this with you. I thought you might want to get away for a moment." Lowering the mask to the side Julia smiled at the young king. Confusion forced George to figure out what had changed in the last few moments. Julia felt confident she knew why the king brought her to the rooftop.

"I am sure that's why you hugged me with such a firm grip just now. Perhaps you are right and we do have a lot in common, but I disagree. I don't think either of us has much in common at all." Taking a step back Julia created space. Sensing the challenge behind the words George responded with a coy grin.

"What leads you to think that we don't share much in common?" Looking back out Julia pointed to the city. Life buzzed through the air of the city. Mixed in with the howling wind were sounds of music and celebration. Protestors bellowed below filling the night air with energy.

"You think this view is tragic. From your point of view that's understandable. You're right that our birthrights do limit our freedoms, but you're wrong when you think we are not free. We just have a different range of opportunities. What I see when I look out is opportunity and choice." George stepped next to Julia leaning against the rail to look out at the cityscape.

New York bustled with activity. Taxis rushed people to their New Year's Eve destination for midnight. People dubbed New York City the city that never sleeps. Some legends live up to the stories. Reality pushed home to George that while most people didn't have security guards it was because they weren't needed.

"I guess whether it's a name, money, or fame people get attacked regardless. Perhaps our lives are blessings instead of curses." Snow blew past both people standing on the roof. Cold air caused Julia to shiver from wind chilling her to the bone. Slipping off the jacket King George placed it on his companion. Julia pulled the jacket tight around herself trying to warm up.

"Thank you for bringing me up here George. This is by far the best New Year's Eve I have ever had." George stood next to his beautiful companion marvelling at her. Julia was unlike any woman the King had ever met. George leaned in face to face with Julia.

"To tell the truth I just wanted a moment alone with you." Wind almost prevented Julia's soft giggle from being heard. Aware of the plan all along Julia waited for George to make his move. The chill of winter urged the two people to stand close to each other. Julia looked into George's big brown eyes.

"Are you always this indirect with women your majesty? I had heard you had a reputation of being quite the ladies' man. If this is your attempt to woo me you're going to need to try harder." Maintaining calm Julia played hard to get enjoying the attention she was receiving. George decided to play along.

"Who says I am trying to woo you Julia?" Standing stoic against the elements George tried to maintain a poker face. Julia couldn't help but smirk watching the king try not to give away his motives. The soft snicker caused George to look at the young woman. The king's face was frozen in grim determination to outlast the provocative stare from Julia.

"You do look kind of cute standing there with that look on your face. You do realize the neural synchronization linked your memories with mine. I knew your whole seduction scheme before we got up here." Julia managed to contain laughter while revealing the truth. Forgetting about the neural link George dropped the charade.

"So then why did you come up here?" The look of bewilderment on George's face looked adorable to Julia. Wind whipped snow between the two people. George searched his companions' eyes searching for any hint of desire. Leaning forward Julia stared into the Kings eyes without flinching.

"Perhaps I just wanted to get away from that party. I just wanted to see how you would sneak us out. You do manage to surprise your majesty." Sensing an opportunity King George leaned into kiss Julia. Before the kiss could meet the young woman's lips she broke free of the King's hold.

"You sure are full of yourself George." Standing only a few feet away Julia lingered in front of the king. George couldn't believe the audacity. Most women fawned for the young king's affections. Caught in the thrill of the hunt George moved forward with a single step.

"I noticed you haven't left to return to the party yet. Are you saying you're not interested in me?" George moved forward with slow and precise steps. Julia didn't break eye contact. Standing right in front of the young woman George paused. Looking up Julia decided to tell her companion her reasons for following him.

"I just want to get to know who you really are George. I don't think you really show yourself to anyone. My mother warned me to beware of a man who seeks you but hides himself from you. I was amazed you sought to hold back certain memories from me during the synchronization." George stood in front of Julia looking at her bright emerald eyes.

"Sounds like wise advice if you ask me. I wasn't trying to hide anything other than the memories surrounding my parents' death. I didn't know if you would want them. I only sought to keep you safe from the pain and suffering of my past. I didn't want you to look at me with pity." Leaning forward King George moved to kiss Julia again. Eyes locked and only a small distance left between lips neither person could break away. Sudden revelation dawned on Julia realizing none of the rooftop guards investigated the noise. George felt the young woman pull away.

"I am sorry if that was too forward." Offering an apology George noticed his companion scanning the roof. Falling snow limited sight across the roof. Unable to discern the problem George felt confused by the situation. Julia turned and whispered to the king.

"My father would have placed security guards on the rooftop. I don't see anyone and no one investigated the noise we've been making." Glancing around George noticed there were no security guards in sight on the rooftop. Activating the neural implant Julia scanned the rooftop finding no active Muse neural implants. George looked back at the door.

"Perhaps it's time to get back to the party." Julia felt the sudden ominous feeling buzz throughout her body.

"Yea I think your right we should return to the party. Beside it's getting really cold outside." Trying to shake off the bad feeling Julia couldn't figure out what was wrong. The door was only a few feet away. George pulled against the wind struggling to open the heavy door.

Creaking open the King used his body to hold the door. A blaring alarm went off inside Julia's mind causing her to freeze in place. A pounding migraine bore down on the young woman. Pain clouded Julia's mind sensing the alarm of her neural implant. Some outside force had begun to breach the barrier maze protecting Julia's neural implant.

George noticed Julia's eyes widen in horror trying to speak but not making a sound. The young woman appeared frozen in time. Grabbing Julia's arms George couldn't move her at all. Some force seemed to hold the woman in place. Trapped in an invisible cage Julia struggled against the consciousness invading her mind.

"What's going on?" George struggled to understand what was happening. Julia didn't panic instead focusing on her hacking knowledge. Pain shot through every nerve in the woman's body. Using the knowledge Julia managed to regain control over her speech.

"I can't move at all please help me. George my neural implant is being hacked!" Pulling out the neural connector cable George moved to insert it into Julia's implant. Neural synchronization would allow the intruder to access Georges' mind. Julia's pupils dilated with horror.

"No if you do that it will give them access to your neural implant. Don't turn your neural implant on or they might hack you as well. Whoever is hacking my implant is far more skilled than you George. We need to get out of here right now!" Looking around in a frantic state George couldn't see anyone.

"I don't' see anything." Julia felt the slow encroach of the invading mind taking over her body. Time raced against the young woman. Struggling back Julia knew she couldn't halt the attack for long. George seemed frozen from uncertainty.

"This is not a joke! Whoever is hacking me is coming right now George. You need to get me out of here right now." Throwing Julia over one shoulder George turned back towards the door. George could see the worry in his companions' eyes.

"I'll get you back to your dad. I promise you'll be fine." George reached out to open the door to the stairwell trying to maintain balance. A loud bang echoed from the distance across the rooftop. Howling wind prevented George from hearing it. Julia heard the noise loud and clear.

"What was that?" Pushing the door all the way open George stopped in the door way.

"What was what?" Julia scanned what little she could see unable to spot anything.

"I heard a loud bang a moment ago." Looking into the snow falling George couldn't see anything either.

"I don't see anything at all. I think you're just hearing things. We need to get going." Sudden glimmering in the distance on the rooftop caught both people's attention. Julia spot the glimmer again when the snow picked up pace.

"Do you see that glimmer out there? What is that?" George felt his stomach sink. Several glimmers appeared to be moving closer. Military training taught George what thermal optical cloaking looked like. Thermal optical cloaking suffered from problems when near water or in severe weather.

"We need to get you out of here." George stopped hearing a loud click nearby. Only a few feet away the distinctive sound of a gun being cocked caught both people's attention. Standing in the door way George glanced around unable to see anyone. Julia's eyes darted around searching for the source of the noise.

A sudden glimmer sparked only a few feet away from the door. Catching the motion Julia's realized the gravity of the situation. Soft footprints echoed in between howls of the wind. The invisible assailant left footprints in the snow. Frozen in place Julia stared out from the limbo of her own mind watching the events unfolding around her. Panic seized Georges' mind.

"I am sorry but the young lady is coming with me." Aiming a fifty calibre pistol at Georges' head the Assailant spoke with a digitized voice. Releasing Julia's muscle controls caused her to topple off the king's shoulder. Caught by the invisible force the young woman landed on her feet. A figure materialized through the snow dressed in dark blue wearing black combat armour.

CHAPTER 30

Minutes to madness

Flashing lights from sirens pulsed against the plaza hotel walls. Police cars formed a barricade. In front of the cars officers formed a wall holding riot shields. Pushing against the barricade of bodies the protestors slung their insults. Waving signs stating the inequality of law, corporate crime, and poverty emphasized the anger of the crowd. Standing back from the barricade line two officers looked out at the throng of protestors through the steady snowfall.

"Wow Joe What a wonderful way to spend New Year's Eve." Holding a pocket watch Joe saw that it was ten minutes until midnight. Both officers held the steaming cup of coffee in hand trying to stay warm. Howling wind blew snow between the cars. Both officers wondered why sane people would stand in this weather to scream insults.

"Certain duties Comes with the uniform Adam. Besides we got hot coffee, cigarettes, and good company." Both officers stood watching the protest raging around them. Shouting louder with each second the crowd pushed harder on the barricade. Adam noticed his fellow officers struggling to hold the line.

"Perhaps we should call for back up?" Scanning the barricade several areas of line of officers looked ready to collapse. Adam pointed out to several groups of protestors beating on officers pulled into the swarm. Loud chants drowned out the officers screams. Protestors swarmed the riot officers slamming against the shields.

"I'll call headquarters for reinforcements. You get whatever men you can to help hold the line." Walking over to the nearby communication unit Adam picked up the receiver. The communication unit reported there was no signal available. Turning back Adam noticed several people acting unusual in the crowd. Protestors began to twitch and spasm becoming enraged.

"Look over there at that protestor Joe. I think someone is neural hacking the protestors to make them attack." Protestors broke through the line tackling an officer before Joe could look. Protestors climbed on top of police cars. Screams of rage filled the city street from the throng of people charging the barricade.

Leaping from the vehicles protesters tackled police officers. Joe watched protestors swarm around his fellow officers. Resembling a pack of wolves the people drove the officers to the ground using numbers. Protestors kicked and stomped on fallen officers with murderous intent. Officers began beating down oncoming protestors with batons trying to fall back.

Surging forward with zealous rage protestors picked off isolated officers. Pure chaos overtook the streets. Gunshots rang out over loud screams. Fear washed through the officers causing them to open fire on the crowd. Joe raced back towards Adam and the communication post. The communication device couldn't get a signal. Joe grabbed Adam's shoulder spinning him around.

"We need reinforcements now!" Turning back to the machine Adam tried to re-establish communications. Diagnostic checks showed the equipment worked. Growing more frustrated by the second Adam couldn't get a signal. Weather didn't account for the inability to get a clear signal.

"There has got to be some kind of jamming signal blocking communications. I can't get a direct line to headquarters from my neural implant or building lines." Overrunning the police barricade the crowd of protestors surged towards the Plaza hotel. Officers retreated towards the hotel main doors. Joe tugged on his friends shoulder seeing the crowd getting closer.

"Come on man we have got to go!" Falling back the officers fired off gas canisters into the crowd trying to slow the horde. Tear gas wafted through the snow filled night sky. Adam and Joe raced towards the front doors of the hotel. Protesters raced behind the two officers trying to catch up to them. The front doors of the Plaza hotel burst open. Cpt. Anderson led his security team to rescue the police officers.

"Everyone make sure you got non-lethal ammunition loaded. Provide suppressing fire to support our withdrawal." Muse soldiers responded to the command with bursts of gunfire. Muse troops tried to suppress the onslaught of people racing towards their position. Cpt. Anderson motioned for officers to get inside the hotel.

"Get these people inside the hotel now. Keep firing men." Rubber rounds struck hard slowing down the protestors rushing forward. Capt. Anderson noticed a round break one of the protestor's ribs failing to stop the man. Protestors close the gap between them and the officers. Adam and Joe worried they wouldn't make it.

Muse troops pushed out from the entrance creating a wedge for the two officers to make it through. Rapid bursts of gunfire continued to fail to stop the surge of people. Racing through the doors Joe and Adam fell to the ground trying to catch their breath. Protestors almost reached the Muse security team when they began to fall back into the building. Cpt. Anderson pulled the doors shut behind with the help of of his soldiers. A loud clunk echoed in the room from the security system locking the doors. One of the police officers marched towards Cpt. Anderson.

"What the hell took you guys so long?" Staring the officer down Cpt. Anderson could understand the anger.

"We came when we heard the gunfire. You need to calm down right now and think. Muse security communications went down because someone activated a jamming field. During that time of distraction the protestors launched their attack. Have anyone of you considered that this was planned?" Authority of command filled Cpt. Andersons' voice. Real questions halted the officer. Adam just caught his breath when the argument broke out.

"Police communications were severed just before the attack." Slamming against the door the protestors smashed against the glass. The force of pressure caused the glass doors to shake. Cpt. Anderson looked at the expression on the protestor's faces. Rage twisted the faces of the people at the doors, but each person's eyes appeared distant. Turning back to the officer's Cpt. Anderson pointed towards the crowd.

"Look at the people's eyes. There is no purpose behind this action to any of those people. Anger and rage is the only thing driving those protestors to attack." Loud thuds echoed through the lobby. Blood smeared the glass from people breaking bones without noticing. Staring in disbelief Joe watched the mindless mass beyond the doors.

"Are you saying those people have been neural hacked?" Glass doors shook again from the throng of people slamming against it. Sound proof glass protected against the mindless screams filling the streets. Protesters sieged the building from all exits. Power cut to the building causing emergency lighting to kick on.

Panic stricken officers looked around wondering what had happened. Anderson knew whoever planned this attack ensured there was no way to escape. Generators would still power the buildings security system for some time. During power loss the security system would seal every exit but designated emergency exits. Pulling Joe and Adam to their feet Cpt. Anderson motioned the officers to follow.

"Available evidence does fit the theory. With the communication block there is no way to dive into one of the protestors mind to be certain. This feels planned to me." Walking up the steps the police officers looked around the main hotel lobby entrance. The entire lobby had been fortified to repel any attack. Joe wished the police barricade had been so well constructed.

"You Muse guys don't mess around do you?" Reinforce steel barricades had been assembled to provide covered positions to fire from. Reinforcing the reception with steel barriers it was now the central command post. Muse troops stood in position throughout the room. Cpt. Anderson stood before his troops to address them.

"You all know the gravity of the situation. Communication is severed between command and us. We have to assume this assault is part of a coordinated attack. I believe the protestors have been neural hacked and cannot be stopped by non-lethal measures. I am hereby ordering the use of lethal ordinance. Our family is depending on us, and so we will hold this position until the last person falls." Clamouring arose among the police officers hearing the order to use lethal force. Rank put Joe in command forcing him to step forward.

"Those are innocent people you can't open fire on them!" Slapping the clip into place with a click Cpt. Anderson looked at the officer's insignia.

"Sergeant I think you need to accept the realities of the situation. Outside there is a mindless horde bent on destruction. Several of your officers are already dead, and it is my duty to ensure that no more people die tonight. You can take up the legal ramifications after I save your life." Unable to accept the truth Joe grabbed Cpt. Anderson by the shoulder stopping him.

"You just gave the order to kill innocent civilians." Adam and the other officers added their support yelling their opinions. The loud clamour drowned out the constant thumping and banging from the door. Muse troops stood watching their commander for an order. Cpt. Anderson looked at Joe with grim resolve.

"I gave no order to kill innocent civilians. I gave the order to use lethal force. The law grants anyone the right to use reasonable force to prevent the loss of life. My troops will try to do as little damage to the people as possible, but my men won't die in vain. We have people to protect."

Without a word Muse troops moved out of formation. Troops placed non-lethal antipersonnel mines on the steps facing towards the door. Security systems were activated humming to life in the lobby entrance. Fire team leaders laid out coordinated fall back plans. Joe watched the troops' activities following behind Cpt. Anderson.

"So what is your exact plan?" Stopping again Cpt. Anderson pointed to the walls.

"First we'll rely on the non-lethal threat deterrence system. Each wall has one hundred darts connected to a powerful electrical generator. If the shock doesn't stop the protestors each step will detonate proximity mines. Each mine launches thousands of rubber balls towards the door. I intend to bottleneck them in this entrance area." Joe admired Cpt. Anderson's resolve at making every attempt to not cause permanent damage.

"What happens if your right and the protestors make it past the steps?" Moving forward Cpt. Anderson pointed to the various positions of cover.

"This will be the neutralization area. When the protestors reach the neutral zone my people will try to incapacitate the people. I'm hoping we can keep the protestors from breaching the neutralization zone to limit civilian casualties." Between the end of the neutralization zone and the first barriers was a wide open space. Joe glanced around the wide open area leading to the rest of the hotel.

"What happens if the protestors make it through the neutralization zone?" Cpt. Anderson's grim expression should have been answer enough.

"Ever read the Sun Tzu? This is called death ground. If the protestors reach the death grounds we do battle until the last person falls. This is where we hold the line." Shaking under the force of the protestors the front doors rattled against the door frame. Thumps escalated to crashes and slams.

Rage drove the protestors against the door with all their might. Police officers followed behind Joe looking for his guidance. Muse troops continued with preparations trying to ignore the loud noise of the impending threat. Everyone moved towards the purpose of preparing a defense. Cpt. Anderson led the group of officers to the command center at the reception.

"Have your men hold this position. Give Sgt. Malarkey a hand restoring communications perhaps so we can get some reinforcements." Police officers took up their positions behind the reception fortifications. Ammunition crates and guns rested against the wall waiting to be needed. Joe looked over at Adam.

"Go lend a hand getting communications working." Adam raced over towards Sgt. Malarkey working on the communication signal booster. Muse soldiers took up positions behind the barriers. Adam and Sgt. Malarkey worked together trying to boost signal strength. Looking down at the wristwatch Cpt. Anderson saw it was only a few minutes until midnight.

"Alright men take your positions. We've prepared the best we can so now we wait." Looking back towards the door Anderson gripped his gun with anticipation. Feeling sweat dripping down Joe wiped his forehead. Each slam against the glass caused the pane to shake.

Bending under the pressure glass creaked under the strain. Each sound sent chills through the police officers heightening the tension in the room. Muse soldiers aimed down guns with unflinching resolve. Each thud brought the dreaded future closer. Joe could see his fellow officers were shaky and unsure.

"Stay calm and focused. Everything will work out." The remaining police officers steadied their nerves by banding together. Marching through Muse troops Cpt. Anderson hopped from behind the reception counter. Soldiers watched their commander march with determination past the barriers. Standing alone out of cover Cpt. Anderson became a steadying symbol of resolve to his troops.

Joe felt terror pulling at his muscles threatening to destroy his calm facade. Staring ahead Muse soldiers stood defiant against the coming storm. Glass continued to shake from the terrible rhythm of pounding fists. Forged in fire and battle these men and women held no fear of death. Cpt. Anderson stared at the doors watching the glass buckling under the protestors force.

Cracks raced across the glass from each thud against the door. Glass shards shot from the door clattering across the white marble floor. Pulling up the rifle Cpt. Anderson kneeled low to the ground aiming down the sight. In unison Muse soldiers cocked their guns in preparation. Joe observed how the soldiers waited with absolute patience. Speaking over the sounds of the hoard Cpt. Anderson's voice resonated throughout the lobby.

"Our duty is to hold this ground and protect the lives of the people in this building. We have sworn to give our lives in defense of others. Remember your purpose. Stay focused on the task at hand. Do not surrender in the face of fear. Stand firm to your duties and hold resolute to your purpose. We will not fall here. WE WILL NOT FAIL!"

Thunderous roaring drew every man and woman into the terrible howl of defiance. Joe watched his fellow officers drawn in by the power of the primal act. Being a police officer meant to put yourself in the line of danger to protect others. Never before had Joe felt such focus in purpose than in this moment. Hundreds of lives of guests attending the party hung in the balance of the next few moments.

Every single person in the lobby felt clear purpose in resisting the murderous horde. Glass shattered inward spraying razor sharp shards across the floor. Doors buckled under the force of the protestor's anger. Metal creaked from the door frame twisting under the force. Shards of sparkling glass littered the floor.

Protestors smashed into the doors filling the air with their furious screams. Men and women tried to push their bodies through the holes in the glass. Jagged glass cut into people causing blood to splatter across the floor. Protestors were unconcerned by the numerous cuts causing rapid blood loss, and continued to slam against the door. Nothing seemed to slow the protestors advanced.

One of the police officers couldn't stop from vomiting at the scene. A fellow officer helped his friend regain composure pulling him back to his feet. Muse troops stood statuesque waiting for the right moment. Joe looked over towards his friend. Too busy trying to fix communication Adam couldn't see the situation. Focused on helping Sgt. Malarkey kept Adam oblivious to the horrors beyond the desk.

"Better you don't see this." Joe felt a measure of peace from the thought allowing him to turn back to the doors. Blood began to pool up on the smooth marble floor inside the door. Cpt. Anderson looked down at his wrist watch. The watch hands showed it was one minute to midnight. One final smash echoed causing the door frame to snap. Glass doors blew inward skipping shards across the ground.

CHAPTER 31

Lethal Force

Protestors charged forward past the glass doors. Several people slipped on the blood crashing into the glass on the floor. The people who fell were trampled into the glass by the flood of protestors. Pushing forward the unorganized horde of people poured into the entrance. Swelling numbers slowed the protestors wading towards the entrance steps.

Clawing over top of each other the horde of people remained oblivious to the mines. Rage propelled each person in the swelling mass of bodies. Internal security sensed the threat activating the suppression system. Hundreds of darts shot from the walls striking different people. Electricity coursed through the wires to each dart zapping the target.

Muscles spasms caused people to collapse to the ground. More protestors charged through the door. Mindless rage drove the people forward trampling over everything in their path. Surging towards the stairs the horde tripped the first anti-personnel mine. Thousands of rubber balls exploded forward. The force of the explosion and impact from the balls threw the first line of protestors backwards.

Rubber balls careened through the lobby shattering vases and smashing into the walls. Protestors flew backwards crashing down onto the people still flowing into the lobby. The mass of people shifted back and forth trying to move against the sudden pressure. After a few seconds of disorientation the horde surged forward again towards the stairs. Charging up the stairs protestors triggered the second mine.

The force of the explosion launched bodies backwards into the air. The second explosion did not have the same effect as the first. Protestors regrouped racing back up the stair way unable to feel pain or broken bones. Some of the people dragged broken legs still hobbling forward. Holes splattered the walls of the plaza lobby. Cracks splintered across the marble floor.

Another explosion rippled through the air from the final mine. Bodies littered the floor of the hotel lobby slowing protestors. Stumbling and crawling over bodies caused less people to be caught in the final blast. White marble floor now shined from the lustre coat of crimson red. Protestors still poured through the door in large numbers.

The main brunt of the attack had been stopped for a moment. Cpt. Anderson watched the horde of people swell building momentum by the second. Nothing remained to impede the onslaught of protestors funnelling into the lobby. Watching down the sight of the pistol Joe could feel his heart beating faster. Coming up the stairs the horde broke into the lobby spreading out.

Muse security opened fire taking single accurate shots. Protestors dropped to the ground from bullets tearing through their legs and knees. One after another people fell to the ground in rapid succession. Each body slowed the rushing horde behind them. Staring down the shaking gun Joe tried to calm his nerves to take a shot.

Bodies accumulated at the top of the stairs creating an unholy damn against the horde. Taking the first shot Joe struck a man in the hip dropping him. With each subsequent squeeze of the trigger another body fell. Joe felt his worry and anxiety slip away with each shot fired at the legion of people before him. Following their commander the other officers opened fire.

Combining fire the officers helped Muse soldier hold the horde in place. Protestors continued to charge forward unable to break through the top of the stairs. Gunfire echoed throughout the hotel. Cpt. Anderson pulled the pin from a concussion grenade lobbing it into the entrance. Concussive force exploded from the grenade knocking people over. Noticing the flow of people breaching the top of the stairs slow Cpt. Anderson analyzed the situation.

None of the people had managed to break through the neutralization zone. Protestors pushed bodies out of the way or trampled over them.

People climbed over the bodies of the fallen trying to rush forward to attack. Muse security and the police force managed to contain the situation so far. Cpt. Anderson threw another concussion grenade scanning the legion outside of the hotel. Several hundred people lay either wounded or dead on the floor, but the vast majority of protestors were still fighting to get inside.

Climbing over the dam of bodies' protestors managed to move further into the lobby. Muse soldiers continued to snipe the person in front of the mass of people. Pouring into the building protestors continued to build up numbers inside the lobby. Those people unable to walk attempted to crawl forward. Swelling numbers of protestors increased the pressure on the defenders. Cpt. Anderson continued to fire looking back at Sgt. Malarkey.

"What's the status on the communications?" Sgt. Malarkey and Adam worked away at the communication signal booster.

"We're trying to get more power right now. It should be up in a minute or so." Adam almost completed a series of batteries salvaged from nearby machines to boost the signal. Placing careful shots Cpt. Anderson surveyed the situation.

"I don't know what fight you're paying attention to Malarkey, but I am not sure we have a minute. Get those damn communications up and working now!"

Another grenade lobbed overhead exploding when it struck the floor by the doors. Force from the blast rushed through the lobby. Protestors still poured forward over the bodies piling up. Firing the assault rifle Cpt. Anderson examined the situation. Shells chimed striking the floor in steady succession.

From the bodies in sight Cpt. Anderson estimated about five hundred people had been stopped. Police reports put the protest at about two thousand people. Cpt. Anderson felt the precarious nature of the untenable position. Protestors surged again towards the top of the stairs. People flooded into the lobby charging towards the barricades.

Continual gunshots only slowed the growing mass of people. Hundreds of people charged into the entrance of the plaza hotel. Keeping count of remaining ammunition Cpt. Anderson knew that the team couldn't last through the firefight. Only one last concussion grenade hung on the captain's belt. Anderson looked at his troops fighting for their lives.

"We are running out of time up here Sgt. Malarkey!"

Dropping the clip from the assault rifle Cpt. Anderson pulled the pin lobbing the last grenade. Force from the explosion would create one final opportunity to regain control for a few moments. Slapping a new clip in Cpt. Anderson opened fire. Pouring into the lobby the horde of protestors seemed endless. A small gap created by the explosion stopped the current wave of people, but the the next wave rushed onward. Screams of rage roared over the cadence of gunfire.

Connecting the series of batteries to the communication booster Adam worked at a feverish pace. The communication device hummed with the addition power. Sgt Malarkey activated the machine trying to overpower the interference. Muse soldiers felt the sudden activation of their combat neural feeds. Neural implants allowed combat teams to know the targets their teammates selected to optimize teamwork. The sudden boost in combat effectiveness allowed the defenders to regain control.

"Sir I have established communications in this area, but I am still struggling to break through interference." Sgt. Malarkeys report came across clear to Cpt. Anderson. Steady gun shots dropped simultaneous targets slowing the protestors advance. Cpt. Anderson began using his neural implant to coordinate fire. Holding firm the Muse forces pushed back the onslaught. Cpt. Anderson confidence flooded across the neural network to his troops.

"Good work Sgt. Malarkey. We need reinforcements so keep working on that interference." Battling to contain the swelling tide of protestors turned into a tug of war. Each time one assault stopped another assaulted broke through. Joe watched the steady stream of protestors pushing closer towards the barricades.

Police officers continued firing into the protestors feeling tensions mounting every second. Wave after wave of people pushed towards the front line held by Muse soldiers. Joe knew it wouldn't be long before the protestors would break through. Everyone could sense the momentum shifting. Protestors gained ground surging forward with renewed effort.

Cpt. Anderson watched the people push into the death ground. Muse security continued to incapacitate people waiting for a new command. Protestors closed in on the barricades. Unable to hesitate any longer Cpt. Anderson looked back at the police officers. Terror filled the eyes of every single officer. Horror gripped Joe when he heard Cpt. Anderson give the signal with a shout.

"Unleash everything you got!" The steady tempo of gunshots increased filling the room with full automatic gunfire. Bullets slammed through the walls and floor flying through the air in every direction. Joe couldn't speak or fire watching the protestors fall under the hail of gunfire. A torrential rain of bullets tore through the protestors splattering blood across the floors, walls, and ceiling.

Brutal force pushed the horde backwards. People twitched and convulsed on the ground riddled with bullets. Joe could only describe what he was seeing as a bloodbath. The rage and fury of the neural hacked protestors countered with pure butchery of professional soldiers. Clips hit the floor creating small lulls in the constant gunfire. Joe couldn't blink or look away from what he was seeing. Horror held the man's eyes fixed on the events transpiring only a few feet away.

Despite constant gunfire the protestors pushed forward without choice. Each person who fell would be replaced by another filling the gap. Protestors had almost reached the barrier wading through gunfire and explosions. Compelled by some unimaginable force Joe became fascinated with the people. Protestor's eyes were red from the tear gas and cut from glass unable to feel a thing. Only when a protestor reached to grab one of the security personnel did Joe break free and open fire. Glancing around Cpt. Anderson could see the turning situation.

"Provide covering fire for the primary positions to fall back." Precise movement and coordinated gunfire allowed the forward muse troops to fall back to their secondary positions. Cpt. Anderson walked backwards firing into the approaching protestors. Joe admired the captain who refused to leave a man behind. Muse soldiers swung their gun fire to keep the protestors away from their commanding officer.

Protestors swarmed through the lobby trying to attack the various positions held by the soldiers. The disorganization in attack allowed Cpt. Anderson to fall back towards the command center. Muse soldiers were able to regain control for a moment. Swelling in the entrance Protestors prepared for another assault. Cpt. Anderson dove behind the cover of the command center looking up at Sgt. Malarkey.

"We need those communications now! We are being overrun." Sgt. Malarkey and Adam almost had solved the power problem. Connecting the building power into the communication signal booster remained the only option. Malarkey knew the surge in power could fry the circuits in the communication equipment. Sgt. Malarkey looked at her commanding officer.

"Either this works or we're going to blow this machine to hell." Adam doubled check the connections giving the signal to activate the power flow. Power rushed to the signal booster. Humming of electricity overtook the sound of gunfire. Sgt. Malarkey accessed the machine and tried to cut through the interference.

"I need a few more seconds. If you believe in god pray this machine doesn't explode first." Protestors managed to cross halfway through the final line of defense. Tension filled the faces of everyone fighting for their lives. Cpt. Anderson knew his troops must be running out of ammunition fast.

"Keep firing we have to hold them here." The vast horde of protestors marched over the bodies of their fallen driven to kill everyone in sight. Rage distorted the faces of the once innocent people. Neural hacking filled the people with inhuman emotions distorting their faces. Sgt. Malarkey spoke over the neural network.

"I got some of the systems working right now. Mr. Williams appears to be heading towards the rooftop. We're just waiting to sync communication channels right now." Time seemed to freeze. Surging forward the relentless horde slammed against the grim determination of the soldiers.

Troops struggled to hold back the wave of enraged protestor's. Bullet casing littered the ground. Caught in the chaos of battle the police and muse soldiers succumbed to the struggle for life against death. Muse soldiers focused their burst of gunfire trying to conserve ammunition. Constant fire from the police officer showed their level of fear. The consequences faded into the minds of each person who decided they wanted to survive.

Continuous fire could only hold the protestors at bay for a few minutes. There was nothing left to do but wait for the signal booster to allow communication channels to connect. Sgt. Malarkey moved forward to the firing line to assist. Protestors filled the plaza lobby. Adam raced over to Joe and set up beside him opening fire.

"You thought this was going to be a boring night. Hell of a way to spend New Year's Eve." Cpt. Anderson activated the team neural network to communicate.

"Fire at will and use everything at your disposal." Muse security followed orders coordinating grenade throws. Successive concussive blast disoriented the protestors for another moment. Humming to life the signal booster broke through the interference. Communication channels opened up. Opening a communication channel Cpt. Anderson reported the situation.

"This is Muse security in the lobby of the plaza hotel. We are under attack by protestors and can't hold out much longer. This is Cpt. Max Anderson of Muse security requesting assistance from anyone who hears this."

CHAPTER 32

Fallen From Grace

Opening the heavy metal door Henry led his team into the stairwell. Robert followed behind wondered why Julia would have gone to the rooftop. Nothing about Julia's disappearance seemed to make sense to either man. Silence in the stairwell heightened the tensions lingering in the air. Ascending the steps Robert looked to Henry with a question burning in his eyes.

"Why would Julia go the rooftop without telling anyone?" Doubts surfaced in Henry's mind from the question posed to him. Julia never tried anything like this before. Ever since the attack nothing had been normal. Charisma could have allowed George to persuade Julia to follow him. Looking back Henry could see the same worry he felt on Roberts face.

"You know Julia always has been rebellious. Don't worry yourself Robert I am sure my daughter will be fine." Trying to convince Robert masked the fathers' attempt to convince himself. Sound of marching footsteps echoed in the stairwell. Glancing at the wrist watch Henry could see it was ten to midnight.

"We've got a ways to go. Let's hurry people." Henry pushed the soldiers forward feeling his stomach churning with worry. Hearing the noise Robert could sense the anxiety emanating from Julia's father. Cold wind rushed down the stairwell from the rooftop door. Feeling the draft both men looked up towards the roof

"I hope you and your team knows you're digging your own graves." King George stared down the barrel of the gun pointed at his head. Several figures materialized across the rooftop aiming their guns at the King. George gritted his teeth still holding the door open. The man holding Julia could see anger seething from George's grimace.

"Perhaps you should be a little more worried about your own safety. Julia is coming with us, but whether you leave this rooftop alive is your choice." George could see fear in the emerald green eyes of the young woman. Unable to speak Julia could only watch and listen to the exchange. Some force prevented George from running.

"You have ten seconds to run or I will kill you." Cybernetic hearing amplified noise allowing the assailant to hear the footsteps in the stairwell. George glanced between Julia and the door. Thoughts churned inside the young kings' mind. Seconds ticked away. Nothing could force George to abandon Julia.

"You are making a grave mistake." Time compelled George to make a decision. The assailant admired the king's determination. George could see the man's finger twitching against the trigger. Horror prevented Julia from looking away from the scene. The assailant could see the resolve in George's eyes. Jumping to life the pistol expelled a thunderous roar spewing fire and metal. A bullet grazed by the King's face slamming into the wall spraying chips of stone in every direction.

George panicked diving into the stairwell away from the gunfire. Knowing the king managed to escape gave Julia some respite from the torment of her emotions. Taking control of Julia's muscles the assailant forced her to follow. Wind caused the heavy door to slam shut. Leaping up George raced down the stairway. Julia unable to move or speak couldn't resist the assailant compelling her to follow him.

"Anyone else got communications with the rest of the team?" Marching up the stairs Henry tried to communicate with the Major. Security personnel looked at each other discovering that communications were not functioning. Robert could sense the worry emanating from the soldiers. Sudden gunfire echoed down the stairwell. Terror shot through the stairwell compelling everyone to race toward the rooftop. Robert looked to Henry for answers.

"Where is that gunfire coming from?" Henry's anxiety escalated to terror when he realized the gunshots were coming from the roof.

"We have to get to that rooftop now!" Bolting up the stairs Henry felt fear pumping through his veins. Racing behind Robert tried to keep pace with the muse troops. Henry felt a strange mix of hope and terror propelling each footstep. Only the thought of Julia's safety remained in the father's mind. Trailing behind neither Robert nor Muse security could see Henry anymore.

Sounds of approaching footsteps descending the stairwell didn't cause the father to pause. Robert and the muse soldiers could hear both footsteps in the near distance. Approaching footsteps caused Henry to draw his pistol out of the jacket. King George ran around the corner panic stricken. Both men collided allowing Henry to pressing the pistol under the young king's chin.

"I thought Julia was with you! Where in the hell is my daughter?" Feeling the barrel of gun George tried to catch his breath.

"We're under attack and they've got Julia!" Henry could see the terror in George's eyes. Catching up Robert could see the two men in the distance. George felt the gun press in harder against his chin. Glaring at the distraught king caused Henry's anger to break free.

"You took my daughter to the rooftop without security. I need you to calm down and tell me what is going on!" King George struggled to catch his breath.

"Julia got bored at the party. I offered to take her away for a few minutes. I didn't think there would be any problems because the building had been secured. We were outside talking. I was just getting ready to bring her back to the party when people attacked us. Someone neural hacked Julia preventing her from escaping. They are using thermal optical camouflage and we didn't see them coming. Before I knew it we were surrounded and I had a gun aimed at my head."

George explained the situation gasping for breath between words. Henry released the king turning his thoughts to discern the best response. Only immediate action could prevent Julia from being abducted. Blocked communication prevented Henry from coordinating a rescue. Robert looked at the young king struggling to breathe.

"So you just left Julia in the hands of those people to save yourself?" George snapped his attention glaring at Robert. Both men exchanged furious looks. Robert stared at George who looked ready to attack. Staring up Henry felt time pressing against him.

"Come on everyone lets go. We have to reach the rooftop before they escape!" Bolting up the stairs Henry felt driven by purpose. Robert shoved the king out of the way. Looking around George noticed everyone held guns.

"Hey I am the only person here unarmed." One of the muse security personnel handed the young king a pistol. Following behind George chambered a round in his gun. Muscles burned trying to tell Henry to stop, but the father refused to slow down. Hearing footsteps growing more distant Robert turned to see the troops falling behind.

"Come on guys we have to catch up. Julia is in danger on the roof and we can't leave Henry alone. Are you coming with us your majesty?" Time seemed to strangle Henry's hope in these few moments. Henry could see the door to the rooftop feeling his heart throbbing in his chest.

Each second diminished any hope to rescue Julia from her assailants. The group of people tried to catch up with the father racing ahead. Slamming into the door Henry's body flung the door open causing it to strike the wall. Cold wind blew snow across the rooftop with a howl. Falling snow created a veil of white. Henry glanced around the rooftop spotting the assailant and his daughter.

"Stop and release my daughter before I kill you!" The assailant stood behind Julia aiming his gun at her father.

"Henry you decided to join us! Your daughter didn't want to leave without saying goodbye first." Cold air racing from the rooftop renewed Robert, George, and Muse troops efforts to reach the roof. Struggling against the neural hack Julia could only watch unable to intervene. Henry aimed his gun at the assailant tracking the target with his cybernetic eyes.

"This rooftop will be crawling with my security forces within a minute or so. There is no escaping this rooftop. What are your plans now that you are corned on the roof?" Henry heard the answer ringing up from the streets below. Sounds of breaking glass echoed up into the night sky.

Arriving on the rooftop Robert and Muse soldiers aimed their guns at the man behind Julia. Sounds of glass shattering blended into the cadence of rage from the protestors below. Robert looked at Henry trying to determine what to do. Falling snow obscured eyesight. Reaching out George tapped Henry on the shoulder.

"There were at least six people on this roof using optical camouflage. Whoever these people are they're well coordinated and have planned this out." Several figures materialized across the roof aiming guns from behind cover. Henry knew the situation looked grim, but there was no other option. Looking across the rooftop the assailant stared at his opponent.

"It would seem this time you do not have the upper hand Mr. Williams." Henry knew his team was exposed and outside of cover facing a fortified enemy.

"You may have the upper hand for the moment, but that still doesn't explain how you intend to escape. There is nowhere for you to go, but if you release Julia I swear no harm will come to you or your people." Loud whooshing of a vector thrust engine roared in the distance. Henry and his people glanced around unable to spot the source of the noise. Snow kicked up off the roof creating a mist around the assailant and Julia.

"Still believe I can't escape?" A glimmering silhouette appeared at the edge of the rooftop. Shutting down optical camouflage the gunship materialized. Hanging just off the edge the gunship doors opened up. Standing at the edge of the rooftop the assailant lowered his gun.

"Well it looks like it about that time to say farewell old friend. We all lose sometimes Henry. That is just life." One at a time the group of assailants moved from cover towards the gunship. Henry and his team could only standby and watch the people board.

"Do you really think there is anywhere you can hide from me?" The assailant handed Julia over to one of his teammates turning back to face Henry.

"I know you won't rest until you find your daughter Mr. Williams. I also know that you have bigger problems to deal with at this moment. As long as you make no attempt to stop or follow us we have no reason to hurt your daughter." An explosion echoed up from the ground emphasizing the troubles below. Henry glared at the audacious assailant standing with his defenses lowered.

"Do you really expect me to just let you leave with my daughter?" Another explosion filled the night sky causing the building to shake again. The assailant stood on the rooftop edge looking down at the sea of protestors assaulting the hotel.

"I know you all too well. Right now you're trying to figure out the exact situation. Let me paint you a picture. Two thousand protestors have besieged the lobby of the hotel because they have been neural hacked." A third explosion roared forth shaking the building. Gunfire erupted again this time from the streets below. The assailant looked back at Henry.

"Right now your men are fighting a mindless horde of people who will overrun them. Without communication you can't send reinforcements to them. You can't call in your nearby reinforcements to follow me. I have placed you on the horns of a dilemma Mr. Williams. I know you want to save your precious daughter, but what about the men and woman loyal to you. Do you save your daughter or your people?"

Grenade explosion resonated in the night air altering the tempo of constant gunshots coming from below. Henry could see the unblinking resolve of the assailant. Cybernetic eyes scanned the man showing extensive body modification. The powerful jamming field continued to prevent communications. Without neural communication Henry couldn't give an order. Robert looked at Henry trying to figure what was going through his mind.

"You can't be considering letting this manic take Julia." Henry knew the situation removed any choice.

"Get to the lobby now! I'll get Julia." Muse troops fell back into the building following orders. Henry charged across the rooftop racing towards the gunship. King George and Robert stood watching Henry run across the rooftop with alarming speed.

Each stride pushed the father closer to his objective. Taking careful aim Henry opened fire. The assailant raised his arm deflected bullets off the metal of his cybernetic arm implant. Several rounds struck the target failing to do any damage. Abandoning all reason Henry continuing to fire.

Raising the fifty calibre pistol the assailant returned fire. Henry felt the first shot strike his left shoulder and the second shot clip his leg. Screams filled Julia's mind seeing her father struck by the bullets. Inertia carried Henry through the air slamming him hard into the rooftop. Snow covered the rooftop creating an icy sheet. Sliding off the edge of the roof Henry grabbed onto the edge to prevent from falling. Looking down at the man dangling over the street the assailant towered above.

"I am sorry it had to come to this, but in all honesty I didn't expect you to just stand and watch me take your daughter. There was never any hope of you stopping me. It would appear the great Henry Williams has fallen from grace. Your enemies circle around you like sharks. I would offer you a helping hand but I must depart."

"I swear I will hunt you down and kill you!" Henry struggled to pull himself back up onto the roof. Stepping on to the gunship the assailant looked back down at Henry.

"I am certain you will hunt me down. Perhaps you will even find me, and I look forward to our next confrontation. If you want to find your daughter figure out who would hire someone to do such a nefarious act. It would seem you have a traitor in your midst." Engines of the gunship roared preparing to depart. Henry pulled himself up onto the rooftop looking at his daughter with tears in his eyes.

"Why not just kill me and be done with it?" Shaking his head the assailant looked at the broken father lying in the cold snow on the roof. Henry watched the man step onto the gunship pressing the button to close the door. Hydraulics activated filling the air with a hiss. The gunship engines whined pulling away from the building. Standing next to Julia her assailant looked down at Henry.

"I am a ghost that survives by being paid to do a job. You should know mercenaries only preform the job they are paid to do. I haven't been paid to kill you yet." Hydraulics closed the gunship door at a slow pace. Both father and daughter eyes filled with tears.

Henry pushed himself up off the ground with his good arm. Robert and King George raced over to help. Rising into the black curtains of darkness the gunship picked up speed. Crimson blood stained the pure white snow on the rooftop. Henry applied pressure to his shoulder wound trying to stop the bleeding. King George looked at Henry unsure of what to do. All three men watched the gunship disappeared from sight into the night sky.

"What are you going to do?" George could see the rage on Henry's face. Tears froze on the father's face from the cold air blowing past. Darkness swallowed the gunship. Henry knew there was nothing he could do at the moment.

"First we are going to go and rescue my troops. Once we contain the situation here I swear I will find my daughter. I will hunt down every person responsible for Julia's abduction. When I find those responsible I will make them pay. I will show the world there are worst things than death when I exact my revenge."

CHAPTER 33

Damage Report

Stinging defeat forced Henry to focus on the only thing he could do. George and Robert looked at each other unsure of what to say or do. Hot blood rushed through Henry pushing the cold air from thought. Winter's fury no longer fazed the man consumed by purpose. The neural connection with Muse security servers reactivated in the man's mind. Henry marched towards the stairwell door activating his neural communications.

"What is your location Maj. Lee?" The elevators stopped moving after the first explosion. Each elevator trapped the Muse and SAS troops. Communications flared to life conveying Henry's voice. Maj. Lee breathed a sigh of relief activating his neural implant to respond.

"Sir it appears the first explosion triggered the earthquake safeguards of the hotel's security system. Colt and I are stuck with the rest of the muse and SAS forces. Where are the gunfire and explosions coming from?" Accessing central security for the hotel revealed that the system had been hacked. Henry manipulated data reactivating the elevator controls.

"I have restored elevator control. Cpt. Anderson needs to be reinforced." Lurching forward the elevator began its descent to the lobby. People shuffled about disorientated by the sudden movement. Maj. Lee pulled his assault rifle and cocked it.

"We're descending to the lobby now sir. We should arrive in about thirty seconds. What is the situation we're going to be facing?" Descending the stair well Henry raced towards the lobby. Following just behind George and Robert kept pace. Henry could hear the footstep of his forces from below echoing up the corridor.

"Cpt. Anderson what is the situation down there?" Protestors isolated the various groups of Muse forces spread throughout the lobby. Joe organized the police forces in the command post. Swarming the reception desks protestors pressed against the defenses. Cpt. Anderson fired his assault rifle activating his neural implant.

"Sir we are under heavy attack! We're running out of ammunition fast. I don't know how much longer we can hold out. Our forces have been isolated and spread out trying to hold the lobby." Hearing desperation in Cpt. Anderson voice Maj. Lee looked to his troops. Years of teamwork told each soldier to get ready for action from one look. Sounds of guns being loaded and cocked filled the small elevator. Colt looked around wondering what was happening.

"Hey you gonna fill this old coot in on what the hell is happening." Maj Lee realized Colt didn't know what was going on hearing his voice over the communicator.

"It looks like the protestors outside have attacked the lobby in force. Cpt. Anderson's force has been pinned down. The lobby position is being overrun. You probably should prepare yourself for combat Mr. Cross. The protestors have been neural hacked leaving us no choice but to use lethal force." Staring at the elevator floors Maj. Lee waited for the doors to open.

Muse forces fired on the protestor standing only a few feet away from the reception barricade. Encroachment of the horde threatened to breach the last line of defense. Cpt. Anderson kept firing trying to hold back the surging wave of people. Protestors overran every position blocking the muse troops from seeing each other. Only the sound of gunfire revealed the fact that Muse forces were still holding their positions. Cpt. Anderson neural implant allowed him to sense the approaching reinforcements.

"Reinforcements are inbound. Just hold out few more seconds!" A ding echoed in the lobby before elevator doors slid open. Maj. Lee charged forward with his team opening fire. Sauntering into the lobby Colt watched SAS charge around him. One of the Muse soldier's was pinned to the ground trying to push off the horde of clawing protestors. Two shots from Maj. Lee dropped a man and woman before he charged past the elevator barricade. Colt pulled the last protestor off the soldier shooting the man in the head at point blank range.

"Never break into a Texans house. We shoot first and ask questions later." Free from being pinned the soldier breathed a sigh of relief. Maj. Lee and his team broke into the lobby firing into the mass crowd of people. Soldiers threw spare clips to their team mates behind enemy's lines.

One of the SAS operatives set up a heavy machine gun position by the elevator barricade. Machinegun fire boomed through the lobby spewing forth fifty calibre rounds. Bullets traced through the air streaking across the lobby in rapid succession. Maj. Lee forced his way through the crowd knocking people aside. Combined fire from the numerous troops pushed the horde of protestors backwards.

Frag grenades exploded tearing the unarmoured targets apart. Shrapnel shot through the air cleaving through anything in the path of the deadly shards. Maj. Lee fought his way through the crowd to the command post. Everyone behind the reception area breathed a sigh of relief except Cpt. Anderson. Grabbing the ammunition from the major the troops reloaded theirs guns. Cpt. Anderson gritted his teeth feeling the assault rifle kick in a burst. Taking position Maj. Lee looked over at this friend.

"Did you order the zombie apocalypse?"

Heavy gunfire tore through the ranks of protestors disorientated by grenade explosions. Almost all the protestors outside gathered in the lobby. Muse thinned the vast horde one by one. Protestors fell under the thunderous roar of automatic gunfire. Maj. Lee accessed the neural network to report the situation.

"Sir we have arrived in the lobby and contained the situation. What is the status on Julia?" Victoria stood on the balcony surrounded by guest watching the streets below. Frozen by the sound of gunfire all the guests hung in suspended terror. Accessing the neural network Victoria accessed her husbands mind.

"Henry is Julia ok?" Unable to answer Henry forced himself to stay focused on getting to his people. Victoria looked to one of the security forces standing nearby.

"Keep the situation contained and hold the perimeter of the door. I am going to head down and assess the situation."

The last few protestors fell to the ground. Joe looked at Adam and the other surviving police officers. Silence filled the lobby for a moment. Everyone looked around at each before breaking into loud cheers of victory. Adam hugged his friend in celebration.

"I can't believe we survived Joe." Joe looked over his friends shoulder at the scene before him. Piles of bodies scattered about. Smoke wafted from craters in the floor. Smell of burning flesh filled the lobby revealing the cost of victory to Joe.

"I can't believe we survived either, but it wasn't without a cost." Adam celebrated with Joe and his fellow police officers. Surviving protestors twitched on the floor. Blood stained the marble floor. Muse security forces moved out applying first aid to wounded survivors.

Survivors clawed at the people trying to help them. Effects from the neural hacking forced troops giving first aid to restrain and sedate the victims. Sounds of sirens from ambulance and police grew closer with each second. New organizations wouldn't be far behind the sirens. Joe and the police officers moved out into the lobby to assist with treating the wounded. The group of men ran down the stairway bursting through the door to the lobby. Several SAS guards reacted to the possible threat pointed their guns. Pushing past the soldiers Henry ran towards the lobby with Robert following behind. Col. Traynor looked at King George.

"Your majesty you're safe and sound."

"Stand down I'm ok." King George brushed Colonel Traynor off.

Henry ran around the corner greeted with sight of the bodies scattered through the lobby. Bullet holes riddled the wall and blood stained the floor. Henry tried to hold back his emotions while surveying the scene of the massacre. Muse forces set up triage operations to save what people they could. Maj Lee approached Henry.

"Sir I have the men preparing the wounded for evacuation when the ambulances arrive." Waiting for orders Maj. Lee empathized with his boss. Henry couldn't think or even speak. No words existed in any language that could capture the true horror spread across the lobby floor. Henry felt powerless staring at the carnage before him.

"Save as many lives as possible major." Police cars and ambulances sat down outside. Within moments officers and paramedics raced into the lobby. Cpt. Anderson tapped on a data pad compiling a damage report. Paramedics worked alongside Muse and SAS to help transport the wounded out of the building. Colt saw Robert and moved to hug him.

"Glad you're ok boy!" Robert hugged his father with all his might trying to fight back the tears.

"Not everyone made it through this dad."

News reporters outside began filming the scene for reports. Police already cordoned off the scene trying to keep reporters at bay. Signalling the arrival of the elevator a chime echoed through the lobby. Victoria pushed past the elevator door spotting her husband standing in the lobby. Caught in the middle of the tragedy Henry saw his wife through the commotion. The couple locked eyes. Victoria ran over and grabbed her husband.

"Where the hell is Julia?" Henry couldn't even look his wife in the eyes. Silence between the couple spoke louder than any words could. Victoria felt her muscles weaken causing her to lose balance. Henry caught his wife pulling her close to his chest. Blood dripped off Henry's fingers pressed against his wife. Cpt. Anderson approached offering the data pad.

"Sir I have completed the post battle damage report for you to look at." Henry held his sobbing wife in his hands glaring out at the scene outside.

"Find my daughter!" Paramedics carried bodies out of the plaza. Terror filled the faces of the officers responding to the emergency. Looking out Henry knew only the future held the hope necessary to survive this ordeal. Muscles tightened in the man's body. Thoughts of revenge brought solace to the Henry staring out at the scene. The future would be stained with the blood of all those responsible for Julia's abduction.

About the Author

Ryan Browning was born in the small town of Wallaceburg, Ontario, and showed his love for writing in grade school. Attending the University of Windsor, he double majored in psychology and political science. Since graduating, Ryan has been using his political science knowledge to fuel his stories. Friends inspired him to self-publish his own work in 2014. Ryan enjoys spending his time reading on the subjects of law, philosophy, and history.

Printed in the United States
by Baker & Taylor Publisher Services